A TEXT BOOK OF

ELECTRICAL AND ELECTRONICS ENGINEERING

FOR
SEMESTER – II

SECOND YEAR DEGREE COURSE IN MECHANICAL, MECHANICAL (SANDWICH) AND AUTOMOBILE ENGINEERING

Strictly According to New Revised Credit System Syllabus of Savitribai Phule Pune University
(w.e.f June 2016)

B. H. DESHMUKH
M. E. (Electrical), B. E. (Mechanical)
Retired Assistant Professor of Electrical Engineering,
Government College of Engineering, Pune - 411 005.

S. S. PATIL
M. Tech. (VLSI Design)
Assistant Professor, E & TC Department
Pune Institute of Computer Technology,
Dhankawadi, Pune.

NIRALI PRAKASHAN
ADVANCEMENT OF KNOWLEDGE

N 3570

Elect. & Electronics Engg. (SE Mech., Mech. (Sw) & Auto.)   **ISBN 978-93-86353-28-3**

First Edition   :   January 2017
©   :   **Authors**

Published By :   Polyplate
NIRALI PRAKASHAN
Abhyudaya Pragati, 1312, Shivaji Nagar,
Off J.M. Road, Pune – 411005
Tel - (020) 25512336/37/39, Fax - (020) 25511379
Email : niralipune@pragationline.com

☞ **DISTRIBUTION CENTRES**

PUNE

Nirali Prakashan   :   119, Budhwar Peth, Jogeshwari Mandir Lane, Pune 411002, Maharashtra
Tel : (020) 2445 2044, 66022708, Fax : (020) 2445 1538
Email : bookorder@pragationline.com, niralilocal@pragationline.com

Nirali Prakashan   :   S. No. 28/27, Dhyari, Near Pari Company, Pune 411041
Tel : (020) 24690204 Fax : (020) 24690316
Email : dhyari@pragationline.com, bookorder@pragationline.com

MUMBAI

Nirali Prakashan   :   385, S.V.P. Road, Rasdhara Co-op. Hsg. Society Ltd.,
Girgaum, Mumbai 400004, Maharashtra
Tel : (022) 2385 6339 / 2386 9976, Fax : (022) 2386 9976
Email : niralimumbai@pragationline.com

☞ **DISTRIBUTION BRANCHES**

JALGAON

Nirali Prakashan   :   34, V. V. Golani Market, Navi Peth, Jalgaon 425001,
Maharashtra, Tel : (0257) 222 0395, Mob : 94234 91860

KOLHAPUR

Nirali Prakashan   :   New Mahadvar Road, Kedar Plaza, 1st Floor Opp. IDBI Bank
Kolhapur 416 012, Maharashtra. Mob : 9850046155

NAGPUR

Pratibha Book Distributors :   Above Maratha Mandir, Shop No. 3, First Floor,
Rani Jhanshi Square, Sitabuldi, Nagpur 440012, Maharashtra
Tel : (0712) 254 7129

DELHI

Nirali Prakashan   :   4593/21, Basement, Aggarwal Lane 15, Ansari Road, Daryaganj
Near Times of India Building, New Delhi 110002
Mob : 08505972553

BENGALURU

Pragati Book House   :   House No. 1, Sanjeevappa Lane, Avenue Road Cross,
Opp. Rice Church, Bengaluru – 560002.
Tel : (080) 64513344, 64513355,Mob : 9880582331, 9845021552
Email:bharatsavla@yahoo.com

CHENNAI

Pragati Books   :   9/1, Montieth Road, Behind Taas Mahal, Egmore,
Chennai 600008 Tamil Nadu, Tel : (044) 6518 3535,
Mob : 94440 01782 / 98450 21552 / 98805 82331,
Email : bharatsavla@yahoo.com

niralipune@pragationline.com | www.pragationline.com

Also find us on [f] www.facebook.com/niralibooks

PREFACE

It gives us great pleasure in publishing this text book on "**Electrical and Electronics Engineering**" for the students of Second Year Degree Course in Mechanical, Mechanical Sandwich and Automobile. This book is strictly written according to **New Revised Credit System Syllabus** of Savitribai Phule Pune University (2015 Pattern).

As per the policy of the University, Engineering Syllabi is revised every five years. Last revision was in the year 2012. New revision is coming little earlier, as university has introduced **Online System of Examination** from year 2012.

As per the **New Credit System**, the **Online Examinations** Phase-I will be conducted based on First & Second Units and Phase II on Third & Fourth Units. The **Online** examinations will have objective types of questions with multiple choices. End Sem. Theory Examination will be based on all the six units and that will be conducted in traditional way and the Theory Course will have 4 credits.

The subject of **'Electrical and Electronics Engineering'** is one of the core technology subjects included in the curriculum of the above courses. This book is specially designed to serve as a Text-Book for this subject.

The Electrical Engineering part covers the topics on D.C. Generators, D.C. Motors, Three-Phase Induction Motors and Special Purpose Motors. Electronics Engineering part covers the topics on Introduction to Arduino(ATmega328p) Microcontrollers, Peripheral Interface-I, Peripheral Interface-II.

Numerous illustrative diagrams and solved problems are included in the book wherever necessary to clarify the concepts and reinforce the understanding of the subject. A large number of review questions and graded unsolved problems with answers are also added at the end of each chapter. We are sure that student fraternity as well as faculty members will find the book extremely useful.

Main feature of this book is, **Complete Coverage** of the New Credit System Syllabus with large number of **Worked (Solved) Examples, Programs and Exercises.**

We have brought out Separate Book of Multiple Choice Questions (MCQ's) which will be very useful to the students especially for Online Examinations.

We take this opportunity to express our sincere thanks to Shri. Dineshbhai Furia, Shri. Jignesh Furia, Mrs. Nirali Verma and Shri. M. P. Munde and entire team of Nirali Prakashan namely Mrs. Deepali Lachake (Co-ordinator), who really have taken keen interest and untiring efforts in publishing this text.

The advice and suggestions of our esteemed readers to improve the text are most welcomed, and will be highly appreciated.

Pune   **Authors**

SYLLABUS

Unit I : D. C. Machines   (6Hrs)

Construction, working principle of D.C. generator, emf equation of D. C. generator (derivation not expected), working principle of D.C. motor, types of D.C. motor, back emf, torque equation for D.C. motor, characteristics of D.C. motor (series and shunt only), three-point starter for D.C shunt motor, methods for speed control of D.C. shunt and series motors, industrial applications.

Unit II : Three Phase Induction Motors   (6Hrs)

Constructional feature, working principle of three phase induction motors, types; torque equation, torque slip characteristics; power stages; efficiency, starters (auto transformer starter, star delta starter); methods of speed control and industrial applications.

Unit III : Special Purpose Motors   (6 Hrs)

Construction, working principle, characteristic and applications of stepper motors, A.C. and D.C servomotors, universal motors, industrial applications, brushless DC motors, linear induction motors, single phase induction motors,(types, construction, working principle of split phase and shaded pole type induction motors), descriptive treatment for AC series motor (difference between AC series and DC series motor, construction and working).

Unit IV : Introduction to Microcontrollers   (6 Hrs)

Introduction to microcontroller and microprocessors, role of embedded systems, open source embedded platforms, Atmega 328P- features, architecture, portstructure, sensors and actuators, data acquisition systems, introduction to Arduino IDE- features, IDE overview, programming concepts: variables, functions, conditional statements.

Unit V : Peripheral Interface-I   (6 Hrs)

Concept of GPIO in Atmega 328P based Arduino board, digital input and output, UART concept, timers, interfacing with LED, LCD and keypad, serial communication using Arduino IDE

Unit VI : Peripheral Interface-II   (6Hrs)

Concept of ADC in Atmega 328P based Arduino board, interfacing with temperature sensor (LM35), LVDT, strain gauge, accelerometer, concept of PWM, DC motor interface using PWM

CONTENTS

Part-I : Electrical Engineering

Unit - I

Unit - III

Part-II : Electronics Engineering

Unit - IV

Unit - I

CHAPTER

ONE

D.C. GENERATORS

1.1 INTRODUCTION

An electric current whether d.c. or a.c. is now commonly produced by means of an electrical machine known as *generator* which converts mechanical energy supplied to it into electrical energy. This mechanical energy is provided by a steam turbine, an internal combustion engine, a water turbine or other prime mover which drives the generator. The *motor*, on the other hand, is a device which converts electrical energy into mechanical energy. The process of conversion of electrical energy into mechanical energy and vice versa using a suitable device is known as *electromechanical energy conversion*. This process is always a reversible one i.e. any motor can be made to run as a generator or any generator can be made to deliver mechanical power as a motor. In this chapter, we shall study the principle of working, construction, types, characteristics and various applications of d.c. generators.

1.2 PRINCIPLE OF GENERATOR

The operation of all electrical generators, whether d.c. or a.c. is based on the fact that when a conductor is moved in magnetic field or a magnetic field moved with respect to the conductor, according to Faraday's law of electromagnetic induction, an electromotive force is set up in the conductor. Thus, as long as there is relative motion between a conductor and a magnetic field, a voltage will always be generated in the conductor.

1.3 ELEMENTARY ALTERNATOR

A.C. generators are normally known as *alternators*. The preliminary knowledge of working of an alternator is very helpful in understanding the working of a d.c. generator. Let us therefore first study the working of an elementary 2-pole alternator shown in Fig. 1.1.

Construction : It consists of a single turn rectangular coil (AB) made up of some conducting material like copper or aluminium. The coil is so placed that it can be rotated about its own axis at a constant speed in a uniform magnetic field provided by the North and South poles of the magnet. This coil is known as *armature* of the alternator. The ends of the armature coil are connected to rings (R_1 and R_2) called *slip-rings* which rotate with the armature. Two carbon brushes (B_1 and B_2) pressed against the slip-rings collect the current induced in the coil and carry it to the external resistor (R).

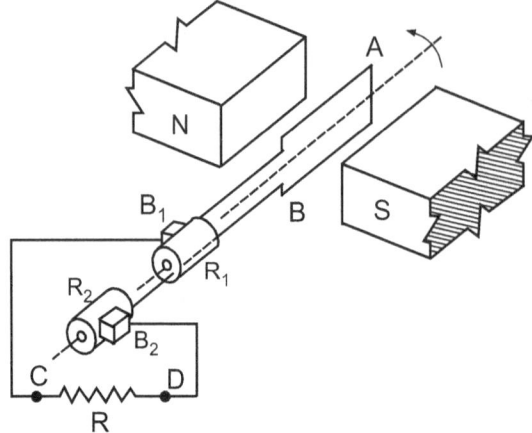

Fig. 1.1 : An elementary alternator with two poles

Operation : Assume that the armature coil is rotating in an anticlockwise direction. As the conductors (A and B) of the coil cut through the magnetic field, according to Faraday's law of electromagnetic induction, an e.m.f. is produced in them, which causes a current to flow through the external circuit. The magnitude of this e.m.f. is dependent on the position of the armature coil in relation to the magnetic field. Let us consider the few selected positions of the coil as shown in Fig. 1.2.

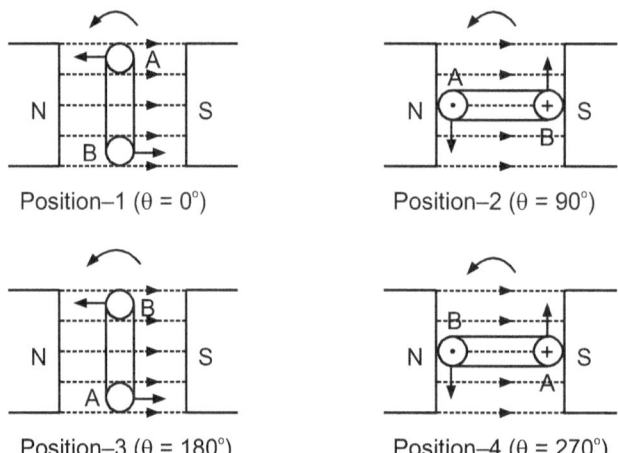

Fig. 1.2 : The end views of the armature coil in different positions

Position No. 1 : This is the initial position of the coil. The plane of the coil being perpendicular to the magnetic field, the conductors (A and B) of the coil move parallel to the magnetic field. Since there is no flux cutting, no e.m.f. is generated in the conductors and therefore, no current flows through the external circuit.

Position No. 2 : As the coil rotates from Position-1 ($\theta = 0°$) to Position-2 ($\theta = 90°$), more and more lines of force are cut by the conductors. In the Position-2, both the conductors of the coil move at right angles to the magnetic field and cut through a maximum number of lines of force, so the e.m.f. induced in them is also maximum. In other words, between zero and 90°, the e.m.f. generated in the conductors builds up from zero to a maximum value. The e.m.f.s in both conductors being in series, the resultant coil e.m.f. is the sum of the two conductor e.m.f.s. It is therefore, twice that of one of the conductors, since the voltages are equal.

The current through the circuit varies just as the e.m.f. varies, being zero at a 0° and rising to a maximum at 90°. In Position-2 of the coil, according to Fleming's right hand rule, the direction of the induced current in conductor A is towards the observer (i.e. out of the plane of paper) and in conductor B, it is away from the observer (i.e. into the plane of paper) as indicated. Therefore, the current flows through external resistor from the terminal C to the terminal D.

Position No. 3 : As the coil continues to rotate further from Position-2 (θ = 90°) to Position-3 (θ = 180°), the lines of force cut by the conductors gradually reduce. This decreases the generated e.m.f. in them. In Position-3, the conductors again move parallel to the field and hence no e.m.f. is induced in them. Therefore, the current through the external resistor is also zero. It should be noted that during the rotation of the coil from 0° to 180° (i.e. during the first half revolution), the conductors of the coil move in the same direction through the magnetic field. Therefore, throughout this period, the polarity of the generated e.m.f. remains same and current flows through the external resistor from C to D only.

Position No. 4 : As the coil rotates beyond Position-3, the direction of the cutting action of the conductors through the magnetic field reverses. Now, the conductor A cuts up through the field and the conductor B cuts down through the field. In consequence both, the polarity of the generated e.m.f. and the current flow reverse. To make it more clear, consider the coil in Position-4 (θ = 270°). By applying Fleming's right hand rule, it is seen that direction of induced current in conductor A is away from the observer and in conductor B it is towards the observer. As such, current flows through the external resistor from D to C. Thus during the entire second half revolution i.e. when the coil rotates from the Position-3 to Position-4 and back to Position-1, the current flows in the opposite direction to that in the first half revolution. Also similar to Position-2, e.m.f. in the coil is maximum in Position-4. In general, the variations in the magnitude of e.m.f. of the alternator when the armature coil rotates from 180° to 360° are exactly similar to those in the first half revolution.

The graph of e.m.f. or current for the complete revolution of the coil under consideration is shown in Fig. 1.3.

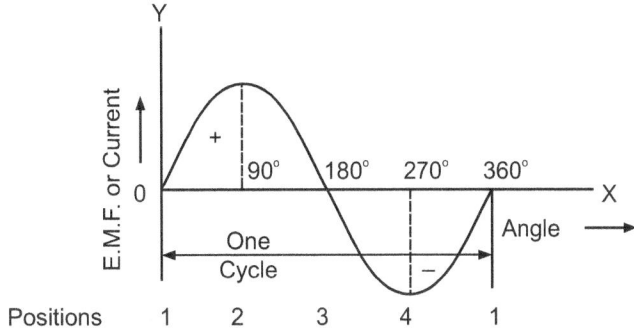

Fig. 1.3 : Graphical representation of e.m.f. or current

From the above graph it will be readily seen that the voltage and the current supplied by such alternator are alternating and follow a sine curve.

1.4 ELEMENTARY D.C. GENERATOR

The elementary alternator, as already seen above, necessarily supplies an alternating current. If a *unidirectional* or *direct current* is desired, then this alternating current must be rectified or commutated as it enters the external circuit. This rectification can be accomplished by replacing the slip-rings R_1 and R_2 of the elementary alternator in Fig. 1.1 by a single split-ring M generally known as a *commutator*, as illustrated in Fig. 1.4. The elementary 2-pole alternator then becomes an elementary 2-pole d.c. generator. Let us therefore see how we get direct current from such an elementary d.c. generator. The commutator in the form of split-ring M of this generator is made by cutting a cylindrical piece of some conducting material such as copper into two halves or segments (a and b). These segments are insulated from each other by a thin sheet of mica or some other insulating material. The ends of the armature coil AB are joined to these segments. The external load resistor R is connected to the split-ring M through brushes B_1 and B_2 as shown in Fig. 1.4.

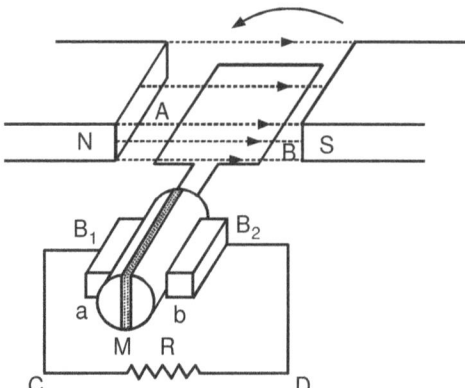

Fig. 1.4 : An elementary 2-pole d.c. generator

Action of a Commutator : Fig. 1.5 (a) shows the condition when the coil is undergoing the first half revolution. In this case, the current flows through the load resistor R from C to D. During the next half revolution, the direction of the current in the coil reverses as illustrated in Fig. 1.5 (b).

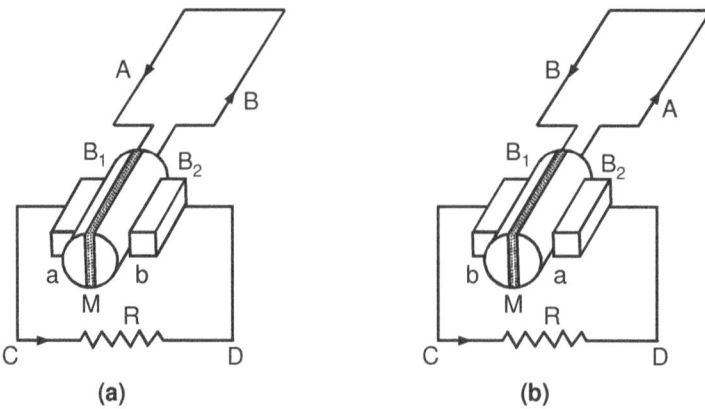

Fig. 1.5 : Action of a commutator

But at the same time, the positions of the segments a and b also reverse. Therefore, the current through the load resistor again flows from C to D. Thus, even though the current induced in the armature coil AB is alternating, due to rectifying action of the commutator, the direction of the current supplied to the external circuit is always the same. Fig. 1.6 shows the waveform of the unidirectional current output of an elementary d.c. generator under consideration. In the commercial d.c. generator, by using a number of coils evenly distributed around the armature core and connecting these coils to the commutator having a corresponding number of segments, a more steady direct current is obtained in the external circuit.

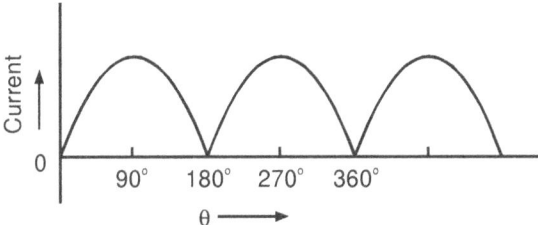

Fig. 1.6 : Unidirectional current output from an elementary d.c. generator

1.5 CONSTRUCTIONAL FEATURES OF A PRACTICAL D.C. GENERATOR

Fig. 1.7 shows a cross-section of a typical 4-pole d.c. generator with its principal parts labelled. It essentially consists of a stationary part generally referred to as *field system* and the rotating part generally referred to as *armature*.

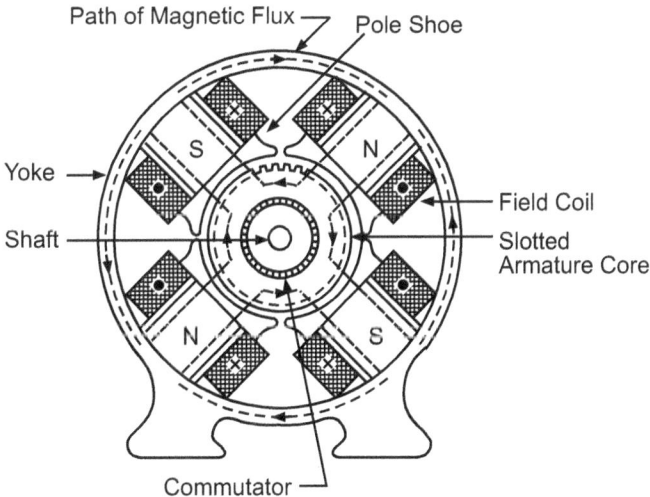

Fig. 1.7 : A cross-section of a typical d.c. machine

1.5.1 Field System

In almost all the practical d.c. generators (except very small ones fitted with permanent magnets), the magnetic field is produced electromagnetically. In these generators, the field system as a whole consists of following components :

(a) Yoke : The main frame of the machine is called the *yoke*. The yokes may be of cast iron or cast steel for small machines, but for large machines, they are fabricated from rolled steel having higher permeability and better mechanical strength. The yoke serves the following two purposes :

- It supports the other components such as poles and provides mechanical protection for the whole machine.

- It forms a part of the magnetic circuit and provides the path of low reluctance for the magnetic flux.

(b) Field Poles : Each field pole consists of a pole core and its exciting winding called the *field coil*.

Pole Cores : These are usually made of steel plates rivetted together under hydraulic pressure and bolted to the yoke. Laminated construction is used to reduce the eddy current loss. Each pole core has an extension at one end with a larger cross-section known as *pole shoe*. The pole shoes serve two purposes :

- They support the field coils.

- Being of larger cross-section, they reduce the reluctance of the magnetic path and spread out the flux in the air gap over a large portion of the armature periphery.

Field Coils : The field coils are usually former wound with cotton covered enamelled copper wire. After drying in a vacuum and impregnating with an insulating compound, these coils are then mounted on the pole cores. When current is passed through these coils, the field poles work as electromagnets and produce the magnetic flux necessary for generator action. All the field coils are connected in series and referred to collectively as the *field winding* of a generator. These field coils are so connected that alternately N and S poles are formed.

1.5.2 Armature Assembly

The armature assembly usually is made up of a shaft, armature core, armature winding and commutator (Fig. 1.8 a).

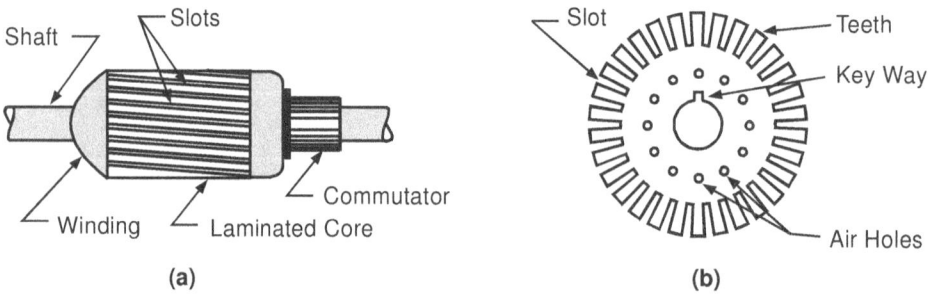

(a)   (b)

Fig. 1.8 : (a) Armature assembly of a d.c. generator,

(b) Single circular lamination

(a) **Armature Core :** The armature core is a cylindrical structure built up of circular steel laminations (Fig. 1.8 b) having thickness of about 0.35 to 0.5 mm and insulated from each other by a thin layer of paper or varnish. Use of laminations keep the eddy current loss to a low value. The built-up armature core has a series of longitudinal slots on its periphery for housing the conductors of the armature winding and may have a radial and axial air ducts for cooling purposes. It should be remembered that the armature core not only serves the purpose of housing the armature winding but also provides the path of low reluctance to the magnetic flux.

(b) **Armature Winding :** The armature winding consists of a large number of coils suitably connected together. These coils are usually wound separately on suitable formers with cotton covered enamelled copper wire and then placed in the core slots lined with tough insulating material. Special hard wooden or fibre wedges are used to prevent the armature conductors from flying out from slots under the action of centrifugal forces during the rotation of the armature. We know that when the armature rotates between the field poles, it is the armature winding where the useful e.m.f. is produced due to flux cutting by its conductors.

(c) **Commutator :** The commutator is made of wedge-shaped segments of hard-drawn or drop forged copper with V-grooves. These segments are insulated from one another by thin layers of mica and held together by steel V-rings or clamping flanges. These V-rings are insulated from the segments using two cone-shaped collars or rings of built-up mica. The commutator segments may have small longitudinal slits at one end for soldering the leads from the armature coils or may have risers for that purpose. Fig. 1.9 shows a sectional view of the commutator.

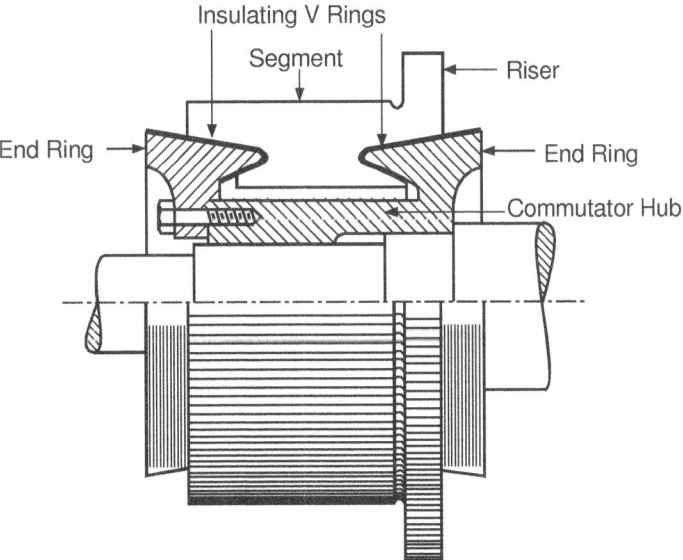

Fig. 1.9 : A sectional view of the commutator

As already seen, the function of the commutator is to facilitate the collection of current from the armature conductors. It is the commutator which converts the alternating current induced in the armature coils into unidirectional current as it enters the external circuit.

1.5.3 Miscellaneous Parts

(a) Brush Assembly : Brushes are used to conduct the current from the commutator to the external circuit. These brushes are usually made of carbon or copper and held in place by brush holders. For proper contact, each brush is pressed on the commutator surface by a spring and is free to slide in its holder in order that it may follow any irregularities in the commutator. A flexible braided conductor called *a pig tail* is used to connect the brush to the external circuit. Fig. 1.10 shows the complete brush assembly.

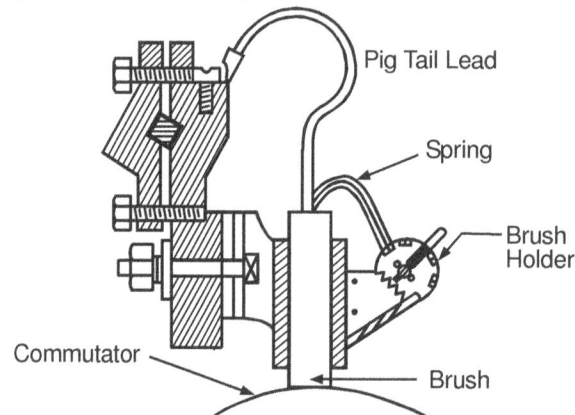

Fig. 1.10 : Brush assembly

(b) Cooling Fan : In some machines, a fan is fitted to the shaft on the side opposite to that of the commutator for cooling purposes.

(c) End Covers : These are attached to the ends of the main frame and contain bearings for the armature. The end cover on the commutator side also supports the brush assemblies.

1.6 TYPES OF ARMATURE WINDING

Depending upon the manner in which the ends of the armature coils are connected to the commutator segments, following are the two general types of the armature winding :

(a) Lap Winding : In this type of winding, the two ends of each armature coil are connected to adjacent commutator segments. The coils used may be single-turn or multi-turn[*] (Fig. 1.11).

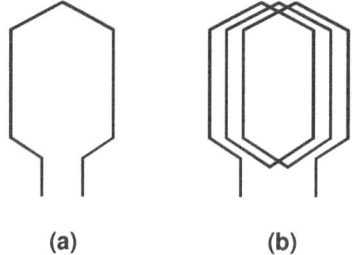

(a)   (b)

Fig. 1.11 : (a) Single-turn coil, lap winding,

(b) Multi-turn coil, lap winding

---

[*]   *For definitions refer to Section 1.7.*

Fig. 1.12 (a) shows the developed view[*] of a part of simple lap winding using single-turn coils. From this developed view, it will be observed that in this case the starting end of first coil is connected to Segment-1, while its finishing end is brought back to Segment-2. To the same segment is also connected the starting end of the adjacent coil and its finishing end is connected to Segment-3 and so on, each coil being connected between adjacent commutator segments. This winding derives its name from the fact that successive coils overlap each other.

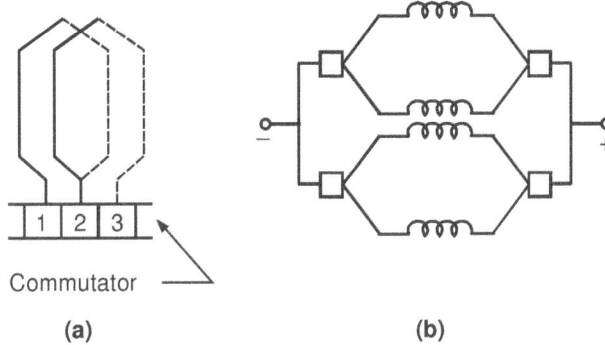

Commutator

(a)	(b)

Fig. 1.12 : (a) Developed view of a part of simple lap winding,

(b) Equivalent circuit, lap winding, 4-pole machine

General Characteristic Features : Following are some of the important characteristic features of the lap winding :

- The total number of brushes required is equal to the number of poles.

- A lap winding has as many paths (or circuits) in parallel between the negative and positive brushes as the number of poles. Due to this typical characteristic of the lap winding, it is also known as *multiple circuit or parallel winding*. Fig. 1.12 (b) shows the equivalent circuit for lap winding in the case of a 4-pole machine.

- The total e.m.f. of the machine is equal to the e.m.f. generated in any one of the parallel paths.

- The total current output divides equally among the different paths in parallel.

(b) Wave Winding : In this type of winding, the two ends of each armature coil are bent in opposite directions and these ends are then connected to those commutator segments which are nearly two pole-pitches apart. Here a pole-pitch as will be seen in Section 1.7, means the distance between two adjacent field poles. Fig. 1.13 shows single and multi-turn coils used in the wave winding and Fig. 1.14 (a) shows the developed view of a part of simple wave winding using single-turn coils. Since the winding advances from pole to pole in the same direction round the armature in a manner similar to that of a wave, it is called the *wave winding*.

---

[*] *The connections between various coils are conveniently illustrated with the help of a developed winding diagram. This is a diagram in which the winding, together with the commutator, poles and brushes, is assumed to be cut and opened out flat.*

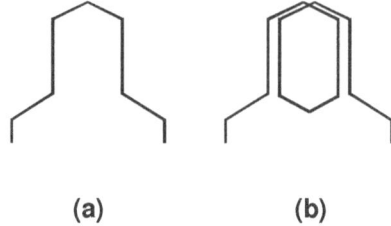

(a)   (b)

Fig. 1.13 : (a) Single-turn coil, wave winding,

(b) Multi-turn coil, wave winding

General Characteristic Features : Some of the important characteristic features of the wave winding are as follows :

- Only two brushes are necessary, although as many brushes as number of poles are frequently employed for lowering current carried per brush. This decreases the size of the brushes and reduces the length of the commutator.

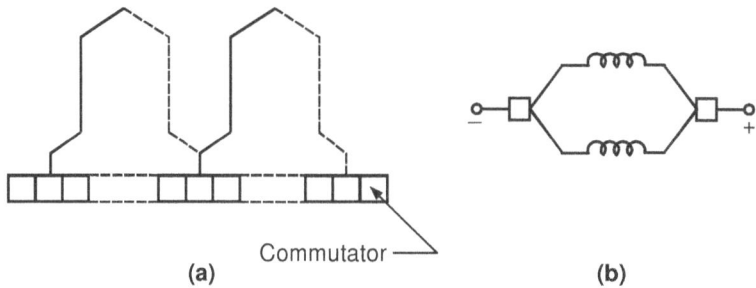

Commutator
(a)   (b)

Fig. 1.14 : (a) Developed view of a part of simple wave winding,

(b) Equivalent circuit, wave winding

- The number of parallel paths between the positive and negative brushes is always two, regardless of the number of poles. Because of this characteristic of the wave winding, it is also called *two circuit or series winding*. Fig. 1.14 (b) shows the equivalent circuit for the wave winding.

- The total e.m.f. of the machine is equal to the e.m.f. generated in any one of the parallel paths.

- Each parallel path supplies half of the total current output.

1.7 WINDING TERMINOLOGY

Before we study the armature winding in detail, it is necessary to get acquainted with some of the commonly used terms in connection with the windings.

- **Conductor :** It is the *active length* (part actually lying in the magnetic field and in which an e.m.f. is induced) of wire or strip embedded in the slot on the armature periphery.

- **Turn :** Every two conductors laid in a pair of slots and connected to each other form one *turn*.

• **Coil :** A coil may consist of a single turn or may consist of many turns connected in series. A coil with one turn is called a *single-turn coil* while a coil with more than one turn is known as *multi-turn coil.*

• **Pole-Pitch :** The pole-pitch is the centre to centre distance (over the armature periphery) between two adjacent poles. It is usually expressed in terms of *slots per pole or coil sides per pole.* e.g. if there are 24 slots, 24 coils, and 4 poles, then pole-pitch is,

$$\frac{24}{4} = 6 \text{ slots } \text{ or } \frac{24 \times 2}{4} = 12 \text{ coil sides}$$

• **Coil Span :** It is the distance on the periphery of the armature spanned by the two sides of the coil. It is usually expressed in terms of corresponding *armature slots* (or *coil sides*).

If the coil span is exactly equal to the pole-pitch, then such a coil is called a *full-pitch coil.* On the other hand, if its span is less than a pole-pitch, it is said to be a *fractional-pitch coil.* Alternatively, this type of coil is also called a *short-pitch or chorded coil.* For example, in a 6-pole armature having 96 slots, a coil spanning 15 teeth would obviously be a fractional-pitch or chorded coil (since pole-pitch is 16). Such a coil is said to be short-pitched or chorded by one *slot-pitch.* Here slot-pitch means the centre to centre distance between two consecutive slots.

The e.m.f. induced in the coil is maximum if the span of the coil is equal to the pole-pitch. This is because under this condition, the coil embraces almost whole of the useful flux per pole. However, sometimes the span is deliberately reduced as it effects a substantial saving in the copper used for end connections and gives improved performance.

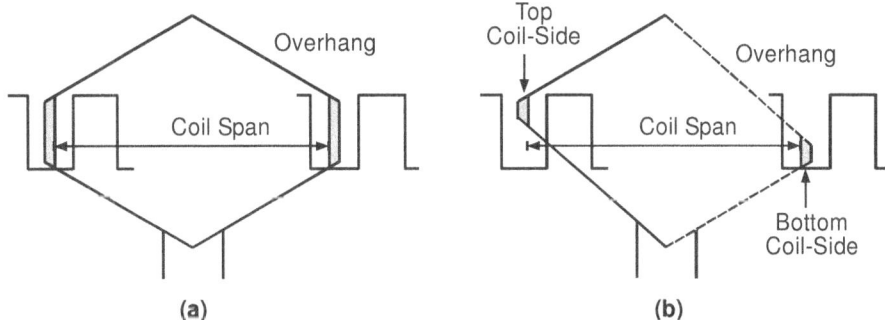

Fig. 1.15 : Single and double layer windings

• **Single Layer Winding :** In this type of winding, the two sides of each coil are placed in the two slots separated by a distance of approximately one pole-pitch as shown in Fig. 1.15 (a). In this type of winding arrangement, since each side of a coil fully occupies the slot in which it is placed, there is only one coil side per slot. Single layer windings are rarely used for armatures of d.c. machines.

• **Double Layer Winding :** In this type of winding arrangement, one side of every coil lies in the top half of one slot and its other side lies in the bottom half of some other slot, normally at a distance of about one pole-pitch (Fig. 1.15 b). Thus, there are at least two coil sides per slot.

1.8 CHOICE OF WINDING

With a given number of poles (except for two poles) and armature conductors, the wave winding gives a higher e.m.f. than the lap winding. This is because with fewer parallel paths, wave winding has a greater number of series connected conductors per parallel path. On the other hand, the number of parallel paths in a lap winding being more, for a given output current, the current per parallel path and hence the current per conductor is smaller than a corresponding value for the wave winding. Hence a smaller cross-sectional area is required for the conductor. In other words, for a given cross-sectional area of the armature conductor, current carrying capacity of the lap winding is comparatively greater. In general, *the wave windings are used for high-voltage, low-current machines whereas lap windings are used for low-voltage, heavy-current machines.*

1.9 E.M.F. EQUATION OF A D.C. GENERATOR

After studying the principle of generation of e.m.f. in an armature, now let us derive the quantitative relationship between the e.m.f. and the various factors involved in its generation. Let

ϕ = Useful flux per pole, in webers

Z = Total number of armature conductors

N = Speed of rotation of the armature, in revolutions per minute (r.p.m.)

P = Number of poles of a generator

A = Number of parallel paths through the armature winding between the positive and negative brushes (remember, A = 2 for wave winding and A = P for lap winding)

When the armature completes its one revolution, each conductor on it cuts the magnetic flux leaving all the North poles and also that entering all the South poles. Therefore, flux cut by one conductor per revolution

$$= \text{Flux per pole} \times \text{Number of poles}$$

$$= \phi \, P \text{ webers}$$

and　　　Time for one revolution　$= \dfrac{60}{N}$ seconds

Hence, according to Faraday's law of electromagnetic induction,

Average e.m.f. induced in one conductor due to flux cutting

$$= \frac{\text{Flux cut}}{\text{Time taken}} = \frac{\phi \, P}{60/N}$$

$$= \frac{\phi \, PN}{60} \text{ volts}$$

Now, number of parallel paths being A,

Number of conductors in series per parallel path $= \dfrac{Z}{A}$

∴　Resultant e.m.f. per parallel path

$$= \begin{bmatrix} \text{Average e.m.f.} \\ \text{per conductor} \end{bmatrix} \times \begin{bmatrix} \text{Number of conductors in} \\ \text{series per parallel path} \end{bmatrix}$$

$$= \frac{\phi\,PN}{60} \times \frac{Z}{A} = \frac{\phi\,ZN}{60} \cdot \frac{P}{A} \text{ volts} \qquad \ldots (1.1)$$

∴　　E.M.F. of a generator,　E = Resultant e.m.f. per parallel path

$$= \frac{\phi\,ZN}{60} \cdot \frac{P}{A} \text{ volts} \qquad \ldots (1.2)$$

Example 1.1 : *An 8-pole d.c. generator has a flux of 40 mWb per pole and a lap-connected armature with 960 conductors. Calculate the generated e.m.f. on open circuit when it runs at 400 r.p.m. If the armature were wave connected, at what speed must the machine be driven to generate the same voltage ?*

Solution :

Case 1 : Lap Connected Armature : From Equation (1.2),

$$E = \frac{\phi\,ZN}{60} \cdot \frac{P}{A}$$

With　$\phi = 40 \times 10^{-3}$ Wb,　Z = 960,　N = 400 r.p.m.,　P = 8　and　A = 8

$$E = \frac{40 \times 10^{-3} \times 960 \times 400}{60} \times \frac{8}{8}$$

$$= \textbf{256 V} \qquad \qquad \textbf{... Ans.}$$

Case 2 : Wave Connected Armature : Let N be the speed at which the machine with wave wound armature would generate a voltage of 256 V. Therefore, from the e.m.f. equation of a generator, we get

$$256 = \frac{40 \times 10^{-3} \times 960 \times N}{60} \times \frac{8}{2} \qquad (\because A = 2)$$

∴　　　　$N = \textbf{100 r.p.m.}$ 　　　　　　　**... Ans.**

1.10 TYPES OF D.C. GENERATORS

As already mentioned previously, in almost all the practical d.c. generators, the magnetic field is produced by electromagnetic means i.e. by using field poles. The direct current necessary to energise the field poles is called the *exciting current*. Depending upon the way in which the field windings are supplied with exciting current, the d.c. generators are classified into following two basic categories.

1.10.1 Separately Excited Generators

If the field winding of a generator is supplied with exciting current from an external d.c. source such as a battery, another generator or indeed any suitable d.c. supply, then such a generator is said to be *separately excited*. Fig. 1.16 shows diagrammatically the separately excited generator using battery for the supply of field current. In this diagram, F-FF represents the field winding and A-AA the armature. The field winding of a separately excited generator normally has a large number of turns of fairly thin wire and hence the high resistance in order to limit the field current to a small value. This is helpful in reducing the power loss in the field circuit. It should be remembered that when the required flux is to be produced with small current, the number of turns required for the winding is obviously large.

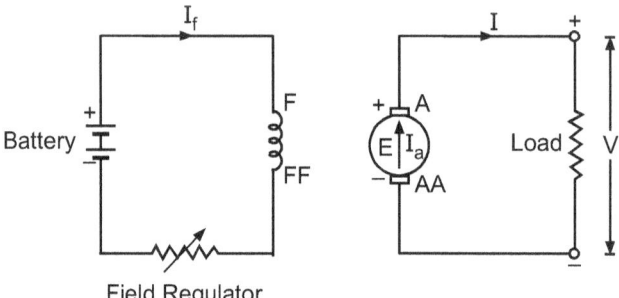

Fig. 1.16 : Schematic representation of a separately excited d.c. generator

1.10.2 Self-Excited Generators

If the field winding of a generator is supplied with the exciting current from the armature of the generator itself, it is said to be *self-excited*. In the normal condition, the field poles of such a generator always possess some *residual* or *remanent magnetism*. This enables the armature to generate small e.m.f. initially when the generator is started. This e.m.f. circulates small amount of current through the field winding thereby the original residual flux is strengthened and more e.m.f. is produced. This process being cumulative, ultimately generator voltage is built up to its full value.

Based on the manner in which field winding is connected to the armature winding, the self-excited generators are further classified as follows :

(i) Shunt Generators : When the field winding (Z-ZZ) is connected across the armature winding (A-AA) forming a parallel or shunt circuit, the generator is said to be a *shunt generator* (Fig. 1.17). The shunt field has a comparatively large number of turns of the fine gauge copper wire and hence the high resistance for the same reason as already discussed in the case of a separately excited generator.

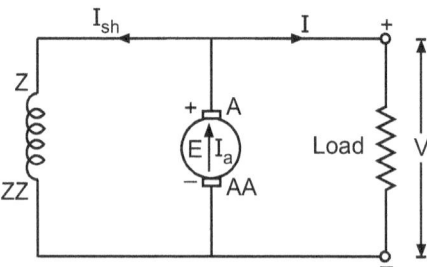

Fig. 1.17 : Schematic representation of a d.c. shunt generator

(ii) Series Generators : In this type of a d.c. generator, the field winding (Y-YY) is connected in series with the armature winding (A-AA) as shown in Fig. 1.18. The series field winding Y-YY has comparatively few turns of thick copper wire (or strip) and consequently a low resistance. It should be noted that in this case, the field current being large (= load current), the required flux can be produced even with a small number of turns.

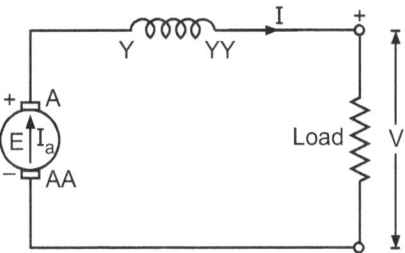

Fig. 1.18 : Schematic representation of a d.c. series generator

(iii) Compound Generators : A compound generator is a combination of a series and a shunt generator. In this type of a generator, both the shunt and series field windings are employed. The coils of both these windings are mounted on the same poles. If the series field winding (Y-YY) is connected in series with the armature winding (A-AA) and the shunt field winding (Z-ZZ) is connected across the armature only as illustrated in Fig. 1.19 (a), the generator is said to be a *short-shunt compound generator*. However, if the shunt field is connected across the armature and series field together as illustrated in Fig. 1.19 (b), the generator is called the *long-shunt compound generator.*

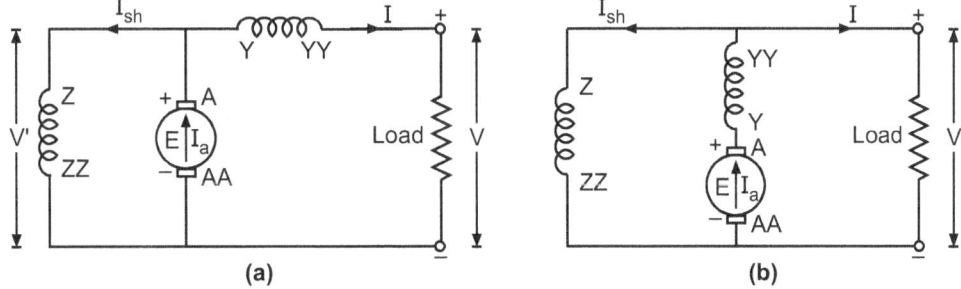

(a)   (b)

Fig. 1.19 : Schematic representation of (a) a short-shunt compound generator,

(b) a long-shunt compound generator

1.11 VOLTAGE AND CURRENT RELATIONSHIPS

When the machine runs as a generator, the generated e.m.f. (E) must be sufficient to supply both the terminal voltage (V) and the internal voltage drop. Voltage and current relationships for different types of generators can be easily derived from their connection diagrams (Figs. 1.16 to 1.19). These relationships are as follows :

(i) Separately Excited Generator :

$$I_a = I \qquad \qquad \text{... (1.3)}$$

and $\qquad\qquad E = V + I_a R_a \qquad\qquad \text{... (1.4)}$

(ii) Shunt Generator : $I_{sh} = \dfrac{V}{R_{sh}}$ ... (1.5)

$$I_a = I + I_{sh}$$ ... (1.6)

and $E = V + I_a R_a$ ... (1.7)

(iii) Series Generator : $I_a = I$ ... (1.8)

$$E = V + I_a (R_a + R_{se})$$ ... (1.9)

(iv) Short-shunt Compound Generator :

Voltage across the shunt field

$$V' = V + IR_{se}$$ ... (1.10)

$$I_{sh} = \frac{V'}{R_{sh}} = \frac{V + IR_{se}}{R_{sh}}$$ ... (1.11)

$$I_a = I + I_{sh}$$ ... (1.12)

$$E = V' + I_a R_a = (V + IR_{se}) + I_a R_a$$ ... (1.13)

(v) Long-shunt Compound Generator :

$$I_{sh} = \frac{V}{R_{sh}}$$ ... (1.14)

$$I_a = I + I_{sh}$$ ... (1.15)

$$E = V + I_a (R_a + R_{se})$$ ... (1.16)

where, E is the generated e.m.f., V the terminal voltage, I the load current, I_{sh} the shunt field current, I_a the armature current, R_a the armature resistance, R_{sh} the shunt field resistance and R_{se} the series field resistance.

Example 1.2 : *A series generator supplies a load of 50 kW at 200 V. If the resistances of the armature and the series field are 0.04 Ω and 0.02 Ω respectively, find the generated e.m.f.*

Solution : Fig. 1.18 shows the connection diagram for a series generator. Since the power supplied by the generator is 50 kW at 200 V,

$$\text{Load current, } I = \frac{\text{Power output}}{\text{Voltage}} = \frac{50 \times 10^3}{200} = 250 \text{ A}$$

Now, for a series generator,

$$\text{Armature current, } I_a = I = 250 \text{ A}$$

Therefore, from Equation (1.9),

$$E = V + I_a (R_a + R_{se})$$

With $V = 200 \text{ V}, R_a = 0.04 \text{ Ω} \text{ and } R_{se} = 0.02 \text{ Ω}$

$$E = 200 + 250 (0.04 + 0.02)$$

$$= \mathbf{215 \ V}$$ **... Ans.**

Example 1.3 : *A 4-pole, wave wound, 750 r.p.m. shunt generator has armature and field resistances of 0.4 Ω and 200 Ω respectively. The armature has 720 conductors and the flux per pole is 0.03 Wb. Find the terminal voltage when a load resistance of 10 Ω is connected across the generator.*

Solution : Fig. 1.17 shows the necessary connection diagram for a shunt generator. Since

$$E = \frac{\phi\, ZN}{60} \cdot \frac{P}{A}$$

With $\phi = 0.03$ Wb, Z = 720, N = 750 r.p.m., P = 4 and A = 2 (for wave winding)

$$E = \frac{0.03 \times 720 \times 750}{60} \times \frac{4}{2} = 540 \text{ V}$$

Now, let V be the terminal voltage. Then with a load resistance,

$$R_L = 10 \ \Omega \text{ and } R_{sh} = 200 \ \Omega$$

Load current, $I = \dfrac{V}{R_L} = \dfrac{V}{10}$ amperes

Shunt field current, $I_{sh} = \dfrac{V}{R_{sh}} = \dfrac{V}{200}$ amperes

∴   Armature current, $I_a = I + I_{sh} = \dfrac{V}{10} + \dfrac{V}{200}$

$$= (0.105 \text{ V}) \text{ amperes}$$

Therefore from Equation (1.7),

$$V = E - I_a\, R_a$$

$$= 540 - (0.105 \text{ V}) \times 0.4 \qquad (\because\ R_a = 0.4\ \Omega)$$

$$= 540 - 0.042 \text{ V}$$

∴ $V = \textbf{518.2 volts}$ **... Ans.**

Example 1.4 : *A long-shunt compound generator has a full-load output of 75 kW at 250 V. If the armature resistance is 0.075 Ω, the series field resistance 0.025 Ω and the shunt field resistance 50 Ω, find,*

(a) Armature current,

(b) E.M.F. generated.

Solution : Fig. 1.19 (b) shows the connection diagram for a long-shunt compound generator. Since the generator supplies a power of 75 kW at 250 V,

Load current, $I = \dfrac{75 \times 10^3}{250} = 300 \text{ A}$

Also, with shunt field resistance, $R_{sh} = 50 \ \Omega$

Shunt field current, $I_{sh} = \dfrac{V}{R_{sh}} = \dfrac{250}{50} = 5 \text{ A}$

∴   Armature current, $I_a = I + I_{sh} = 300 + 5 = \textbf{305 A}$ **... Ans.**

Now, as armature resistance, $R_a = 0.075 \ \Omega$ and series field resistance, $R_{se} = 0.025 \ \Omega$, from Equation (1.16), we have

$$E = V + I_a (R_a + R_{se})$$
$$= 250 + 305 (0.075 + 0.025)$$
$$= \textbf{280.5 V} \qquad \qquad \textbf{... Ans.}$$

Example 1.5 : *A 25 kW, short-shunt compound generator works on full load with a terminal voltage of 250 V. If its armature, shunt field and series field resistances are 0.05 Ω, 110 Ω and 0.06 Ω respectively, calculate the total e.m.f. generated in the armature of the machine under this condition.*

Solution : Fig. 1.19 (a) shows the necessary connection diagram of a short-shunt compound generator. Under full-load conditions, the generator delivers a power of 25 kW at 250 V. Hence, under this condition,

$$\text{Full-load current, } I = \frac{25 \times 10^3}{250} = 100 \text{ A}$$

$\therefore$ Voltage across the shunt field,

$$V' = V + IR_{se} = 250 + 100 \times 0.06$$
$$= \textbf{256 V} \qquad \qquad \textbf{... Ans.}$$

$\therefore$ $\quad$ Shunt field current, $I_{sh} = \dfrac{V'}{R_{sh}} = \dfrac{256}{110} = 2.33$ A

$\therefore$ $\quad$ Armature current, $I_a = I + I_{sh} = 100 + 2.33 = 102.33$ A

Therefore from Equation (1.13),

$$\text{Generated e.m.f., } E = V' + I_a R_a = 256 + 102.33 \times 0.05$$
$$= \textbf{261.1165 V} \qquad \qquad \textbf{... Ans.}$$

1.12 CHARACTERISTICS OF D.C. GENERATORS

In general, for any machine, *a performance characteristic* means a graph between two related quantities one of which is considered as the independent variable. Following are the most important characteristics of a d.c. generator :

• **Open Circuit Characteristic (O.C.C.) :** It is a graph between the e.m.f. generated (E) and the field current (I_f) at a given speed. Sometimes, this curve is also called *the no load characteristic or magnetization curve.* When a particular machine is run at constant speed on no load, the induced e.m.f. is proportional to the flux per pole (ϕ) and therefore to the flux density (B). Also the turns on the field being constant, the field m.m.f. and therefore magnetic field strength (H) is a function of the field current. Hence, the graph between the induced e.m.f. and the field current is nothing but the magnetization curve for the material of the field magnets.

• **Load Characteristic or External Characteristic :** The curve showing the variation of terminal voltage (V) with load current (I) under the given conditions of excitation and speed is called *the load or external characteristic* (both the related quantities being external to the armature) of the generator.

• **Internal or Total Characteristic :** It gives the relationship between the induced e.m.f. (E) and the armature current (I_a) at the particular excitation and speed. Both the quantities (E and I_a) being related with the armature, the characteristic is named as *internal characteristic** .

1.13 OPEN-CIRCUIT CHARACTERISTIC OF A D.C. GENERATOR

This is the basic characteristic of a d.c. generator on which all other characteristics depend. It may be obtained experimentally by running the generator at the normal speed on no load (Fig. 1.20 a) and recording the series of values of armature voltage (which under no-load condition is equal to the induced e.m.f.) corresponding to a series of values of field current.

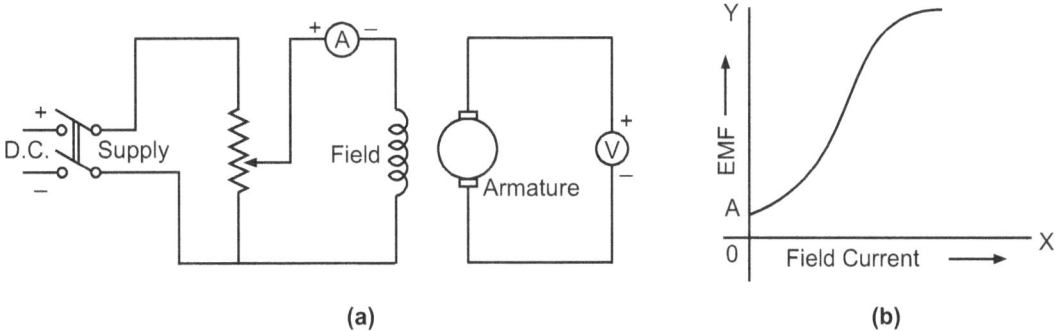

(a)   (b)

Fig. 1.20 : Determination of open-circuit characteristic of a d.c. generator

The field current is gradually increased from zero onwards till the armature voltage attains about 125% of its rated value. The field winding of the machine (even of shunt or series wound machine) is separately excited** to ensure smooth and independent flux control. The characteristic is shown in Fig. 1.20 (b). Due to residual magnetism in the poles, some e.m.f. is generated even when the field current is zero. Hence, the curve does not start from origin but starts at some higher point say A on Y-axis. For low values of field current, the curve is practically a straight line. However, as the field current is increased, the magnetic circuit starts getting saturated and the linear relationship between the e.m.f. and the field current no longer holds good. The curve becomes almost horizontal at the end when the magnetic circuit becomes fully saturated.

In the case of a d.c. generator, since $E \propto N$ when ϕ is constant, the open circuit characteristic at any speed can be derived from the open circuit characteristic at any other speed.

---

* *Very often the shunt field current is so small compared with the load current that it can be neglected. Hence there is also a practice to consider the internal characteristic as the plot between the induced e.m.f. (E) and the load current (I) at a particular excitation and speed.*

** *Sometimes, the test for experimental determination of O.C.C. of a shunt generator is conducted with the machine shunt connected. This is because the small field current supplied by the armature does not produce appreciable voltage drop in the armature circuit.*

1.14 VOLTAGE BUILDING IN SELF-EXCITED GENERATORS

Self-excited generators may have their field windings connected either in parallel or in series with the armature circuit. The process of voltage building, in the case of these generators requires that the field system should always have some residual magnetism. To understand the process of voltage building, consider the case of a shunt generator shown in Fig. 1.21 (a). When the machine is run to full speed on no load (with the main circuit left open), the e.m.f. induced in the armature, due to its rotation through the residual magnetic flux, sends a current through the field winding. This current may be in such a direction as to tend to increase the magnetic flux, or such as to tend to decrease it. With correct connections, this current gradually strengthens the magnetic field, and as a result the induced e.m.f. is increased. This, in turn, increases the field current, and so the voltage builds up until steady conditions are obtained. The maximum voltage that can be built up depends, for a given speed, entirely upon the total resistance of the field circuit and upon the open-circuit characteristic of the machine. To make this more clear, assume that the open-circuit characteristic and field circuit resistance line (a graph of terminal voltage V against field current I_{sh}) for the shunt machine under consideration are as shown in Fig. 1.21 (b). As the generator comes upto speed, as said earlier, there is a small e.m.f. OA induced in the armature due to residual magnetism in the magnetic circuit. This voltage when applied across the field winding sends a current OB through it. If the connections are proper, this current strengthens the magnetic flux, and as a result the induced e.m.f. is increased to OC. This voltage OC increases the field current to OD which in turn generates a still higher induced e.m.f. This process is cumulative. The e.m.f. continues to build up until point P is reached, where the field circuit resistance line crosses the open-circuit characteristic. The generator cannot build up beyond this point. This is because during the entire process of voltage building until point P, the e.m.f. generated by a given field current is always greater than that required to send that current through the field circuit. This will not be the case after point P. Hence the generator cannot build up the voltage beyond this point.

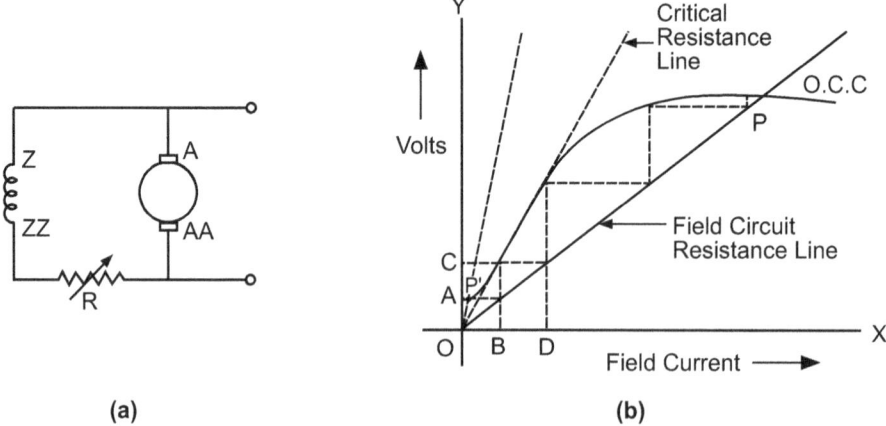

(a)   (b)

Fig. 1.21 : Building up of voltage in a d.c. shunt generator

If the slope of the field circuit resistance line is reduced by decreasing the field circuit resistance, the maximum voltage that can be built up (decided by the point of intersection of open-circuit characteristic and field circuit resistance line) will be higher. Similarly, if the slope of the field circuit resistance line is increased, the final voltage will be lower. If the field circuit resistance is increased to such an extent that field circuit resistance line cuts the open-circuit characteristic at point say p', then the machine will fail to excite at the given speed. If the field circuit resistance is such that the field circuit resistance line becomes tangential to the lower part of open circuit characteristic, then the machine just excites. This value of the field circuit resistance is called the *critical resistance* of the shunt field circuit at the given speed.

With a series generator, self-excitation and subsequent voltage building is not possible until the load circuit is completed. In the case of series generator also the final value of the voltage attained, for any speed of operation, is determined by the resistance of the field circuit which now forms the complete load circuit. Further, in this case also, appreciable building of voltage does not take place until the resistance of the entire circuit is reduced to a certain *critical* value determined by the speed of operation and the magnetization characteristic of the machine. Thus, the following conditions must be satisfied for self-excitation and subsequent voltage building in the case of self-excited d.c. generators.

- There must be some residual magnetism in the field system. The absence of residual magnetism is indicated by the zero reading of the voltmeter connected across the armature terminals. In such a condition, it may be necessary to connect the field terminals temporarily across a separate power supply such as that from a battery to build the residual magnetism. This is called *flashing the field*.

- The connection of the field circuit must be proper so that the field current that is established in it strengthens the magnetic field already existing.

- For a shunt generator, the total resistance of the field circuit must be less than the critical resistance corresponding to the given speed.

- For a series generator, the resistance of the complete load circuit must be less than the critical resistance at the given speed.

1.15 CHARACTERISTICS OF A SEPARATELY EXCITED GENERATOR

External Characteristic : Suitability of a generator for particular application is mainly decided by the nature of its external (or load) characteristic. The important information regarding how the terminal voltage of the generator varies with the load current can be obtained from this characteristic. The external characteristic of a separately excited generator can be experimentally obtained by conducting a load test on it as follows :

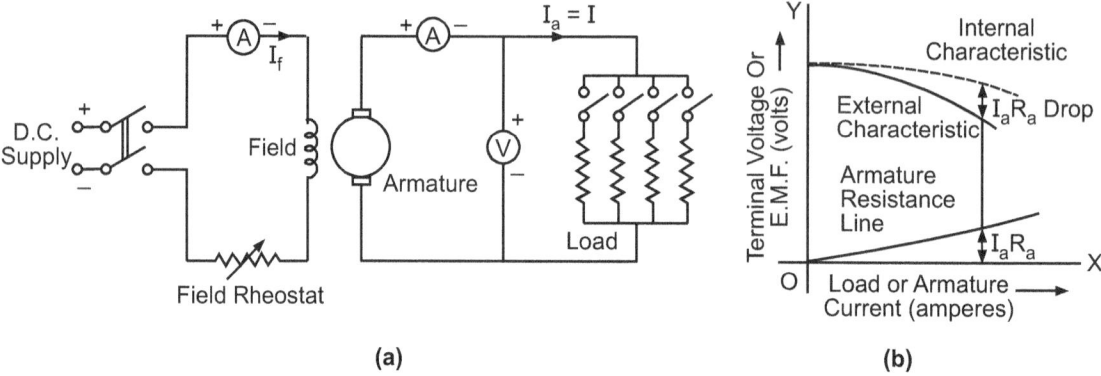

(a)　　　　　　　　　　　　(b)

Fig. 1.22 : (a) Load test on a separately excited d.c. generator,

(b) Characteristics of a separately excited generator

The connections are made as shown in Fig. 1.22 (a), the field being connected to a separate d.c. supply source. The machine is driven at a normal speed with the help of a suitable prime mover and the field current is adjusted to give the rated no-load voltage.[*] Since normally the rated no-load voltage of a machine is not known, first the field current is so adjusted that the rated voltage is obtained with full load applied on the machine using a variable loading resistance or a lamp bank. The machine is run for about 20 minutes under this condition so as to allow the field to reach its ultimate operating temperature. The load is then removed. The terminal voltage under this condition being the rated no-load voltage, the corresponding field current is the desired field current in this case. Keeping this excitation and the speed constant throughout, the machine is then again gradually loaded. The terminal voltage (V) and the load current (I) are measured at regular intervals and then plotted so as to obtain the external characteristic as shown in Fig. 1.22 (b). The characteristic is slightly drooping. As the load current increases, the terminal voltage of a generator falls due to :

- The increased voltage drop caused by the armature resistance.　　　$(\because V = E - I_a R_a)$

- Reduction of main flux and therefore of e.m.f. caused by the demagnetizing effect of armature reaction.[**]

Internal Characteristic : As said earlier, the internal characteristic of a d.c. generator gives the relationship between the induced e.m.f. (E) and the armature current (I_a). This characteristic can be easily obtained from the data of the load test conducted on a d.c. generator. The values of induced e.m.f. are obtained by adding $I_a R_a$ drop to the corresponding values of terminal voltage $(\because E = V + I_a R_a)$. These values of induced e.m.f. are then plotted against the corresponding

---

[*]　*As the value of the rated voltage on full load is known from the name plate of the machine, for all practical purposes, it is sufficient to adjust the voltage on no load as equal to or slightly more than this rated value.*

[**] *The effect of armature flux on the value and the distribution of the main magnetic field (produced by the main poles) of the machine is called armature reaction.*

values of armature current. Internal characteristic of a generator always lies above its external characteristic. Fig. 1.22 (b) shows the internal characteristic of a separately excited generator with dotted line. It should be remembered that in the case of a separately excited generator, armature current is same as the load current. Hence, by drawing the armature drop ($I_a R_a$) line and adding its ordinates at different points to the corresponding ordinates of the external characteristic, internal characteristic can also be obtained graphically.

Internal or total characteristic of a generator has very little practical importance and is of interest mainly to the designer.

1.16 VOLTAGE REGULATION

The voltage regulation of a d.c. generator (irrespective of the kind of excitation employed) is defined as *the change in its terminal voltage when the load is reduced from rated value to zero, expressed as a percentage of the rated-load voltage.* This change in voltage should be observed under the following conditions :

(i) The test should be conducted at rated speed allowing for the change in speed inherent in the prime mover.

(ii) After adjusting the rated-voltage at rated-load, the excitation should remain constant during the test for separately excited machines and external resistance in the field circuit shall remain constant for self-excited machine.

Thus, if   V = Rated-load voltage

and V_o = No-load voltage

Then,

$$\text{Voltage regulation} = \frac{V_o - V}{V} \times 100 \qquad \qquad \dots (1.17)$$

As an example, let us consider the generator having rated-load voltage of 230 V and no-load voltage of 250 V. Then by definition, the voltage regulation for this generator is

$$\text{Voltage regulation} = \frac{250 - 230}{230} \times 100 = \textbf{8.7 per cent}$$

1.17 CHARACTERISTICS OF A SHUNT GENERATOR

External Characteristic : The external characteristic of a shunt generator can be obtained by conducting a load test on it in a manner similar to that described for a separately excited generator. The connections are made as shown in Fig. 1.23 (a). The machine is driven at a normal speed and field current is adjusted to obtain rated no-load voltage. The position of the field rheostat is then kept undisturbed throughout. After this, the load is gradually applied and for different values of load current, corresponding values of terminal voltage are noted. The plot of terminal voltage against load current then gives the external characteristic of a shunt generator (Fig. 1.23 b).

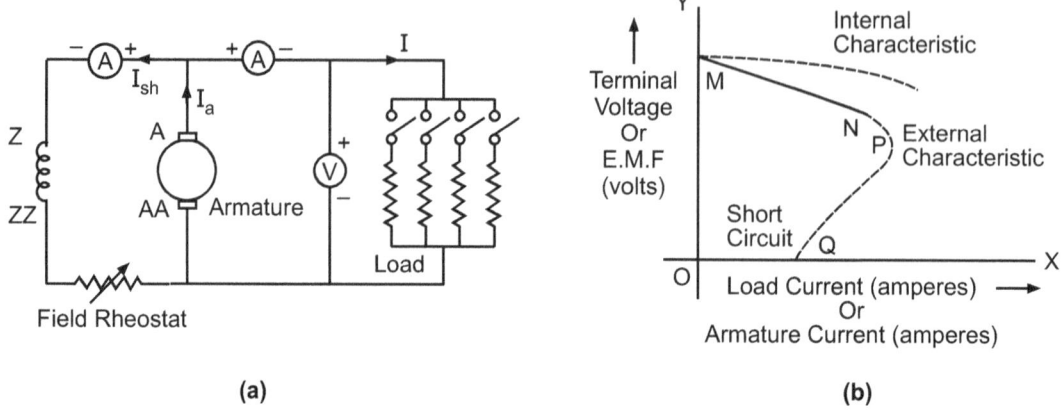

(a)   (b)

Fig. 1.23 : (a) Load test on a d.c. shunt generator,

(b) Characteristics of a shunt generator

The causes which contribute to the drop in terminal voltage as the load current is increased in the case of a separately excited generator are also present in the case of a shunt generator. However, reduction in the field current due to the decreased terminal voltage on account of the above mentioned factors further drops the terminal voltage of a shunt generator. Hence, the external characteristic of a shunt generator is more drooping in comparison with that of a separately excited generator as illustrated in Fig. 1.24 (a).

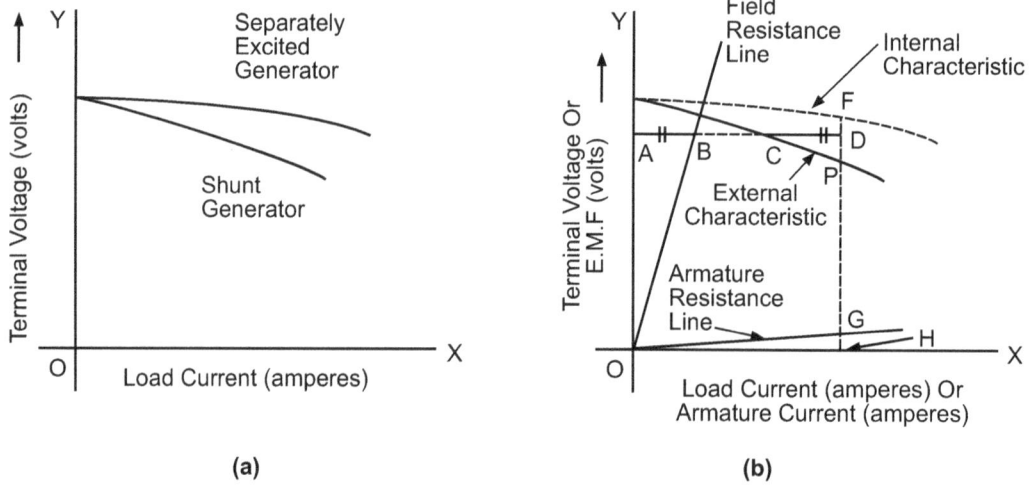

(a)   (b)

Fig. 1.24 : (a) Comparison of external characteristics of
separately excited and shunt generators,

(b) Graphical determination of internal characteristic of a shunt generator
from its external characteristic

Now again refer to the external characteristic of a d.c. shunt generator shown in Fig. 1.23 (b). The portion MN is the part of the external characteristic over a normal working region of a generator. Over this portion, as the load current is increased by progressive reduction in the load resistance, the terminal voltage falls due to the various reasons mentioned above. Further, this terminal voltage falls rapidly over the portion NP. Beyond point P, the increasing effects of armature reaction, resistance drop and decreasing field current cause the terminal voltage and hence the load current to reduce more rapidly than the increase in the load current due to decreased load resistance. This ultimately results into decreased load current and therefore the characteristic turns back as shown in the figure. Finally, when the load resistance is reduced to almost zero, the terminals of the generator get short circuited. As a result, the terminal voltage and hence the field current reduces to zero. This condition corresponds to point Q. The short circuit current OQ under this condition is considerably less than the normal full load current and is merely due to the weak residual magnetism (weakened by armature reaction) of the generator. If the shunt generator has to build up its field with the load circuit closed, the load resistance should not be below a certain minimum value called *critical resistance* for the load. Otherwise it will fail to excite. Thus the shunt generator has two critical resistances, one for the field circuit (refer to Section 1.14) and the other for the load.

Internal Characteristic : In the case of a d.c. shunt generator, we know that

$$I_a = I + I_{sh} \quad \text{and} \quad E = V + I_a R_a$$

The values of E and I_a therefore, can be calculated from the data of the load test conducted on the shunt generator and then plotted to obtain the internal characteristic as illustrated in Fig. 1.23 (b). Very often the field current is so small compared with the load current that it can be neglected.

Graphical Determination of Internal Characteristic : The internal characteristic may also be found graphically from the external characteristic as follows :

As seen earlier, plot the external characteristic from the data of the load test (Fig. 1.24 b). Similarly draw the field resistance line (V/I_{sh} curve) and the armature resistance line ($I_a R_a$/I_a curve). After this, select the different points on the external characteristic and find the corresponding points on the internal characteristic one by one. To illustrate the method, consider any point C on the external characteristic. Draw a horizontal line AC through C. For a load current AC at a terminal voltage OA, the shunt field current as given by the field-resistance line is then AB. Extend AC to D such that CD is equal to AB. Then AD is the corresponding armature current ($\because I_a = I + I_{sh}$). Next, draw the ordinate DGH. Then GH is the armature drop for a current AD. Finally, draw DF equal to GH. Then F is a point on the internal characteristic ($\because E = V + I_a R_a$). Number of points are obtained in a similar manner which when joined give the internal characteristic.

1.18 CHARACTERISTICS OF A SERIES GENERATOR

External Characteristic : As in the case of a separately excited or shunt generator, for a series generator also, external characteristic is obtained experimentally by conducting a load test. Connections are made as shown in Fig. 1.25 (a). The generator is driven at normal speed.

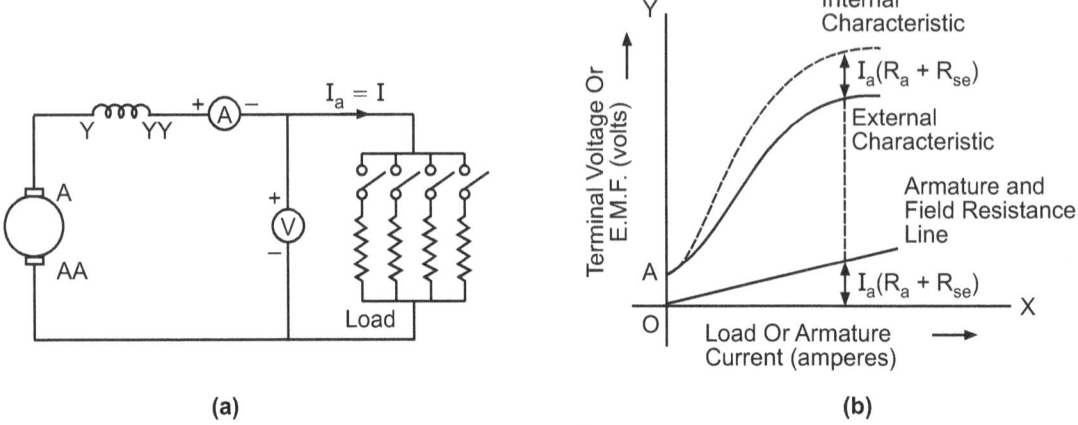

Fig. 1.25 : (a) Load test on a d.c. series generator,

(b) Characteristics of a series generator

The load current is then increased in steps and readings are taken at each step of the value of the load current and of the terminal voltage of the machine. These readings, when plotted, give the external characteristic. Fig. 1.25 (b) shows the typical external characteristic of a series generator. When the load current (or field current) is zero, the terminal voltage has some small value due to residual magnetism. Hence, the curve starts from A, and not from O. After loading, the load current entirely passes through the field winding. Therefore, as the load current increases, due to increased excitation, the induced e.m.f. increases. This ultimately results into increased terminal voltage. Thus the terminal voltage is directly dependent on the load current and is almost proportional to it until saturation of the magnetic circuit starts. At high loads, a stage comes when the terminal voltage starts decreasing due to excessive demagnetizing effect of armature reaction and rapidly increasing armature and field resistance drops.

Internal Characteristic : The values of the induced e.m.f. corresponding to different values of the armature currents can be obtained from the data of the load test conducted on a generator using the following relationship :

$$E = V + I_a (R_a + R_{se})$$

The plot between induced e.m.f. and armature current then gives the internal characteristic (Fig. 1.25 b). This characteristic can also be obtained graphically by adding ordinates of the ohmic drop line to the corresponding ordinates of the external characteristic.

1.19 CHARACTERISTICS OF A COMPOUND GENERATOR

In the compound generator, when the shunt field m.m.f. assists the series field m.m.f. i.e. when the fluxes produced by these two m.m.f.s are additive, it is said to be *cumulatively compounded*. Fig. 1.26 (a) shows the relative current directions in the series and shunt field coils on each pole of a cumulative compound generator and Fig. 1.26 (b) shows diagrammatically the short-shunt type cumulative compound generator connected to a load.

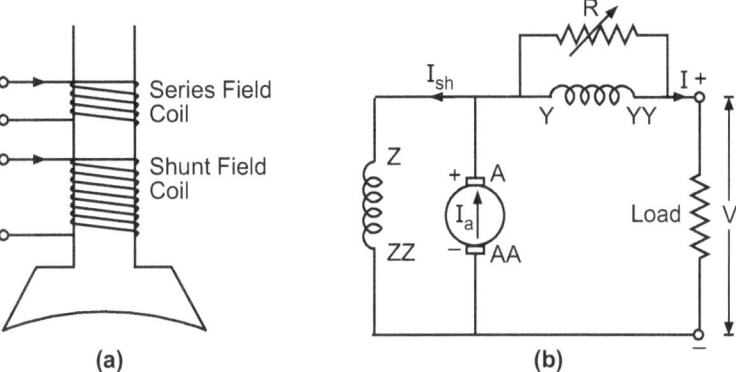

(a)   (b)

Fig. 1.26 : (a) Relative current directions in series and shunt field coils on each pole of a cumulative compound generator,

(b) Schematic representation of a cumulative compound generator (short-shunt)

From the study of the external characteristics of shunt and series generators, it follows that the shunt field alone gives the drooping characteristic while the series field alone gives the rising characteristic. Any characteristic in between these two can be obtained in a cumulative compound generator by the judicious combination of m.m.f.s provided by shunt and series fields (Fig. 1.27).

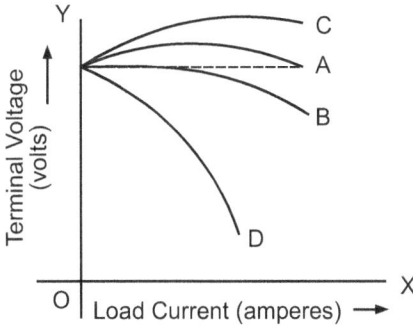

Fig. 1.27 : External characteristics of a compound generator

If the series field m.m.f. is so adjusted that the generator maintains its terminal voltage practically constant between no load and full load, then such a generator is said to be *level compounded* (curve A). When the m.m.f. provided by the series field is such that the rated load voltage of the generator is less than its no-load voltage, the generator is said to be *under compounded* (curve B) and when the rated load voltage of the generator is greater than its no-load voltage, the generator is said to be *over compounded* (curve C).

If the series field m.m.f. opposes the shunt field m.m.f. (Fig. 1.28 a), a drooping characteristic as illustrated by curve D (Fig. 1.27) is obtained, and this is referred to as *differential compounding*.

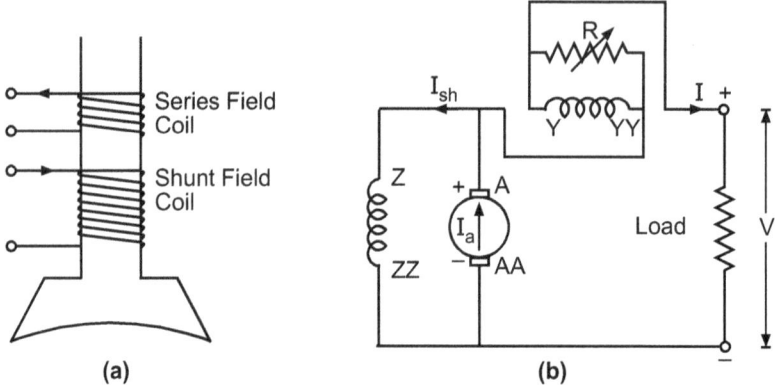

Fig. 1.28 : (a) Relative current directions in series and shunt field coils on each pole of a differential compound generator,

(b) Schematic representation of a differential compound generator (short-shunt)

All the above characteristics (external) of a compound generator can be experimentally determined by conducting a load test on it in a manner similar to that in other types of generators. While conducting this test, the degree of compounding is regulated by shunting more or less current away from the series field. To do this, a variable low resistance, called *diverter* (R), is used in parallel with the series field as illustrated in Figs. 1.26 and 1.28 (b).

1.20 COMPARISON OF EXTERNAL CHARACTERISTICS OF DIFFERENT TYPES OF D.C. GENERATORS

For comparison, the external characteristics of different types of d.c. generators are drawn together in Fig. 1.29. While drawing these characteristics, the rated voltage is assumed to be same for all the generators.

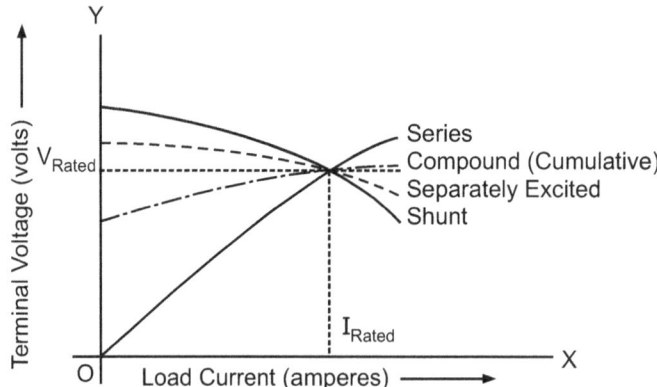

Fig. 1.29 : External characteristics of different types of d.c. generators

1.21 APPLICATIONS OF D.C. GENERATORS

• **Separately Excited Generators :** Separate excitation requires a separate source of direct current and is therefore, usually more expensive than self-excitation. Therefore, it is used only in special applications where voltage variation over a wide range is required or where a quick and definite response to control is important e.g. in automatic motor control system, main generators in d.c. ship propulsion, electroplating, electro-refining of metals.

- **Shunt Generators :** Because of their constant voltage characteristic, these generators are commonly used for ordinary lighting and power purposes. They are also useful for charging of batteries.

- **Series Generators :** Because of their rising voltage characteristic, series generators have very limited field of applications. They are normally used for constant current application. These generators were used quite extensively for lighting arc lamps. Presently, they are commonly used as boosters on d.c. feeders for compensating line drops.

- **Cumulative Compound Generators :** Over compounded generators are commonly used for ordinary lighting and power purposes. Over compounding is made to take care of the voltage drop in the distribution networks so that the voltage at consumer's premises may be approximately constant. They are more suitable in the situation where the variation in load is abrupt and large e.g. in traction.

- **Differential Compound Generators :** These generators are used only in some special applications e.g. electric arc welding.

1.22 POINTS TO REMEMBER

- Generator converts mechanical energy supplied to it into electrical energy.

- The operation of all electrical generators, whether d.c. or a.c., is based on the fact that when a conductor is moved in the magnetic field or a magnetic field moved with respect to the conductor, according to Faraday's law of electromagnetic induction, an electromotive force is set up in the conductor.

- Wave windings are used for high-voltage, low-current machines whereas lap windings are used for low-voltage, heavy-current machines.

- If the field winding of a generator is supplied with the exciting current from an external d.c. source (e.g. battery, suitable d.c. supply), then such a generator is said to be *separately excited.*

- If the field winding of a generator is supplied with the exciting current from the armature of the generator itself, it is said to be *self-excited.*

- A compound generator is combination of a series and shunt generator.

- For self-excitation and subsequent voltage building in the case of a self-excited d.c. generator, there must be some residual magnetism in the field system. In the absence of residual magnetism (as indicated by zero reading of the voltmeter connected across the armature terminals), it becomes necessary to connect the field terminals temporarily across a separate d.c. power supply such as that from a battery to build the residual magnetism. This is called *flashing the field.*

- Voltage regulation of a d.c. generator is defined as the change in its terminal voltage when the load is reduced from rated value to zero, expressed as a percentage of the rated voltage. This change in voltage is observed under constant speed and constant excitation conditions.

- In a compound generator, when the shunt field m.m.f. assists the series field m.m.f. (i.e. when the fluxes produced by these two m.m.fs are additive), it is said to be *cumulatively compounded.*

- In a compound generator, when the series-field m.m.f. opposes the shunt-field m.m.f., it is said to be *differentially compounded.*

1.23 IMPORTANT FORMULAE AT A GLANCE

- E.M.F. of a generator, $E = \dfrac{\phi ZN}{60} \cdot \dfrac{P}{A}$ volts

  where

  ϕ = Useful flux per pole, in webers

  Z = Total number of armature conductors

  N = Speed of rotation of the armature, in r.p.m.

  P = Number of poles of a generator

  A = Number of parallel paths through the armature winding between the positive and negative brushes ($A = 2$ for wave winding and $A = P$ for lap winding)

- **Voltage and Current Relationships for Different Types of D.C. Generators :**

  (i) Separately Excited Generator :

  $$I_a = I$$

  $$E = V + I_a \cdot R_a$$

  (ii) Shunt Generator :

  $$I_{sh} = \frac{V}{R_{sh}}$$

  $$I_a = I + I_{sh}$$

  $$E = V + I_a \cdot R_a$$

  (iii) Series Generator :

  $$I_a = I$$

  $$E = V + I_a (R_a + R_{se})$$

  (iv) Short-Shunt Compound Generator :

  Voltage across the shunt field,

  $$V' = V + I \cdot R_{se}$$

  $$I_{sh} = \frac{V'}{R_{sh}} = \frac{V + I \cdot R_{se}}{R_{sh}}$$

  $$I_a = I + I_{sh}$$

  $$E = V' + I_a R_a = (V + I \cdot R_{se}) + I_a \cdot R_a$$

(v) Long-Shunt Compound Generator :

$$I_{sh} = \frac{V}{R_{sh}}$$

$$I_a = I + I_{sh}$$

$$E = V + I_a (R_a + R_{se})$$

where E is the generated e.m.f. (in volts), V the terminal voltage (in volts), I the load current (in amperes), I_{sh} the shunt-field current (in amperes), I_a the armature current (in amperes), R_a the armature resistance (in ohms), R_{sh} the shunt-field resistance (in ohms) and R_{se} the series-field resistance (in ohms).

- Voltage regulation of a d.c. generator $= \dfrac{V_0 - V}{V} \times 100$ per cent

where   V = Rated load voltage, in volts

           V_0 = No-load voltage, in volts

1.24 EXERCISES

1.24.1 Review Questions

1. Draw a neat labelled diagram of the cross-section of a four-pole, d.c. shunt connected generator. What are the essential functions of the field coils, armature, commutator and brushes ?

2. Differentiate between lap and wave windings and name their fields of application.

3. Develop from first principles, an expression for the e.m.f. of a d.c. generator.

4. Distinguish clearly between a separately excited and a self-excited generator.

5. State the different types of self-excited generators and mention their fields of application.

6. Explain the process of building up of voltage in a self-excited d.c. generator.

7. What are the necessary conditions for the generators to be self-excited ?

8. Name the different types of characteristics of a d.c. generator and state which of them is of most practical importance.

9. Define the term critical resistance with reference to a d.c. shunt generator and bring out its role in the process of self-excitation of d.c. machine.

10. Sketch the load characteristics of separately excited, shunt and series type d.c. generators and give reasons for the particular shape in each case.

11. What is voltage regulation of a d.c. generator ? Explain.

12. Distinguish between the internal characteristic and external characteristic of a d.c. generator. How can the internal characteristic be derived from the external characteristic of (a) Separately excited generator, (b) Shunt generator, (c) Series generator ?

13. What do you understand by a compound generator ? How is the generator made cumulative and differential compound ? Differentiate between over, level and under compounding.

1.24.2 Examples for Practice

1. The armature of a 4-pole d.c. generator is required to generate an e.m.f. of 500 V on open circuit, when running at 600 r.p.m. Calculate the magnetic flux per pole required if the armature has 160 slots with two coil sides per slot, each coil containing three turns. The armature is wave wound   (26.04 mWb)

2. A series generator supplies a load of 100 kW at 200 V. Its armature resistance is 0.04 Ω and series field resistance is 0.02 Ω. What is the e.m.f. generated ?   (230 V)

3. A separately excited, 4-pole, lap wound d.c. generator has 960 armature conductors and total resistance of the armature circuit is 0.05 Ω. Calculate the useful flux per pole required to generate an open circuit e.m.f. of 500 V at a speed of 1000 r.p.m. The generator armature is now connected to an external load of resistance 9.5 Ω, the speed and flux being maintained constant. Calculate the terminal voltage and output.

                           (0.0312 Wb, 497.38 V, 26040.7 W)

4. The armature of a 4-pole, lap wound, shunt generator has 128 slots with four conductors pet slot. Its shunt field resistance is 50 Ω and the armature resistance is 0.025 Ω. If the flux per pole is 0.05 Wb, find the speed of the machine when supplying 100 kW at a terminal voltage of 250 V.   (610 r.p.m)

5. A 4-pole long-shunt compound generator has 600 lap connected conductors on its armature. The armature, series field and shunt field resistances are 0.1, 0.1 and 250 Ω respectively. The machine is delivering a load of 50 kW at 500 V. If the flux per pole is 0.05 Wb, calculate the speed of a machine.   (1041 r.p.m.)

6. A short-shunt compound generator feeds a load taking 100 A at 250 V. The resistance of the leads is 0.1 Ω, armature resistance 0.05 Ω, shunt field resistance 100 Ω and series field resistance 0.015 Ω. Find the e.m.f. generated.   (266.631 V)

D.C. MOTORS

2.1 INTRODUCTION

As said earlier, the electric motor is a machine which converts electrical energy into mechanical energy and so its function is exactly the reverse of that of a generator. In fact, the same machine can be interchangeably used as a generator or motor depending upon whether the electrical energy is supplied by it or supplied to it. Present day large scale utilization of electrical energy is possible only because of the development of the various types of electrical motors to suit different industrial and domestic applications. Every modern industry of today incorporates such motors either into its products, or its manufacturing processes. The number of homes equipped with domestic appliances using electric motors is also increasing very fastly. Study of electric motors is, therefore, of vital importance.

Among the different types of electric motors that are available, induction type a.c. motors are most widely adopted in industrial drives. Even then, use of d.c. motors becomes essential in many industrial applications due to their typical performance characteristics and precise speed control over a wide range. Hence, various aspects like operating principle, types, characteristics, starting, reversal of rotation, speed control and industrial applications of d.c. motors are discussed in this chapter.

2.2 GENERAL PRINCIPLE OF AN ELECTRIC MOTOR

We know that *when a conductor carrying current is placed in a magnetic field, it experiences a mechanical force.* The action of an electric motor is based on this principle. It has some suitable mechanical arrangement to utilize this force in producing the motion (rotation) of the conductors as illustrated in Fig. 2.1.

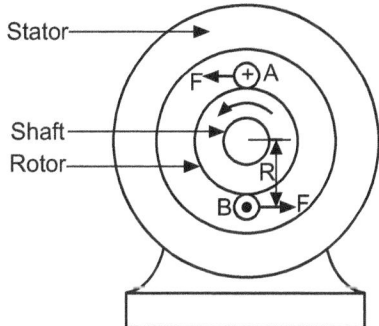

Fig. 2.1 : Production of torque in a motor

The turning or twisting moment of a force about an axis is known as *torque*. It is measured by the product of the force (F) and the radius (R) at which this force acts, the unit being *newton-metre (Nm)*.

The production of the torque requires the interaction of two sets of magnetic fields produced by two sets of windings both carrying currents. One set of windings is placed on the stationary outer member called *stator* and the other set on the rotating member called *rotor*. The principle is illustrated in Fig. 2.2 which shows a rotating member in the form of a coil (AB) free to rotate about its axis in a uniform magnetic field produced by the current carrying winding on the outer stationary member.

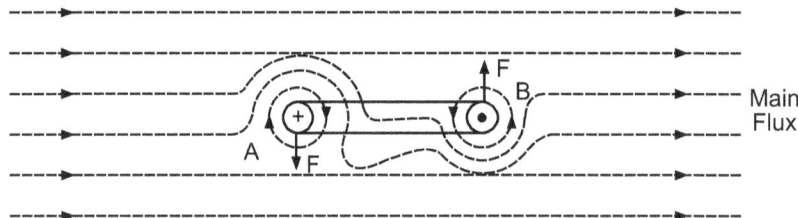

Fig. 2.2 : Principle of torque production in a motor

If this coil is supplied with current directly or by induction, the magnetic flux associated with this current will interact with the main magnetic flux resulting into a motion of the coil due to force and subsequent torque experienced by each coil side. With the current in the direction as indicated, the motion of the coil will be in an anticlockwise direction. This is obvious from the resultant flux pattern shown in Fig. 2.2. The direction of the force (F) which will be experienced by each coil side can also be found by using Fleming's left hand rule. The principle of torque production is basically the same whether the currents producing the two fields originate from a.c. or d.c. supplies.

In all the commonly encountered varieties of practical electric motors, either or both the sets of windings mentioned above are excited by alternating or direct current. When direct current (d.c.) is supplied to both rotor and stator windings, the motors are known as *d.c. motors*. On the other hand, in *induction motors*, alternating current is supplied directly to the stator winding and by induction (i.e. by transformer action) to the rotor winding. In synchronous motors, alternating current is supplied to the stator winding and direct current (d.c.) to the rotor winding. We shall begin our study of electric motors firstly with the study of d.c. motors.

2.3 PRINCIPLE OF WORKING OF A D.C. MOTOR

As mentioned previously, a d.c. motor utilizes the direct current in its operation to produce the torque required for driving the mechanical load. The study of an elementary d.c. motor will be very helpful in understanding the working principle of a d.c. motor. Let us therefore first study the elementary d.c. motor.

2.4　ELEMENTARY D.C. MOTOR

Fig. 2.3 shows an elementary d.c. motor.

Construction : The construction of this elementary d.c. motor is exactly similar to that of an elementary d.c. generator shown in Fig. 1.4 except that the armature coil (AB) is now supplied with direct current through the brushes B_1 and B_2 in contact with the commutator segments using some direct current source like battery.

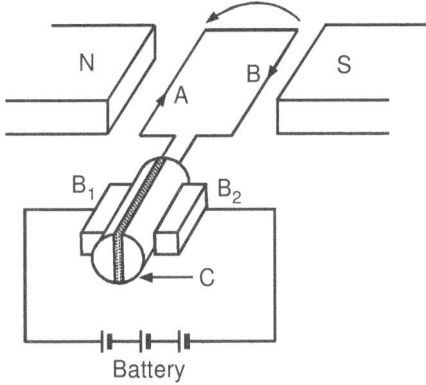

Fig. 2.3 : An elementary d.c. motor

Working : Being in the magnetic field of the magnet, each current carrying conductor (A and B) of the armature coil experiences a force which ultimately results into rotation of the armature coil. To understand how unidirectional torque is produced in a d.c. motor, consider the armature coil in its different positions as shown in Fig. 2.4.

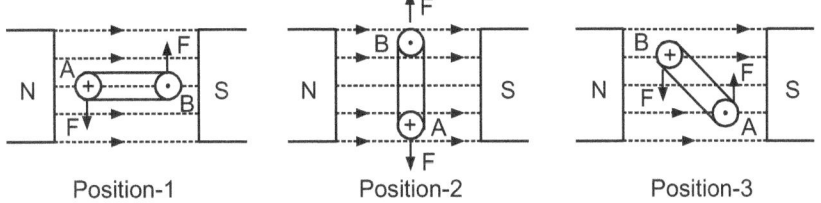

Position-1　　　　Position-2　　　　Position-3

Fig. 2.4 : Torque developed at different positions of the coil

Position No. 1 : In this position, plane of the coil lies parallel to a magnetic field. The direction of the current in the conductor A is into the plane of the paper and in the conductor B it is out of the plane of the paper. Therefore, the conductor A tends to move downward and the conductor B tends to move upward with equal force F (by Fleming's left hand rule or considering the resultant field pattern). These two forces thus produce a torque tending to rotate the coil about its axis in a counterclockwise direction. In this position, the coil experiences maximum torque because the perpendicular distance between two forces is also maximum.

Position No. 2 : When the coil reaches this position, the two forces being opposite to each other and the perpendicular distance between them being zero, the torque experienced by the coil is also zero. Therefore, the coil tends to remain stationary in this position.

Position No. 3 : Even though the coil has tendency to remain stationary in Position-2, because of its inertia, it crosses this position and at the same time, the direction of the current in the coil is reversed by the commutator. Therefore, the coil continues to experience the torque in the counterclockwise direction only. Thus the commutator plays a very important part in the operation of the d.c. motor. *It reverses the current in each conductor of the armature as it passes from one pole to another and thus helps to develop a continuous and unidirectional torque.*

2.5 PRACTICAL D.C. MOTORS

A single coil elementary d.c. motor shown in Fig. 2.3 is almost impractical because of pulsating torque developed by it. In the practical d.c. motor, by using number of coils evenly distributed around the armature core and connecting these coils to a commutator having a corresponding number of segments, a more uniform torque is obtained. Practical d.c. motors are similar in construction to direct current generators. In fact, as already mentioned previously, the same machine can be interchangeably used as a generator or motor.

2.6 BACK OR COUNTER E.M.F.

We have seen that when the current carrying conductors of the armature winding are placed in the magnetic field produced by the field winding, each of them experiences a force and as a result, the armature of the motor starts rotating. When these armature conductors start rotating, the flux which is responsible for their rotation is cut and consequently an e.m.f. is induced in them in accordance with Faraday's law of electromagnetic induction. This e.m.f. always acts in opposition with the applied voltage (V) as per Lenz's law and therefore it is known as *back e.m.f. (E_b) or counter e.m.f.* (Fig. 2.5). Since the counter e.m.f. opposes the applied voltage across the armature, the net voltage acting in the armature circuit is the difference between the two (i.e. $V - E_b$). It is this effective voltage which determines the value of the armature current (I_a). If R_a is the armature resistance, then from Ohm's law,

$$I_a = \frac{V - E_b}{R_a} \text{ amperes} \qquad \qquad \dots (2.1)$$

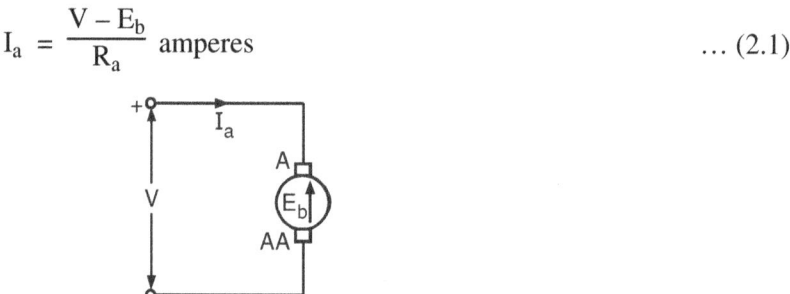

Fig. 2.5 : Back e.m.f. or counter e.m.f. in the armature of a d.c. motor

In the running condition, E_b is nearly equal to V. The internal resistance of the armature of a d.c. motor being very low, it is the back e.m.f. which mainly limits the armature current in the running condition of the motor. The Equation (2.1) can be rewritten as

$$V = E_b + I_a R_a \qquad \qquad \dots (2.2)$$

This is known as *voltage equation* of the motor. It shows that in order to maintain the current supply to armature, the applied voltage has to overcome not only the resistance of the armature winding but also the back e.m.f.

Similar to generator, the magnitude of the back e.m.f. generated in the armature of a d.c. motor is given by the following expression :

$$E_b = \frac{\phi\, Z \cdot N}{60} \cdot \frac{P}{A} \text{ volts} \qquad \qquad \dots (2.3)$$

where,　　　　　　　　ϕ = Flux per pole, in webers

　　　　　　　　　　　　N = Speed, in revolutions per minute

　　　　　　　　　　　　Z = Number of armature conductors

　　　　　　　　　　　　P = Number of poles

　　　　　　　　　　　　A = Number of parallel paths

Example 2.1 : *A 230 V, 4-pole d.c. motor has an armature circuit resistance of 0.5 Ω. Find the back e.m.f. in the motor when the armature current is 25 A. If the armature winding is lap connected with 320 conductors and the useful flux per pole is 50 mWb, calculate the speed.*

Solution : Equation (2.2) gives,

$$E_b = V - I_a R_a$$

With　V = 230 V, R_a = 0.5 Ω and I_a = 25 A,

$$E_b = 230 - 25 \times 0.5 = \mathbf{217.5\ V} \qquad \qquad \textbf{... Ans.}$$

Now, from Equation (2.3),

$$E_b = \frac{\phi\, Z \cdot N}{60} \cdot \frac{P}{A}$$

With　$\phi = 50 \times 10^{-3}$ Wb, Z = 320, P = 4, A = 4 (for lap connection),

$$E_b = 217.5 = \frac{50 \times 10^{-3} \times 320 \times N}{60} \times \frac{4}{4}$$

$\therefore$　　　　　　　　　N = **816 r.p.m.** 　　　　　　　　　　**... Ans.**

2.7 TORQUE EQUATION OF A D.C. MOTOR

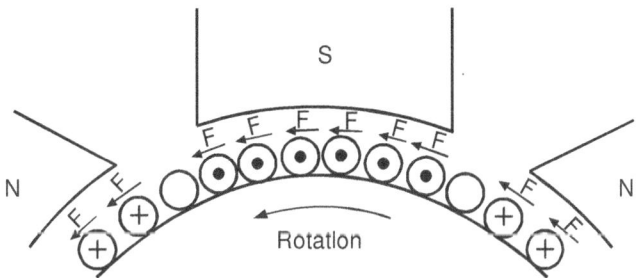

Fig. 2.6 : Torque on motor armature

In a d.c. motor, each armature conductor by virtue of the force experienced by it, exerts a torque tending to turn the armature (Fig. 2.6). The sum of all these torques due to individual conductors is called *gross* or *armature torque* (T). Let us now derive the expression for this torque. For this, let

ϕ = Flux per pole, in webers

Z = Total number of armature conductors

I_a = Total armature current, in amperes

P = Number of poles

A = Number of parallel paths in the armature winding

D = Diameter of the armature, in metres

L = Length of the armature, in metres

(giving the effective length of each armature conductor)

Then,

Average flux density under a pole face,

$$B = \frac{P\phi}{\pi DL} \text{ teslas}$$

Current per armature conductor,

$$I = \frac{I_a}{A} \text{ amperes}$$

$\therefore$ Force on each armature conductor,

$$F = BIl = \frac{P\phi}{\pi DL} \cdot \frac{I_a}{A} \cdot L$$

$$= \frac{P\phi I_a}{\pi DA} \text{ newtons}$$

Hence, Torque due to each conductor

$$= F \times \frac{D}{2} = \frac{P\phi I_a}{\pi DA} \times \frac{D}{2}$$

$$= \frac{P\phi I_a}{2\pi A} \text{ newton-metres}$$

$\therefore$ Total armature torque, $T = \left(\frac{P\phi I_a}{2\pi A}\right) \times Z$

$$= \frac{1}{2\pi} \phi Z I_a \cdot \frac{P}{A}$$

$$= 0.159 \, \phi Z I_a \cdot \frac{P}{A} \text{ newton-metres} \qquad \ldots (2.4)$$

For a particular machine, Z, P and A being fixed,

$$T \propto \phi \cdot I_a \qquad \ldots (2.5)$$

Thus it should be noted that *the torque of a d.c. motor is proportional to the product of the flux per pole and the armature current.*

Alternative Method : The torque equation of a d.c motor can also be derived as follows :

From Equation (2.2), we know that for a d.c. motor,

$$E_b = V - I_a \cdot R_a$$

Multiplying both the sides by I_a, we have

$$E_b \cdot I_a = VI_a - I_a^2 \cdot R_a \qquad \ldots (2.6)$$

In the above expression,

$$V.I_a = \text{Total electrical power supplied to the armature.}$$

$$I_a^2 .R_a = \text{Power loss due to the resistance of the armature circuit (armature copper loss).}$$

Therefore, the difference between the above two quantities, namely $E_b.I_a$ represents the mechanical power developed by the armature. Now if T is the corresponding torque in newton-metres developed by the armature and ω is the angular velocity of the armature in radians/second, then it is obvious that

$$E_b \cdot I_a = T \cdot \omega \qquad \ldots (2.7)$$

But (with usual notations), $\omega = \dfrac{2\pi N}{60}$

and $E_b = \dfrac{\phi ZN}{60} \cdot \dfrac{P}{A}$ (Refer to Equation 2.3)

Substituting these values of ω and E_b in the Equation (2.7), we get

$$\frac{\phi ZN}{60} \cdot \frac{P}{A} \cdot I_a = T \cdot \frac{2\pi N}{60}$$

$\therefore$ $$T = \frac{1}{2\pi} \phi ZI_a \cdot \frac{P}{A} = 0.159 \, \phi \, ZI_a \cdot \frac{P}{A} \text{ newton-metres}$$

Shaft Torque : The whole of the torque developed by the armature is not available at the shaft for doing useful work since a part of it is used in overcoming the friction, windage and iron losses. The torque which is available at the shaft for doing useful work is known as *shaft torque (T_{sh}).*

Example 2.2 : *A 4-pole d.c. motor has lap connected armature winding with 576 conductors and draws an armature current of 25 A. If the flux per pole is 0.02 Wb, calculate the gross torque developed by the motor.*

Solution :   We know that, $T = 0.159 \, \phi \, ZI_a \cdot \dfrac{P}{A}$ newton-metres

Here, $\phi = 0.02$ Wb, $Z = 576$, $I_a = 25$ A, $P = 4$, $A = 4$

Substituting these values in the above equation, we get

$$T = 0.159 \times 0.02 \times 576 \times 25 \times \frac{4}{4} = \textbf{45.79 Nm} \qquad \ldots \textbf{Ans.}$$

2.8 TYPES OF D.C. MOTORS

Similar to d.c. generators, depending upon the way of connecting the field winding with the armature winding, the d.c. motors may be series wound, shunt wound or compound wound as illustrated schematically in Fig. 2.7.

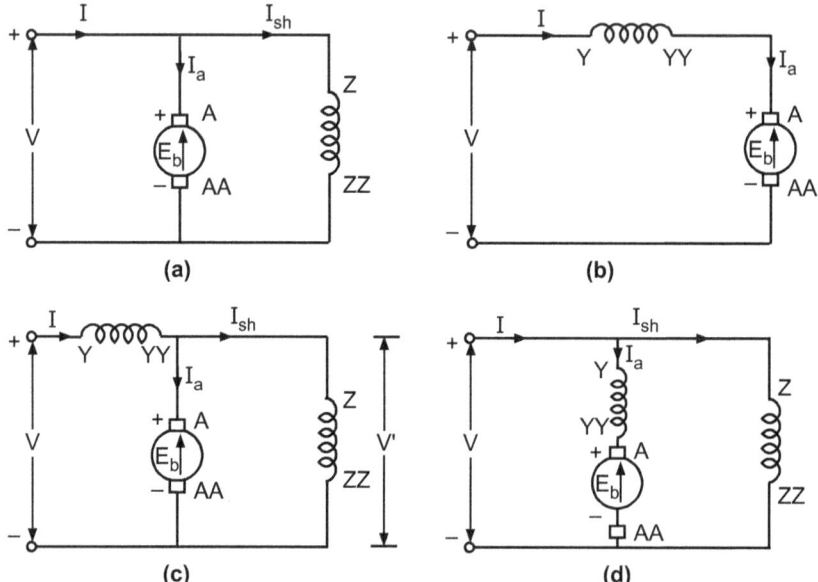

Fig. 2.7 : Schematic representation of

(a) a d.c. shunt motor,   (b) a d.c. series motor,

(c) a short-shunt compound motor, (d) a long-shunt compound motor

2.9 VOLTAGE AND CURRENT RELATIONSHIPS

When the d.c. machine runs as a motor, the applied voltage (V) across its terminals must be sufficient to overcome the back e.m.f. (E_b) and supply the internal voltage drop. Voltage and current relationships for different types of motors can be very easily derived from their connection diagrams shown in Fig. 2.7. These relationships are as follows :

(i) Shunt Motor :
$$I_{sh} = \frac{V}{R_{sh}} \qquad \qquad \ldots (2.8)$$

$$I_a = I - I_{sh} \qquad \qquad \ldots (2.9)$$

$$E_b = V - I_a R_a \qquad \qquad \ldots (2.10)$$

(ii) Series Motor :
$$I_a = I \qquad \qquad \ldots (2.11)$$

$$E_b = V - I_a (R_a + R_{se}) \qquad \qquad \ldots (2.12)$$

(iii) Short-shunt Compound Motor :

Voltage across the shunt field, $V' = V - I R_{se}$ $\qquad \ldots (2.13)$

$$I_{sh} = \frac{V'}{R_{sh}} = \frac{V - I R_{se}}{R_{sh}} \qquad \qquad \ldots (2.14)$$

$$I_a = I - I_{sh} \qquad \qquad \ldots (2.15)$$

$$E_b = V' - I_a R_a = V - I R_{se} - I_a R_a \qquad \qquad \ldots (2.16)$$

(iv) Long-shunt Compound Motor :

$$I_{sh} = \frac{V}{R_{sh}} \qquad \qquad \text{... (2.17)}$$

$$I_a = I - I_{sh} \qquad \qquad \text{... (2.18)}$$

$$E_b = V - I_a (R_a + R_{se}) \qquad \qquad \text{... (2.19)}$$

where, E_b is the back e.m.f., V the supply voltage, I the line current, I_{sh} the shunt field current, I_a the armature current, R_a the armature resistance, R_{sh} the shunt field resistance and R_{se} the series field resistance.

2.10 CHARACTERISTICS OF D.C. MOTORS

The performance of the d.c. motor under different operating conditions is revealed by the following characteristics :

• **Torque-Armature Current Characteristic :** The curve which shows the relation between the torque (T) and the armature current (I_a) is known as torque-armature current characteristic.

• **Speed-Armature Current Characteristic :** This curve shows the relation between the speed (N) and the armature current (I_a).

• **Speed-Torque Characteristic :** The curve showing the relation between the speed (N) and the torque (T) is called the speed-torque characteristic of a motor. This characteristic can be derived from the above two characteristics.

These characteristics play very important role in determining the suitability of a motor for any particular application. Therefore, let us study these characteristics of different types of d.c. motors.

2.10.1 Characteristics of Shunt Motors

• **Torque-Armature Current Characteristic :** From Expression (2.5), we know that the resultant torque (T) produced by all the armature conductors together due to the force experienced by each of them is

$$\propto \phi \cdot I_a \qquad \qquad \text{(With usual notations)}$$

Field current and hence the flux per pole is practically constant for a shunt motor. Therefore, the torque-armature current characteristic of a shunt motor is a straight line passing through the origin (Fig. 2.8 a).

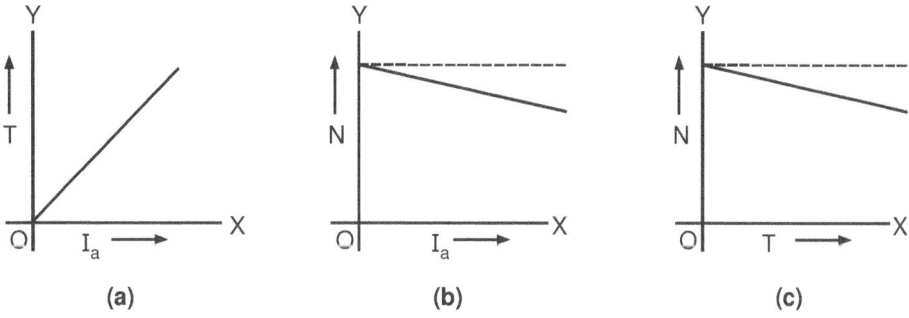

(a)   (b)   (c)

Fig. 2.8 : Characteristics of a d.c. shunt motor

● **Speed-Armature Current Characteristic :**

From Equation (2.3),

$$N \propto \frac{E_b}{\phi}$$ (Other things being constant)

But for a shunt motor, flux being practically constant,

$$N \propto E_b \propto V - I_a R_a$$ (Refer to Equation 2.10)

As I_a increases, E_b reduces. Consequently, the speed drops down. Hence the speed curve is slightly drooping as shown in Fig. 2.8 (b). However, the drop in speed from no load to full load being very small, a shunt motor is considered to be a constant speed motor for all practical purposes.

● **Speed-Torque Characteristic :** The relation between speed and torque can be derived from the above two characteristics. It is shown in Fig. 2.8 (c). This curve shows that the motor speed is fairly constant from no load to full load. This type of speed-torque characteristic is generally referred to as *shunt characteristic*.

2.10.2 Characteristics of Series Motors

● **Torque-Armature Current Characteristic :** The field winding of a series motor being in series with the armature, carries the armature current. Hence, before the saturation of the magnetic circuit,

$$\phi \propto I_a$$

∴ $$T \propto \phi I_a \propto I_a^2$$

The torque under this condition is thus nearly proportional to the square of the armature current and the torque-armature current characteristic is a *parabola* as illustrated in Fig. 2.9 (a). After the saturation of the magnetic circuit, ϕ remains practically constant. Hence $T \propto I_a$ only. Consequently, the characteristic becomes a straight line. Because of this typical characteristic, a series motor can exert a high torque at starting and at low speeds. It is, therefore, most suitable for the applications where a large starting torque is required.

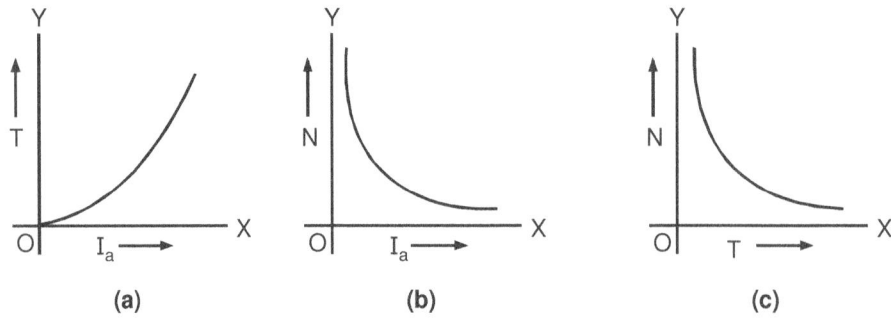

(a)　　　　　　　　　(b)　　　　　　　　　(c)

Fig. 2.9 : Characteristics of a d.c. series motor

- **Speed-Armature Current Characteristic :** For a series motor,

$$E_b = V - I_a (R_a + R_{se})$$　　　　　(Refer to Equation 2.12)

$I_a (R_a + R_{se})$ drop being very small, E_b is nearly constant.

∴　　　　　　$$N \propto \frac{E_b}{\phi} \propto \frac{1}{\phi} \propto \frac{1}{I_a}$$　　　　($\because \; \phi \propto I_a$)

Hence, the speed is inversely proportional to the armature current and the speed curve approximates to a *rectangular hyperbola* as illustrated in Fig. 2.9 (b). This curve shows that the series motor is a variable speed motor. It has a tendency for speed to rise to a dangerously high value on no load or even on light load. The centrifugal force developed at such a high speed can damage the motor. Hence, a d.c. series motor is never started without some mechanical load on it or never run on light load. For the same reason, it is seldom used for belt drive as breaking or slipping of the belt throws off the load on the motor.

- **Speed-Torque Characteristic :** Speed-torque curve shown in Fig. 2.9 (c) can be easily derived from the torque-armature current and speed-armature current curves. It shows that the speed of the motor falls as the torque increases. This type of speed-torque characteristic is commonly known as a *series characteristic.*

2.10.3 Characteristics of Compound Motors

Similar to a compound generator, a compound motor can also be cumulatively or differentially compounded. If the series field winding of a d.c. compound motor is arranged to assist the shunt field winding, it is said to be *cumulatively compounded.* On the other hand, if the series field winding opposes the shunt field winding, the motor is said to be *differentially compounded.* All the characteristics of the compound motor are a combination of the shunt and series motor characteristics. The exact shape of these characteristics depends upon the relative values of the shunt and series field m.m.f.s. These characteristics are shown in Fig. 2.10.

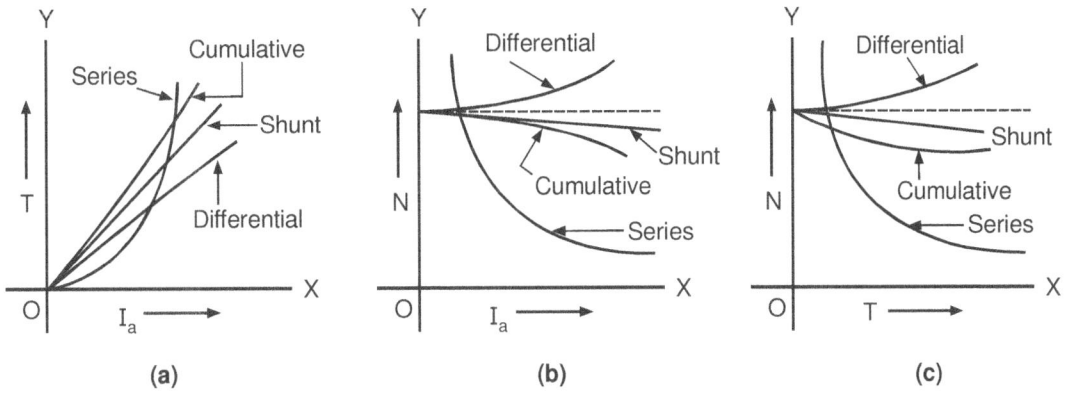

Fig. 2.10 : Characteristics of a d.c. compound motor

2.11 SPEED REGULATION OF D.C MOTORS

For a d.c. motor, speed regulation is defined as the change in its speed when the load on it is reduced from rated value to zero, expressed in per cent of rated load speed. Thus

$$\text{Speed regulation} = \frac{(\text{Speed on no load}) - (\text{Speed on rated load})}{(\text{Speed on rated load})} \times 100 \quad \dots (2.20)$$

The speed regulation is a measure of the ability of a motor to maintain its speed on application of load and hence considered as a criterion of performance particularly for the constant speed motors, such as shunt motors.

Example 2.3 : *A 250 V shunt motor on no load runs at 1000 r.p.m. and takes 5 A. The total armature and shunt field resistances are respectively 0.2 Ω and 250 Ω. Calculate the speed when loaded and taking a current of 50 A, if the flux remains practically constant.*

Solution : We have seen that for any d.c. motor,

$$N \propto \frac{E_b}{\phi}$$

If N_1, ϕ_1 and E_{b1} denote respectively the speed of the motor, flux per pole and the back e.m.f. in one condition and N_2, ϕ_2 and E_{b2} denote the corresponding quantities in the second condition, then from the above relation, we get

$$\frac{N_1}{N_2} = \frac{E_{b1}}{E_{b2}} \times \frac{\phi_2}{\phi_1}$$

In a d.c. shunt motor, since the flux is practically constant,

$$\frac{N_1}{N_2} = \frac{E_{b1}}{E_{b2}}$$

Now from the given data, in this case, $N_1 = 1000$ r.p.m., $I_1 = 5$ A, $I_2 = 50$ A, V = 250 V, $R_{sh} = 250$ Ω and $R_a = 0.2$ Ω

$\therefore$ $I_{sh} = \dfrac{V}{R_{sh}} = \dfrac{250}{250} = 1$ A

$\therefore$ $I_{a1} = I_1 - I_{sh} = 5 - 1 = 4$ A

and $I_{a2} = I_2 - I_{sh} = 50 - 1 = 49$ A

Hence, $E_{b1} = V - I_{a1} R_a = 250 - 4 \times 0.2 = 249.2$ V

and $E_{b2} = V - I_{a2} R_a = 250 - 49 \times 0.2 = 240.2$ V

Therefore, using the speed relationship which we have already developed, the speed N_2 during the load condition can be calculated as follows :

$$\frac{1000}{N_2} = \frac{249.2}{240.2}$$

$\therefore$ $N_2 = 963.88 \approx$ **964 r.p.m.**   **... Ans.**

Example 2.4 : *A d.c. series motor has an armature resistance of 0.25 Ω and a field resistance of 0.5 Ω. The speed is 700 r.p.m. when the current is 24 A and the terminal voltage 230 V. Assuming the flux to be proportional to current, calculate the speed of the motor when it takes 40 A from the supply.*

Solution : As already seen, for any d.c. motor,

$$\frac{N_1}{N_2} = \frac{E_{b1}}{E_{b2}} \times \frac{\phi_2}{\phi_1}$$

In a series motor, armature current passes through the field winding and if the flux is assumed to be proportional to the current,

$$\phi \propto I_a$$

Therefore, from the above mentioned speed relationship,

$$\frac{N_1}{N_2} = \frac{E_{b1}}{E_{b2}} \times \frac{I_{a2}}{I_{a1}}$$

where I_{a1} and I_{a2} are the armature currents in the two conditions.

Now from the given data, in this case,

$N_1 = 700$ r.p.m., $I_{a1} = 24$ A, $I_{a2} = 40$ A, $R_a = 0.25 \Omega$, $R_{se} = 0.5 \Omega$, and $V = 230$ V

$\therefore$ $E_{b1} = V - I_{a1} (R_a + R_{se}) = 230 - 24 (0.25 + 0.5)$

            $= 212$ V

and $E_{b2} = V - I_{a2} (R_a + R_{se}) = 230 - 40 (0.25 + 0.5)$

            $= 200$ V

Let N_2 be the speed when $I_{a2} = 40$ A

Then from the above speed relationship,

$\therefore$ $\dfrac{700}{N_2} = \dfrac{212}{200} \times \dfrac{40}{24}$

$\therefore$ $N_2 = $ **396 r.p.m.**   **... Ans.**

Example 2.5 : *A 200 V, 6-pole, d.c. shunt motor has 600 lap-connected armature conductors. Its armature resistance is 0.1 Ω and shunt field resistance is 100 Ω. Assuming the flux per pole as 0.06 Wb, calculate the speed of the motor when it draws 20 A from the supply.*

Solution : $I_{sh} = \dfrac{V}{R_{sh}} = \dfrac{200}{100} = 2$ A

            $I_a = I - I_{sh} = 20 - 2 = 18$ A

$\therefore$ $E_b = V - I_a R_a = 200 - 18 \times 0.1 = 198.2$ volts

Now, $E_b = \dfrac{\phi ZN}{60} \times \dfrac{P}{A}$

$\therefore$ $198.2 = \dfrac{0.06 \times 600 \times N}{60} \times \dfrac{6}{6}$ $(\because \ A = 6)$

$\therefore$ Speed of the motor, $N = $ **330.33 r.p.m.**   **... Ans.**

Example 2.6 : *A 460 V, d.c. series motor runs at 500 r.p.m., taking a current of 40 A. Calculate the speed and percentage change in the torque, if the load is reduced so that the motor takes 30 A. The armature resistance is 0.5 Ω and field resistance is 0.3 Ω.*

Solution :

$$I_{a1} = I_1 = 40 \text{ A}$$

$\therefore$

$$E_{b1} = V - I_{a1}(R_a + R_{se}) = 460 - 40(0.5 + 0.3) = 428 \text{ volts}$$

$$I_{a2} = I_2 = 30 \text{ A}$$

$\therefore$

$$E_{b2} = V - I_{a2}(R_a + R_{se}) = 460 - 30(0.5 + 0.3) = 436 \text{ volts}$$

Now, $\quad \dfrac{N_1}{N_2} = \dfrac{E_{b1}}{E_{b2}} \times \dfrac{\phi_2}{\phi_1} = \dfrac{E_{b1}}{E_{b2}} \times \dfrac{I_{a2}}{I_{a1}}$ $\qquad$ (Assuming, $\phi \propto I_a$)

$\therefore$

$$\frac{500}{N_2} = \frac{428}{436} \times \frac{30}{40}$$

$\therefore$ Motor speed with reduced load, $N_2 = $ **679 r.p.m.** $\qquad\qquad$ **... Ans.**

Further, $\quad T \propto \phi \cdot I_a \propto I_a^2$ $\qquad\qquad$ ($\because \ \phi \propto I_a$)

$\therefore$

$$\frac{T_1}{T_2} = \left(\frac{I_{a1}}{I_{a2}}\right)^2 = \left(\frac{40}{30}\right)^2 = 1.78$$

$\therefore$

$$T_2 = 0.562\, T_1 \ \text{ i.e. } \ 56.2 \ \% \text{ of } T_1$$

$\therefore$ Reduction in torque $= $ **43.8 %** $\qquad\qquad\qquad\qquad$ **... Ans.**

Example 2.7 : *A 120 V, d.c. shunt motor having an armature circuit resistance of 0.2 Ω and a field circuit resistance of 60 Ω draws a line current of 40 A at full load. The brush voltage drop is 2 V and rated full-load speed is 1800 r.p.m. Calculate the speed at half load.*

Solution :

$$I_{sh} = \frac{V}{R_{sh}} = \frac{120}{60} = 2 \text{ A}$$

$$I_{a1} = I_1 - I_{sh} = 40 - 2 = 38 \text{ A}$$

$\therefore$

$$E_{b1} = V - (I_{a1}R_a + \text{Brush drop}) = 120 - (38 \times 0.2 + 2)$$

$$= 110.4 \text{ volts}$$

Further, $\quad T \propto \phi \cdot I_a \propto I_a$ $\qquad\qquad$ ($\because \ \phi = \text{Constant}$)

$\therefore$ At half load, $I_{a2} = 0.5\, I_{a1} = 0.5 \times 38 = 19 \text{ A}$

$\therefore$

$$E_{b2} = V - (I_{a2}R_a + \text{Brush drop}) = 120 - (19 \times 0.2 + 1)$$

$$= 115.2 \text{ volts}$$

Now, $\quad \dfrac{N_1}{N_2} = \dfrac{E_{b1}}{E_{b2}} \times \dfrac{\phi_2}{\phi_1} = \dfrac{E_{b1}}{E_{b2}}$ $\qquad\qquad$ ($\because \ \phi = \text{Constant}$)

$\therefore$

$$\frac{1800}{N_2} = \frac{110.4}{115.2}$$

$\therefore$ Half-load motor speed, $\quad N_2 = $ **1878 r.p.m.** $\qquad\qquad$ **... Ans.**

Example 2.8 : *Armature resistance of a d.c. shunt motor is 5.75 Ω. On full load, it runs at 1725 r.p.m. taking armature current of 10 A from 230 V, d.c. supply. Find full-load torque and starting torque. Assume constant flux.*

Solution : Full-Load Condition :

$$E_b = V - I_{afl}R_a = 230 - 10 \times 5.75 = 172.5 \text{ V}$$

Now,

$$E_b \cdot I_{afl} = T_{fl} \times \frac{2\pi N}{60}$$

$$\therefore \qquad 172.5 \times 10 = T_{fl} \times \frac{2\pi \times 1725}{60}$$

$$\therefore \qquad T_{fl} = \textbf{9.55 Nm} \qquad \qquad \textbf{... Ans.}$$

Starting Condition :

$$E_b = 0 = V - I_{ast} R_a = 230 - I_{ast} \times 5.75$$

$$\therefore \qquad I_{ast} = \frac{230}{5.75} = 40 \text{ A}$$

Now,

$$T \propto \phi \cdot I_a \propto I_a \qquad \qquad (\because \quad \phi = \text{Constant})$$

$$\therefore \qquad \frac{T_{st}}{T_{fl}} = \frac{I_{ast}}{I_{afl}}$$

$$\therefore \qquad T_{st} = T_{fl} \times \frac{I_{ast}}{I_{afl}} = 9.55 \times \frac{40}{10} = \textbf{38.2 Nm} \qquad \qquad \textbf{... Ans.}$$

Example 2.9 : *A 230 V, 4-pole, d.c. shunt motor has wave winding with 600 conductors. Under certain load conditions, motor draws a current of 75 A and runs at 1200 r.p.m. The armature and shunt field resistances are 0.2 Ω and 75 Ω respectively. Calculate flux/pole and torque developed.*

Solution :   Field current, $I_{sh} = \dfrac{V}{R_{sh}} = \dfrac{230}{75} = 3.07 \text{ A}$

$\therefore$ Armature current, $I_a = I - I_{sh} = 75 - 3.07 = 71.93 \text{ A}$

$\therefore$ Back e.m.f., $E_b = V - I_a R_a = 230 - 71.93 \times 0.2 = 215.61 \text{ V}$

But,

$$E_b = \frac{\phi Z N}{60} \times \frac{P}{A}$$

$$\therefore \qquad 215.61 = \frac{\phi \times 600 \times 1200}{60} \times \frac{4}{2} \qquad \qquad (\because \quad A = 2)$$

$\therefore$ Flux per pole, $\phi = \textbf{8.98} \times \textbf{10}^{-3} \textbf{ Wb or 8.98 mWb}$ **... Ans.**

Further, Torque developed,

$$T = 0.159 \, \phi Z I_a \times \frac{P}{A}$$

$$= 0.159 \times 8.98 \times 10^{-3} \times 600 \times 71.93 \times \frac{4}{2} \qquad (\because \quad A = 2)$$

$$= \textbf{123.24 Nm} \qquad \qquad \textbf{... Ans.}$$

Example 2.10 : *A 4-pole, 250 V, d.c. shunt motor takes 4 A on no load, running at 1200 r.p.m. The armature resistance is 0.1 Ω and shunt field resistance is 125 Ω. Total brush drop is 2 V. If it takes total current of 61 A on full load, calculate its full-load speed. Assume that flux gets weakened by 5% on full-load condition due to armature reaction.*

Solution : Given : $P = 4$, $V = 250$ volts, $I_1 = 4$ A, $R_a = 0.1 \Omega$, $R_{sh} = 125 \Omega$,

Brush drop $= 2$ V, $I_2 = 61$ A, $\phi_2 = 0.95 \phi_1$

No-Load Condition : 　　$I_{sh} = \dfrac{V}{R_{sh}} = \dfrac{250}{125} = 2$ A

$$I_{a1} = I_1 - I_{sh} = 4 - 2 = 2 \text{ A}$$

$$E_{b1} = V - (I_{a1} R_a + \text{Brush drop}) = 250 - (2 \times 0.1 + 2)$$

$$= 247.8 \text{ V}$$

Load Condition : 　　$I_{sh} = 2$ A 　　　　　　　　　(As before)

$$I_{a2} = I_2 - I_{sh} = 61 - 2 = 59 \text{ A}$$

$$E_{b2} = V - (I_{a2} R_a + \text{Brush drop}) = 250 - (59 \times 0.1 + 2)$$

$$= 242.1 \text{ V}$$

Now, 　　　　$\dfrac{N_1}{N_2} = \dfrac{E_{b1}}{E_{b2}} \times \dfrac{\phi_2}{\phi_1}$

$\therefore$ 　　　　$\dfrac{1200}{N_2} = \dfrac{247.8}{242.1} \times \dfrac{0.95 \, \phi_1}{\phi_1}$

$\therefore$ Full-load speed of the motor,

$$N_2 = \textbf{1234 r.p.m.} \qquad\qquad \textbf{... Ans.}$$

Example 2.11 : *A 120 V, d.c. shunt motor draws a current of 200 A. The armature resistance is 0.02 Ω and shunt field resistance 30 Ω. Find the back e.m.f. and speed at which motor will run, if the lap wound armature has 90 slots with four conductors per slot and flux per pole is 0.04 Wb.*

Solution : Given : $V = 120$ volts, $I = 200$ A, $R_a = 0.02 \Omega$, $R_{sh} = 30 \Omega$,

Number of slots $= 90$, Conductors/slot $= 4$, $\phi = 0.04$ Wb.

(i) 　　　　　　　　　　　$I = 200$ A

$$I_{sh} = \dfrac{V}{R_{sh}} = \dfrac{120}{30} = 4 \text{ A}$$

$\therefore$ 　　Armature current, $I_a = I - I_{sh} = 200 - 4 = 196$ A

$$E_b = V - I_a R_a = 120 - 196 \times 0.02 = \textbf{116.08 V} \qquad \textbf{... Ans.}$$

(ii) Let the number of poles be P.

$$\therefore \qquad A = P \qquad (\because \text{Lap wound armature})$$

$$Z = (\text{Conductors/Slot}) \times \text{Number of Slots}$$

$$= 4 \times 90 = 360$$

Now,

$$E_b = \frac{\phi ZN}{60} \times \frac{P}{A}$$

$$\therefore \qquad 116.08 = \frac{0.04 \times 360 \times N}{60} \times 1 \qquad (\because \ A = P)$$

$$\therefore \qquad \text{Motor speed, N} = \textbf{483.67 r.p.m.} \qquad \textbf{... Ans.}$$

2.12 STARTERS FOR D.C. MOTORS

From the discussion in Section 2.6, we know that the armature current of a d.c. motor is given by the relation,

$$I_a = \frac{V - E_b}{R_a} \qquad \text{(Refer to Equation 2.1)}$$

In the running condition, back e.m.f. (E_b) being nearly equal to the voltage applied across the armature (V), armature current is very small. But when the motor is at rest at the beginning, armature conductors do not cut any flux lines.

Hence,

$$E_b = 0$$

$$\therefore \qquad I_a = \frac{V}{R_a}$$

As already mentioned previously, the resistance of the armature is normally very small. Therefore, if the motor is switched directly across the supply, the starting armature current will be excessively high in the absence of the back e.m.f. This excessive current blows out the fuses and prior to that may damage the armature. The large voltage drop caused by this current in the line also affects the performance of the other equipments connected to the same line. It is therefore absolutely necessary to limit this current. This is achieved by connecting a variable resistance called the *starting resistor* in series with the armature at starting (Fig. 2.11). As the speed and the back e.m.f. increase, the starting resistor is gradually cut off from the armature circuit. The complete starting resistor assembly is called *a starter*. In addition to a starting resistor which limits the starting current, the d.c. motor starter usually contains some protective devices. These devices provide protection to the motor in case the field circuit becomes open or the applied voltage becomes too low or load exceeds its predetermined value. The starter also ensures that the starting resistance is automatically reconnected into the armature circuit every time the motor stops.

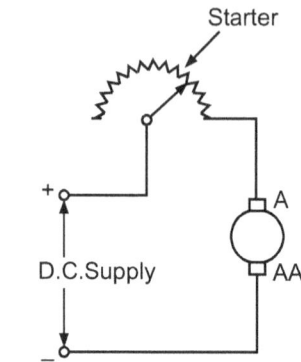

Fig. 2.11 : Starting of a d.c. motor

All d.c. motors except very small motors need starters. Small fractional kilowatt d.c. motors normally do not require starters because :

(i) In comparison with large motors, they have high armature resistance. This helps in limiting the starting current.

(ii) Being small with low moment of inertia, they pick-up speed very quickly and thereby fastly develop back e.m.f.

(iii) Disturbance caused due to their momentary starting current to the other equipments connected to the lines is minimum.

Various types of manually operated face-plate starters are commonly used for starting d.c. motors. All these starters have a face-plate fitted with a rotary type of switch connected to a group of current limiting resistors. Push-button type automatic starters are also available now-a-days. These starters use electromagnetic contactors and time-delay relays for automatically cutting out the starting resistors from the armature circuit in a predetermined time sequence or when the armature current drops to a preset value. Manually operated face-plate type starters suitable for d.c. shunt motors are described in the following section.

2.12.1 Shunt Motor Starters

Following two varieties of manually operated face-plate type starters are in common use for starting d.c. shunt motors.

(i) Three-point starter, (ii) Four-point starter.

(i) Three-Point Starter : Fig. 2.12 shows this type of starter. Since this starter has three terminals L, A and F as illustrated in the figure, it is called *three-point starter*. Terminal L is connected to the line, terminal A to the armature and terminal F to the field. Now, let us first see the construction of the starter.

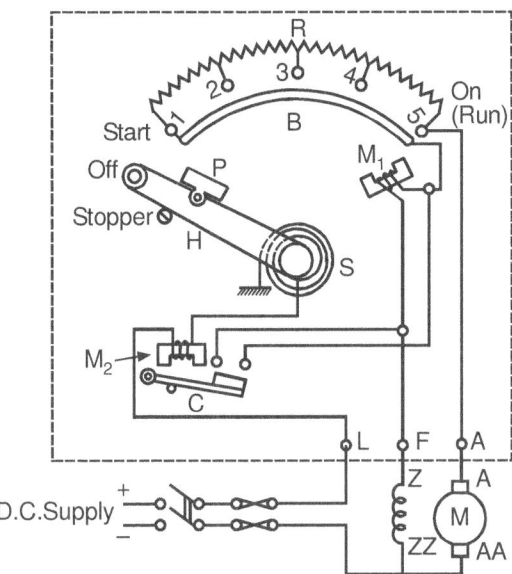

Fig. 2.12 : Three-point starter for a d.c. shunt motor

Construction : It consists of a starting resistor R sub-divided between number of contact studs (1 to 5). The starting handle (H) is pivoted on one side and its other side is free to move against a strong spring S and make contact with each stud and at the same time with the brass arc B, during the starting operation. The starter is also provided with two protective devices called *no-volt release* and *over-load release*. The no-volt release consists of an electromagnet M_1 and a hinged soft iron piece P carried by the starting handle. The coil of this electromagnet has a large number of turns wound on a U-shaped iron core and it is connected in series with the field winding. The over-load release consists of another small electromagnet M_2 and soft iron armature C. The coil of this electromagnet has few turns and it is connected in series with the motor. One end of the armature C is pivoted and its other side carries a link of some conducting material. The two brass studs facing this link are connected to the two ends of the coil of the electromagnet M_1. Fig. 2.12 also illustrates the internal wiring of such a starter.

Operation : To start the motor, the d.c. supply is first switched on. The starting handle is then slowly moved against spring in the clockwise direction. When the handle makes connection with the first stud, the field winding of the motor gets connected directly across the line through the coil of the no-volt release and at the same time the entire starting resistor comes in series with the armature. As the handle is moved further, the starting resistor is gradually cut off from the armature circuit. Finally, when the handle reaches the running position (i.e. final stud), the starting resistor is completely cut off and the motor starts operating on full speed. Handle is held in this position against spring tension by the electromagnet M_1 of no-volt release.

Functions of No-Volt Release : Following important functions are carried out by the no-volt release.

- When the handle is in the RUN (or ON) position, a small iron piece P on it is attracted by the electromagnet M_1 of no-volt release energized by the field current flowing through its coil. Thus the handle is held in ON position against the pull of a spring. Because of this specific function which is carried out by the no-volt release, electromagnet M_1 is called *hold-up* magnet and its coil is termed *hold-on coil*.

- If the supply fails, or is switched off, or if the field circuit is broken, the demagnetized electromagnet of the no-volt release no longer attracts the iron piece and a return spring brings the handle to OFF position. This prevents the starting of the motor without any starting resistance in its armature circuit when the supply is again restored.

- The pull of the electromagnet of the no-volt release also becomes insufficient under low-voltage condition and the handle returns to the OFF position, thus providing protection against low voltage. This is the reason why no-volt release is also sometimes called *low-voltage release.*

Function of Over-Load Release : Since the coil of the electromagnet M_2 of the over-load release is connected in series with the motor, it always carries the line current. If the current exceeds certain predetermined value due to over-load (or some fault), the electromagnet M_2 of the over-load release attracts the armature C which when lifted, bridges two brass studs connected to the two ends of the coil of the electromagnet M_1 of the no-volt release. As soon as the coil of the electromagnet M_1 of the no-volt release holding the starting handle in the RUN position is short circuited, it gets demagnetized. The spring then pulls the handle back to OFF position and thus disconnects the motor from the supply. The overload release can be set for different values of the current by adjusting the position of its armature with the help of a set screw provided for this purpose.

A slightly modified form of a three-point starter as shown in Fig. 2.13 is also in use in which the brass arc (B) is eliminated and the field circuit is connected to the supply through the starting resistor. With this modification, it will be seen that when the starting handle is moved from first stud to the last stud, the portion of the starting resistor which is cut off from the armature circuit is included in the field circuit. But as the resistance of the starting resistor is very small as compared to that of shunt field circuit, the inclusion of starting resistor in the field circuit has very little effect on the field current.

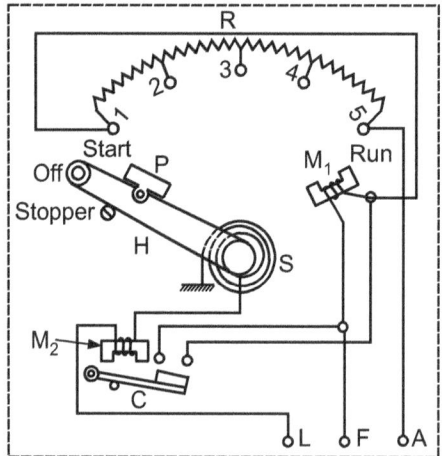

Fig. 2.13 : Three-point starter, a modified form

Three-point starter is not suitable for the variable-speed motors using field control. Because in the case of such a motor, when the speed is increased by reducing the field current with the help of field regulator $\left(\because N \propto \dfrac{1}{\phi} \propto \dfrac{1}{I_{sh}} \right)$, it causes weakening of the hold-up magnet. This weakening may be to such an extent that hold-up magnet fails to keep the starting handle in ON position and the motor is thus disconnected from the supply when it is not desired. This difficulty is overcome by using a four-point starter.

(ii) Four-Point Starter : This type of starter is similar to a three-point starter except that the hold-on coil along with its protective resistance R' is connected across the supply line instead of in series with the shunt field circuit and thus have four points L_1, L_2, A, F as shown in Fig. 2.14. This arrangement permits variation of motor speed with the help of a field regulator R_f without affecting the current through the hold-on coil. The disadvantage of this type of starter is that the hold-on coil being independent of field circuit connection, no protection is provided against over speed if for some reason field circuit is open circuited.

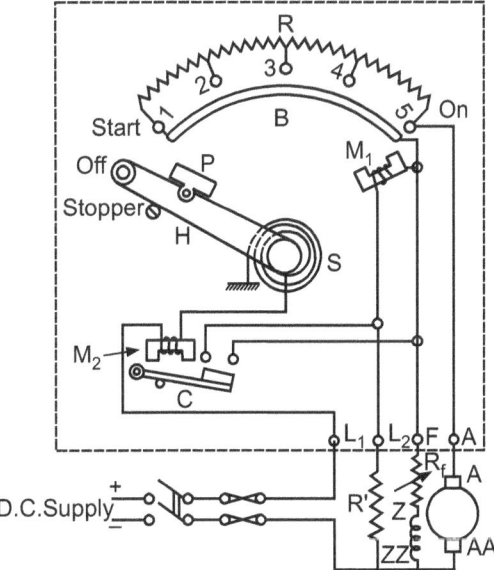

Fig. 2.14 : Four-point starter for a d.c. shunt motor

It is important to note here that the three-point and four-point starters described above are also used for starting *d.c. compound motors.*

2.13 REVERSAL OF ROTATION IN D.C. MOTORS

We know that in a d.c. motor, every current carrying conductor of the armature being in the magnetic field produced by the stationary field poles, experiences a mechanical force which ultimately results into rotation of the armature in a particular direction (Fig. 2.6).

Now, we know that the direction of the force experienced by the current carrying conductor placed in the magnetic field depends upon the direction of field and the direction of the current flow in the conductor. From this, it follows that the direction of the force experienced by each conductor of the armature and therefore the direction of rotation of a motor depends on the direction of the field and the direction of the current flow in the armature.

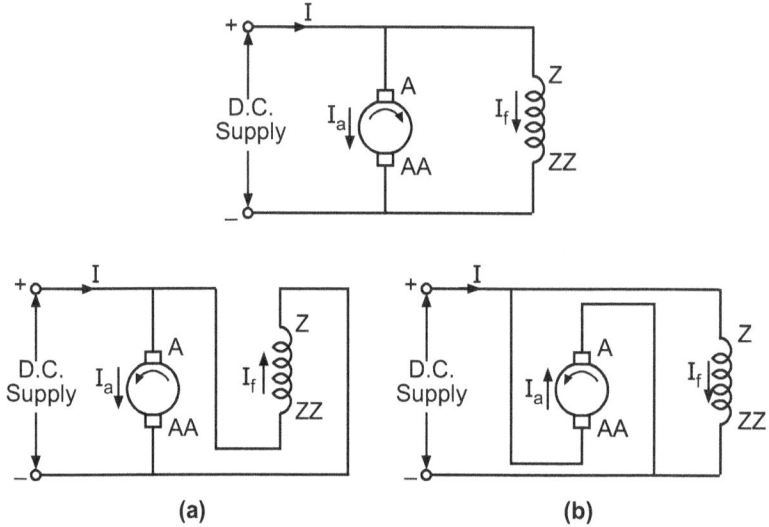

**Fig. 2.15 : Reversal of direction of rotation of a d.c. shunt motor by
(a) Reversal of field connections, (b) Reversal of armature connections**

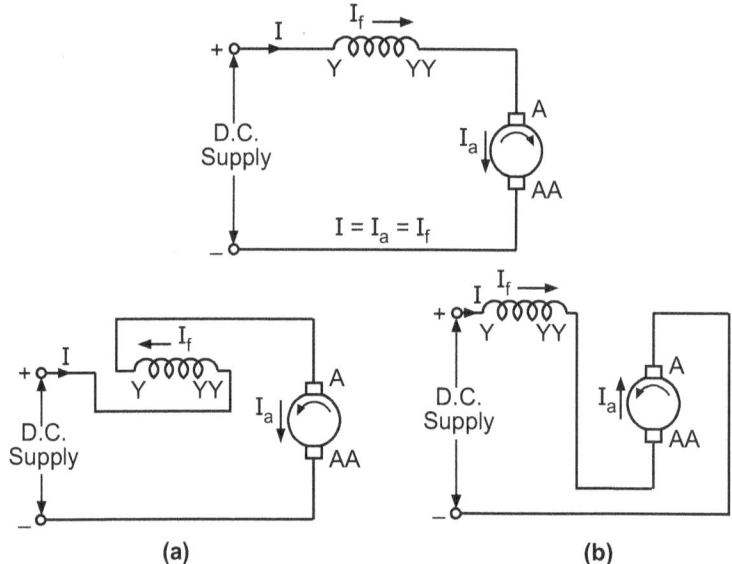

**Fig. 2.16 : Reversal of direction of rotation of a d.c. series motor by
(a) Reversal of field connections, (b) Reversal of armature connections**

The direction of the field in turn is decided by the direction of the field current. Therefore, if either the direction of the field current (I_f) or the direction of armature current (I_a) is reversed, the rotation of the motor will reverse. However, if both of the above two factors are reversed at the same time, there will be no effect on the direction of rotation.

Thus, whenever it becomes necessary to change the direction of rotation of a d.c. motor, this can be achieved simply by reversing the connections of either the armature or the field (but not both) as illustrated in Fig. 2.15 and Fig. 2.16 for d.c. shunt and series motors respectively.

2.14 SPEED CONTROL OF D.C. MOTORS

From the relationship between the back e.m.f., speed, flux, etc. given by the Equation (2.3), we have

$$N \propto \frac{E_b}{\phi} \qquad \qquad \ldots (2.21)$$

This is because for a particular machine Z, A and P are fixed. Also from Equation (2.2),

$$E_b = V - I_a R_a$$

∴

$$N \propto \frac{E_b}{\phi} \propto \frac{V - I_a R_a}{\phi} \qquad \qquad \ldots (2.22)$$

Resistance of the armature is normally very small. Therefore, the value of $I_a R_a$ is also small in comparison with the voltage applied across the armature. If this voltage drop in the armature resistance is neglected, then

$$N \propto \frac{V}{\phi} \qquad \qquad \ldots (2.23)$$

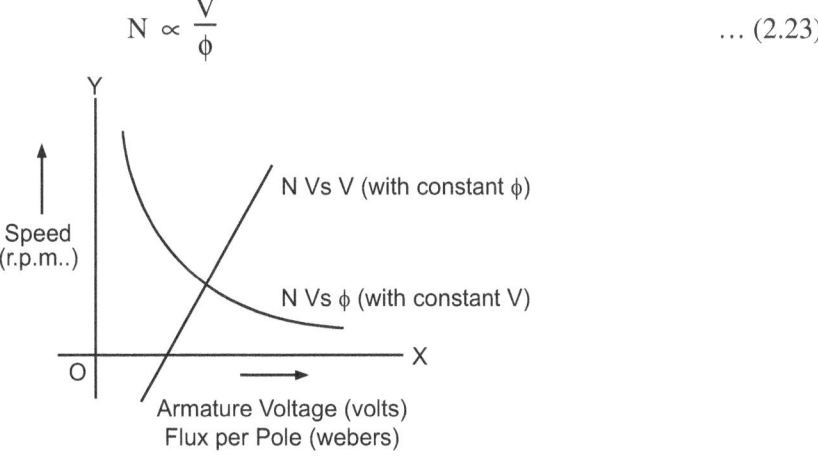

Fig. 2.17 : Variation of speed with the armature voltage and flux per pole

The above expression shows that the speed of a d.c. motor is approximately proportional to the voltage applied across the armature and inversely proportional to the flux per pole as illustrated graphically in Fig. 2.17. This gives two basic methods for varying the speed of a d.c. motor, namely :

(i) Armature voltage control,

(ii) Flux control.

These methods as applied to d.c. shunt and series motors are discussed below. These methods are also applicable for compound motors.

2.14.1 Speed Control of Shunt Motors

Armature Voltage Control : In this method, the voltage applied across the armature of a d.c. shunt motor is changed to change its speed. Following schemes are commonly used for controlling the armature voltage :

(a) **Rheostatic Control :** Since the supply voltage is normally constant, the voltage applied across the armature is changed by simply connecting a variable resistance (R) called *controller* in series with the armature as shown in Fig. 2.18 (a). As this external resistance is increased, the voltage applied across the armature decreases and the speed falls. By changing the value of the resistance, different motor speeds can be obtained (Fig. 2.18 b). This rheostatic method of changing the armature voltage for speed control purposes has following merits and demerits :

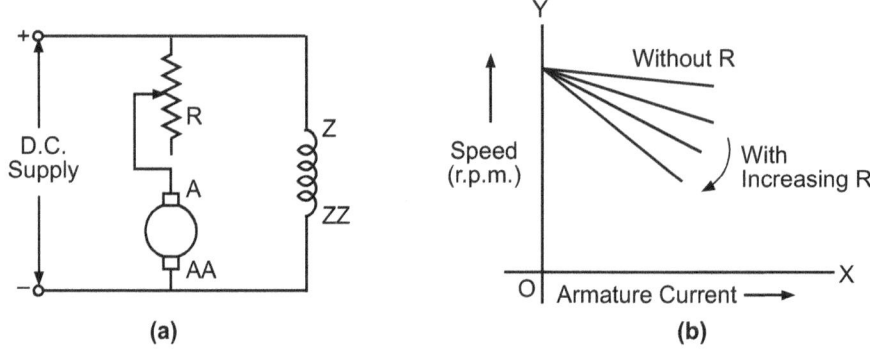

(a)　　　　　　　　　　　　　　　　(b)

Fig. 2.18 : Rheostatic control for a d.c. shunt motor

Merits : Simple method to obtain any speed below normal[*] down to crawling.

Demerits :

- This method cannot give speeds above normal as controller can only decrease the armature voltage.

- Considerable amount of power is wasted in the controller which lowers the efficiency of the motor.

- This method needs costly controller with proper heat dissipation arrangement.

- With the controller in the circuit, speed of the motor varies greatly with the variation in load (Fig. 2.18 b). Thus the motor has poor speed regulation.

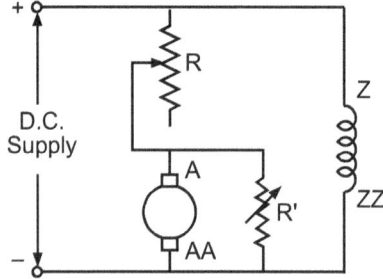

Fig. 2.19: Rheostatic control for a d.c. shunt motor with shunted armature

---

[*] *Normal speed is that speed which is obtained when rated voltage is applied across the armature and full excitation is provided to the field winding.*

Because of the above drawbacks, this method is used in the applications where slow speeds are required for a short period only and where efficiency is of secondary importance e.g. hoists, cranes, trams, printing machines, etc. If a diverter R' (variable resistance) is placed across the armature in addition to the series resistance (Fig. 2.19), the rheostatic control gives more stable operation. This is because under this condition, a change in armature current (due to alteration in load torque) is not so effective in changing the voltage drop across the armature and hence the speed of the motor. This gives better speed regulation particularly in the low speed range.

(b) Multiple Voltage Control : In this method, the excitation is held constant by permanently connecting the shunt field of the motor across a definite voltage, but the armature is supplied with different voltages by means of suitable switch gear. The speeds are then approximately proportional to these voltages. Fig. 2.20 (a) illustrates the method when the motor is fed from a 3-wire system and Fig. 2.20 (b) shows the speed characteristics corresponding to two working voltages that are available. In large factories, special 3 or 4 wire systems giving a number of graded values for the armature voltage are sometimes employed for the purpose of speed control. Since this method of speed control involves considerable investment on auxiliary equipments, it is used only where a wide range of speed is necessary, as in some machine-tool operations.

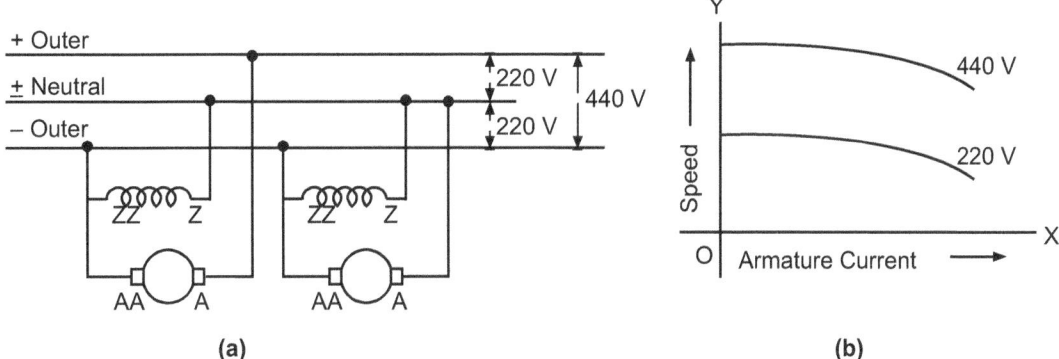

(a)   (b)

Fig. 2.20 : Multiple voltage control for a d.c. shunt motor fed from a 3-wire system

(c) Series-Parallel Control : Even though this method is more commonly used for d.c. series motors (in traction), it may also be used for controlling the speed of the d.c. shunt motors. In this method, two identical motors are mechanically coupled to a common load. When the motor armatures are connected in series as shown in Fig. 2.21 (a), each motor armature receives one-half the normal supply voltage $\left(\text{i.e. } \dfrac{V}{2}\right)$. On the other hand, when they are connected in parallel as shown in Fig. 2.21 (b), the terminal voltage across each motor armature rises to the normal value of the supply voltage (i.e. V). Thus two operating characteristics are possible with this method (Fig. 2.21 c). The voltage applied across the field winding is maintained to the same value during both series and parallel working. For that the fields may be connected in parallel across the full voltage or in series as shown in the figure. So far as efficiency is concerned, this method is superior to the rheostatic control. However, only two operating speeds are possible.

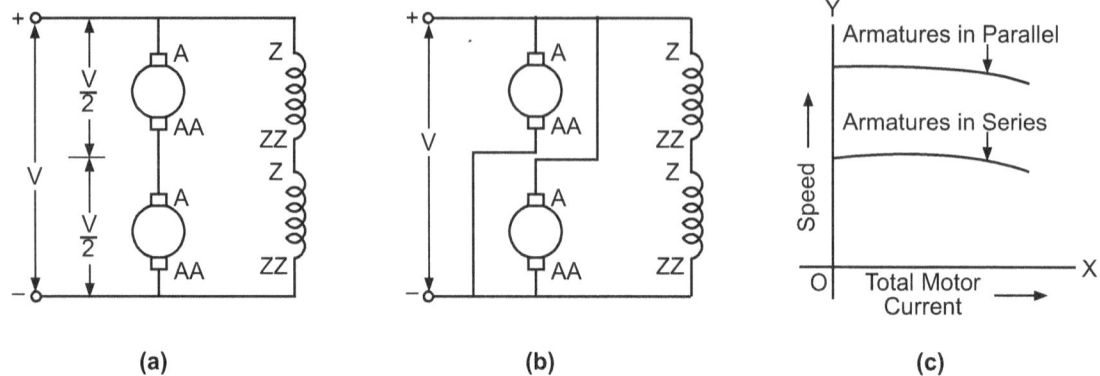

(a)   (b)   (c)

Fig. 2.21 : Series-parallel control for d.c. shunt motors

(d) Ward-Leonard System : Fig. 2.22 shows the complete scheme of connections used in Ward-Leonard system. M_1 is the main motor whose speed is to be controlled. The field winding of this motor is permanently connected across the supply mains and its armature is provided with the variable voltage for the purpose of speed control using a separate generator G. This generator is driven at constant speed by a d.c. motor M_2 as shown or any suitable a.c. motor can be used for this purpose. The output voltage of the generator (which is fed to the armature of the main motor) is varied from nearly zero to a certain maximum value by means of its field regulator. A reversing switch is also included in the field circuit of the generator to reverse the direction of its field current and thereby to change the direction of rotation of the main motor.

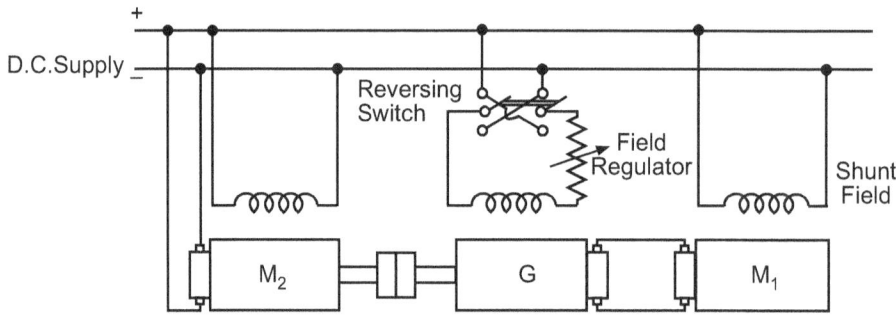

Fig. 2.22 : Ward-Leonard system

The principal merits and demerits of the Ward-Leonard system are listed below :

Merits :

- This is one of the most precise methods of speed control with a wide speed range in either direction of rotation.

- No special starting gear is required and speed reversal can be carried out very smoothly and with ease. As such, the method is ideal for the applications requiring frequent starting, stopping, reversals and smooth acceleration.

Demerits :

- Two extra machines are necessary. This makes the system most expensive.

- The absence of external resistance in the armature circuit of the motor under control considerably improves the efficiency. However, still the overall efficiency is low, particularly at light loads.

Even though costly, this type of control is extensively used for rolling mill motors, colliery winding motors, elevators, hoists, large shears, paper mills, electric shovels, etc.

Flux Control : A wide variation in speed can be obtained by changing the flux per pole of the d.c. motor. The flux per pole depends upon the value of the field current. Therefore, to change the field current, a variable resistance (R) termed as *field regulator* is connected in series with the field winding of a d.c. shunt motor as illustrated in Fig. 2.23 (a). When this resistance is increased, the field current and the flux are reduced. Consequently, the speed increases and vice versa (Fig. 2.23 b).

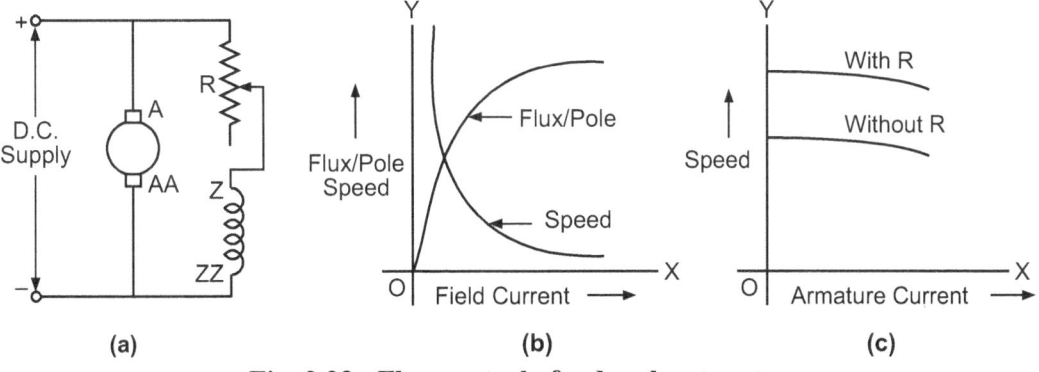

Fig. 2.23 : Flux control of a d.c. shunt motor

Some principal merits and demerits of this method of speed control are given below :

Merits :

- Speeds above normal can be obtained with ease.

- Because of small current, power loss involved in the external resistor is also comparatively small. Hence, the method is more convenient, economical and efficient.

- For any particular speed adjustment, speed regulation is excellent (Fig. 2.23 c).

Demerits :

- This method cannot give speeds below normal as field can only be weakened and cannot be made stronger.

- For motors requiring a wide range of speed control, weakening of flux for high speeds increases sparking at the brushes and hence puts a limit to the maximum speed obtainable with this method. Therefore with non-interpolar machines, speed range (the ratio of maximum to minimum speeds) is limited to about 2 : 1, whereas in motors fitted with interpoles*, it can be as great as 6 : 1.

In actual practice, by combining the above two methods i.e. armature voltage control and flux control, speed above and below the normal may be obtained.

---

*   *These are the small auxiliary poles placed mid-way between the main poles to improve the performance of the machine. The exciting coils of the interpoles are connected in series with the armature.*

Example 2.12 : *A 250 V, d.c. shunt motor has an armature circuit resistance of 0.5 Ω and a field circuit resistance of 125 Ω. It drives a load at 1000 r.p.m. and takes 25 A. The field circuit resistance is then slowly increased to 150 Ω. If the load torque remains constant, calculate the new speed and armature current. Assume the magnetization curve to be linear.*

Solution : We know that for a d.c. motor,

$$\text{Speed, } N \propto \frac{E_b}{\phi}$$

$$\therefore \qquad \frac{N_2}{N_1} = \frac{E_{b2}}{E_{b1}} \times \frac{\phi_1}{\phi_2}$$

where the symbols used have usual meaning and the suffixes represent the two sets of conditions.

Further, since the motor works on the linear portion of the magnetization curve,

$$\phi \propto \text{Field current, } I_{sh}$$

$$\therefore \qquad \frac{N_2}{N_1} = \frac{E_{b2}}{E_{b1}} \times \frac{I_{sh1}}{I_{sh2}}$$

Now, $$I_{sh1} = \frac{V}{R_{sh1}} = \frac{250}{125} = 2 \text{ A}$$

$$I_{a1} = I_1 - I_{sh1} = 25 - 2 = 23 \text{ A}$$

$$E_{b1} = V - I_{a1} R_a = 250 - 23 \times 0.5 = 238.5 \text{ V}$$

$$I_{sh2} = \frac{250}{150} = 1.67 \text{ A}$$

Since $T \propto \phi \cdot I_a$ and it is constant,

$$\phi_1 \cdot I_{a1} = \phi_2 \cdot I_{a2}$$

i.e. $$I_{sh1} \cdot I_{a1} = I_{sh2} \cdot I_{a2} \qquad\qquad (\because \ \phi \propto I_{sh})$$

$$\therefore \qquad I_{a2} = I_{a1} \times \frac{I_{sh1}}{I_{sh2}} = 23 \times \frac{2}{1.67}$$

$$= \mathbf{27.55 \text{ A}} \qquad\qquad \textbf{... Ans.}$$

$$E_{b2} = V - I_{a2} \cdot R_a = 250 - 27.55 \times 0.5$$

$$= 236.23 \text{ V}$$

Substituting all these values in the above equation, we have

$$\frac{N_2}{1000} = \frac{236.23}{238.5} \times \frac{2}{1.67}$$

$$\therefore \qquad N_2 = \mathbf{1186 \text{ r.p.m.}} \qquad\qquad \textbf{... Ans.}$$

Example 2.13 : *A 250 V shunt motor is taking current of 75 A. Resistances of the shunt field and armature are 50 Ω and 0.025 Ω respectively. There is a resistance of 0.5 Ω in series with the armature and the speed is 1000 r.p.m. What alteration must be made in the armature circuit to raise the speed to 1050 r.p.m., the torque remaining the same ?*

Solution :
$$I_{sh} = \frac{V}{R_{sh}} = \frac{250}{50} = 5 \text{ A}$$

$$I_{a1} = I_1 - I_{sh} = 75 - 5 = 70 \text{ A}$$

$$E_{b1} = V - I_{a1}(R_a + R_1) = 250 - 70(0.025 + 0.5)$$

$$= 213.25 \text{ V}$$

Now,
$$\frac{T_1}{T_2} = \frac{\phi_1 \cdot I_{a1}}{\phi_2 \cdot I_{a2}} \qquad (\because T \propto \phi \cdot I_a)$$

But as the torque is constant,

$$T_1 = T_2$$

$\therefore$
$$I_{a_1} = I_{a_2} = 70 \text{ A} \qquad \text{(Assuming } \phi_1 = \phi_2)$$

Further,
$$\frac{N_2}{N_1} = \frac{E_{b2}}{E_{b1}} \times \frac{\phi_1}{\phi_2} = \frac{E_{b2}}{E_{b1}} \qquad (\because \phi_1 = \phi_2)$$

$\therefore$
$$E_{b2} = E_{b1} \times \frac{N_2}{N_1} = 213.25 \times \frac{1050}{1000} = 224 \text{ V}$$

Let the new value of the external resistance in the armature circuit be R_2. Then obviously,

$$E_{b2} = V - I_{a2}(R_a + R_2)$$

$\therefore$
$$224 = 250 - 70(0.025 + R_2)$$

$\therefore$
$$R_2 = 0.346 \ \Omega$$

Hence, the value of the external resistance in the armature circuit must be reduced by $(0.5 - 0.346) = \mathbf{0.154 \ \Omega}$ **... Ans.**

Example 2.14 : *A 230 V, d.c. shunt motor takes an armature current of 20 A on a certain load. Resistance of the armature is 0.5 Ω. Find the resistance required in series with the armature to halve the speed, if the load torque is proportional to the square of the speed.*

Solution :
$$E_{b1} = V - I_{a1} R_a = 230 - 20 \times 0.5 = 220 \text{ volts}$$

Now,
$$\frac{N_1}{N_2} = \frac{E_{b1}}{E_{b2}} \times \frac{\phi_2}{\phi_1} = \frac{E_{b1}}{E_{b2}} \qquad (\because \phi = \text{Constant})$$

$\therefore$ $\dfrac{N_1}{0.5\,N_1} = \dfrac{220}{E_{b2}}$

$\therefore$ $E_{b2} = 110\text{ V}$

Further, $T \propto \phi \cdot I_a \propto I_a$ $(\because \ \phi = \text{Constant})$

$\therefore$ $\dfrac{T_1}{T_2} = \dfrac{I_{a1}}{I_{a2}}$ $\dots$ (I)

Also, $\dfrac{T_1}{T_2} = \left(\dfrac{N_1}{N_2}\right)^2$ $\dots$ (II)

Therefore, from equations (I) and (II), we have

$$\dfrac{I_{a1}}{I_{a2}} = \left(\dfrac{N_1}{N_2}\right)^2$$

$\therefore$ $\dfrac{20}{I_{a2}} = \left(\dfrac{N_1}{0.5\,N_1}\right)^2$

$\therefore$ $I_{a2} = 5\text{ A}$

Let R be the resistance required in series with the armature to halve the speed. Then,

$$E_{b2} = V - I_{a2}\,(R_a + R)$$

$\therefore$ $110 = 230 - 5\,(0.5 + R)$

$\therefore$ **R = 23.5 Ω**   ... Ans.

Example 2.15 : *A 300 V, d.c. shunt motor is taking 50 A. Resistances of the shunt field and the armature are 150 Ω and 0.03 Ω respectively. Motor is running with a speed of 1000 r.p.m. If now an additional resistance of 0.25 Ω is added in series with the armature, calculate the new value of the speed. Assume load to be constant.*

Solution : $I_{sh} = \dfrac{V}{R_{sh}} = \dfrac{300}{150} = 2\text{ A}$

$I_{a1} = I_1 - I_{sh} = 50 - 2 = 48\text{ A}$

$\therefore$ $E_{b1} = V - I_{a1}\,R_a = 300 - 48 \times 0.03 = 298.56\text{ volts}$

Further, $T \propto \phi \cdot I_a \propto I_a$ $(\because \ \phi = \text{Constant})$

$\therefore$ $\dfrac{T_1}{T_2} = 1 = \dfrac{I_{a1}}{I_{a2}}$ $(\because \ T = \text{Constant})$

$\therefore$ $I_{a1} = I_{a2} = 48\text{ A}$

$\therefore$ $E_{b2} = V - I_{a2}\,(R_a + R) = 300 - 48\,(0.03 + 0.25)$

       $= 286.56\text{ volts}$

$$\text{Now,} \quad \frac{N_1}{N_2} = \frac{E_{b1}}{E_{b2}} \times \frac{\phi_2}{\phi_1} = \frac{E_{b1}}{E_{b2}} \qquad (\because \ \phi = \text{Constant})$$

$$\therefore \qquad \frac{1000}{N_2} = \frac{298.56}{286.56}$$

$$\therefore \qquad \text{New speed, } N_2 = \textbf{959.81 r.p.m.} \qquad \textbf{... Ans.}$$

Example 2.16 : *A 240 V, d.c. shunt motor takes a current of 20 A and runs at 600 r.p.m. while driving a load whose torque remains constant. Its armature circuit resistance is 0.5 Ω and field circuit resistance is 240 Ω. It is desired to raise the speed to 800 r.p.m. by flux variation. Calculate the required resistance to be added in the field circuit.*

Solution :

$$I_{sh1} = \frac{V}{R_{sh}} = \frac{240}{240} = 1 \text{ A}$$

$$I_{a1} = I_1 - I_{sh1} = 20 - 1 = 19 \text{ A}$$

$$\therefore \qquad E_{b1} = V - I_{a1} R_a = 240 - 19 \times 0.5 = 230.5 \text{ volts}$$

$$\text{Further,} \quad T \propto \phi \cdot I_a \propto I_{sh} \cdot I_a \qquad (\because \ \phi \propto I_{sh})$$

$$\therefore \qquad \frac{T_1}{T_2} = 1 = \frac{I_{sh1} \cdot I_{a1}}{I_{sh2} \cdot I_{a2}} \qquad (\because \ T = \text{Constant})$$

$$\therefore \qquad I_{sh1} \cdot I_{a1} = I_{sh2} \cdot I_{a2}$$

$$\therefore \qquad I_{a2} = \frac{I_{sh1} \cdot I_{a1}}{I_{sh2}} = \frac{1 \times 19}{I_{sh2}} = \frac{19}{I_{sh2}}$$

$$\therefore \qquad E_{b2} = V - I_{a2} R_a = 240 - \frac{19}{I_{sh2}} \times 0.5 = 240 - \frac{9.5}{I_{sh2}}$$

$$\text{Now,} \quad \frac{N_1}{N_2} = \frac{E_{b1}}{E_{b2}} \times \frac{\phi_2}{\phi_1} = \frac{E_{b1}}{E_{b2}} \times \frac{I_{sh2}}{I_{sh1}} \qquad (\because \ \phi \propto I_{sh})$$

$$\therefore \qquad \frac{600}{800} = \frac{230.5}{\left(240 - \dfrac{9.5}{I_{sh2}} \right)} \times \frac{I_{sh2}}{1}$$

$$\therefore \qquad 230.5 \ I_{sh2}^2 - 180 \ I_{sh2} + 7.125 - 0$$

Solving the above quadratic equation, we get

$$I_{sh2} = 0.739 \text{ A or } 0.042 \text{ A}$$

Rejecting the second value being impractical, we have

$$I_{sh2} = 0.739 \text{ A}$$

Let R be the required resistance to be added in the field circuit. Then,

$$I_{sh2} = \frac{V}{R_{sh} + R}$$

$$\therefore \qquad 0.739 = \frac{240}{240 + R}$$

$$\therefore \qquad R = \textbf{84.76 Ω} \qquad \qquad \textbf{... Ans.}$$

2.14.2 Speed Control of Series Motors

Armature Voltage Control : As in the case of a d.c. shunt motor, following schemes are commonly used for changing the voltage applied across the armature terminals of a d.c. series motor for speed control purposes :

(a) Rheostatic Method : In this method, a variable resistance R (called *controller*) is inserted in series with the motor circuit as shown in Fig. 2.24 (a). Increase in this external resistance reduces the voltage across the motor terminals (hence across the armature terminals) and consequently the speed drops. Fig. 2.24 (b) shows the operating characteristics of a motor with and without such series resistance in the circuit. The merits and demerits of this method are same as those mentioned earlier in the case of rheostatic control for a d.c. shunt motor. An improved performance can be obtained by using a diverter R' across the armature as shown in Fig. 2.25. Since now the current taken from the mains is shared by the diverter and the armature, the current through the armature is reduced. But for a given load torque, when I_a reduces, ϕ must increase ($\because T \propto \phi \cdot I_a$). Hence the motor draws more current from supply mains and speed falls. This scheme is, therefore, very helpful in getting slow speeds at light loads and no-load speed of finite and reasonable value.

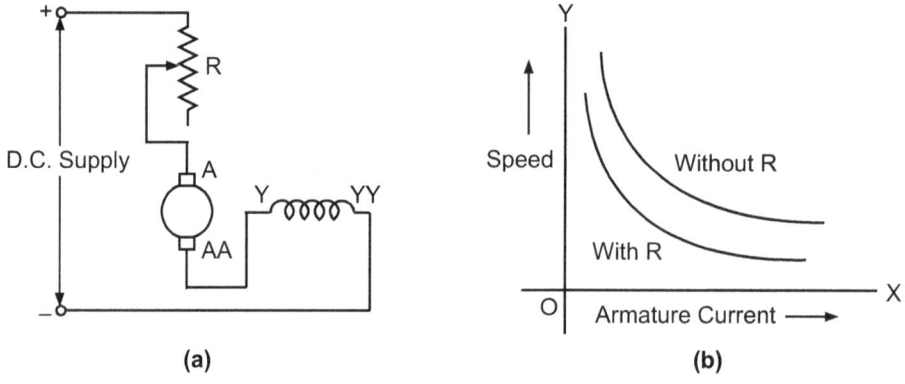

(a)   (b)

Fig. 2.24 : Rheostatic control for a d.c. series motor

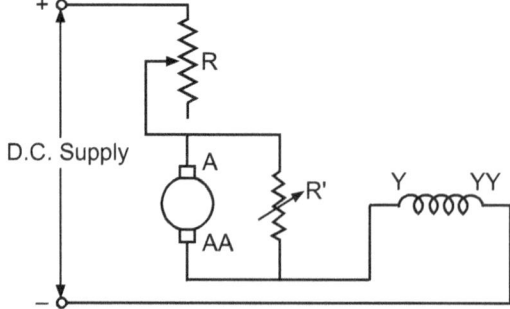

Fig. 2.25 : Rheostatic control for a d.c. series motor with shunted armature

(b) Series-Parallel Control : Figs. 2.26 (a) and (b) show the scheme of connections for series-parallel control for two identical mechanically coupled d.c. series motors. With the series connection of the motors, speed is lower because the voltage applied across the terminals of each motor is one-half the supply voltage $\left(\text{i.e. } \dfrac{V}{2}\right)$. On the other hand, parallel connection of motors gives higher speed as voltage applied across each motor gets doubled. Thus two operating characteristics are possible using this method (Fig. 2.26 c). This method of speed control is widely used in electric traction.

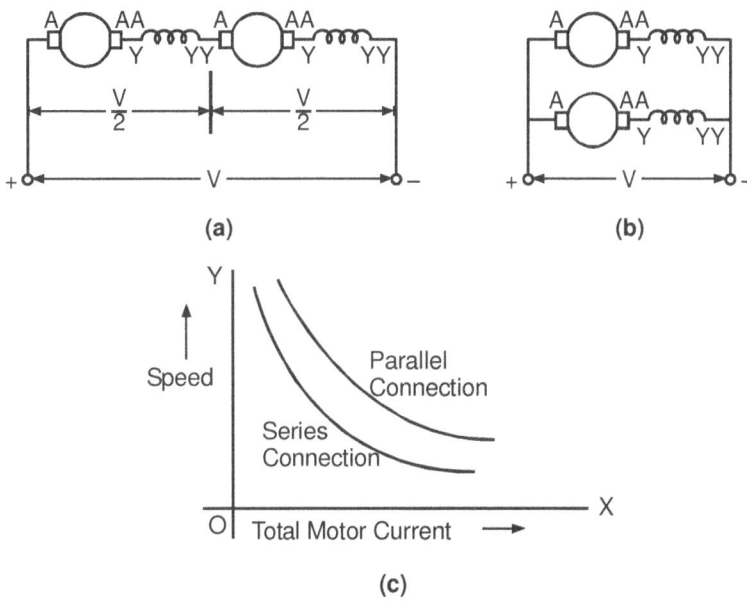

Fig. 2.26 : Series-parallel control for d.c. series motors

(c) Variable-Voltage Control : A modified form of the conventional Ward-Leonard system of speed control as shown in Fig. 2.27 may be used for a series motor. Variation of the speed of the series motor is achieved with the help of a field-diverter of a series generator. This generator is driven at constant speed with the help of a suitable a.c. or d.c. motor. The usual range of speed with this arrangement is about 10 : 1.

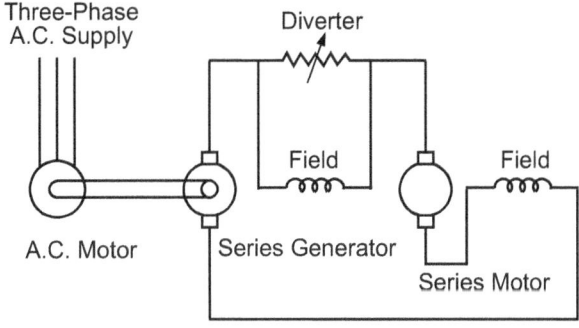

Fig. 2.27 : Variable-voltage control for a series motor

Flux Control : In a series motor, variation in flux for speed control purposes can be achieved by using any one of the following methods :

(a) Diverter Control : A change in field current and hence in the flux can be achieved by placing a variable resistance R called *diverter* in parallel with the field winding of a series motor as shown in Fig. 2.28 (a). By adjusting this resistance, any desired portion of the current can be diverted from the field and thereby the speed can be increased above normal (Fig. 2.28 b).

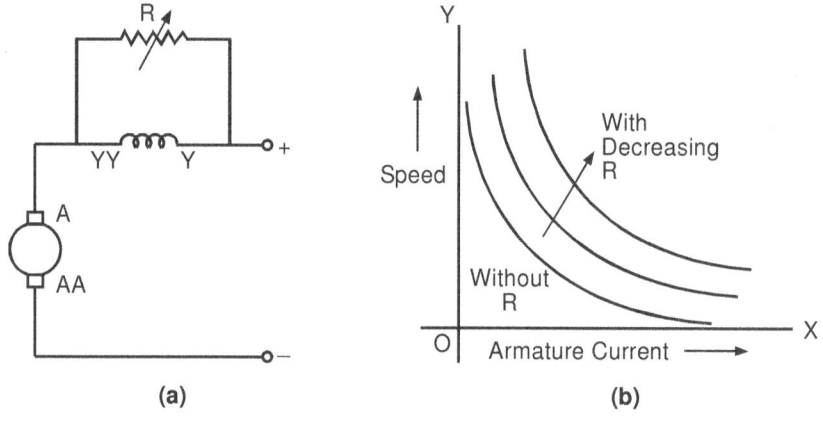

Fig. 2.28 : Diverter field control

(b) Tapped-Field Control : In this method, variation in flux is achieved by changing the number of turns of the field winding. For that number of taps are provided on the field winding as shown in Fig. 2.29 (a). With full field winding in the circuit, the motor runs at its minimum speed. For higher speeds, some of the series turns are cut out in steps. Fig. 2.29 (b) shows the operating characteristics with different number of series turns in the circuit. This method is often used in electric traction.

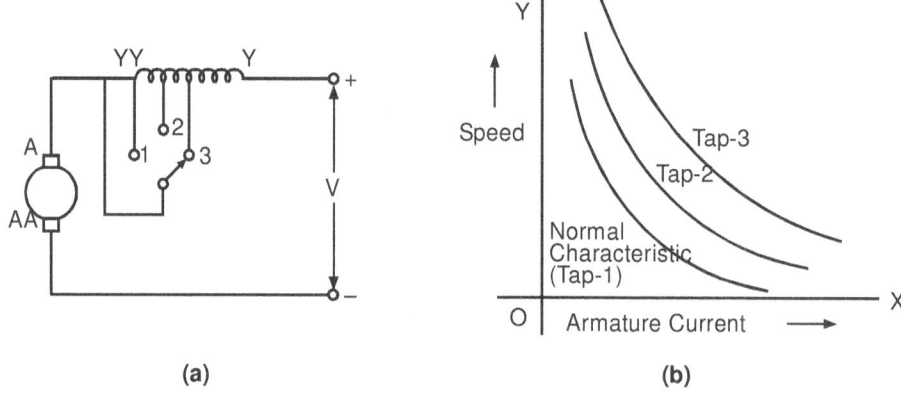

Fig. 2.29 : Tapped-field control

(c) **Series-Parallel Connections of Field Coils :** In this method, field m.m.f. and hence the flux is varied by series-parallel grouping of field coils and thereby several fixed speeds are obtained. If the field winding is divided into two equal halves, then by connecting these halves in series or in parallel as illustrated in Fig. 2.30 (a) and (b), two operating characteristics can be obtained (Fig. 2.30 c). Obviously, parallel field connection gives the higher speed for the same torque. This method is usually employed in the case of fan motors.

The various limitations of flux control method discussed earlier for shunt motors also stand in all the above cases of flux control for series motors. In actual practice, as said earlier, combination of armature voltage control and flux control is normally employed for speed variation over a wide range.

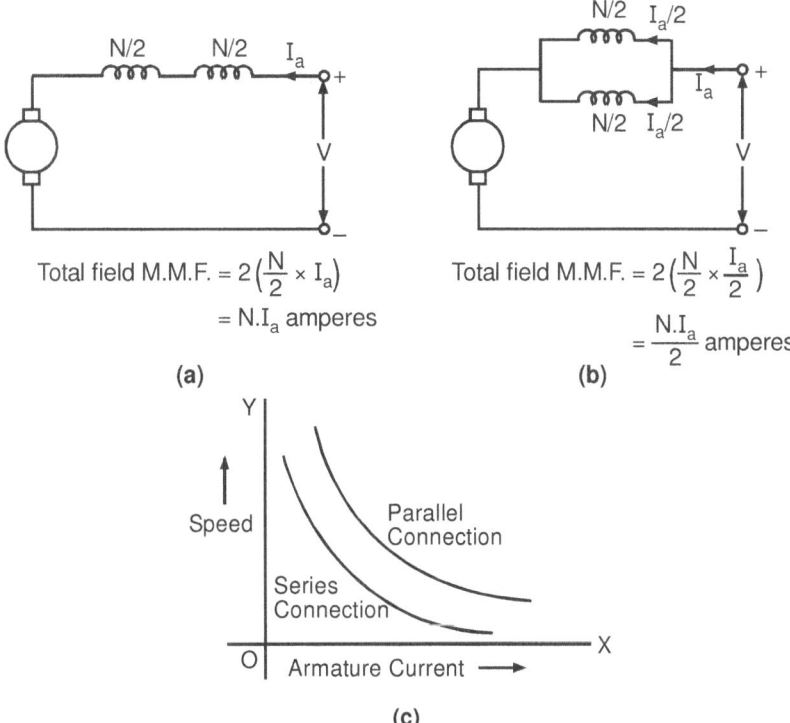

(a)   (b)

(c)

Fig. 2.30 : Flux control by series-parallel connections of field coils

Example 2.17 : *A 500 V, d.c. series motor has armature and series field resistances of 0.08 Ω and 0.02 Ω respectively and takes a current of 50 A at a speed of 500 r.p.m. What resistance should be connected in series with the armature to reduce the speed to 350 r.p.m. ? Load torque at this new speed is 75 % of its previous value. Assume flux to be proportional to the load current.*

Solution : In a series motor, before magnetic saturation,

$$T \propto \phi \cdot I_a \propto I_a^2$$

$$\therefore \qquad \frac{T_1}{T_2} = \frac{I_{a1}^2}{I_{a2}^2} \qquad \qquad \text{(With usual notations)}$$

With I_{a1} = 50 A and T_2 = 0.75 T_1, we have

$$\frac{T_1}{0.75 \, T_1} = \frac{50^2}{I_{a2}^2}$$

$\therefore$ $\qquad\qquad\qquad\qquad\qquad I_{a2}$ = 43.3 A

Now, for a d.c. motor, $\qquad\qquad N \propto \dfrac{E_b}{\phi}$

$$\frac{N_2}{N_1} = \frac{E_{b2}}{E_{b1}} \times \frac{\phi_1}{\phi_2}$$

$$= \frac{E_{b2}}{E_{b1}} \times \frac{I_{a1}}{I_{a2}} \qquad\qquad (\because \text{ In this case, } \phi \propto I_a)$$

$$E_{b1} = V - I_{a1} \, (R_a + R_{se}) = 500 - 50 \, (0.08 + 0.02)$$

$$= 495 \text{ V}$$

Let R be the resistance to be connected in series with the armature to reduce the motor speed to 350 r.p.m. Then,

$$E_{b2} = V - I_{a2} \, (R_a + R_{se} + R)$$

$$= 500 - 43.3 \, (0.08 + 0.02 + R)$$

Therefore substituting these values in the above equation, we get

$$\frac{350}{500} = \frac{500 - 43.3 \, (0.1 + R)}{495} \times \frac{50}{43.3}$$

$\therefore$ $\qquad\qquad\qquad\qquad$ **R = 4.517 Ω** $\qquad\qquad\qquad\qquad\qquad$ ... Ans.

Example 2.18 : *A series motor runs at 800 r.p.m. when taking a current of 75 A at 440 V. The resistance of its armature circuit is 0.2 Ω and that of the field winding is 0.05 Ω. At what speed will this motor run while developing half-full load torque with its field winding shunted by a resistor of 0.1 Ω ? Assume flux to be proportional to the field current.*

Solution : Initially when the field is without diverter,

$\qquad N_1$ = 800 r.p.m., $\qquad I_{a1}$ = 75 A

$$E_{b1} = V - I_{a1} \, (R_a + R_{se}) = 440 - 75 \, (0.2 + 0.05)$$

$$= 421.25 \text{ V}$$

When the diverter is in parallel with the field winding,

$$\text{Equivalent resistance, } R'_{se} = \frac{0.05 \times 0.1}{(0.05 + 0.1)} = 0.033 \, \Omega$$

Let I_{a2} be the new armature current when the diverter is in parallel with the field winding. Under this condition,

$$\text{Current through field winding} = \frac{0.1}{(0.05 + 0.1)} \times I_{a2}$$

$$= 0.667 \, I_{a2}$$

Now,
$$\frac{T_1}{T_2} = \frac{\phi_1 \cdot I_{a1}}{\phi_2 \cdot I_{a2}}$$
$\qquad (\because \ T \propto \phi \cdot I_a)$

$\therefore$
$$\frac{T_1}{0.5\,T_1} = \frac{75 \times 75}{0.667\,I_{a2} \times I_{a2}}$$
$\qquad (\because \ \phi \propto \text{Field current})$

$\therefore$
$$I_{a2} = 64.94 \text{ A}$$

and
$$E_{b2} = V - I_{a2}(R_a + R'_{se})$$
$$= 440 - 64.94\,(0.2 + 0.033) = 424.87 \text{ V}$$

Hence, we have
$$\frac{N_2}{N_1} = \frac{E_{b2}}{E_{b1}} \times \frac{\phi_1}{\phi_2}$$

$\therefore$
$$N_2 = N_1 \times \frac{E_{b2}}{E_{b1}} \times \frac{\phi_1}{\phi_2}$$

$$= 800 \times \frac{424.87}{421.25} \times \frac{75}{0.667 \times 64.94} \quad (\because \ \phi \propto \text{Field current})$$

$$= \textbf{1397 r.p.m.} \qquad\qquad\qquad \textbf{... Ans.}$$

Example 2.19 : *A d.c. series motor having a resistance of 1 Ω drives a fan for which the torque varies as the square of the speed. At 220 V, the set runs at 350 r.p.m. and takes 25 A current. The speed is to be raised to 500 r.p.m. by increasing the voltage. Calculate the new voltage required.*

Solution : Since,
$$N \propto \frac{E_b}{\phi}$$

$$\frac{N_2}{N_1} = \frac{E_{b2}}{E_{b1}} \times \frac{\phi_1}{\phi_2} = \frac{E_{b2}}{E_{b1}} \times \frac{I_{a1}}{I_{a2}} \quad (\because \ \phi \propto I_a) \qquad \text{... (I)}$$

Now,
$$E_{b1} = V_1 - I_{a1}(R_a + R_{se}) = 220 - 25\,(1.0) = 195 \text{ V}$$

For a series motor,
$$T \propto \phi \cdot I_a \propto I_a^2 \qquad\qquad (\because \ \phi \propto I_a)$$

$\therefore$
$$\frac{T_1}{T_2} = \frac{I_{a1}^2}{I_{a2}^2} \qquad\qquad\qquad \text{... (II)}$$

But for fan,
$$\frac{T_1}{T_2} = \frac{N_1^2}{N_2^2} \qquad\qquad\qquad \text{... (III)}$$

Therefore, from equations (II) and (III), we get
$$\left(\frac{I_{a1}}{I_{a2}}\right)^2 = \left(\frac{N_1}{N_2}\right)^2$$

$\therefore$
$$\frac{I_{a1}}{I_{a2}} = \frac{N_1}{N_2}$$

$\therefore$
$$I_{a2} = I_{a1} \times \frac{N_2}{N_1} = 25 \times \frac{500}{350} = 35.71 \text{ A}$$

Substituting the relevant values in Equation (I), we get

$$\frac{500}{350} = \frac{E_{b2}}{195} \times \frac{25}{35.71}$$

$\therefore$ $\qquad\qquad\qquad E_{b2} = 397.91$ V

Let the corresponding voltage to be applied be V_2. Then,

$$E_{b2} = V_2 - I_{a2} (R_a + R_{se})$$

$\therefore$ $\qquad\qquad\qquad 397.91 = V_2 - 35.71 (1.0)$

$\therefore$ $\qquad$ Voltage to be applied, $V_2 = \mathbf{433.62}$ **V** ... **Ans.**

Example 2.20 : *A 200 V, d.c. series motor drives a load at a certain speed and takes a current of 30 A. The resistance between its terminals is 1.5 Ω. Find the extra resistance to be added in series with the motor circuit to reduce the speed to 60% of its original value. Assume that the torque produced is proportional to the cube of the speed.*

Solution : Given : V = 200 volts, I_1 = 30 A, $R_a + R_{se}$ = 1.5 Ω, N_2 = 0.6 N_1.

$$E_{b1} = V - I_{a1} (R_a + R_{se})$$

$$= 200 - 30 (1.5) = 155 \text{ V} \qquad (\because I_1 = I_{a1})$$

Now, $\qquad\qquad T \propto \phi \cdot I_a \propto I_a^2 \qquad (\because \text{With unsaturated field, } \phi \propto I_a)$

$\therefore$ $\qquad\qquad\qquad \dfrac{T_1}{T_2} = \left(\dfrac{I_{a1}}{I_{a2}}\right)^2 \qquad\qquad$ ... (I)

Also, $\qquad\qquad T \propto N^3$

$\therefore$ $\qquad\qquad\qquad \dfrac{T_1}{T_2} = \left(\dfrac{N_1}{N_2}\right)^3 \qquad\qquad$ ... (II)

Hence, from equations (I) and (II), we have

$$\left(\frac{I_{a1}}{I_{a2}}\right)^2 = \left(\frac{N_1}{N_2}\right)^3$$

$\therefore$ $\qquad \left(\dfrac{30}{I_{a2}}\right)^2 = \left(\dfrac{N_1}{0.6 N_1}\right)^3 = \left(\dfrac{1}{0.6}\right)^3$

$\therefore$ $\qquad\qquad\qquad I_{a2} = 13.94$ A

Further, $\qquad \dfrac{N_1}{N_2} = \dfrac{E_{b1}}{E_{b2}} \times \dfrac{\phi_2}{\phi_1} = \dfrac{E_{b1}}{E_{b2}} \times \dfrac{I_{a2}}{I_{a1}} \qquad (\because \phi \propto I_a)$

$\therefore$ $\qquad \dfrac{N_1}{0.6 N_1} = \dfrac{155}{E_{b2}} \times \dfrac{13.94}{30}$

$\therefore$ $\qquad\qquad\qquad E_{b2} = 43.21$ V

But $\qquad\qquad\qquad E_{b2} = V - I_{a2} (R_a + R_{se} + R)$

$\therefore$ $\qquad\qquad 43.21 = 200 - 13.94 (1.5 + R)$

$\therefore$ Extra resistance required in series with the motor circuit,

$\qquad\qquad\qquad R = \mathbf{9.75} \; \mathbf{\Omega}$ ... **Ans.**

2.15 APPLICATIONS OF D.C. MOTORS

• **D.C. Shunt Motors :** Being constant speed motors, they are commonly employed for the following applications :

Lathes, drilling machines, grinders, shapers, planers, milling machines, metal cutting machines, wood working machines, fans, blowers, compressors, conveyors, vacuum cleaners, centrifugal and reciprocating pumps, etc.

• **D.C. Series Motors :** These motors are very useful for the applications requiring high starting torque like traction, lifts, hoists, cranes. They are also commonly used for conveyors and in rolling mills.

• **D.C. Compound Motors :** Cumulative compound motors are suitable for applications requiring a high starting torque and particularly under fluctuating load conditions. They have the advantage over the series motors of a stable no-load speed. Some of their applications are :

Driving of steel rolling mills, elevators, punches, shears, conveyors, heavy planers, strokers, presses.

Differential compound motors have low starting torque. They are, therefore, rarely used in actual practice.

2.16 POINTS TO REMEMBER

• An electric motor is a machine which converts electrical energy into mechanical energy.

• When a conductor carrying current is placed in a magnetic field, it experiences a mechanical force. The action of an electric motor is based on this principle.

• Commutator plays very important role in the operation of a d.c. motor. It reverses the current in each conductor of the armature as it passes from one pole to another and thus helps to develop a continuous and unidirectional torque.

• As per Lenz's law, the e.m.f. induced in the rotating armature conductors of a d.c. motor always acts in opposition with the applied voltage and therefore known as *back e.m.f. (E_b)* or *counter e.m.f.*

• Torque of a d.c. motor is proportional to the product of the flux per pole (ϕ) and the armature current (I_a).

• The net torque available at the shaft of a d.c. motor for doing useful work (after providing for friction, windage and iron losses) is known as *shaft torque (T_{sh})*.

• If the series field winding of a d.c. compound motor is arranged to assist the shunt field winding, it is said to be *cumulatively compounded*. On the other hand, if the series field winding opposes the shunt field winding, the motor is said to be *differentially compounded*.

- Speed regulation of a d.c. motor is defined as the change in its speed when the load on it is reduced from rated value to zero, expressed in per cent of rated load speed.

- The complete starting resistor assembly including protective devices such as no-volt release and over-load release, is called *a starter*.

- If either the direction of field current (I_f) or the direction of armature current (I_a) is reversed, the rotation of motor is reversed. However, if both are reversed at the same time, there is no effect on the direction of rotation.

- The speed of a d.c. motor is approximately proportional to the voltage applied (V) across the armature and inversely proportional to the flux per pole (ϕ).

2.17 IMPORTANT FORMULAE AT A GLANCE

- Back e.m.f.,
$$E_b = \frac{\phi ZN}{60} \cdot \frac{P}{A} \text{ volts}$$

where

ϕ = Flux per pole, in webers

Z = Number of armature conductors

N = Speed of the motor, in r.p.m.

P = Number of poles

A = Number of parallel paths in the armature winding (A = 2 for wave winding and A = P for lap winding).

- Gross torque of a motor,
$$T = \frac{1}{2\pi} \phi ZI_a \cdot \frac{P}{A} = 0.159 \, \phi ZI_a \cdot \frac{P}{A} \text{ newton-metres}$$

where

ϕ = Flux per pole, in webers

Z = Total number of armature conductors

I_a = Armature current, in amperes

P = Number of poles

A = Number of parallel paths in the armature winding (A = 2 for wave winding and A = P for lap winding)

- **Voltage and Current Relationships for Different Types of Motors :**

  (i) Shunt Motor :
$$I_{sh} = \frac{V}{R_{sh}}$$
$$I_a = I - I_{sh}$$
$$E_b = V - I_a \cdot R_a$$

(ii) Series Motor :

$$I_a = I$$

$$E_b = V - I_a (R_a + R_{se})$$

(iii) Short-Shunt Compound Motor :

Voltage across the shunt field,

$$V' = V - I \cdot R_{se}$$

$$I_{sh} = \frac{V'}{R_{sh}} = \frac{V - I \cdot R_{se}}{R_{sh}}$$

$$I_a = I - I_{sh}$$

$$E_b = V' - I_a \cdot R_a = V - I \cdot R_{se} - I_a \cdot R_a$$

(iv) Long-Shunt Compound Motor :

$$I_{sh} = \frac{V}{R_{sh}}$$

$$I_a = I - I_{sh}$$

$$E_b = V - I_a (R_a + R_{se})$$

where E_b is the back e.m.f. (in volts), V the supply voltage (in volts), I the line current (in amperes), I_{sh} the shunt-field current (in amperes), I_a the armature current (in amperes), R_a the armature resistance (in ohms), R_{sh} the shunt-field resistance (in ohms) and R_{se} the series-field resistance (in ohms).

•
$$\frac{N_1}{N_2} = \frac{E_{b1}}{E_{b2}} \times \frac{\phi_2}{\phi_1}$$

where N_1, ϕ_1 and E_{b1} are respectively the speed of the motor (in r.p.m.), flux per pole (in webers) and the back e.m.f. (in volts) in one condition and N_2, ϕ_2 and E_{b2} denote the corresponding quantities in the second condition.

2.18 EXERCISES

2.18.1 Review Questions

1. In what way does a motor differ from a generator in the function which it performs ?

2. State the general principle on which the electrical motors work.

3. Explain the principle of operation of a d.c. motor.

4. Explain the function of the commutator in a d.c. motor. In what respect is it different from that in generator ?

5. State the factors on which electromagnetic torque developed in a d.c. motor depends. Deduce the expression for the torque developed in a d.c. motor.

6. What are the various types of d.c. motors ? Show diagrammatically these motors and give their industrial applications.

7. Compare the operating characteristics of different types of d.c. motors.

8. Why are d.c. series motors suitable for traction ?

9. D.C. series motor is always started with some mechanical load on it. Why ?

10. What is the difficulty in starting a d.c. motor without a starter ? State the functions of a starter.

11. Draw a neat sketch of any one type of starter suitable for d.c. shunt motor. Name the various parts and state the function of each of them.

12. Suggest the methods to change the direction of rotation of a d.c. motor.

13. Explain the different methods of controlling the speed of (a) a d.c. shunt motor, (b) a d.c. series motor. Mention the limitations of each method.

2.18.2 Examples for Practice

1. A 230 V shunt motor takes 5 A on no load and runs at 750 r.p.m. Its shunt field and armature resistances are 115 Ω and 0.25 Ω respectively. Calculate the speed of the motor when loaded and taking a current of 55 A. Assume that the flux becomes weak by 4 per cent under load condition.   (739 r.p.m.)

2. A series motor runs at 650 r.p.m. when taking 100 A from a 230 V supply. The resistance of the armature circuit is 0.15 Ω and that of the series field is 0.05 Ω. Calculate the speed when the current has fallen to 50 A. Assume the flux to be proportional to current.

                                    (1362 r.p.m.)

3. A 200 V, d.c. shunt motor has a shunt field resistance of 200 Ω and an armature resistance of 0.5 Ω. For a given load torque and no additional resistance included in the shunt field circuit, the motor runs at 1500 r.p.m. drawing an armature current of 25 A. If a resistance of 200 Ω is inserted in series with the field, the load torque remaining the same, find out the new speed and armature current. Assume the magnetization curve to be linear.   (50 A, 2800 r.p.m.)

4. A 230 V, d.c. shunt motor takes an armature current of 20 A on a certain load. Resistance of the armature is 0.5 Ω. Find the resistance required in series with the armature to halve the speed if the load torque is proportional to the square of the speed.   (23.5 Ω)

5. A 200 V, d.c. series motor when fully loaded runs at 1000 r.p.m. and draws 20 A from the mains. The resistance of armature winding is 0.5 Ω and that of the field winding 0.2 Ω. Find the speed when 0.2 Ω resistor is joined in parallel with the field winding. Assume the torque to remain unaltered and the flux to be proportional to the field current.   (1392 r.p.m.)

6. A 220 V, d.c. series motor takes 7.5 A and runs at 1000 r.p.m. The resistance of its armature circuit is 0.5 Ω and that of the field winding is 0.2 Ω. At what speed will it run when a 2.5 Ω resistance is connected in series, the motor current remaining the same ?

                                    (913 r.p.m.)

CHAPTER

THREE

THREE-PHASE INDUCTION MOTORS

3.1 INTRODUCTION

As already mentioned previously in Section 2.2, induction motor operates with alternating current supplied directly to the stator winding and by induction, or transformer action, to the rotor winding. It is for this reason that motors of this type are known as *induction motors*. In fact, an induction motor can be considered as a sort of rotating transformer i.e. one in which a stationary winding on stator is connected to the a.c. source, while the other winding mounted on a rotor receives its power by transformer action while it rotates. Motors of this type are designed to operate either on single-phase or on three-phase a.c. supply and accordingly called *single-phase induction motors* and *three-phase induction motors*. Of all the types of a.c. motors, the three-phase induction motor is by far the most common type. This chapter deals with three-phase induction motors in details.

3.2 PRODUCTION OF ROTATING MAGNETIC FIELD

The action of three-phase induction motor is based on the fact that *if a stationary system of coils suitably wound, is supplied with polyphase a.c., then a uniformly rotating magnetic field of constant magnitude is produced.* This rotating magnetic field is in effect, similar to the rotation of field poles in space by some mechanical means. The principle of rotating magnetic field is, therefore, of fundamental importance. It can be very easily understood by considering the elementary three-phase, two-pole stator illustrated in Fig. 3.1.

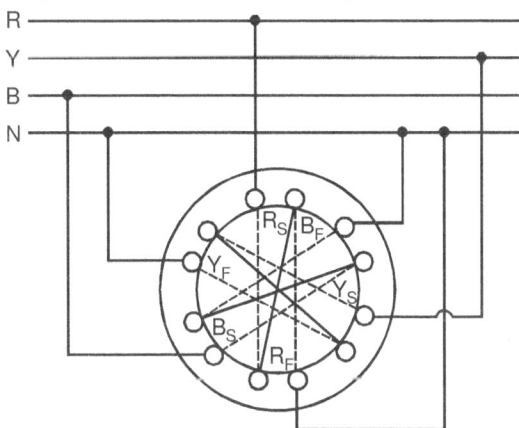

Fig. 3.1 : An elementary three-phase, two-pole stator

It consists of three coils 120° apart in space i.e. the starting terminals R_S, Y_S and B_S or the finishing terminals R_F, Y_F and B_F of the three coils are 120° apart. Each coil thus forms one phase of a three-phase winding of a stator. Let this winding be supplied with three-phase currents and let the phase-sequence for these currents be R-Y-B. Since the currents in the three coils are alternating and 120 degrees out of phase with respect to time, the magnetic fields generated by them will also be alternating and 120 degrees out of phase. Fig. 3.2 (a) shows the waveforms for alternating magnetic fields generated by the three coils. At any instant, these magnetic fields will act along the magnetic axes of the respective coils and therefore will be displaced from each other through 120 degrees in space. Assumed positive directions of these fluxes in space are shown in Fig. 3.2 (b). It should be remembered that the choice of a particular direction as positive is merely conventional.

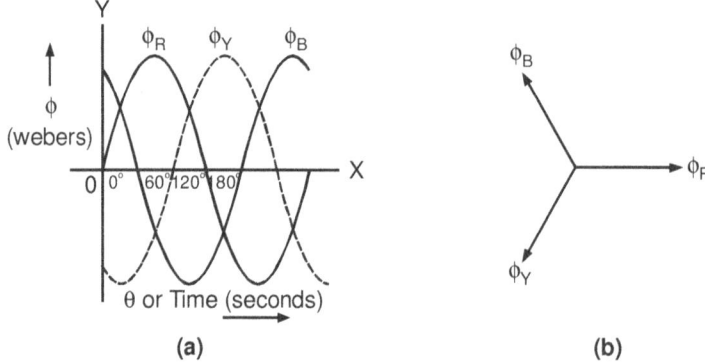

(a)   (b)

Fig. 3.2 : (a) Waveforms for alternating magnetic fields generated by three phases of the stator winding.

(b) Diagram showing positive directions of fluxes in space

Now, let ϕ_R, ϕ_Y and ϕ_B be the instantaneous values of the fluxes produced by three-phases. Then, the total flux ϕ_T at any instant will be given by vectorially combining ϕ_R, ϕ_Y and ϕ_B in space. We will consider values of ϕ_T at four instants at intervals of 1/6 of a period corresponding to 0°, 60°, 120° and 180° in Fig. 3.2 (a).

(i) **When $\theta = 0^0$:** At this instant, $\phi_R = 0$. To find the instantaneous values of other fluxes, consider the corresponding phasor diagram shown in Fig. 3.3 (a), where ϕ_{Rm}, ϕ_{Ym} and ϕ_{Bm} are the maximum values of the fluxes by three phases. We obtain instantaneous value of a particular alternating quantity by projecting a rotating phasor representing that alternating quantity on a fixed OY-axis. Therefore, in this case,

$$\phi_Y = -\phi_{Ym} \cos 30^0 = -\frac{\sqrt{3}}{2} \phi_{Ym}$$

If $\qquad \phi_{Rm} = \phi_{Ym} = \phi_{Bm} = \phi_m$, then

$$\phi_Y = -\frac{\sqrt{3}}{2} \phi_m$$

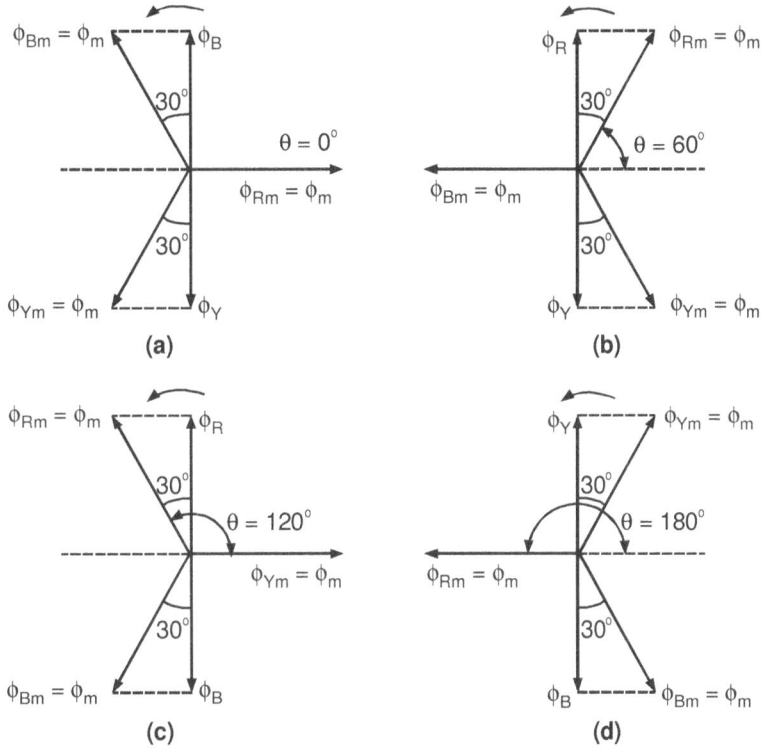

Fig. 3.3 : Phasor diagrams for the alternating fluxes produced by three phases at the instants when (a) $\theta = 0°$, (b) $\theta = 60°$, (c) $\theta = 120°$, (d) $\theta = 180°$

Similarly, $\qquad \phi_B = \phi_{Bm} \cos 30° = \dfrac{\sqrt{3}}{2} \phi_{Bm} = \dfrac{\sqrt{3}}{2} \phi_m$

Combining ϕ_Y and ϕ_B vectorially* in space as illustrated in the vector diagram of Fig. 3.4 (a), we get

$$\text{Total flux, } \phi_T = 2 \times \dfrac{\sqrt{3}}{2} \phi_m \cos \dfrac{60°}{2} - \sqrt{3} \times \dfrac{\sqrt{3}}{2} \phi_m = \dfrac{3}{2} \phi_m$$

It should be noted that ϕ_Y being equal to $-\dfrac{\sqrt{3}}{2} \phi_m$, it is drawn in its negative direction in space with a magnitude of $\dfrac{\sqrt{3}}{2} \phi_m$ in the vector diagram of Fig. 3.4 (a).

(ii) When $\theta = 60°$: From the corresponding phasor diagram shown in Fig. 3.3 (b),

$$\phi_R = \phi_{Rm} \cos 30° = \dfrac{\sqrt{3}}{2} \phi_{Rm} = \dfrac{\sqrt{3}}{2} \phi_m,$$

$$\phi_Y = -\phi_{Ym} \cos 30° = -\dfrac{\sqrt{3}}{2} \phi_{Ym} = -\dfrac{\sqrt{3}}{2} \phi_m,$$

and $\qquad \phi_B = 0$

---

* *It should be remembered that while the phasor represents a sinusoidally time-varying quantity, the vector represents a quantity with definite space direction.*

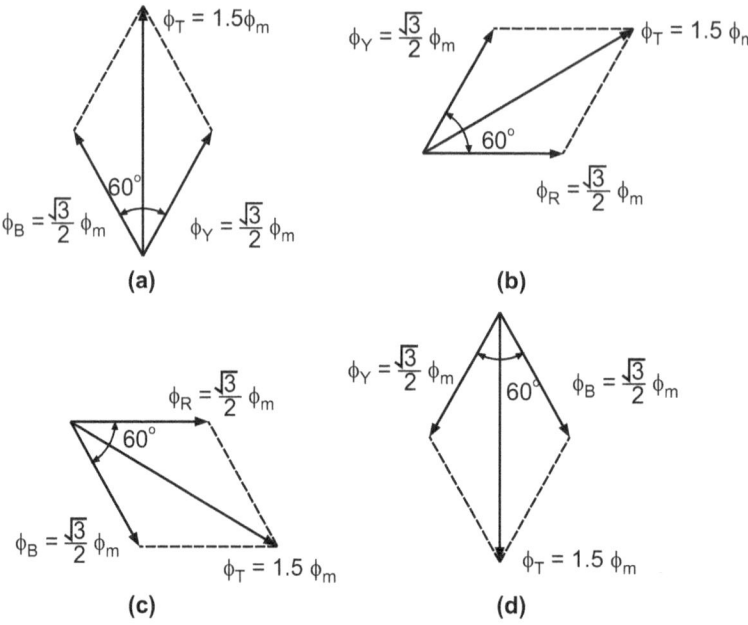

Fig. 3.4 : Vector diagrams of fluxes in space at the instants when

(a) θ = 0°, (b) θ = 60°, (c) θ = 120°, (d) θ = 180°

Therefore, from the vector diagram of Fig. 3.4 (b), total flux ϕ_T in space at this instant

$$= 2 \times \frac{\sqrt{3}}{2} \, \phi_m \, \cos \frac{60^0}{2} = \frac{3}{2} \, \phi_m$$

Thus, the resultant flux ϕ_T is again $\frac{3}{2} \phi_m$. However, from the vector diagram, it will be observed that this resultant flux has now rotated clockwise through an angle of 60^0 from its previous position at $\theta = 0^0$.

(iii) When θ = 120° : Fig. 3.3 (c) shows the phasor diagram for the fluxes at this instant. From this phasor diagram,

$$\phi_R = \phi_{Rm} \cos 30^0 = \frac{\sqrt{3}}{2} \, \phi_{Rm} = \frac{\sqrt{3}}{2} \, \phi_m,$$

$$\phi_Y = 0,$$

and $\qquad\qquad \phi_B = -\phi_{Bm} \cos 30^0 = -\frac{\sqrt{3}}{2} \, \phi_{Bm} = -\frac{\sqrt{3}}{2} \, \phi_m$

Hence, from vector diagram (Fig. 3.4 c),

$$\phi_T = 2 \times \frac{\sqrt{3}}{2} \, \phi_m \, \cos \frac{60^0}{2} = \frac{3}{2} \, \phi_m$$

Thus, the resultant flux has still the magnitude of $\frac{3}{2} \phi_m$, but has its position shifted further through 60^0 in a clockwise direction from its previous position at $\theta = 60^0$.

(iv) When θ = 180⁰ : From the phasor diagram, (Fig. 3.3 d),

$$\phi_R = 0,$$

$$\phi_Y = \phi_{Ym} \cos 30^\circ = \frac{\sqrt{3}}{2} \phi_{Ym} = \frac{\sqrt{3}}{2} \phi_m,$$

and

$$\phi_B = -\phi_{Bm} \cos 30^\circ = -\frac{\sqrt{3}}{2} \phi_{Bm} = -\frac{\sqrt{3}}{2} \phi_m$$

Vector diagram of Fig. 3.4 (d) shows that the resultant flux ϕ_T in space at this instant also is $\frac{3}{2} \phi_m$ and has rotated still further through 60⁰ in a clockwise direction from its previous position at θ = 120⁰ or through 180⁰ from its starting position at θ = 0⁰.

From the above discussion, following important conclusions can be drawn :

(i) When the three phase windings displaced in space through 120⁰ electrical* are supplied with three-phase currents, they produce uniformly rotating magnetic field of constant magnitude. The resultant field in space at any instant has magnitude equal to 1.5 times the maximum flux produced by one phase i.e. $\phi_T = \frac{3}{2} \phi_m$

(ii) The resultant flux rotates in space with a speed of two pole pitches** per cycle. In the case of the elementary three-phase, two-pole stator which we have considered, 2 pole-pitches correspond to 1 revolution. If the stator is wound for P pole, then 2-pole pitches will correspond to $\frac{2}{P}$ revolution.

Therefore, with a supply frequency of f cycles per second, number of revolutions of the magnetic field per second will be $\frac{2}{P} \times f$. If N is the speed of the magnetic field in revolutions per minute, then

$$N - \frac{120\,f}{P} \qquad\qquad \text{... (3.1)}$$

Thus the speed with which the flux rotates bears a fixed relation with the supply frequency and the number of poles.

(iii) The direction of rotation of the resultant flux is from the axis of the *leading* phase of the stator winding to that of its *lagging* phase. In the example under consideration, the phase sequence of three-phase currents supplied to the three-phase, two-pole stator is assumed to be R-Y-B. Therefore in this case, phase R leads phase Y and phase Y leads phase B. Hence, the direction of the resultant flux is from the axis of phase R (i.e. of a coil with starting terminal R_S and finishing terminal R_F) of the stator winding to the axis of phase Y and then to the axis of phase B. Thus, it is in the clockwise direction. It can be shown that direction of rotation of the resultant flux reverses when the phase sequence of currents is reversed. This can be easily accomplished by interchanging the supply connections to any two terminals of the stator.

---

*   *For 2-pole machine, 1° Mechanical = 1° Electrical*

**   *Refer to the Section 1.7.*

3.2.1 Determination of the Magnitude and Speed of the Rotating Magnetic Field by Analytical Method

The production of rotating magnetic field can also be studied using analytical method. For that consider again an elementary three-phase, two-pole stator illustrated in Fig. 3.1. Let each phase of the stator produce an alternating flux of maximum value ϕ_m along its axis. Then the instantaneous values of the alternating fluxes produced by three phases can be represented by the following equations :

$$\phi_R = \phi_m \sin \omega t$$
$$\phi_Y = \phi_m \sin (\omega t - 120°)$$
$$\phi_B = \phi_m \sin (\omega t - 240°)$$

These fluxes which have a time phase difference of 120 electrical degrees with respect to each other are oriented in space along the magnetic axes of their respective phases and thus are displaced from each other through 120° in space as illustrated in Fig. 3.5.

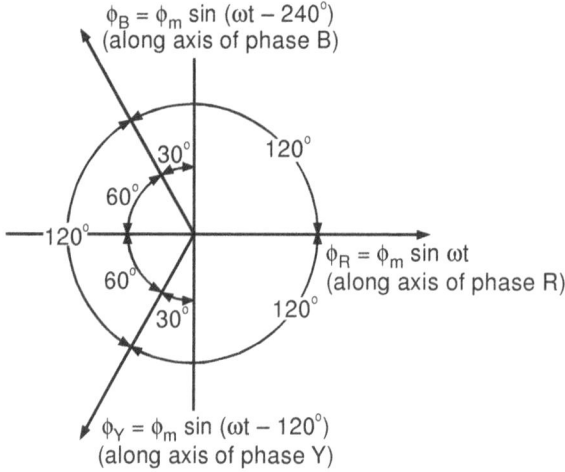

Fig. 3.5 : Relative orientation in space of fluxes produced by
three phases of the stator winding

The value of the resultant flux ϕ_T in space at any particular instant can be obtained by resolving the component fluxes along the axis of phase R and the axis perpendicular to it. Thus,

Resultant horizontal component,

$$\bar{X} = \phi_R - \phi_Y \cos 60° - \phi_B \cos 60°$$

$$= \phi_m \sin \omega t - \frac{1}{2} \phi_m \sin (\omega t - 120°) - \frac{1}{2} \phi_m \sin (\omega t - 240°)$$

$$= \phi_m [\sin \omega t - \frac{1}{2} (\sin \omega t \cos 120° - \cos \omega t \sin 120°)$$

$$- \frac{1}{2} (\sin \omega t \cos 240° - \cos \omega t \sin 240°)]$$

$$= \phi_m \left[\sin \omega t - \frac{1}{2} \left(-\frac{1}{2} \sin \omega t - \frac{\sqrt{3}}{2} \cos \omega t \right) - \frac{1}{2} \left(-\frac{1}{2} \sin \omega t + \frac{\sqrt{3}}{2} \cos \omega t \right) \right]$$

$$= \frac{3}{2} \phi_m \sin \omega t \qquad\qquad \text{... (3.2)}$$

Resultant vertical component,

$$\overline{Y} = 0 - \phi_Y \cos 30° + \phi_B \cos 30°$$

$$= -\frac{\sqrt{3}}{2} \phi_m \sin (\omega t - 120°) + \frac{\sqrt{3}}{2} \phi_m \sin (\omega t - 240°)$$

$$= \frac{\sqrt{3}}{2} \phi_m [-(\sin \omega t \cos 120° - \cos \omega t \sin 120°)$$

$$+ (\sin \omega t \cos 240° - \cos \omega t \sin 240°)]$$

$$= \frac{\sqrt{3}}{2} \phi_m \left[-\left(-\frac{1}{2} \sin \omega t - \frac{\sqrt{3}}{2} \cos \omega t \right) + \left(-\frac{1}{2} \sin \omega t + \frac{\sqrt{3}}{2} \cos \omega t \right) \right]$$

$$= \frac{3}{2} \phi_m \cos \omega t \qquad \qquad \text{... (3.3)}$$

Hence, in view of Equations (3.2) and (3.3), we have

The resultant flux, $\phi_T = \sqrt{(\overline{X})^2 + (\overline{Y})^2}$

$$= \frac{3}{2} \phi_m \qquad \qquad \text{... (3.4)}$$

This clearly shows that the magnitude of resultant flux is independent of time and hence is constant all the while. Now for finding the direction of the resultant flux, let us find the angle θ made by this flux with the reference axis i.e. the axis of phase R.

$$\tan \theta = \frac{\overline{Y}}{\overline{X}} = \frac{\cos \omega t}{\sin \omega t} = \tan (90° - \omega t)$$

∴ $\theta = 90° - \omega t$ or $(90° - \theta) = \omega t$ ... (3.5)

Thus the angle $(90° - \theta)$ which is the angle made by resultant flux with the axis perpendicular to the axis of phase R (i.e. with Y-axis in this case) is directly proportional to the time. The resultant field therefore rotates in space with uniform angular velocity ω ($= 2\pi f$) and its direction of rotation is clearly *clockwise*. The angular distance travelled by this rotating field in a period of one cycle is 2π electrical radians which is equivalent to 2-pole pitches. Hence, as already seen previously in Section 3.2, with a stator wound for P poles and a supply frequency of f cycles per second, the speed of the magnetic field in revolutions per minute will be

$$N = \frac{120 \, f}{P}$$

3.2.2 Essential Conditions to be Satisfied for Obtaining a Rotating Magnetic Field

We have seen that when the three-phase windings displaced in space through 120 electrical degrees are supplied with the three-phase currents having time phase difference of 120 electrical degrees, they produce a uniformly rotating magnetic field. Similarly, it can be shown that when a two-phase supply is applied across two phase windings displaced in space through 90 electrical degrees, a rotating magnetic field is produced. In general, following conditions should be satisfied for obtaining a rotating magnetic field :

- A polyphase supply must be available i.e. say 2-phase, 3-phase, etc.

- A polyphase winding across which a polyphase supply is being applied for obtaining the rotating magnetic field should have phases equal to number of supply phases.

- The various phases of the polyphase winding must be displaced from each other by an angular distance (in electrical degrees) in space equal to the electrical phase difference (with respect to time) between the currents supplied to them by the polyphase supply.

3.3 OPERATING PRINCIPLE OF A THREE-PHASE INDUCTION MOTOR

This type of motor (Fig. 3.6) consists of a set of three phase windings distributed in slots around the stationary outer member called *stator*. The rotating member which is known as *rotor* also carries the other set of windings. When the stator windings are connected to the three-phase a.c. supply, then as already seen, the rotating magnetic field of constant magnitude is produced.

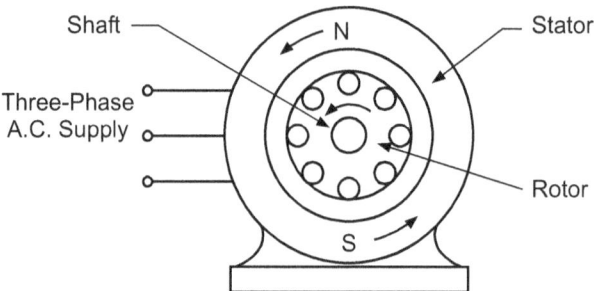

Fig. 3.6 : Three-phase induction motor

When this rotating field is cut by the stationary rotor conductors, according to Faraday's law of electromagnetic induction, an e.m.f. is induced in the rotor conductors. Since all the rotor conductors together form a closed circuit, the induced e.m.f. in the rotor conductors sets up rotor currents. Thus, being in the magnetic field produced by the stator windings, each current carrying conductor of the rotor experiences a mechanical force which ultimately results into rotation of the rotor. The rotating field due to stator currents and the rotor currents react basically in the same manner as described in the Section 2.2 to produce force on the rotor conductors and the torque. To understand this more clearly, assume that the stator field is rotating in an anticlockwise direction and the rotor is stationary as illustrated in Fig. 3.7 (a). The relative motion of the rotor, with respect to the stator field is then obviously in the clockwise direction (Fig. 3.7 b). In other words, this means that if the field is made stationary, the rotor can be assumed to be rotating in the clockwise direction. Under this condition, the direction of the induced e.m.f. in the rotor conductor shown in the figure, as given by Fleming's right-hand rule is in the plane of the paper. The current set up by this induced e.m.f. is also in the same direction. Fig. 3.7 (b) also shows the direction of the flux due to the rotor current alone and the resultant flux pattern is shown in Fig. 3.7 (c). The stretched flux lines exert the force on the rotor conductor due to which the rotor rotates in the anticlockwise direction. Thus the rotor rotates in the same direction as that of the stator flux.

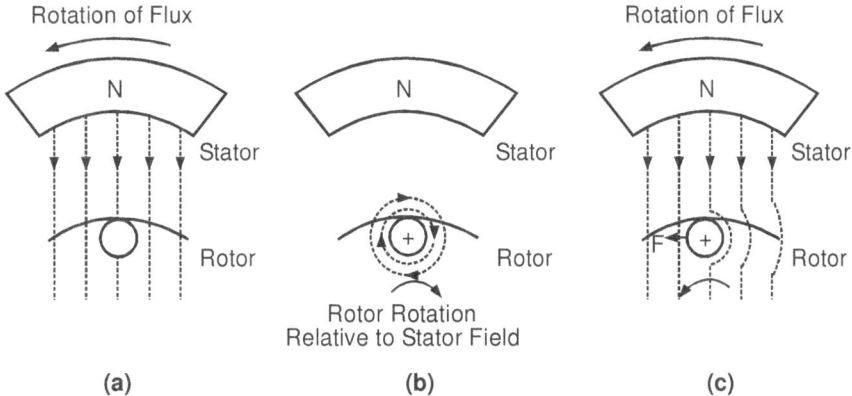

Fig. 3.7 : Production of torque in a three-phase induction motor

This can be explained in another way also. According to Lenz's law, the direction of the induced current in the rotor conductors is always such as to oppose the very cause producing it. In this case, the cause producing the current in the rotor conductors being the relative speed between the rotating flux of the stator and the stationary rotor conductors, the rotor starts rotating in the same direction as that of the flux to reduce the relative speed between them. It should be noted that no electrical connection exists between the two sets of windings, on the stator and the rotor. Thus the motor purely works on the induction principle.

3.4 SYNCHRONOUS SPEED

We have seen that the speed of the rotating magnetic field produced by the stator winding of the three-phase induction motor depends upon the supply frequency (f) and the number of poles (P) for which the motor is wound. From Equation (3.1), the relation among speed (N), frequency and number of poles is given by the expression,

$$N = \frac{120\,f}{P} \text{ r.p.m.}$$

This speed of rotating magnetic field is known as the *synchronous speed* of the motor and denoted by N_S.

Thus, $$N_S = \frac{120\,f}{P} \text{ r.p.m}$$ ... (3.6)

3.5 SLIP

In an induction motor, it is impossible for the rotor to run at synchronous speed.[*] If it runs at synchronous speed, there will be no relative motion between the rotating magnetic field produced by the stator and the rotor conductors. As a result, there will be no induced e.m.f. and no current in the rotor conductors. Therefore, no torque will be produced. Actually, the speed of the motor

---

[*] *For this reason, induction motor is sometimes called an asynchronous motor.*

adjusts itself so that the magnitude of the rotor current is just sufficient to produce a torque equal to that required by the rotor losses and the load if any on the motor. For example at no load, the retarding torque is only due to the mechanical (friction and windage) and other no-load losses. Therefore, the speed very nearly reaches synchronous value. On the application of a load, the speed falls. Thereby the rotor e.m.f. and the current are increased. Thus the motor meets the increased demand for the torque.

The speed of the rotor relative to that of the rotating magnetic field produced by the stator is known as *absolute slip* or only *slip* (or sometimes, *slip speed*). In other words, slip is the difference between the synchronous speed (N_S) and the actual speed (N) of the rotor. It is usually expressed as a fraction or percentage of the synchronous speed. Thus,

$$\text{Fractional slip, } S = \frac{N_S - N}{N_S} \qquad \qquad \ldots (3.7)$$

and

$$\text{Percentage slip} = \frac{N_S - N}{N_S} \times 100 \qquad \qquad \ldots (3.8)$$

Rearranging the Equation (3.7), we get

$$N = N_S (1 - S) \qquad \qquad \ldots (3.9)$$

At starting, N = 0. Therefore, value of the slip is 1. The value of the full load slip is about 4 to 5 % for small motors and about $1\frac{1}{2}$ to 2 % for large motors.

Example 3.1 : *A 3-phase, 4-pole, 50 Hz induction motor works with a full load slip of 3%. Find : (i) Synchronous speed, (ii) Actual speed of the motor.*

Solution :

(i) Synchronous speed, $N_S = \dfrac{120\,f}{P}$

With f = 50 Hz and P = 4,

$$N_S = \frac{120 \times 50}{4} = \textbf{1500 r.p.m.} \qquad \qquad \textbf{... Ans.}$$

(ii) From Equation (3.9),

Actual speed of the motor, $N = N_S (1 - S)$

Since the percentage slip is 3, fractional slip, S = 0.03.

Therefore, from the above equation,

$$N = 1500 (1 - 0.03) = \textbf{1455 r.p.m.} \qquad \qquad \textbf{... Ans.}$$

3.6 TYPES OF THREE-PHASE INDUCTION MOTORS

As already mentioned, a three-phase induction motor consists essentially of two main parts, namely a *stator* and *a rotor*. Depending on the type of rotor used, there are two principal varieties available of the three-phase induction motor.

3.6.1 Squirrel-Cage Induction Motors

The stator of the squirrel-cage induction motor (Fig. 3.8 a) has a laminated core provided with slots on its inner surface. The slots used may be open, semi-closed or totally closed type as illustrated in Fig. 3.9.

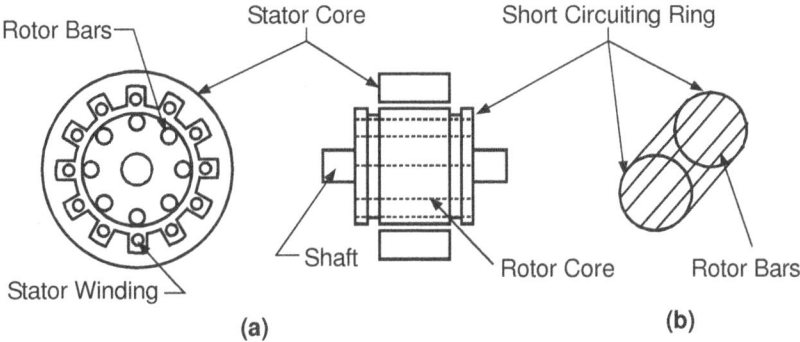

Fig. 3.8 : (a) Induction motor with a cage rotor, (b) The squirrel-cage winding

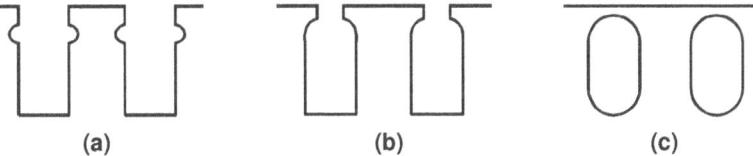

Fig. 3.9 : Various forms of stator and rotor slots

(a) Open, (b) Semi-closed, (c) Totally closed

A typical ring stamping (lamination) used for the stator core with open slots is also illustrated in Fig. 3.10 (a). These stampings are usually 0.4 to 0.5 mm thick and made from high grade silicon steel. They are insulated from each other by varnish or oxide coating. Such laminated construction for the core ensures low iron loss. The built-up core is fitted in either a cast or fabricated steel frame which provides the necessary mechanical protection and carries a terminal box and end covers housing the bearings.

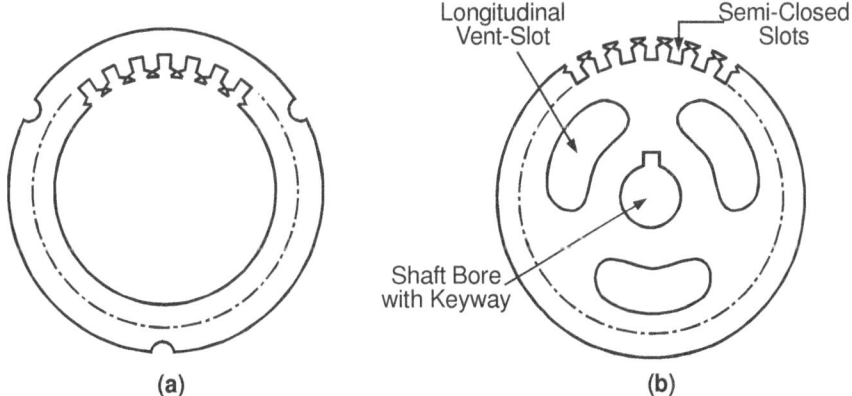

Fig. 3.10 : Typical core laminations for (a) Stator, (b) Rotor

The radial ventilating ducts are provided along the length of the core with the help of spacer plates. The slotted stator core carries a three-phase winding connected either in star or delta and wound for definite number of poles depending on the speed required.

The rotor core also has laminated construction. In small motors, each circular lamination is of one piece (Fig. 3.10 b). The punched laminations are stacked and directly keyed to the shaft.

On the other hand, in large motors, the laminations are segmented and dovetailed to a central spider. As in the stator core, ventilating ducts (both radial and axial) are also provided in the rotor core. The rotor winding of the motor consists of a series of uninsulated aluminium or copper bars, accommodated in the slots of the rotor core and permanently short-circuited at each end by a conducting ring called the *end-ring*. The bars are usually welded or brazed to the end rings. Thus, the rotor construction resembles a *squirrel-cage* (Fig. 3.8 b) and hence this type of rotor is called a *cage rotor* or *squirrel-cage rotor*. For the motors having ratings upto about 50 kW, the entire rotor winding is often of die-cast aluminium. The aluminium bars, the end rings and even the fan blades are cast in one operation. The remarkable feature of the cage winding is that it is adaptable to any number of stator poles. This feature is important in connection with speed control. Fan blades are generally provided at the ends of the rotor core for forcing circulating air through the machine. The air gap between the stator and the rotor is kept uniform and made as small as is mechanically possible. The rotor slots are sometimes skewed (i.e. made somewhat non-parallel to the shaft) to reduce the magnetic hum (noise) and prevent possible magnetic locking (called *cogging*) between the stator and rotor teeth at the time of starting. Fig. 3.11 shows the schematic representation of a three-phase, squirrel-cage induction motor.

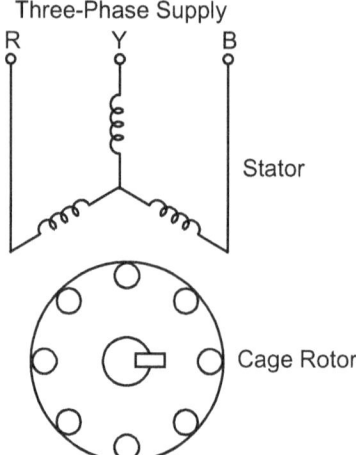

Fig. 3.11 : Schematic representation of a three-phase, squirrel-cage induction motor

3.6.2 Slip-Ring or Wound-Rotor Induction Motors

The stator and rotor of this type of motor (Fig. 3.12) also have laminated construction for their cores. The stator of this motor has three-phase star or delta connected winding similar to the stator of the squirrel-cage induction motor. The rotor also carries a similar three-phase, star-connected winding. Both stator and rotor are wound for the same number of poles. The open ends of the rotor windings are brought out to three insulated rings called *slip-rings*. These slip-rings are mounted on the motor shaft and bear the brushes. This arrangement allows the insertion of external resistance in series with each phase of the rotor for starting or speed control purposes. When running normally, the slip-rings are short circuited. Thus under running condition, even the wound rotor is short circuited on itself just like squirrel-cage rotor. Fig. 3.13 shows the schematic representation of a three-phase, slip-ring induction motor.

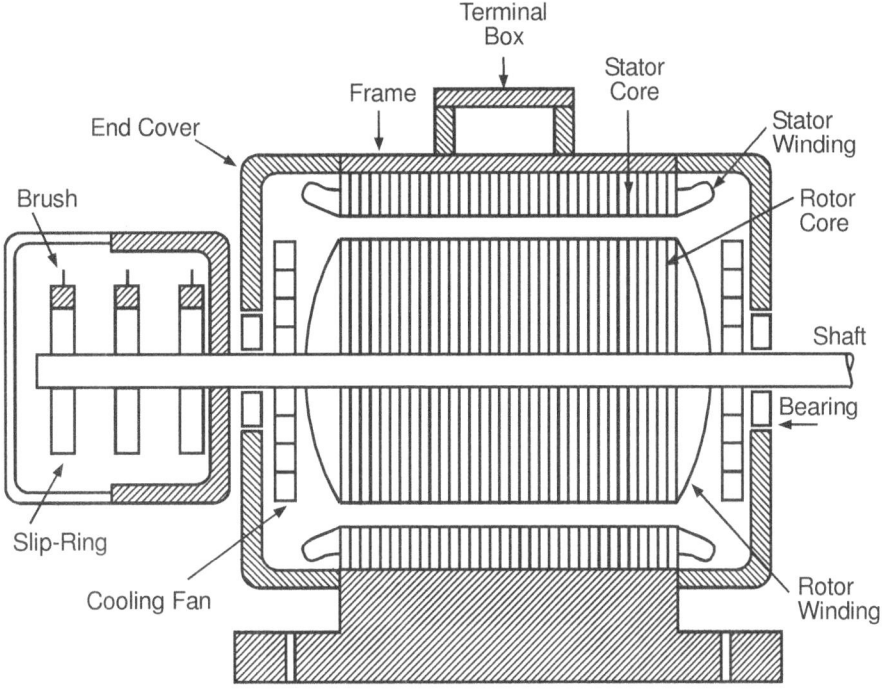

Fig. 3.12 : Induction motor with a wound rotor

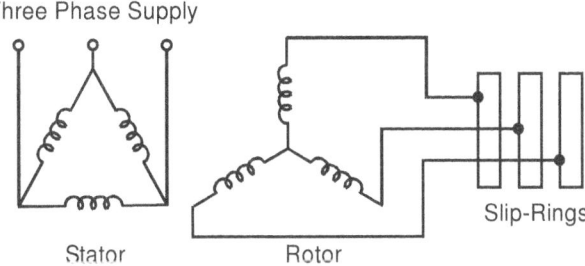

Fig. 3.13 : Schematic representation of a three-phase, slip-ring induction motor

3.7 ROTOR FREQUENCY, ROTOR E.M.F., ROTOR CURRENT AND ROTOR POWER FACTOR UNDER STANDSTILL CONDITION

Rotor Frequency : It is obvious that the e.m.f. induced in each rotor conductor will complete one cycle as one pair of stator poles (comprising one N-pole and one S-pole) sweeps past this rotor conductor. If

N = Speed of the rotor, in r.p.m. (the corresponding slip being S)

P = Total number of stator poles

Then, the speed (in r.p.m.) with which synchronously rotating stator field will sweep past the rotor conductors is

$$= N_S - N$$

Number of cycles of rotor e.m.f. per revolution of the rotating magnetic field with respect to rotor conductors is

$$= \frac{P}{2}$$

∴ Frequency of rotor e.m.f. (i.e. number of cycles per second) at a slip S,

$$f_{2S} = \begin{bmatrix} \text{Number of cycles per} \\ \text{revolution of the rotating} \\ \text{magnetic field with} \\ \text{respect to rotor conductors} \end{bmatrix} \times \begin{bmatrix} \text{Number of revolutions} \\ \text{per second of the} \\ \text{rotating magnetic field} \\ \text{with respect to rotor conductors} \end{bmatrix}$$

$$= \frac{P}{2} \times \frac{N_S - N}{60}$$

$$= \frac{P(N_S - N)}{120} \qquad \qquad \dots (3.10)$$

Thus *the frequency of the rotor e.m.f. is proportional to the relative speed $(N_S - N)$ of rotating stator field to rotor.* Now at standstill (i.e. when the rotor is stationary), $N = 0$.

∴ $$f_2 = \frac{PN_S}{120}$$

But we know that the stator supply frequency,

$$f = \frac{PN_S}{120}$$

∴ $$f_2 = f \qquad \qquad \dots (3.11)$$

Thus, it will be observed that under standstill condition, the induction motor acts as a simple polyphase static transformer, the stator being the primary and the short-circuited rotor being the secondary, the frequency on either side remaining the same.

Rotor E.M.F. : The rotating magnetic field produced by the stator induces e.m.f.s in both stator and the rotor windings. The magnitudes of these e.m.f.s obviously depend upon the magnitude of the rotating flux and the speed at which the flux cuts the stator and rotor conductors. Under standstill condition, these conductors are cut by the rotating flux at synchronous speed N_S. Let us therefore derive the expressions for the e.m.f.s induced in the stator and rotor windings under this condition. For that let

V_1 = Stator applied voltage per phase, in volts

T_1 = Number of stator winding turns in series per phase

T_2 = Number of rotor winding turns in series per phase

P = Number of poles

ϕ = Stator flux per pole, in webers

Magnetic flux cut by a conductor (either of stator or rotor) per revolution of rotating magnetic flux is

$$= \phi . P \text{ webers}$$

Time for one revolution of the rotating flux is

$$= \frac{60}{N_S} \text{ seconds}$$

Hence, according to Faraday's law of electromagnetic induction,

Average e.m.f. induced per conductor

$$= \frac{\text{Flux cut}}{\text{Time taken}} = \frac{\phi \cdot P}{60/N_S} = \frac{\phi PN_S}{60} \text{ volts}$$

But we know that, $N_S = \frac{120 f}{P}$

$\therefore$ Average e.m.f. induced per conductor

$$= 2 \phi \cdot f \text{ volts}$$

If the e.m.f. wave is assumed to be sinusoidal, then

R.M.S. value of the induced e.m.f. per conductor

$$= 1.11 \times 2 \phi \cdot f = 2.22 \phi \cdot f \text{ volts}$$

Hence, for a stator with T_1 turns (i.e. $2T_1$ conductors) in series per phase, if all the corresponding coils were full-pitch* and the winding is concentrated in 1 slot per pole per phase,

Stator induced e.m.f. per phase,

$$E_1 = 4.44 \phi f T_1 \text{ volts}$$

In general, if K_{d1} is the distribution factor ** of the stator winding and K_{p1} is its pitch factor, then

$$E_1 = 4.44 K_{p1} K_{d1} \phi f T_1 \text{ volts} \qquad \qquad \dots (3.12)$$

Since the stator induced e.m.f. is approximately equal to the applied voltage across the stator terminals,

$$V_1 \approx 4.44 K_{p1} K_{d1} \phi f T_1 \text{ volts} \qquad \qquad \dots (3.13)$$

Similarly, the induced e.m.f. per phase in the rotor at standstill,

$$E_2 = 4.44 K_{p2} K_{d2} \phi f T_2 \text{ volts} \qquad \qquad \dots (3.14)$$

where K_{p2} and K_{d2} are respectively the pitch factor and distribution factor of the rotor winding. If these factors are the same for the stator and rotor windings, then as in a transformer, from Equations (3.12) and (3.14), we have

$$E_2 = E_1 \times \frac{T_2}{T_1} \approx V_1 \times \frac{T_2}{T_1} \qquad \qquad \dots (3.15)$$

The ratio $\frac{T_2}{T_1}$ is called the *standstill voltage-transformation ratio* of the motor.

Rotor Current : If $R_2 =$ Rotor resistance per phase, in ohms

$L_2 =$ Leakage inductance of the rotor per phase, in henrys

---

*   *For definition, refer to Section 1.7.*

**   *Distribution factor and pitch factor are the factors which take into account the reduction in emf induced in each phase winding respectively due to its distribution in two or more slots per pole and using short-pitch coils.*

then, rotor leakage reactance per phase,

$$X_2 = 2\pi f\, L_2 \qquad (\because\ f_2 = f) \qquad\qquad \ldots (3.16)$$

Rotor impedance per phase,

$$Z_2 = \sqrt{R_2^2 + X_2^2} \qquad\qquad \ldots (3.17)$$

Therefore from Fig. 3.14, Rotor current per phase,

$$I_2 = \frac{E_2}{Z_2} = \frac{E_2}{\sqrt{R_2^2 + X_2^2}} \qquad\qquad \ldots (3.18)$$

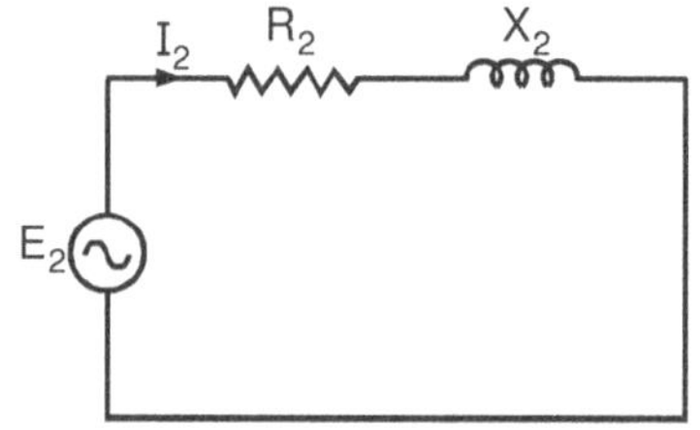

Fig. 3.14 : Rotor circuit, at standstill (i.e. when S = 1)

Rotor Power Factor : If the phase difference between the rotor induced e.m.f. E_2 and rotor current I_2 is ϕ_2, then obviously,

Rotor power factor,

$$\cos \phi_2 = \frac{R_2}{Z_2} = \frac{R_2}{\sqrt{R_2^2 + X_2^2}} \qquad\qquad \ldots (3.19)$$

3.8 ROTOR FREQUENCY, ROTOR E.M.F., ROTOR CURRENT AND ROTOR POWER FACTOR UNDER RUNNING CONDITION

Rotor Frequency : We have seen in the previous section that the frequency of the rotor e.m.f. is proportional to the relative speed of rotating stator field to rotor, and when the rotor is running at speed N, i.e. with slip S, it is given by

$$f_{2S} = \frac{P\,(N_S - N)}{120}$$

Now,
$$N_S - N = \frac{N_S - N}{N_S} \times N_S = S \cdot N_S \qquad\qquad \ldots (3.20)$$

Substituting this in the above equation, we have

$$f_{2S} = S \times \left(\frac{P \cdot N_S}{120}\right) = S.\,f \qquad \left(\because\ f = \frac{P \cdot N_S}{120}\right) \qquad \ldots (3.21)$$

Thus under running condition, *the rotor frequency is equal to the stator supply frequency multiplied by the slip* and therefore it is sometimes referred to as *slip frequency*.

Rotor E.M.F. : As already mentioned previously, the magnitude of the rotor e.m.f. depends upon the speed at which the rotating stator flux cuts the rotor conductors. The value of the rotor e.m.f. is maximum at start when the rotor is stationary because under this condition, the relative speed between the rotating stator flux and the rotor is maximum ($= N_S$). When the rotor starts rotating, the relative speed between the field and rotor is decreased. Hence, the rotor e.m.f. is also reduced proportionately. To derive the relationship between the e.m.f.s induced in the rotor under these two conditions, let E_2 be the induced e.m.f. per phase in the rotor under standstill condition. When the rotor starts rotating at a speed (in r.p.m.) say N, the relative speed between the field and rotor reduces to $(N_S - N)$ i.e. $S.N_S$. Hence, the rotor e.m.f. which is directly proportional to this relative speed will reduce to $S.E_2$. Thus,

Rotor e.m.f. per phase under running condition (at slip S),

$$E_{2S} = S \cdot E_2 \qquad \qquad \text{... (3.22)}$$

From Equation (3.14), since

$$E_2 = 4.44 \, K_{p2} \cdot K_{d2} \, \phi \, f \, T_2 \text{ volts}$$

Rotor e.m.f. per phase under running condition,

$$E_{2S} = S \, (4.44 \, K_{p2} \cdot K_{d2} \, \phi \, f \, T_2)$$

$$= 4.44 \, K_{p2} \cdot K_{d2} \, \phi \, f_{2S} \, T_2 \text{ volts} \quad (\because \ f_{2S} = S \cdot f) \qquad \text{... (3.23)}$$

Rotor Current :

Rotor reactance per phase under running condition (at slip S),

$$X_{2S} = 2\pi f_{2S} \, L_2 = 2\pi \, (S \cdot f) \, L_2 \qquad \qquad (\because \ f_{2S} = S \cdot f)$$

$$= S \, (2\pi f \, L_2) = S \, X_2 \qquad \qquad \text{... (3.24)}$$

where X_2 is the rotor reactance per phase under standstill condition.

Further, Rotor impedance per phase under running condition (at slip S),

$$Z_{2S} = \sqrt{R_2^2 + (S \cdot X_2)^2} \qquad \qquad \text{... (3.25)}$$

Then from Fig. 3.15, Rotor current per phase under running condition (at slip S),

$$I_{2S} = \frac{E_{2S}}{Z_{2S}} = \frac{S \cdot E_2}{\sqrt{R_2^2 + (S \cdot X_2)^2}} \qquad \qquad \text{... (3.26)}$$

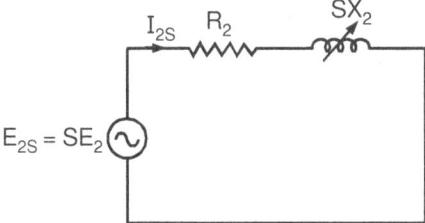

Fig. 3.15 : Rotor circuit, at slip S

Rotor Power Factor :

Rotor power factor under running condition (at slip S),

$$\cos \phi_{2S} = \frac{R_2}{Z_{2S}} = \frac{R_2}{\sqrt{R_2^2 + (S \cdot X_2)^2}} \qquad \qquad \text{... (3.27)}$$

where ϕ_{2S} is the phase difference between the rotor e.m.f. E_{2S} and rotor current I_{2S}.

Under standstill condition, rotor being stationary, S = 1. Therefore putting this value of S in the above equations for rotor frequency, rotor e.m.f., rotor reactance, rotor current and rotor power factor under running condition, we can easily obtain the expressions for these quantities under standstill condition derived earlier in Section 3.7.

Example 3.2 : *A 4-pole induction motor is connected to a 50 Hz supply. If the frequency of rotor e.m.f. at full load is 3 Hz, find (i) full-load slip, (ii) speed of the motor.*

Solution : Here, f = 50 Hz, f_{2S} = 3 Hz.

(i) Now, we have seen that under running condition (at slip S),

$$\text{Rotor frequency, } f_{2S} = S \cdot f$$

$\therefore$ $\qquad\qquad\qquad 3 = S \times 50$

$\therefore$ $\qquad\qquad\qquad S = \dfrac{3}{50} = \mathbf{0.06 \ or \ 6\%}$ $\qquad\qquad$ ... Ans.

(ii) $\qquad\qquad N_S = \dfrac{120\,f}{P} = \dfrac{120 \times 50}{4} = 1500 \text{ r.p.m.}$

$\therefore$ $\qquad\qquad N = N_S(1-S) = 1500(1-0.06) = \mathbf{1410 \ r.p.m.}$ $\qquad$ ... Ans.

Example 3.3 : *A star-connected rotor of a 3-phase, 4-pole, 50 Hz induction motor has a resistance and standstill reactance of 0.35 Ω and 2 Ω per phase respectively. With stator connected to normal supply voltage, the e.m.f induced between slip-rings at standstill is 160 V. Find :*

(a) *Rotor phase current and power factor at starting when the rings are*

    (i) *short-circuited,*

    (ii) *joined to a star-connected resistance of 3 Ω per phase.*

(b) *Rotor phase current and power factor at full load if the corresponding motor speed (with slip-rings shorted) is 1410 r.p.m.*

Solution : (a) Starting Condition (with rotor at standstill) :

Phase e.m.f. in rotor at standstill, $E_2 = \dfrac{160}{\sqrt{3}} = 92.38 \text{ V}$

(i) Slip-Rings Short-Circuited :

$$I_2 = \frac{E_2}{\sqrt{R_2^2 + X_2^2}} = \frac{92.38}{\sqrt{0.35^2 + 2^2}}$$

$$= \mathbf{45.5 \ A} \qquad\qquad\qquad \text{... Ans.}$$

$$\cos\phi_2 = \frac{R_2}{\sqrt{R_2^2 + X_2^2}} = \frac{0.35}{\sqrt{0.35^2 + 2^2}}$$

$$= \mathbf{0.17} \qquad\qquad\qquad \text{... Ans.}$$

(ii) Slip-Rings Joined to Star-Connected Resistance :

The total resistance in the rotor circuit per phase,

$$(R_2 + R) = 0.35 + 3 = 3.35 \ \Omega$$

$$I_2 = \frac{E_2}{\sqrt{(R_2 + R)^2 + X_2^2}} = \frac{92.38}{\sqrt{3.35^2 + 2^2}} = 23.68 \ A \qquad \text{... Ans.}$$

$$\cos \phi_2 = \frac{(R_2 + R)}{\sqrt{(R_2 + R)^2 + X_2^2}} = \frac{3.35}{\sqrt{3.35^2 + 2^2}} = 0.86 \qquad \text{... Ans.}$$

(b) Full-load Condition :

$$N_S = \frac{120 \ f}{P} = \frac{120 \times 50}{4} = 1500 \ \text{r.p.m.}$$

$$S = \frac{1500 - 1410}{1500} = 0.06$$

$$I_{2S} = \frac{S \cdot E_2}{\sqrt{R_2^2 + (S \cdot X_2)^2}} = \frac{0.06 \times 92.38}{\sqrt{0.35^2 + (0.06 \times 2)^2}}$$

$$= 14.98 \ A \qquad \text{... Ans.}$$

$$\cos \phi_{2S} = \frac{R_2}{\sqrt{R_2^2 + (S \cdot X_2)^2}}$$

$$= \frac{0.35}{\sqrt{0.35^2 + (0.06 \times 2)^2}}$$

$$= 0.95 \qquad \text{... Ans.}$$

3.9 FACTORS DETERMINING TORQUE

In the d.c. motor,[*] the torque is proportional to the product of the flux per pole and the armature current $(T \propto \phi \cdot I_a)$. Similarly in the induction motor also, the torque is proportional to the product of the flux per stator pole and the rotor current provided that the instantaneous values of flux and current are considered. The average torque produced by an induction motor, however, is dependent on one more factor i.e. the rotor power factor. Let us therefore study the relation between the torque and rotor power factor.

Torque and Rotor Power Factor : The space distribution of the flux set up in the air gap due to the rotating stator field may be represented approximately by a sine wave. This rotating flux induces in each rotor conductor an e.m.f. which is proportional to the flux density in which the conductor is lying ($\because$ e = Blv) at a particular instant. Hence, the space distribution of the induced e.m.f. in the rotor is also sinusoidal. Now, if the rotor is assumed to be non-inductive, the rotor current will be in time phase with the rotor e.m.f. The resulting current distribution curve will therefore be a sine wave in space phase with the e.m.f. wave as shown in Fig. 3.16 (a). The corresponding torque distribution curve (at any slip S) obtained by plotting the product of the instantaneous values of the flux (ϕ) and the rotor current (i_{2S}) for each conductor ($\because$ F = Bil)

---

[*] *Refer to the Section 2.7.*

is also shown in the figure. From this torque curve, it will be seen that the torque under this condition is always positive i.e. unidirectional.

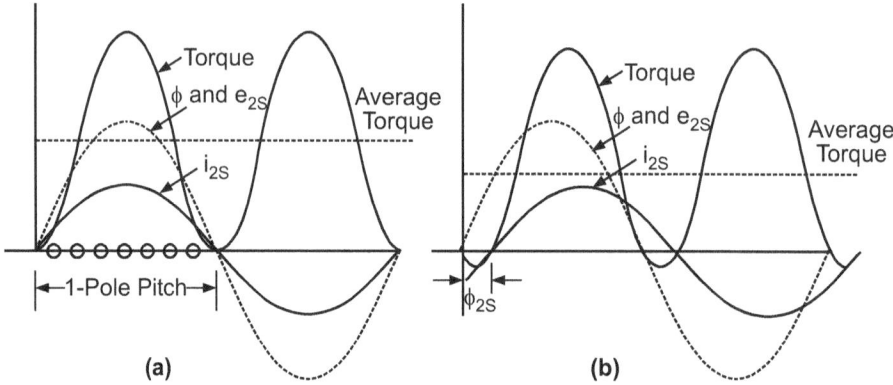

Fig. 3.16 : Torque and rotor power factor

Further, if the rotor circuit is assumed to be inductive (as is the usual case), the rotor current will lag behind the rotor e.m.f. by certain angle, say ϕ_{2S}. Fig. 3.16 (b) shows the e.m.f., current and torque distribution curves for this condition. From the torque distribution curve, it will be observed that for some part of the pole pitch, the torque is negative i.e. in the reverse direction, and hence the average torque taken over a period is considerably reduced. If the rotor current lags behind the rotor e.m.f. by 90°, the average torque would be zero. Thus, *the average torque depends not only on the flux per stator pole and the rotor current but also on the rotor power factor.*

3.10 TORQUE DEVELOPED BY AN INDUCTION MOTOR

From the above discussion, it can be concluded that the average torque developed by an induction motor at any slip S basically depends on three factors namely the flux per stator pole, the rotor current per phase and the rotor power factor i.e.

$$\text{The average torque, } T \propto \phi \, I_{2S} \cos \phi_{2S} \qquad \dots (3.28)$$

where,
$$\phi = \text{Flux per stator pole (r.m.s. value)}$$
$$I_{2S} = \text{Rotor current per phase (r.m.s. value) at slip S}$$
$$\cos \phi_{2S} = \text{Corresponding rotor power factor.}$$

But since the rotor e.m.f. per phase at standstill $E_2 \propto \phi$, the above expression for the torque can be written as

$$T \propto E_2 \cdot I_{2S} \cos \phi_{2S}$$

Or,
$$T = KE_2 \cdot I_{2S} \cos \phi_{2S}$$

where K is the constant of proportionality.

Further substituting the values of I_{2S} and $\cos \phi_{2S}$ in terms of the parameters of the rotor circuit from Equations (3.26) and (3.27) in the above expression, we have

$$T = KE_2 \cdot \frac{SE_2}{\sqrt{R_2^2 + (SX_2)^2}} \cdot \frac{R_2}{\sqrt{R_2^2 + (SX_2)^2}}$$

$$= \frac{KSE_2^2 \, R_2}{R_2^2 + (SX_2)^2} \qquad \dots (3.29)$$

The expression for the torque in the above generalized form is very useful in studying the relationship between the torque and slip of the induction motor.

3.11 CONDITION FOR MAXIMUM TORQUE

Usually the supply voltage is always constant. Under such conditions, the flux per stator pole (ϕ) and hence the e.m.f. induced by it in each phase of the rotor at standstill (E_2) are constant. Hence from the Expression (3.29) giving the torque developed by an induction motor at any slip S, we have

$$T \propto \frac{SR_2}{R_2^2 + (SX_2)^2} \qquad \qquad \ldots (3.30)$$

The condition for maximum torque can be obtained by differentiating the above expression with respect to S (assuming R_2 to remain constant) and then equating it to zero.

$$\therefore \qquad \frac{d}{dS}\left(\frac{SR_2}{R_2^2 + S^2 X_2^2}\right) = \frac{(R_2^2 + S^2 X_2^2)\, R_2 - SR_2 \times 2\, SX_2^2}{(R_2^2 + S^2 X_2^2)^2} = 0$$

i.e. $\qquad\qquad R_2^2 - S^2 X_2^2 = 0$

Or, $\qquad\qquad\qquad R_2 = SX_2$

Hence, *the torque is maximum when the reactance per phase of the rotor at any slip S (i.e. SX_2) is equal to the resistance per phase of the rotor (i.e. R_2).* If the slip corresponding to the maximum torque is denoted by S_m, then obviously,

$$S_m = \frac{R_2}{X_2} \qquad \qquad \ldots (3.31)$$

Substituting this value for the slip in Expression (3.29) for the torque, we have

$$\text{Maximum torque, } T_m = \frac{K\,(R_2/X_2)\,E_2^2\,R_2}{R_2^2 + (R_2/X_2)^2\,X_2^2} = \frac{K\,E_2^2}{2\,X_2} \qquad \qquad \ldots (3.32)$$

From the expressions (3.31) and (3.32), we can draw the following important conclusions :

(i)   Maximum torque is inversely proportional to the rotor reactance.

(ii) The value of the maximum torque is independent of the rotor resistance but the slip at which the maximum torque occurs is a function of the rotor resistance.

3.12 RELATION BETWEEN FULL-LOAD TORQUE AND MAXIMUM TORQUE

Let $\qquad\qquad\qquad S_f$ = Slip at full load.

$\qquad\qquad\qquad\qquad S_m$ = Slip corresponding to maximum torque

Then from Equation (3.29), we have

$$\text{Full-load torque, } T_f = \frac{KS_f\, E_2^2\, R_2}{R_2^2 + (S_f X_2)^2}$$

and from Equation (3.32),

$$\text{Maximum torque, } T_m = \frac{KE_2^2}{2X_2}$$

$$\therefore \qquad \frac{T_f}{T_m} = \frac{KS_f\, E_2^2\, R_2}{R_2^2 + (S_f X_2)^2} \times \frac{2X_2}{KE_2^2} = \frac{2S_f\, R_2 X_2}{R_2^2 + S_f^2\, X_2^2}$$

Dividing both the numerator and denominator by X_2^2, we get

$$\frac{T_f}{T_m} = \frac{2S_f \, (R_2/X_2)}{(R_2/X_2)^2 + S_f^2} = \frac{2S_m \, S_f}{S_m^2 + S_f^2} \left(\because S_m = \frac{R_2}{X_2} \right) \qquad \ldots (3.33)$$

3.13 EFFECT OF CHANGE IN SUPPLY VOLTAGE ON TORQUE AND SLIP

From Equation (3.29), at any slip S, the torque acting on the rotor of an induction motor is given by,

$$T = \frac{KSE_2^2 \, R_2}{R_2^2 + (SX_2)^2}$$

As $E_2 \propto \phi \propto V$, where V is the supply voltage,

$$T \propto \frac{SV^2 R_2}{R_2^2 + (SX_2)^2}$$

Now, since the slip at or near full load is very low, the term $S^2 X_2^2$ in the denominator of the above expression can be neglected in comparison with the term R_2^2.

$$\therefore \qquad\qquad T \propto \frac{SV^2}{R_2}$$

Or, $\qquad\qquad T \propto SV^2 \qquad\qquad (\because \; R_2 \text{ is constant}) \quad \ldots (3.34)$

Thus, if the supply voltage falls, the torque decreases. Hence in order to maintain the same torque, the slip increases i.e. the speed falls. Reverse is the effect if the supply voltage increases.

3.14 STARTING TORQUE

Since the slip at the instant of starting is equal to 1, from Expression (3.29), we have

$$\text{Starting torque, } T_{st} = \frac{KE_2^2 \, R_2}{R_2^2 + X_2^2} \qquad\qquad \ldots (3.35)$$

3.15 RELATION BETWEEN STARTING TORQUE AND MAXIMUM TORQUE

From Equation (3.35), we know that

$$T_{st} = \frac{KE_2^2 \, R_2}{R_2^2 + X_2^2}$$

Also, from Equation (3.32), we have

$$T_m = \frac{KE_2^2}{2X_2}$$

$$\therefore \qquad \frac{T_{st}}{T_m} = \frac{KE_2^2 \, R_2}{R_2^2 + X_2^2} \times \frac{2X_2}{KE_2^2} = \frac{2R_2X_2}{R_2^2 + X_2^2}$$

Dividing both the numerator and the denominator by X_2^2, we get

$$\frac{T_{st}}{T_m} = \frac{2(R_2/X_2)}{(R_2/X_2)^2 + 1} = \frac{2S_m}{S_m^2 + 1} \qquad \left(\because S_m = \frac{R_2}{X_2} \right) \quad \ldots (3.36)$$

3.16 EFFECT OF CHANGE IN SUPPLY VOLTAGE ON STARTING TORQUE

From Equation (3.35),

$$T_{st} = \frac{KE_2^2 R_2}{R_2^2 + X_2^2}$$

Since $E_2 \propto \phi \propto V$, where V is the supply voltage,

$$T_{st} \propto \frac{V^2 R_2}{R_2^2 + X_2^2} \propto V^2 \qquad (\because R_2 \text{ and } X_2 \text{ are constant}) \dots (3.37)$$

Thus, the starting torque of an induction motor is proportional to the square of the applied voltage. Hence, it is very sensitive to any changes in the supply voltage.

3.17 TORQUE-SLIP CHARACTERISTIC OF AN INDUCTION MOTOR

As the rotor of an induction motor speeds up from rest after starting, the slip and therefore rotor e.m.f., frequency and reactance gradually decrease. Consequently, the rotor current is decreased and the rotor power factor is improved. Initially, the increase in rotor power factor causes the torque to increase. But in the later stages, when the reactance becomes very small, the effect of the decrease in rotor current predominates. Hence, the torque decreases rapidly and finally becomes zero at synchronous speed. If the torque (T) is plotted against the slip (S) from $S = 1$ (standstill condition) to $S = 0$ (synchronous speed condition), we get the curve known as *torque-slip characteristic* of an induction motor. This curve is very important as it reveals lot of information with regard to the behaviour of the motor. Fig. 3.17 (a) shows one such typical curve. The nature of the curve can be very well explained from the torque equation as follows :

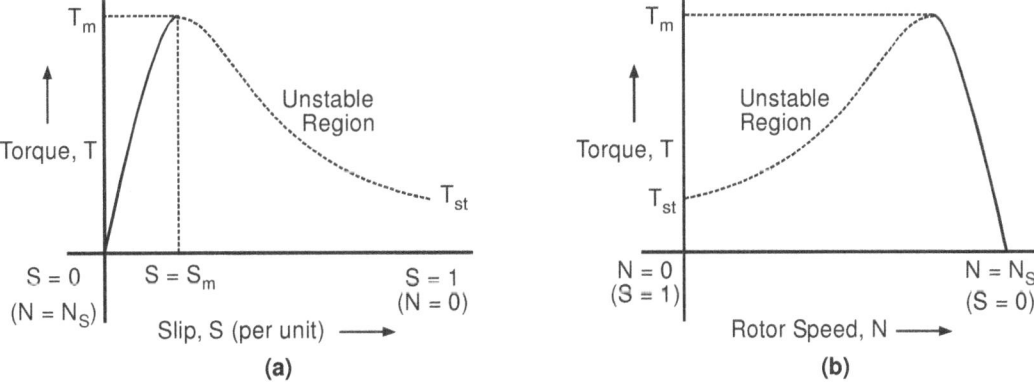

Fig. 3.17 : Torque-slip and torque-speed characteristics of an induction motor

We have seen that for a given supply voltage, flux per stator pole (ϕ) and hence the standstill rotor e.m.f. per phase (E_2) being constant,

$$T \propto \frac{SR_2}{R_2^2 + (SX_2)^2} \qquad \text{(Refer to Equation 3.30)}$$

From the above equation, it is evident that when $S = 0$ (at synchronous speed), $T = 0$. Hence the torque-slip curve starts from the origin (0, 0).

For small values of slip (at normal speeds close to synchronism), the term $(SX_2)^2$ in the denominator of the above expression is very small in comparison with the term R_2^2 and hence can be neglected. In such a case,

$$T \propto \frac{S}{R_2} \propto S \text{ if } R_2 \text{ is constant} \qquad \dots (3.38)$$

Thus, for small values of slip, the torque is directly proportional to the slip and hence the torque-slip curve is a straight line. As the slip increases with the increase in the load on the motor, the torque increases. It becomes maximum when $S = S_m = \dfrac{R_2}{X_2}$. This torque is known as *pullout* or *break down torque.*

For higher values of slip (resulting from further increase in the motor load), the term R_2^2 in the denominator of the torque expression becomes negligible in comparison with the term $(SX_2)^2$.

$$\therefore \qquad T \propto \frac{R_2}{SX_2^2} \propto \frac{1}{S}, \text{ if } R_2 \text{ and } X_2 \text{ are constant.} \qquad \dots (3.39)$$

So, for higher values of slip (beyond the value that corresponds to maximum torque), the torque is inversely proportional to the slip and the torque-slip curve is a *rectangular hyperbola* as shown in the figure.

Thus, it will be seen that when the load on the motor is increased, the slip increases and therefore the torque increases until it attains the maximum value. However, any further increase in the motor load results in decrease of torque developed by the motor. As a result, the motor slows down and eventually stops. Hence, the dotted portion of the curve represents unstable conditions.

It should be noted that the torque can also be plotted against the rotor speed as illustrated in Fig. 3.17 (b).

3.18 EFFECT OF ROTOR RESISTANCE ON TORQUE-SLIP CHARACTERISTIC

We have seen that the value of the maximum torque is independent of the rotor resistance (refer to Expression 3.32). Further, from Expression (3.39), it will be seen that with high values of slip i.e. when the rotor resistance R_2 is small compared with the rotor reactance SX_2, the torque of the motor for a given slip is directly proportional to the value of the rotor resistance. On the other hand, Expression (3.38) shows that with small values of slip i.e. when the rotor resistance R_2 is large compared with the rotor reactance SX_2, the torque of the motor for a given slip is inversely proportional to the value of the rotor resistance. Fig. 3.18 shows the torque-slip curves for different values of rotor resistance.

The effect of the rotor resistance on the shape of the torque-slip curve can be very well seen from these curves. If a large starting torque is required, the rotor must have a relatively high resistance. If it is made sufficiently large (with $R_2 = X_2$), maximum torque may be obtained at starting itself. However, with such a high rotor resistance, slip for full-load torque would be very large.

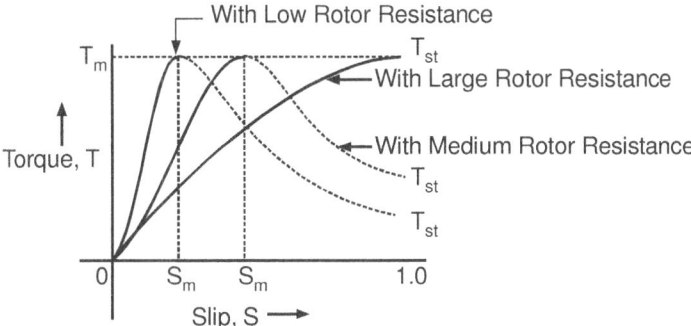

Fig. 3.18 : Effect of rotor resistance on torque-slip characteristic of an induction motor

The copper loss (i.e. I^2R loss) in the rotor winding would be high and therefore temperature rise would be excessive. Also the efficiency and speed regulations of the motor would be poor. In practice, when a motor is required to exert its maximum torque at starting, initially the extra resistance is inserted into the rotor circuit and subsequently this resistance is gradually cut out as the motor accelerates. Thus good performance under starting as well as running conditions becomes possible. Such an arrangement is possible only with wound rotors. The motors with low resistance cage type rotors, therefore, have inherently low starting torque.

3.19 OPERATION OF AN INDUCTION MOTOR ON LOAD

The behaviour of the motor under changing load can be very well studied from its speed-torque characteristic. The fall in speed from no-load to full-load condition being only about 4 to 5 % in small motors and 1.5 to 2 % in large motors, the induction motor is practically a *constant-speed motor*. Hence, over the normal operating range, the speed-torque characteristic of a three-phase induction motor (Fig 3.19) is similar to that of a d.c. shunt motor[*]. As said earlier, at no load, the torque required is only to overcome friction, windage and other no-load losses, and speed is very nearly synchronous. When the load on the motor is increased, the speed falls. This causes an increase in relative speed between the rotating magnetic field produced by the stator and the rotor conductors and hence increase in rotor e.m.f. and current. This results into increased motor torque. Correspondingly, the motor draws increased current from the supply. Thus, the motor meets the increased demand for the torque by the load. The load may be increased until the speed is such that maximum value for the torque is reached. As said earlier, this limiting torque is known as *breakdown torque or pullout torque*. If the load is increased beyond this limit, the motor is unable to supply the necessary torque and it stops. Hence, the dotted portion of the characteristic curve represents this unstable condition.

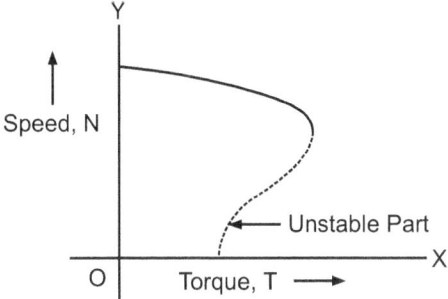

Fig. 3.19 : Speed-torque characteristic of a three-phase induction motor

---

[*]　*Refer to the Section 2.10.1.*

Example 3.4 : *A 24-pole, 50 Hz, star-connected induction motor has rotor resistance of 0.016 Ω per phase and rotor reactance of 0.256 Ω per phase at standstill. It is achieving its full-load torque at speed of 247 r.p.m. Calculate the ratios of,*

(i) T_{FL}/T_{max} and (ii) T_{st}/T_{max}.

Solution : (i)

$$S_m = \frac{R_2}{X_2} = \frac{0.016}{0.256} = 0.0625 \text{ or } 6.25\%$$

Synchronous speed, $N_S = \frac{120\,f}{P} = \frac{120 \times 50}{24} = 250 \text{ r.p.m.}$

∴

$$S_f = \frac{N_S - N}{N_S} = \frac{250 - 247}{250} = 0.012 \text{ or } 1.2\%$$

∴

$$\frac{T_{FL}}{T_{max}} = \frac{2S_m \cdot S_f}{S_m^2 + S_f^2} = \frac{2 \times 0.0625 \times 0.012}{(0.0625)^2 + (0.012)^2}$$

$$= \mathbf{0.37} \qquad \qquad \text{... Ans.}$$

(ii)

$$\frac{T_{st}}{T_{max}} = \frac{2\,S_m}{S_m^2 + 1} = \frac{2 \times 0.0625}{(0.0625)^2 + 1}$$

$$= \mathbf{0.125} \qquad \qquad \text{... Ans.}$$

Example 3.5 : *A 400 V, 4-pole, 50 Hz, 3-phase, star-connected induction motor has a wound rotor of resistance 0.02 Ω per phase and standstill reactance of 0.3 Ω per phase. Full-load torque is obtained at a speed of 1455 r.p.m. Calculate :*

(i)   *Ratio of full-load torque to maximum torque,*

(ii) *Speed at maximum torque, and*

(iii) *Ratio of starting torque to full-load torque.*

Solution : (i)

$$S_m = \frac{R_2}{X_2} = \frac{0.02}{0.3} = 0.067 \text{ or } 6.7\%$$

$$N_S = \frac{120\,f}{P} = \frac{120 \times 50}{4} = 1500 \text{ r.p.m.}$$

∴

$$S_f = \frac{N_S - N}{N_S} = \frac{1500 - 1455}{1500} = 0.03 \text{ or } 3\%$$

∴

$$\frac{T_f}{T_m} = \frac{2\,S_m \cdot S_f}{S_m^2 + S_f^2} = \frac{2 \times 0.067 \times 0.03}{(0.067)^2 + (0.03)^2} = \mathbf{0.746} \qquad \qquad \text{... Ans.}$$

(ii)

$$N = (1 - S_m)\,N_S = (1 - 0.067) \times 1500$$

$$= 1399.5 \approx \mathbf{1400 \text{ r.p.m.}} \qquad \qquad \text{... Ans.}$$

(iii)

$$\frac{T_{st}}{T_m} = \frac{2\,S_m}{S_m^2 + 1} = \frac{2 \times 0.067}{(0.067)^2 + 1} = 0.1334$$

∴

$$\frac{T_{st}}{T_f} = \frac{T_{st}}{T_m} \times \frac{T_m}{T_f} = 0.1334 \times \frac{1}{0.746} = \mathbf{0.1788} \qquad \qquad \text{... Ans.}$$

Example 3.6 : *A 3-phase, 440 V, 4-pole, 50 Hz induction motor has a rotor resistance of 0.025 Ω per phase and rotor reactance of 0.15 Ω per phase at standstill. The motor develops full-load torque of 150 Nm at 1440 r.p.m.*

Calculate :

(i) Maximum torque and speed at which it will occur,

(ii) Value of the resistance to be inserted in each phase winding of the rotor in order to obtain the maximum torque at starting.

Solution :

(i)   Synchronous speed, $N_S = \dfrac{120\,f}{P} = \dfrac{120 \times 50}{4} = 1500$ r.p.m.

Full-load speed $= 1440$ r.p.m.

$\therefore$ Full-load slip, $S_f = \dfrac{1500 - 1440}{1500} = 0.04$

Slip at maximum torque, $S_m = \dfrac{R_2}{X_2} = \dfrac{0.025}{0.15} = 0.1667$

Now, from Equation (3.33), we have

$$\frac{T_f}{T_m} = \frac{2 S_m \cdot S_f}{S_m^2 + S_f^2}$$

Substituting the values of S_m and S_f, we get

$$\frac{T_f}{T_m} = \frac{2 \times 0.1667 \times 0.04}{(0.1667)^2 + (0.04)^2} = 0.4538$$

As full-load torque, $T_f = 150$ Nm (given)

Maximum torque, $T_m = \dfrac{T_f}{0.4538} = \dfrac{150}{0.4538} = \mathbf{330.5\ Nm}$ **... Ans.**

Speed at maximum torque, $N = N_S (1 - S_m)$

$= 1500\,(1 - 0.1667)$

$= \mathbf{1250\ r.p.m.}$ **... Ans.**

(ii) To obtain maximum torque at starting (when $S = 1$), let the extra resistance to be inserted in each phase winding of the rotor be r ohms.

Then obviously under this condition,

$$R_2 + r = X_2 \qquad (\because\ S_m = 1)$$

$\therefore$ Extra resistance per phase, $\quad r = X_2 - R_2$

$= 0.15 - 0.025$

$= \mathbf{0.125\ \Omega}$ **... Ans.**

Example 3.7 : *A 3-phase induction motor has a slip-ring rotor with a resistance and standstill reactance of 0.04 Ω and 0.2 Ω per phase respectively. Find the amount of resistance to be inserted in each rotor phase to obtain a pullout torque at one-half of the full-load speed. What is then the rotor power factor ? The slip at full load is 3 per cent.*

Solution : Let N_S be the synchronous speed of the motor.

The full-load slip, $\; S_f = 0.03$ (given)

Full-load speed, $\; N_f = N_S (1 - S_f) = N_S (1 - 0.03)$

$$= 0.97 \, N_S$$

One-half of the full-load speed,

$$N = \frac{1}{2} N_f = \frac{0.97 \, N_S}{2} = 0.485 \, N_S$$

Slip at one half of the full-load speed,

$$S = \frac{N_S - 0.485 \, N_S}{N_S} = 0.515$$

Let r be the required resistance to be inserted in each rotor phase for torque to be maximum at $S = 0.515$ (slip corresponding to one half of full-load speed),

$$(R_2 + r) = SX_2$$

i.e. $\qquad\qquad 0.04 + r = 0.515 \times 0.2$

$$r = \mathbf{0.063 \; \Omega} \qquad\qquad\qquad\qquad \textbf{... Ans.}$$

The corresponding rotor power factor,

$$\cos \phi_{2S} = \frac{R_2 + r}{\sqrt{(R_2 + r)^2 + (SX_2)^2}}$$

$$= \frac{0.04 + 0.063}{\sqrt{(0.04 + 0.063)^2 + (0.515 \times 0.2)^2}}$$

$$= \mathbf{0.707 \; lagging} \qquad\qquad\qquad \textbf{... Ans.}$$

Alternatively, $\qquad\qquad \tan \phi_{2S} = \dfrac{R_2 + r}{SX_2} = \dfrac{0.04 + 0.063}{0.515 \times 0.2} = 1$

$\therefore \qquad\qquad\qquad\qquad \cos \phi_{2S} = \mathbf{0.707 \; lagging} \qquad\qquad\qquad \textbf{... Ans.}$

Example 3.8 : *A 3-phase, 4-pole, 50 Hz, slip-ring induction motor develops a maximum torque of 125 Nm at 1350 r.p.m. The resistance of the star-connected rotor is 0.2 Ω per phase.*
Calculate :
(i) Torque exerted by the motor at 5 % slip.
(ii) Value of the additional resistance that must be inserted in series with each rotor phase to produce a starting torque equal to half the maximum torque.

Solution :

(i)   Synchronous speed, $\; N_S = \dfrac{120 \, f}{P} = \dfrac{120 \times 50}{4} = 1500$ r.p.m.

Slip at maximum torque, $\; S_m = \dfrac{1500 - 1350}{1500} = 0.1$

Also, $\qquad\qquad\qquad\qquad S_m = \dfrac{R_2}{X_2}$

$\therefore \qquad\qquad\qquad\qquad X_2 = \dfrac{R_2}{S_m} = \dfrac{0.2}{0.1} = 2 \, \Omega$

Now, from Equation (3.32), we have

$$\text{Maximum torque,} \quad T_m = \frac{KE_2^2}{2X_2} = \frac{KE_2^2}{2 \times 2} = \frac{KE_2^2}{4} \qquad \ldots \text{(I)}$$

Let T be the torque at S = 0.05. Then from Equation (3.29), we have

$$T = \frac{KSE_2^2 R_2}{R_2^2 + (SX_2)^2} = \frac{K \times 0.05 \times E_2^2 \times 0.2}{0.2^2 + (0.05 \times 2)^2}$$

$$= 0.2 \, KE_2^2 \qquad \ldots \text{(II)}$$

Dividing Equation (II) by Equation (I), we get

$$\frac{T}{T_m} = \frac{0.2 \, KE_2^2 \times 4}{KE_2^2} = 0.8$$

As $T_m = 125$ Nm (given),

$$T = 125 \times 0.8 = \textbf{100 Nm} \qquad \textbf{... Ans.}$$

Alternative Method : If T is the torque exerted by the motor at S = 0.05, then from Equation (3.33), we have

$$\frac{T}{T_m} = \frac{2 \, S_m \cdot S}{S_m^2 + S^2} = \frac{2 \times 0.1 \times 0.05}{0.1^2 + 0.05^2} = 0.8$$

Therefore, as seen above, $T = 125 \times 0.8 = \textbf{100 Nm}$ **... Ans.**

(ii) If r is the additional resistance to be inserted in series with each rotor phase, then from Equation (3.35),

$$\text{Starting torque,} \quad T_{st} = \frac{KE_2^2 (R_2 + r)}{(R_2 + r)^2 + X_2^2}$$

Substituting the values of R_2 and X_2, we have

$$T_{st} = \frac{KE_2^2 (0.2 + r)}{(0.2 + r)^2 + 2^2}$$

Now, since $T_{st} = \frac{1}{2} T_m$ (given),

$$\frac{KE_2^2 (0.2 + r)}{(0.2 + r)^2 + 4} = \frac{1}{2} \times \frac{KE_2^2}{4} \qquad \text{(Refer to Equation I)}$$

Or, $\qquad\qquad r^2 - 7.6 \, r + 2.44 = 0$

$$\therefore \qquad\qquad r = \frac{7.6 \pm \sqrt{57.76 - 4 \times 2.44}}{2} = 7.2641, \ 0.3359$$

The first value being too high, it should be rejected. Hence,

Additional resistance per rotor phase,

$$r = \textbf{0.3359} \, \boldsymbol{\Omega} \qquad\qquad \textbf{... Ans.}$$

Alternative Method : Let S_m' be the new slip at maximum torque corresponding to rotor circuit resistance $(R_2 + r)$. Then from Equation (3.36), we have

$$\frac{T_{st}}{T_m} = \frac{2S_m'}{(S_m')^2 + 1}$$

But since

$$\frac{T_{st}}{T_m} = \frac{1}{2} \text{ (given)}$$

$$\frac{1}{2} = \frac{2S_m'}{(S_m')^2 + 1}$$

Or,

$$(S_m')^2 - 4S_m' + 1 = 0$$

$\therefore$

$$S_m' = \frac{4 \pm \sqrt{16 - 4}}{2} = 0.268, 3.7321$$

Rejecting the larger value, we have

$$S_m' = \frac{R_2 + r}{X_2} = 0.268$$

$\therefore$

$$\frac{0.2 + r}{2} = 0.268$$

$\therefore$ $r = \mathbf{0.3359\ \Omega}$ ... Ans.

Example 3.9 : *A 6-pole, 50 Hz, 3-phase induction motor runs at 4 percent slip while delivering full-load torque. It has standstill rotor resistance of 0.2 Ω and reactance of 0.6 Ω per phase. Calculate the speed of the motor if an additional resistance of 0.25 Ω is inserted in each phase of the rotor circuit, the full-load torque remaining constant.*

Solution : Let S_{f1} and S_{f2} be the full-load slips with rotor circuit resistances of R_2 and $(R_2 + r)$ respectively (Fig. 3.20). Then from Equation (3.29), the torque developed by the motor under these two conditions can be expressed as

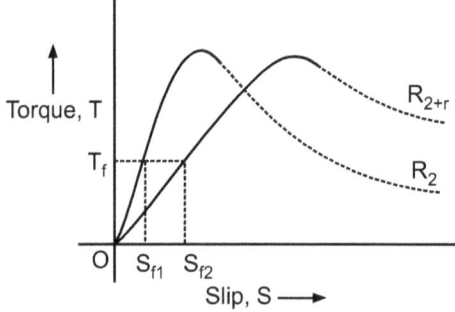

Fig. 3.20 : Torque-slip characteristics for different values of rotor resistance, Example 3.9

$$T_1 = \frac{KS_{f1}\ E_2^2\ R_2}{R_2^2 + (S_{f1} \cdot X_2)^2}$$

$$T_2 = \frac{KS_{f2}\ E_2^2\ (R_2 + r)}{(R_2 + r)^2 + (S_{f2} \cdot X_2)^2}$$

Since the motor is on full load in both the conditions,

$$T_1 = T_2 = T_f$$

$$\therefore \quad \frac{S_{f1} R_2}{R_2^2 + (S_{f1} \cdot X_2)^2} = \frac{S_{f2} (R_2 + r)}{(R_2 + r)^2 + (S_{f2} \cdot X_2)^2}$$

Now, $S_{f1} = 0.04$, $R_2 = 0.2\ \Omega$, $X_2 = 0.6\ \Omega$, $r = 0.25\ \Omega$

Substituting the above values, we have

$$\frac{0.04 \times 0.2}{(0.2)^2 + (0.04 \times 0.6)^2} = \frac{S_{f2} (0.2 + 0.25)}{(0.2 + 0.25)^2 + (S_{f2} \times 0.6)^2}$$

$$\therefore \quad 2.88\ S_{f2}^2 - 18.26\ S_{f2} + 1.62 = 0$$

Solution of the above quadratic equation gives,

$$S_{f2} = \frac{18.26 \pm \sqrt{(18.26)^2 - 4 \times 2.88 \times 1.62}}{2 \times 2.88}$$

$$= 6.25,\ 0.09$$

Neglecting the higher value, being impractical, we have

$$S_{f2} = 0.09$$

Alternatively, using Equation 3.38, we have

$$\frac{S_{f1}}{S_{f2}} = \frac{R_2}{R_2 + r}$$

$$\therefore \quad \frac{0.04}{S_{f2}} = \frac{0.2}{0.2 + 0.25}$$

$$\therefore \quad S_{f2} = 0.09$$

$$\text{Synchronous speed,}\ N_S = \frac{120\ f}{P} = \frac{120 \times 50}{6} = 1000\ \text{r.p.m.}$$

$$\therefore \quad \text{New speed of the motor,}\ N_2 = N_S (1 - S_{f2}) = 1000 (1 - 0.09)$$

$$= \mathbf{910\ r.p.m.} \qquad \qquad \text{... Ans.}$$

Example 3.10 : *A 10 kW, 400 V, 4-pole, 3-phase, 50 Hz slip-ring induction motor has the full-load slip of 5 % and its starting torque is equal to full-load torque. Calculate : (i) its starting torque if the supply voltage falls to 375 V, (ii) the slip when developing full-load torque at this voltage.*

Solution :

$$\text{Synchronous speed,}\ N_S = \frac{120\ f}{P} = \frac{120 \times 50}{4} = 1500\ \text{r.p.m.}$$

$$\text{Full-load speed,}\ N = N_S (1 - S) = 1500 (1 - 0.05) = 1425\ \text{r.p.m.}$$

If T_f is the full-load torque at 400 V, then

$$\frac{T_f \times 2\pi N}{60} = 10 \times 10^3$$

$$\therefore \quad T_f = \frac{10 \times 10^3 \times 60}{2\pi \times 1425} = 67.01\ \text{Nm}$$

$$\therefore \quad \text{Starting torque at 400 V} = T_f = 67.01\ \text{Nm}$$

(i) Now from Equation (3.37), we know that

$$\text{Starting torque,}\ T_{st} \propto V^2$$

$$\therefore \quad \text{Starting torque at 375 V} = 67.01 \times \left(\frac{375}{400}\right)^2$$

$$= \mathbf{58.9\ Nm} \qquad \qquad \text{... Ans.}$$

(ii) For small slips, $T \propto SV^2$ (Refer to Equation 3.34)

Since the motor develops full-load torque in both the cases,

$$S_{fl} \cdot V_1^2 = S_{f2} \cdot V_2^2$$

$\therefore$ Full-load slip at 375 V, $S_{f2} = S_{fl} \times \left(\dfrac{V_1}{V_2}\right)^2 = 0.05 \times \left(\dfrac{400}{375}\right)^2$

$$= \mathbf{0.0569 \ or \ 5.69 \ \%} \qquad \textbf{... Ans.}$$

Example 3.11 : *A 6-pole, 50 Hz, 3-phase, slip-ring induction motor has rotor resistance of 0.08 Ω per phase. If the stalling speed is 500 r.p.m., calculate the additional resistance to be added in the rotor circuit so as to obtain maximum starting torque.*

Solution : Motor stalling speed, $N = 500$ r.p.m.

$$\text{Synchronous speed, } N_S = \frac{120 \ f}{P} = \frac{120 \times 50}{6} = 1000 \ \text{r.p.m.}$$

$\therefore$ $S_m = \dfrac{N_S - N}{N_S} = \dfrac{1000 - 500}{1000} = 0.5$

But $S_m = \dfrac{R_2}{X_2}$

$\therefore$ $X_2 = \dfrac{R_2}{S_m} = \dfrac{0.08}{0.5} = 0.16 \ \Omega$

To get maximum torque at starting,

$$R_2 + R = X_2 = 0.16 \ \Omega$$

$\therefore$ Additional resistance required,

$$R = 0.16 - 0.08 = \mathbf{0.08 \ \Omega} \qquad \textbf{... Ans.}$$

Example 3.12 : *A 4-pole, 50 Hz, 7.46 kW, three-phase induction motor has at rated voltage of 415 V, starting torque of 160 % and maximum torque of 200 % of full-load torque. Determine :*

(i)   Full-load speed.

(ii) Speed at maximum torque.

Solution : (i) $\dfrac{T_{st}}{T_f} = 1.6 \ $ and $\ \dfrac{T_m}{T_f} = 2$

$\therefore$ $\dfrac{T_{st}}{T_f} \times \dfrac{T_f}{T_m} = 1.6 \times \dfrac{1}{2} = 0.8$

$\therefore$ $\dfrac{T_{st}}{T_m} = 0.8$

Now, $\dfrac{T_{st}}{T_m} = \dfrac{2 \ S_m}{S_m^2 + 1}$

$\therefore$ $0.8 = \dfrac{2 \ S_m}{S_m^2 + 1}$

$\therefore$ $0.8 \ S_m^2 - 2 \ S_m + 0.8 = 0$

Solving the above quadratic equation, we get

$$S_m = 2 \text{ or } 0.5$$

Rejecting the first value being impractical, we have

$$S_m = 0.5$$

Further,

$$\frac{T_f}{T_m} = \frac{2\,S_m\,S_f}{S_m^2 + S_f^2}$$

$\therefore$

$$\frac{1}{2} = \frac{2 \times 0.5 \times S_f}{(0.5)^2 + S_f^2}$$

$\therefore$

$$0.5\,S_f^2 - S_f + 0.125 = 0$$

Solving the above quadratic equation, we get

$$S_f = 1.866 \text{ or } 0.134$$

Rejecting the first value being impractical, we have

$$S_f = 0.134$$

$$\text{Synchronous speed, } N_S = \frac{120\,f}{P} = \frac{120 \times 50}{4} = 1500 \text{ r.p.m.}$$

$\therefore$

$$\text{Full-load speed, } N = (1 - S_f)\,N_S = (1 - 0.134) \times 1500$$

$$= \textbf{1299 r.p.m.} \qquad \textbf{... Ans.}$$

(ii)

$$S_m = 0.5$$

$\therefore$ Speed at maximum torque $= (1 - S_m)\,N_S = (1 - 0.5) \times 1500 = \textbf{750 r.p.m.} \textbf{ ... Ans.}$

Example 3.13 : *Rotor resistance and reactance of a 3-phase, 4-pole, 415 V, 50 Hz, star-connected induction motor, are 0.024 Ω and 0.12 Ω respectively, on per phase basis. Calculate :*

(i) Speed at which the maximum torque occurs.

(ii) External resistance required to be added in the rotor circuit to get 75 % of the maximum torque at start.

Solution :

(i)   Slip at maximum torque, $S_m = \dfrac{R_2}{X_2} = \dfrac{0.024}{0.12} = 0.2$

$$\text{Synchronous speed, } N_S = \frac{120\,f}{P} = \frac{120 \times 50}{4} = 1500 \text{ r.p.m.}$$

$\therefore$ Speed at maximum torque, $N = (1 - S_m)\,N_S = (1 - 0.2) \times 1500$

$$= \textbf{1200 r.p.m.} \qquad \textbf{... Ans.}$$

(ii)

$$\frac{T_{st}}{T_m} = 0.75 = \frac{2\,S_m}{S_m^2 + 1}$$

$\therefore$

$$0.75\,S_m^2 - 2\,S_m + 0.75 = 0$$

Solving the above quadratic equation, we get

$$S_m = 2.21 \text{ or } 0.45$$

Rejecting the first value being impractical, we have

$$S_m = 0.45$$

Let r be the external resistance required to be added in the rotor circuit to achieve the above condition. Then, obviously under this condition,

$$\frac{R_2 + r}{X_2} = 0.45$$

∴
$$\frac{0.024 + r}{0.12} = 0.45$$

∴
$$r = \mathbf{0.03 \ \Omega} \qquad\qquad \textbf{... Ans.}$$

Example 3.14 : *A 4-pole, 50 Hz, slip-ring induction motor has rotor resistance of 0.24 Ω/phase and runs at 1445 r.p.m. Calculate external resistance per phase that must be added to lower the speed to 1200 r.p.m., torque being constant.*

Solution : For an induction motor working at or near full-load slip, the torque and the slip are related approximately as,

$$T \propto \frac{S}{R_2} \qquad\qquad \text{(Refer to Equation 3.38)}$$

∴
$$T_1 \propto \frac{S_1}{R_2} \quad \text{and} \quad T_2 \propto \frac{S_2}{R_2 + r}$$

Or,
$$\frac{T_1}{T_2} = \frac{S_1}{S_2} \times \frac{R_2 + r}{R_2}$$

where suffixes represent the two sets of conditions, one with normal resistance R_2 and the other with external resistance r added in the rotor circuit. Under the given condition, since $T_1 = T_2$,

$$\frac{S_1}{S_2} = \frac{R_2}{R_2 + r}$$

Now,   Synchronous speed, $N_S = \dfrac{120 \, f}{P} = \dfrac{120 \times 50}{4} = 1500 \text{ r.p.m.}$

∴
$$S_1 = \frac{1500 - 1445}{1500} = 0.0367$$

$$N_2 = 1200 \text{ r.p.m.}$$

∴
$$S_2 = \frac{1500 - 1200}{1500} = 0.2$$

Also,
$$R_2 = 0.24 \ \Omega$$

Substituting all these values in the above referred equation, we have

$$\frac{0.0367}{0.2} = \frac{0.24}{0.24 + r}$$

∴ External resistance per phase needed, $r = \mathbf{1.068 \ \Omega}$ **... Ans.**

Example 3.15 : *A 4-pole, 3-phase, 50 Hz induction motor has rotor resistance and reactance per phase of 0.01 Ω and 0.1 Ω respectively. Rotor induced e.m.f. at standstill per phase is 57.75 V. If maximum torque is twice that of the full-load torque, then find full-load speed of the motor.*

Solution : Slip corresponding to maximum torque,

$$S_m = \frac{R_2}{X_2} = \frac{0.01}{0.1} = 0.1$$

Now,

$$\frac{T_f}{T_m} = \frac{2 S_m \cdot S_f}{S_m^2 + S_f^2}$$

$\therefore$

$$\frac{1}{2} = \frac{2 \times 0.1 \times S_f}{(0.1)^2 + S_f^2} \qquad (\because T_m = 2 T_f)$$

$\therefore$

$$S_f^2 - 0.4\, S_f + 0.01 = 0$$

Solving the above quadratic equation, we have

$$S_f = 0.373, \ 0.027$$

Rejecting the larger value, we have

$$S_f = 0.027$$

Synchronous speed of the motor,

$$N_S = \frac{120\, f}{P} = \frac{120 \times 50}{4} = 1500 \text{ rpm}$$

$\therefore$ Full-load speed, $N = N_S (1 - S_f) = 1500\,(1 - 0.027) = \mathbf{1460 \ r.p.m.}$ ... **Ans.**

3.20 LOSSES IN AN INDUCTION MOTOR

Different types of losses which occur in an induction motor are as follows :

- Copper losses

- Iron losses or Core losses

- Mechanical losses

Copper Losses : These are the I^2R losses which occur due to current flow through the resistance of the stator and rotor windings of the motor. These losses depend on the load on the motor. Use of the material with good conductivity, like copper, for the windings of the motor helps in reducing these losses.

Iron Losses or Core Losses : These losses (consisting of hysteresis and eddy current losses) occur in the stator and rotor cores. The stator core loss depends on supply frequency and flux density in the stator core. Since the rotor frequency under normal operating condition is very small, the rotor core loss is negligibly small. As already mentioned previously, in view to reduce the core losses, both stator and rotor cores are built up using high grade silicon steel laminations. Under constant voltage conditions, core losses together are always assumed to be constant at all loads and speeds.

Mechanical Losses : These losses include friction and windage losses. Since the speed of the induction motor varies slightly over the working range, these losses are assumed to be constant regardless of the load.

It should be noted that the core and mechanical losses together are sometimes referred to as *constant losses* or *rotational losses*.

3.21 POWER FLOW DIAGRAM FOR AN INDUCTION MOTOR

As any other electrical motor, the induction motor also converts the electrical power supplied to it into mechanical power. Various stages of this power conversion and the accompanying losses are diagrammatically represented in Fig. 3.21. From this figure, it will be clear that a small part of the electrical power supplied to the motor (i.e. its stator) is utilized to supply the stator losses consisting of stator core and copper losses. The remaining power is transferred magnetically to the rotor through the air gap. From this rotor input power (P_2), different rotor losses (rotor core and copper losses) are provided and the remaining power is converted into mechanical power (P_m). All the mechanical power developed by the rotor is not available at the shaft because part of it is always lost in supplying friction and windage losses.

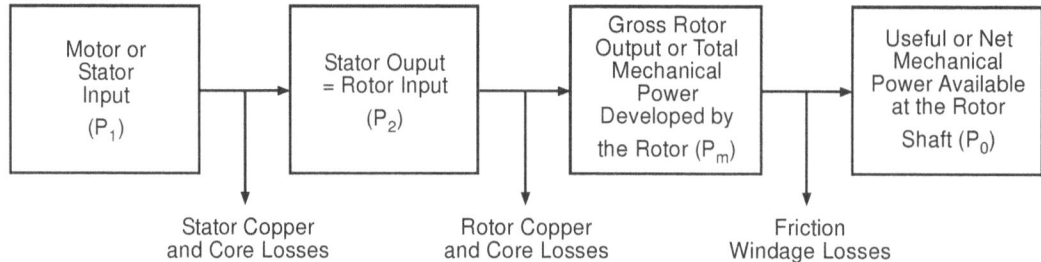

Fig. 3.21 : Power flow diagram for an induction motor

3.22 RELATIONSHIP BETWEEN ROTOR INPUT, ROTOR COPPER LOSS, TOTAL MECHANICAL POWER DEVELOPED BY THE ROTOR AND SLIP

To derive the relationship between the rotor input, rotor copper loss, total mechanical power developed by the rotor and slip, let

T = Total torque developed by the motor, in newton-metres.

This means that the torque exerted by the synchronously rotating stator field on the rotor is T. Hence,

Stator output (i.e. power transferred from stator to rotor)

$$= \text{Rotor input, } P_2$$

$$= T \times \frac{2\pi N_S}{60} \text{ watts} \qquad \ldots (3.40)$$

If the rotor speed (in r.p.m.) is N, then

Gross rotor output or total mechanical power developed by the rotor,

$$P_m = T \times \frac{2\pi N}{60} \text{ watts} \qquad \ldots (3.41)$$

Now, from the power flow diagram shown in Fig. 3.21, it will be observed that the difference between the input and gross output of the rotor represents practically the rotor copper loss (rotor core loss being negligibly small). Hence,

Rotor copper loss = Rotor input – Gross rotor output

$$= T \times \frac{2\pi N_S}{60} - T \times \frac{2\pi N}{60}$$

$$= T \times \frac{2\pi (N_S - N)}{60}$$

$$= S \left[T \times \frac{2\pi N_S}{60} \right] \qquad (\because N_S - N = SN_S)$$

$$= S \times \text{Rotor input} \qquad \qquad \dots (3.42)$$

The above equation for rotor copper loss may be written as

$$\frac{\text{Rotor copper loss}}{\text{Rotor input}} = S$$

Or, $$\frac{\text{Rotor copper loss}}{\text{Rotor input} - \text{Rotor copper loss}} = \frac{S}{1-S}$$

$$\therefore \quad \frac{\text{Rotor copper loss}}{\left[\begin{array}{l} \text{Gross rotor output or total} \\ \text{mechanical power developed} \\ \text{by the rotor, } P_m \end{array} \right]} = \frac{S}{1-S} \qquad \dots (3.43)$$

Thus combining Equations (3.42) and (3.43), we have

$$P_2 : (\text{Rotor copper loss}) : P_m = 1 : S : (1-S) . \qquad \dots (3.44)$$

The above expression concisely gives the relationship between rotor input (P_2), rotor copper loss, total mechanical power developed by the rotor (P_m) and slip. From this expression, it will be observed that lesser the slip for the given rotor input, lesser is the rotor copper loss. Consequently, more is the mechanical power developed and efficiency of the motor. Thus, it is always advantageous to run the motor at small slips.

It is important to note here that torque (T) in the above discussion is the total torque developed by the motor. The *useful* or *shaft torque* (T_{sh}) is always less than the total torque. This is because some part (even though small) of the total torque developed by the motor is always lost in overcoming the friction and windage.

3.23 TORQUE EQUATION OF AN INDUCTION MOTOR

The exact mathematical expression for the torque developed by an induction motor can be derived from the relationship between the rotor input, rotor copper loss, total mechanical power developed by the rotor and slip seen in the previous section. Let T be the total torque (in newton-metres) developed by an induction motor while operating at a speed of N r.p.m. and let S be the corresponding slip. Then

$$\text{Rotor input, } P_2 = \frac{\text{Rotor copper loss}}{S} = \frac{3I_{2S}^2 R_2}{S}$$

$$= \frac{3}{S} \left[\frac{SE_2}{\sqrt{R_2^2 + (SX_2)^2}} \right]^2 \times R_2$$

$$= \frac{3SE_2^2 R_2}{R_2^2 + (SX_2)^2} \text{ watts}$$

$\therefore$ Total mechanical power developed by the motor,

$$P_m = (1 - S)(\text{Rotor input}) = (1 - S) \times \frac{3SE_2^2 R_2}{R_2^2 + (SX_2)^2} \text{ watts}$$

But total mechanical power developed by the motor is also given by,

$$P_m = T \times \frac{2\pi N}{60} \text{ watts}$$

$\therefore$

$$T \times \frac{2\pi N}{60} = (1 - S) \times \frac{3SE_2^2 R_2}{R_2^2 + (SX_2)^2}$$

Or,

$$T = \frac{60(1 - S)}{2\pi N} \times \frac{3SE_2^2 R_2}{R_2^2 + (SX_2)^2}$$

However, we know that

$$N = N_s (1 - S)$$

Substituting this in the above equation, we have

$$T = \frac{60}{2\pi N_s} \times \frac{3SE_2^2 R_2}{R_2^2 + (SX_2)^2}$$

Or,

$$T = \frac{3}{2\pi n_s} \times \frac{SE_2^2 R_2}{R_2^2 + (SX_2)^2} \text{ newton-metres} \qquad \dots (3.45)$$

where n_s = Synchronous speed of the motor in r.p.s.

The above expression is known as torque equation of an induction motor. Comparing this equation with the Expression (3.29) for the torque derived earlier in Section (3.10), it is obvious that

$$K = \frac{3}{2\pi n_s}$$

It should also be noted that from Expression (3.32),

$$\text{Maximum torque, } \quad T_m = \frac{KE_2^2}{2X_2}$$

$$= \frac{3}{2\pi n_s} \cdot \frac{E_2^2}{2X_2} \text{ newton-metres} \qquad \dots (3.46)$$

3.24 TORQUE IN SYNCHRONOUS WATTS

From Equation (3.40), it is evident that the total torque developed by the induction motor is directly proportional to the rotor power input, regardless of actual speed of the motor. For this reason, it is common practice to express the torque in terms of *synchronous watts*. The synchronous watt is defined *as that torque which, at the synchronous speed of the motor, would develop a power of 1 W*. Hence,

$$\text{Total torque,} \quad T = \frac{P_m}{2\pi N/60} = \frac{60\,(1-S)\,P_2}{2\pi N_S\,(1-S)}$$

$$= \frac{60\,P_2}{2\pi N_S} \text{ newton-metres}$$

$$= P_2 \text{ synchronous watts} \qquad\qquad \dots (3.47)$$

Thus the torque in synchronous watts equals the rotor input in watts. It is important to note here that the two motors having different synchronous speeds, may have identical values for the total torque developed when it is expressed in synchronous watts but will have different values when the same torque is expressed in newton-metres.

3.25 EFFICIENCY OF AN INDUCTION MOTOR

The ratio of net power output at shaft to the power input to motor is known as efficiency of an induction motor. Thus,

$$\text{Efficiency,} \quad \eta = \frac{\text{Net power output at shaft}}{\text{Power input to motor}} \qquad\qquad \dots (3.48)$$

At light loads, for the given input, the constant losses being large as compared with the output, motor efficiency is low. As the load increases, the efficiency increases and ultimately attains its maximum value. The constant and variable losses are equal under this condition. After this, the variable losses become relatively large and hence the efficiency starts decreasing. Thus the shape of the efficiency curve for the motor is as shown in Fig. 3.22.

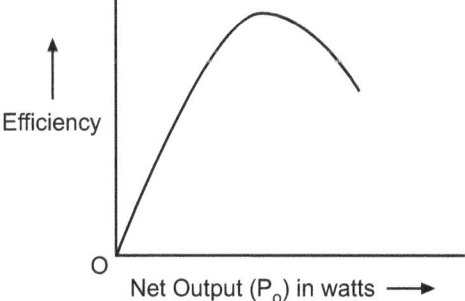

Fig. 3.22 : Efficiency curve for an induction motor

Example 3.16 : *A 4-pole, 3-phase, induction motor runs at a speed of 1440 r.p.m. and the shaft torque is 150 Nm. Calculate the rotor copper loss if the friction and windage losses amount to 300 W. The frequency of supply is 50 Hz.*

Solution : Here, $T_{sh} = 150$ Nm, N = 1440 r.p.m.

$$\text{Power output at shaft} = T_{sh} \times \frac{2\pi N}{60}$$

$$= 150 \times \frac{2\pi \times 1440}{60} = 22619.47 \text{ W}$$

Total mechanical power developed,

$$P_m = \text{Power output at shaft} + \text{Friction and windage losses}$$

$$= 22619.47 + 300 = 22919.47 \text{ W}$$

$$\text{Synchronous speed, } N_S = \frac{120 \, f}{P} = \frac{120 \times 50}{4} = 1500 \text{ r.p.m.}$$

$$\therefore \qquad S = \frac{N_S - N}{N_S} = \frac{1500 - 1440}{1500} = 0.04$$

Now, $$\frac{\text{Rotor copper loss}}{P_m} = \frac{S}{(1 - S)}$$

$$\therefore \qquad \text{Rotor copper loss} = P_m \times \frac{S}{(1 - S)}$$

$$= 22919.47 \times \frac{0.04}{(1 - 0.04)} = \textbf{954.98 W} \qquad \text{... Ans.}$$

Example 3.17 : *A 3-phase, 4 pole, 50 Hz, induction motor runs at 1440 r.p.m. while delivering the power output of 40 kW. The stator losses at this load are equal to rotor losses and mechanical losses amount to 3500 W. Calculate (i) Slip, (ii) Total mechanical power developed by the rotor, (iii) Rotor copper loss, (iv) Rotor input, (v) Stator input, (vi) Efficiency.*

Solution : (i) With f = 50 Hz, P = 4

$$\text{Synchronous speed, } N_S = \frac{120 \, f}{P} = \frac{120 \times 50}{4} = 1500 \text{ r.p.m.}$$

$$\therefore \qquad \text{Slip, } S = \frac{N_S - N}{N_S}$$

$$= \frac{1500 - 1440}{1500} = \textbf{0.04 or 4 \%} \qquad \text{... Ans.}$$

(ii) Total mechanical power developed by the rotor,

$$P_m = \text{Power output} + \text{Mechanical losses}$$

$$= 40000 + 3500$$

$$= \textbf{43500 W} \qquad \text{... Ans.}$$

(iii) Now,

$$\frac{\text{Rotor copper loss}}{P_m} = \frac{S}{(1 - S)}$$

$$\therefore \qquad \text{Rotor copper loss} = P_m \times \frac{S}{(1 - S)} = 43500 \times \frac{0.04}{(1 - 0.04)}$$

$$= \textbf{1812.5 W} \qquad \text{... Ans.}$$

(iv) $\qquad$ Rotor input, $P_2 = P_m + \text{Rotor copper loss}$

$$= 43500 + 1812.5$$

$$= \textbf{45312.5 W} \qquad \text{... Ans.}$$

(v) Assuming the rotor core loss to be negligibly small, we have

$$\text{Stator losses} = \text{Rotor losses} = \text{Rotor copper loss}$$
$$= 1812.5 \text{ W}$$

$\therefore$ Stator input $= \text{Rotor input} + \text{Stator losses}$
$$= 45312.5 + 1812.5$$
$$= \textbf{47125 W} \qquad \qquad \textbf{... Ans.}$$

(vi)   Efficiency, $\eta = \dfrac{\text{Power output}}{\text{Power input}} = \dfrac{40000}{47125}$

$$= \textbf{0.85 or 85 \%} \qquad \qquad \textbf{... Ans.}$$

Example 3.18 : *The input to a 400 V, 6-pole, 50 Hz, 3-phase, star-connected induction motor is 10 kW while running at 950 r.p.m. The stator losses total 600 W and friction and windage losses amount to 400 W. Find the output and efficiency of the motor.*

Solution : It is given that

$$\text{Motor input} = 10 \text{ kW} = 10000 \text{ W}$$
$$\text{Stator losses} = 600 \text{ W}$$

$\therefore$ Stator output $= \text{Rotor input } (P_2)$
$$= \text{Motor input} - \text{Stator losses}$$
$$= 10000 - 600 = 9400 \text{ W}$$

$$N_S = \frac{120 \, f}{P} = \frac{120 \times 50}{6} = 1000 \text{ r.p.m.}$$

$$S = \frac{N_S - N}{N_S} = \frac{1000 - 950}{1000} = 0.05$$

Hence,   Rotor copper loss $= S \times \text{Rotor input} = 0.05 \times 9400$
$$= 470 \text{ W}$$

Total mechanical power developed by the rotor,

$$P_m = \text{Rotor input} - \text{Rotor copper loss}$$
$$= 9400 - 470 = 8930 \text{ W}$$

Net power output at shaft $= P_m - \text{Friction and windage losses}$
$$= 8930 - 400$$
$$= \textbf{8530 W} \qquad \qquad \textbf{... Ans.}$$

$\therefore$ Efficiency, $\eta = \dfrac{\text{Net power output at shaft}}{\text{Power input to motor}}$

$$= \frac{8530}{10000} = \textbf{0.853 or 85.3 \%} \qquad \qquad \textbf{... Ans.}$$

Example 3.19 : *A 440 V, 4-pole, 50 Hz, star-connected, 3-phase induction motor draws the line current of 35 A at 0.8 lagging power factor. Stator resistance per phase is 0.25 Ω. Rotor develops the total torque of 125 Nm making 24 revolutions per second. The useful mechanical power obtained from the rotor shaft is 18 kW. Calculate (a) Slip, (b) Stator iron loss, (c) Efficiency.*

Solution : (a) Here, f = 50 Hz, P = 4. Hence,

$$\text{Synchronous speed, } N_S = \frac{120 \, f}{P} = \frac{120 \times 50}{4}$$

$$= 1500 \text{ r.p.m.}$$

$$\text{Rotor speed, } N = 24 \times 60 = 1440 \text{ r.p.m.}$$

$$\therefore \qquad \text{Slip, } S = \frac{N_S - N}{N_S} = \frac{1500 - 1440}{1500}$$

$$= \textbf{0.04 or 4 \%} \qquad\qquad \text{... Ans.}$$

(b) Total mechanical power developed by the rotor,

$$P_m = T \times \frac{2\pi N}{60} = 125 \times \frac{2\pi \times 1440}{60}$$

$$= 18849.6 \text{ W}$$

Now, $\qquad \dfrac{P_2}{P_m} = \dfrac{1}{(1 - S)}$

$$\therefore \qquad \text{Rotor input, } P_2 = P_m \times \frac{1}{(1 - S)} = 18849.6 \times \frac{1}{(1 - 0.04)}$$

$$= 19635 \text{ W}$$

$$\text{Stator input} = \sqrt{3} \cdot V_L \cdot I_L \cdot \cos\phi$$

$$= \sqrt{3} \times 440 \times 35 \times 0.8$$

$$= 21338.87 \text{ W}$$

$$\therefore \qquad \text{Total stator losses} = \text{Stator input} - \text{Rotor input (i.e. stator output)}$$

$$= 21338.87 - 19635$$

$$= 1703.87 \text{ W}$$

$$\text{Stator copper loss} = 3 \, I_1^2 \cdot R_1 = 3 \times 35^2 \times 0.25$$

$$= 918.75 \text{ W}$$

$$\therefore \qquad \text{Stator iron loss} = \text{Total stator loss} - \text{Stator copper loss}$$

$$= 1703.87 - 918.75$$

$$= \textbf{785.12 W} \qquad\qquad \text{... Ans.}$$

(c) $\qquad\qquad \text{Efficiency, } \eta = \dfrac{\text{Net power output at shaft}}{\text{Power input to motor (i.e. stator)}}$

$$= \frac{18000}{21338.87} = \textbf{0.84 or 84 \%} \qquad\qquad \text{... Ans.}$$

Example 3.20 : *A 3-phase, 400 V, 4-pole, 50 Hz, slip-ring induction motor has a star-connected stator winding. The rotor resistance and standstill reactance per phase are 0.2 Ω and 1.5 Ω respectively. The stator to rotor turns ratio is 2 : 1. The full-load slip is 3 %. Calculate*

(i) The power and the torque developed at full load.

(ii) Maximum torque and the speed at which it occurs.

Solution : (i) **Full-load Condition :**

Supply voltage per phase $= \dfrac{400}{\sqrt{3}} = 230.94$ V

Standstill rotor e.m.f. per phase,

$$E_2 = 230.94 \times \frac{1}{2} = 115.47 \text{ V}$$

$$Z_{2S} = \sqrt{R_2^2 + (SX_2)^2} = \sqrt{(0.2)^2 + (0.03 \times 1.5)^2} = 0.205 \ \Omega$$

$$I_{2S} = \frac{E_{2S}}{Z_{2S}} = \frac{SE_2}{Z_{2S}} = \frac{0.03 \times 115.47}{0.205} = 16.8981 \text{ A}$$

Total rotor copper losses $= 3\,I_{2S}^2\,R_2 = 3 \times 16.8981^2 \times 0.2 = 171.3264$ W

$\therefore$ Total mechanical power developed,

$$P_m = \frac{(1-S)}{S} \times \text{Rotor copper loss}$$

$$= \frac{(1-0.03)}{0.03} \times 171.3264$$

$$= 5539.5536 \text{ W} \qquad\qquad\qquad \text{... Ans.}$$

Synchronous speed, $N_S = \dfrac{120\,f}{P} = \dfrac{120 \times 50}{4} = 1500$ r.p.m.

Rotor speed, $N = N_S(1-S) = 1500(1-0.03) = 1455$ r.p.m.

$\therefore$ Total torque developed,

$$T = \frac{P_m}{(2\pi N/60)} = \frac{5539.5536}{2\pi \times (1455/60)}$$

$$= 36.3566 \text{ Nm} \qquad\qquad\qquad \text{... Ans.}$$

Alternative Method : From Equation (3.45),

$$T = \frac{3}{2\pi n_s} \cdot \frac{SE_2^2\,R_2}{R_2^2 + (SX_2)^2} \quad \text{newton-metres}$$

$$= \frac{3}{2\pi \times (1500/60)} \times \frac{0.03 \times 115.47^2 \times 0.2}{0.2^2 + (0.03 \times 1.5)^2}$$

$$= 36.3566 \text{ Nm} \qquad\qquad\qquad \text{... Ans.}$$

and hence, $\qquad P_m = T \times \dfrac{2\pi N}{60} = 36.3566 \times \dfrac{2\pi \times 1455}{60}$

$$= 5539.5546 \text{ W} \qquad\qquad\qquad \text{... Ans.}$$

(ii) **Maximum Torque Condition :** We know that for maximum torque,

Slip, $S = S_m = \dfrac{R_2}{X_2} = \dfrac{0.2}{1.5} = 0.1333$

Under this condition,

$$Z_{2S} = \sqrt{R_2^2 + (S_m X_2)^2} = \sqrt{(0.2)^2 + (0.1333 \times 1.5)^2}$$

$$- 0.2828 \ \Omega$$

$$I_{2S} = \frac{E_{2S}}{Z_{2S}} = \frac{S_m E_2}{Z_{2S}} = \frac{0.1333 \times 115.47}{0.2828} = 54.4277 \text{ A}$$

Total rotor copper losses $= 3\,I_{2S}^2\,R_2 = 3 \times (54.4277)^2 \times 0.2$

$$= 1777.4247 \text{ W}$$

Total mechanical power developed,

$$P_m = \frac{(1-S)}{S} \times (\text{Rotor copper loss})$$

$$= \frac{(1-0.1333)}{0.1333} \times 1777.4247$$

$$= \textbf{11556.5941 W} \qquad \textbf{... Ans.}$$

Rotor speed, $N = N_S\,(1-S) = 1500\,(1-0.1333)$

$$= \textbf{1300 r.p.m.} \qquad \textbf{... Ans.}$$

$\therefore \qquad T_m = \dfrac{P_m}{(2\pi N/60)} = \dfrac{11556.5941}{(2\pi \times 1300/60)}$

$$= \textbf{84.89 Nm} \qquad \textbf{... Ans.}$$

Alternative Method : From Equation (3.46),

$$T_m = \frac{3}{2\pi n_s} \cdot \frac{E_2^2}{2X_2} \text{ newton-metres}$$

$$= \frac{3}{(2\pi \times 1500/60)} \times \frac{115.47^2}{2 \times 1.5}$$

$$= \textbf{84.88 Nm} \qquad \textbf{... Ans.}$$

Example 3.21 : *A 3-phase induction motor supplies a load of 36.775 kW at 90% efficiency when its stator copper loss and rotor copper loss each equals the iron loss. If its mechanical losses are one-third of no-load loss, estimate the slip. Assume no-load copper losses as negligible.*

Solution :

Power input to the motor $= \dfrac{\text{Power output}}{\text{Efficiency}} = \dfrac{36.775}{0.9} = 40.861 \text{ kW}$

$\therefore \qquad$ Total loss $=$ Power input $-$ Power output $= 40.861 - 36.775$

$$= 4.086 \text{ kW}$$

Now, let $\qquad P_{cu1} =$ Stator copper loss, in kW

$$P_{cu2} = \text{Rotor copper loss, in kW}$$

$P_i =$ Iron loss $=$ Stator iron loss, in kW $\quad$ ($\because$ Rotor iron loss is negligible)

$$P_{mL} = \text{Mechanical loss, in kW}$$

Now, $\qquad P_{mL} = \dfrac{1}{3} \text{ No-load loss} = \dfrac{1}{3}\,(P_{mL} + P_i) \qquad \text{(Given)}$

$\therefore \qquad P_{mL} = \dfrac{P_i}{2}$

$\therefore$ Total loss $= P_{cu1} + P_i + P_{cu2} + P_{mL} = P_i + P_i + P_i + \dfrac{1}{2} P_i$

$$= 3.5 \, P_i = 4.086 \text{ kW}$$

$\therefore$ $P_i = 1.167 \text{ kW} (= P_{cu1} = P_{cu2})$

and $P_{mL} = \dfrac{P_i}{2} = 0.5835 \text{ kW}$

Rotor input, P_2 = Motor input – Stator losses

$$= 40.861 - (P_{cu1} + P_i) = 40.861 - (1.167 + 1.167)$$

$$= 38.527 \text{ kW}$$

$\therefore$ Slip, $S = \dfrac{\text{Rotor copper loss}}{\text{Rotor input}} = \dfrac{P_{cu2}}{P_2} = \dfrac{1.167}{38.527}$

$$= \mathbf{0.0302 \text{ or } 3.02 \%} \qquad \qquad \textbf{... Ans.}$$

Alternatively,

Mechanical power developed by the rotor,

$$P_m = \text{Power output} + \text{Mechanical loss} = 36.775 + 0.5835$$

$$= 37.3585 \text{ kW}$$

Now, $\dfrac{\text{Rotor copper loss}}{P_m} = \dfrac{S}{1-S}$

$\therefore$ $\dfrac{1.167}{37.3585} = \dfrac{S}{1-S}$

$\therefore$ Slip, $S = \mathbf{0.0303 \text{ or } 3.03 \%}$ **... Ans.**

Example 3.22 : *A 6-pole, 50 Hz, 3-phase, induction motor is developing a maximum torque of 30 Nm at 960 r.p.m. Determine the torque exerted by the motor at 5 % slip. Rotor resistance per phase is 0.6 Ω.*

Solution : Synchronous speed, $N_S = \dfrac{120 \, f}{P} = \dfrac{120 \times 50}{6} = 1000 \text{ r.p.m.}$

Slip at maximum torque, $S_m = \dfrac{1000 - 960}{1000} = 0.04$

But $S_m = \dfrac{R_2}{X_2}$

$\therefore$ $0.04 = \dfrac{0.6}{X_2}$

$\therefore$ $X_2 = \dfrac{0.6}{0.04} = 15 \, \Omega$

Now,   Maximum torque, $T_m = \dfrac{3}{2\pi n_s} \times \dfrac{E_2^2}{2 \, X_2}$

$\therefore$ $30 = \dfrac{3}{2\pi \times (1000/60)} \times \dfrac{E_2^2}{2 \times 15}$

$\therefore$ $E_2 = 177.25 \text{ V}$

∴   Torque exerted by the motor at 5 % slip,

$$T = \frac{3}{2\pi n_s} \times \frac{SE_2^2 R_2}{R_2^2 + S^2 X_2^2}$$

$$= \frac{3}{2\pi \times (1000/60)} \times \frac{0.05 \times (177.25)^2 \times 0.6}{(0.6)^2 + (0.05)^2 \times 15^2}$$

$$= 29.2698 \text{ Nm} \qquad \qquad \text{... Ans.}$$

Alternatively, $$\frac{T}{T_m} = \frac{2 S_m S}{S_m^2 + S^2}$$

∴ $$\frac{T}{30} = \frac{2 \times 0.04 \times 0.05}{(0.04)^2 + (0.05)^2}$$

∴   Torque at 5 % slip, $T = 29.268$ Nm   ... Ans.

Example 3.23 : *A 4-pole, three-phase, 50 Hz induction motor has a voltage between the slip-rings on open circuit of 520 V. The star-connected rotor has resistance of 0.4 Ω and standstill reactance of 2 Ω per phase. Determine :*

(i) Full-load torque if full-load speed is 1425 r.p.m.
(ii) The ratio of T_{st} to T_{fl}.
(iii) The ratio of T_m to T_{fl}.
(iv) The external resistance required in the rotor per phase to get maximum torque at start.

Solution : Given : $R_2 = 0.4$ Ω, $X_2 = 2$ Ω, f = 50 Hz, N = 1425 r.p.m., P = 4.

(i) Synchronous speed, $$N_S = \frac{120 \, f}{P} = \frac{120 \times 50}{4} = 1500 \text{ r.p.m.}$$

Hence, $$n_s = \frac{N_S}{60} = \frac{1500}{60} = 25 \text{ r.p.s.}$$

Full-load slip, $$S_{fl} = \frac{N_S - N}{N_S} = \frac{1500 - 1425}{1500} = 0.05$$

Standstill rotor e.m.f. per phase,

$$E_2 = \frac{520}{\sqrt{3}} = 300.22 \text{ V}$$

∴   Full-load torque, $$T_{fl} = \frac{3}{2\pi n_s} \times \frac{S_{fl} E_2^2 R_2}{R_2^2 + (S_{fl} X_2)^2}$$

$$= \frac{3}{2\pi \times 25} \times \frac{0.05 \times (300.22)^2 \times 0.4}{[(0.4)^2 + (0.05 \times 2)^2]}$$

$$= 202.52 \text{ Nm} \qquad \qquad \text{... Ans.}$$

(ii)   Starting torque, $$T_{st} = \frac{3}{2\pi n_s} \times \frac{E_2^2 R_2}{R_2^2 + X_2^2} \qquad (\because S = 1)$$

$$= \frac{3}{2\pi \times 25} \times \frac{(300.22)^2 \times 0.4}{[(0.4)^2 + 2^2]} = 165.52 \text{ Nm}$$

∴ $$\frac{T_{st}}{T_{fl}} = \frac{165.52}{202.52} = 0.82 \qquad \qquad \text{... Ans.}$$

(iii)   Maximum torque, T_m = $\dfrac{3}{2\pi n_s} \times \dfrac{E_2^2}{2X_2}$ = $\dfrac{3}{2\pi \times 25} \times \dfrac{(300.22)^2}{(2 \times 2)}$

$$= 430.35 \text{ Nm}$$

∴ $\dfrac{T_m}{T_{fl}}$ = $\dfrac{430.35}{202.52}$ = **2.125**   ... **Ans.**

(iv) To obtain maximum torque at starting (i.e. when S = 1), let the extra resistance to be inserted in each phase of the rotor be r ohms. Then, obviously under this condition,

$$R_2 + r = X_2 \qquad (\because S_m = 1)$$

∴   External resistance per phase required in the rotor circuit,

$$r = X_2 - R_2 = 2 - 0.4 = \mathbf{1.6\ \Omega} \qquad \text{... \textbf{Ans.}}$$

3.26 MEASUREMENT OF SLIP

Some most commonly used methods of measuring slip of an induction motor are as follows :

(i) By Actual Measurement of Motor Speed : In this method, the motor speed is actually measured with the help of a tachometer. Slip is then calculated from the knowledge of the synchronous speed of the machine using the equation,

$$\text{Slip, } S = \frac{N_S - N}{N_S}$$

(ii) By Measurement of Rotor Frequency : Since the rotor frequency is very low, it can be accurately measured with the help of a centre-zero type d.c. moving-coil millivoltmeter (or galvanometer) inserted in the rotor circuit.

Fig. 3.23 (a) illustrates the method of connecting a millivoltmeter along with its protective resistance across the slip-rings of slip-ring induction motor. In the case of squirrel-cage induction motor, it is possible to pick up inductively some voltage of rotor frequency by connecting a millivoltmeter with its protective resistance across the ends of the motor shaft as illustrated in Fig. 3.23 (b) or by connecting it across a large flat search coil of many turns placed centrally against the end plate on the non-driving end of the motor. Rotor frequency is determined by counting the number of complete oscillations made by the pointer of millivoltmeter about its mean zero position per second. Slip is then found by using the relationship between supply frequency and rotor frequency as follows :

$$\text{Slip, } S = \frac{\text{Rotor frequency}}{\text{Supply frequency}}$$

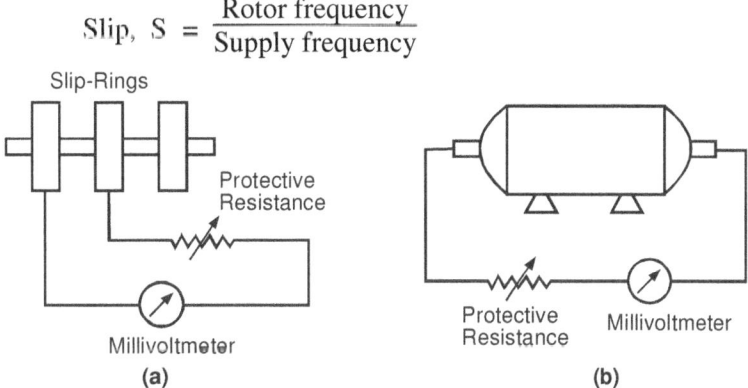

**Fig. 3.23 : Measurement of slip of an induction motor by measuring rotor frequency
(a) Slip-ring induction motor, (b) Squirrel-cage induction motor**

(iii) Stroboscopic Method : In this method, a disc painted with alternate black and white sectors is attached to the end of the motor shaft as shown in Fig. 3.24. The number of black sectors as well as white sectors on the disc are each equal to the number of motor poles. The disc is illuminated by a neon lamp connected across the leads of the motor either directly or through a transformer. Such a lamp has the typical characteristic that it glows twice in a cycle when the voltage is above certain limit. If the speed of the motor were synchronous, each sector on the disc would move forward a pole pitch in a period of half cycle. Hence, one black sector seen by the observer at the instant of first maximum illumination from the lamp would advance to the position of the next black sector, at the instant of next maximum illumination.

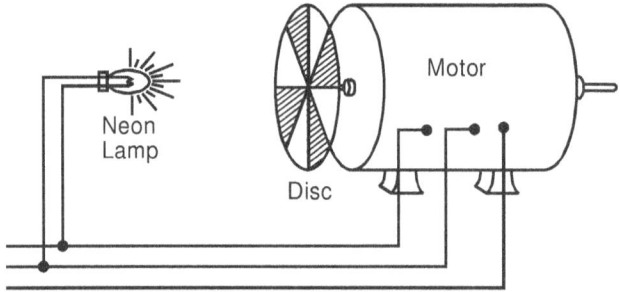

Fig. 3.24 : Stroboscopic method of measuring slip of an induction motor

The same thing would happen in the case of each white sector. Thus in effect, the disc would appear to be stationary. But when there is a slip, each sector in the above situation will fail to reach the position of the next adjacent sector of the same colour. So the disc will not appear to be stationary but will seem to be rotating slowly backward. The speed in r.p.m. with which the disc appears to rotate backward gives the slip-speed $(N_S - N)$ of the motor. The slip may then be found from relation,

$$\text{Slip, } S = \frac{N_S - N}{N_S}$$

3.27 STARTING OF THREE-PHASE INDUCTION MOTORS

In the case of a three-phase induction motor, the magnitude of the induced e.m.f. in the rotor winding depends on the relative speed between the rotating magnetic field produced by the stator and the rotor conductors. Initially when the rotor is stationary, this relative speed is maximum. Therefore, a large e.m.f. is induced in the rotor conductors. Since all the rotor conductors together form a closed circuit, very large current is circulated through the rotor winding. Consequently, the motor draws a very large current of the order of 5 to 7 times its full load current for a short-period from the supply. In this condition, the motor can be regarded as a transformer with a short-circuited secondary. Once the rotor starts running, the relative speed between the rotor conductors and stator field reduces thereby reducing the e.m.f. developed in the rotor. Thus, the rotor current and hence the current drawn by the motor is automatically reduced.

The large starting current drawn by the motor may not cause harm to the motor due to its rugged construction but causes a large voltage drop in the lines. This affects the working of the other equipments connected to the same line. Many supply authorities, therefore, limit the size of the induction motor which can be started directly on line to three or sometimes five kilowatts. Hence, use of starters becomes essential for the motors above this rating for reducing their starting current.

Thus, induction motor starter mainly limits the starting current to the safe value without, at the same time, reducing the starting torque to a value less than that required to start and accelerate the motor and the load. In addition to this, it also provides protection to the motor against over-load and low voltage. For this, it is always fitted with no-volt and over-load releases. It may also be fitted with single phasing preventer for providing protection to the motor against single phasing.

The starting current of the induction motor can be reduced either by applying a reduced voltage to the stator during the starting period or by increasing the resistance of the rotor circuit. Various types of starters have been developed for this purpose to suit squirrel-cage and slip-ring induction motors.

3.27.1 Starting of Squirrel-Cage Induction Motors

In general, the starting methods for squirrel-cage induction motors may be broadly classified as :

(a) Direct-on-line starting,

(b) Reduced-voltage starting.

(a) **Direct-On-Line Starting** : In this method, a squirrel-cage induction motor is started by connecting it directly to the line i.e. without using any special device for reducing the starting current. However, as said earlier, this method is restricted only to small squirrel-cage induction motors.

Direct-On-Line Starter : Fig. 3.25 (a) shows a typical direct-on-line starter called *D.O.L. starter* suitable for a small squirrel-cage induction motor consisting of a magnetic contactor and thermal overload relay and Fig. 3.25 (b) shows a schematic wiring diagram for its control circuit. When *start* push-button is pressed, the contactor coil is energised and its three normally open (N/O) main contacts (M) are closed. Thus, the motor gets connected across the supply mains.

The contactor remains closed even when the *start* push-button is released because its operating coil continues to get supply through the closed auxiliary or hold-on contacts (A) of the contactor.

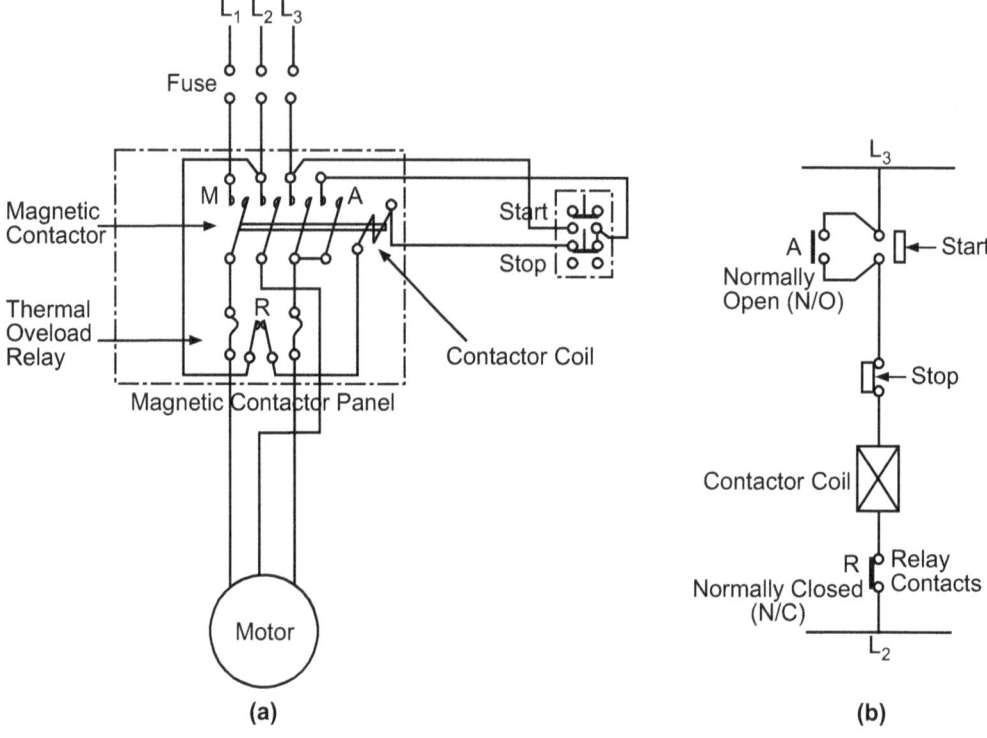

Fig. 3.25 : (a) Typical direct-on-line starter for small squirrel-cage induction motor, (b) Schematic wiring diagram for the control circuit

Motor continues to run until shut down by pressing the *stop* push-button, by the tripping of the overload relay (meaning by opening of its normally closed contacts R) under overload conditions, or by power failure. From the figure, it will be seen that the thermal overload relay has only two thermal elements. This is because an overload or a break in the phase without thermal element can cause an increased current in the other two phases sufficient enough to actuate the relay. Fuses are provided for the protection of the motor against short-circuits. A single phasing preventer may also be provided for protection against single phasing.

(b) Reduced-Voltage Starting : Increasing rotor resistance for limiting the starting current is not feasible in squirrel-cage induction motors. However, in their case, reduction in starting current can be achieved by applying the reduced voltage to the stator terminals during the starting period. The voltage is then increased to its normal value when the motor picks up the full speed. The reduced-voltage starting causes the starting torque to reduce drastically as it is proportional to the square of voltage. Hence, such starting can be carried out only under no or light-load conditions. Different types of starters used for starting squirrel-cage induction motors with reduced voltage are described below :

(i) Stator-Resistance Starter : It essentially consists of a set of variable starting resistors. These resistors are connected in series with each phase of the stator winding during starting as illustrated in Fig. 3.26. Since, some voltage is dropped across the starting resistors, the voltage applied across the motor terminals is reduced. This in turn, reduces the starting current. As the motor picks up speed, the starting resistances are gradually cut off from all the phases of the stator winding. Finally, when the resistances are completely cut off, full voltage is applied across the motor terminals and motor attains its rated speed.

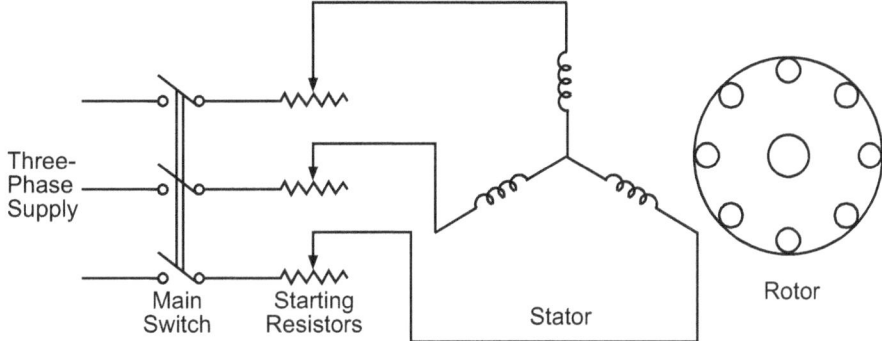

Fig. 3.26 : Stator-resistance starter

This type of starter is simple in construction and cheap. It is useful for both star and delta connected motors. However, because of the large power loss involved in the starting resistors, it is used for smooth starting of small motors only.

(ii) Auto-Transformer Starter : A three-phase, star-connected auto-transformer along with a suitable change-over switch forms an auto-transformer starter (Fig. 3.27). When the switch is in the starting position, the stator of an induction motor is supplied with reduced voltage through the auto-transformer using suitable tap. This limits the starting current to a safe value. Usually three tappings per phase are provided to give 50, 65 or 80 per cent of normal line voltage across the motor terminals. When the motor attains about 80% of its normal speed, the switch is thrown to run position, which connects the motor directly across the supply and cuts out the auto-transformer from the circuit. These actions may be carried out automatically by time-delay relay operated magnetic contactors.

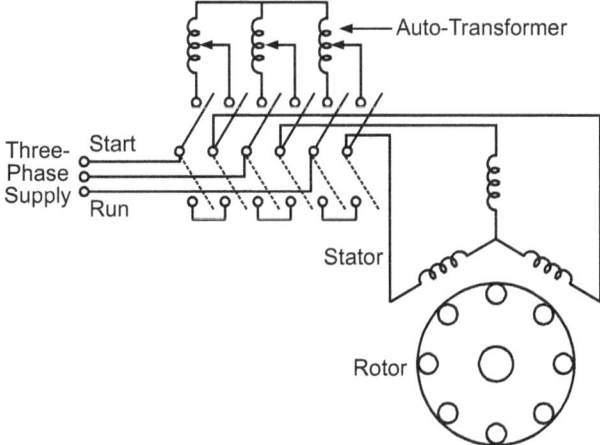

Fig. 3.27 : Auto-transformer starter

The loading of the system during starting and the power loss involved are small with this type of starter. Moreover, it can be used with star as well as delta connected motors. The provision of several taps on the auto-transformer makes the adjustment possible to suit the local conditions. But it is more expensive than a star-delta starter.

(iii) Star-Delta Starter : This starter is essentially a two-way switch as shown in Fig. 3.28. In the starting position, it connects the stator phases in star. Therefore, voltage applied across each phase is only $1/\sqrt{3}$ (i.e. 58%) of line value of the supply voltage. Consequently, the current drawn by the motor is also small. When the motor picks up speed, the switch is moved to the running position. In this position of the switch, the stator phases are reconnected in delta and thereby the voltage applied across each phase is raised to full line value. Thus, the motor attains its full speed. Mechanical interlock is always provided with such a starter so as to prevent starting of the motor directly with delta connection. In automatic type of star-delta starters, all the starting operations are carried out automatically with the help of time-delay relay operated magnetic contactors.

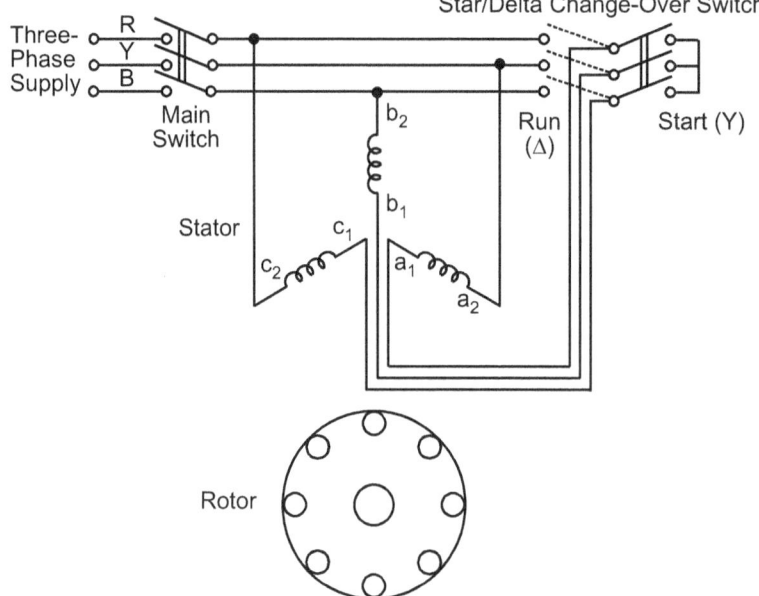

Fig. 3.28 : Star-delta starter

Obviously, this type of starter is useful only for that motor which is designed to run normally with delta connection. Moreover, all the six terminals of the stator phases must be available outside on the terminal board of such motor. Being efficient, simple and cheap, star-delta starters are more commonly used for starting the squirrel-cage induction motors, particularly when the starting torque is not required to exceed about 50% of full-load torque. When induction motors are required to run on light load for long period, star-delta switch permits the motor to be star-connected. This helps in reducing magnetizing current and thereby in improving power factor and efficiency.

3.27.2 Starting of Slip-Ring Induction Motors

Slip-ring induction motors are invariably started with full line voltage applied across the stator terminals. The starting current is limited by introducing a variable resistance in the rotor circuit. The increased rotor resistance not only limits the starting current but also gives high starting torque.

Rotor-Resistance Starter : This type of starter essentially consists of a three-phase, star-connected controlling resistance. The starter unit also includes a line switching contactor for the stator along with usual no-voltage (or low-voltage) and over-current protective devices.

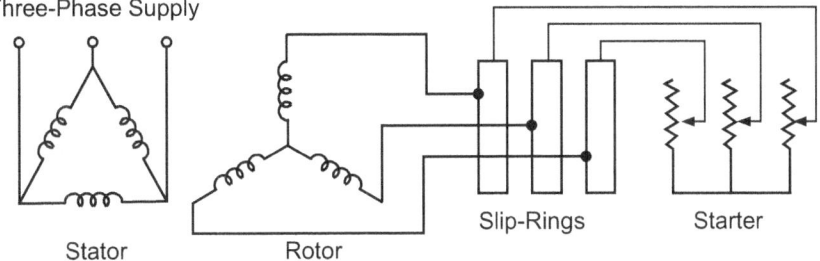

Fig. 3.29 : Rotor-resistance starter

For starting the motor, the controlling resistance is inserted in the rotor circuit through the slip-rings and brushes and full supply voltage is applied across the stator terminals as illustrated in Fig. 3.29. The starting resistance introduced in the rotor circuit is gradually cut out as the motor speeds up. This resistance cutting may be automatic or manual. In large motors, when the resistance is completely cut out from the rotor circuit, the slip-rings are short circuited with the help of a metallic collar and at the same time the brushes are lifted automatically from them. This avoids power loss due to brush friction and the lead resistance. A mechanical interlocking is also normally provided to prevent the starting of the motor without the resistance in the rotor circuit.

3.28 REVERSAL OF ROTATION IN THREE-PHASE INDUCTION MOTORS

The reversal of rotation can be very easily achieved in three-phase induction motors simply by interchanging the supply connections to any two of the three terminals of the stator as illustrated in Fig. 3.30.

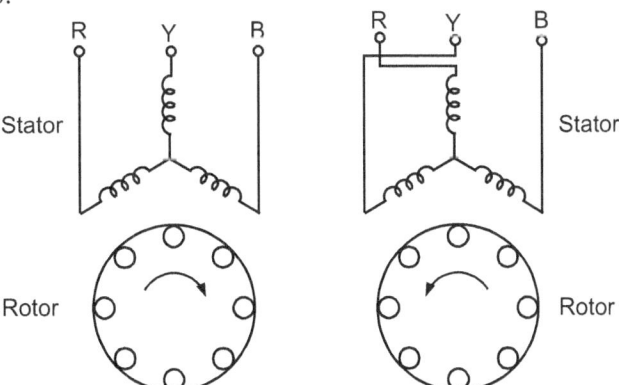

Fig. 3.30 : Reversal of rotation of a 3-phase induction motor

The interchange between the supply connections to any two terminals of the stator reverses the direction of rotation of the magnetic field and thereby reverses the direction of rotation of the motor.

3.29 SPEED CONTROL OF THREE-PHASE INDUCTION MOTORS

From Equation (3.9) seen earlier, we know that the speed of the induction motor is given by

$$N = N_S (1 - S)$$

The above expression clearly shows that the speed of the induction motor can be controlled by varying any one of the two basic factors, namely the synchronous speed of the motor and its slip. The synchronous speed of the motor can be changed by changing the supply frequency or the number of poles $\left(\because N_S = \dfrac{120\,f}{P} \right)$. The slip may be changed by changing the supply voltage, introducing extra resistance in the rotor circuit, injecting e.m.f. in the rotor circuit or by operating the motor in tandem or cascade with another induction motor. Accordingly, we have the following methods for the speed control of induction motors.

(a) Frequency Control : The synchronous (and therefore also running) speed of the induction motor can be varied smoothly over a wide range by changing the supply frequency. In order to maintain the air gap flux at its normal value under varying frequency conditions, it is necessary to keep E_1/f (refer to Equation 3.12) and therefore V/f ratio constant. Therefore, if speed control is to be achieved by changing frequency, the supply voltage is also to be changed simultaneously to meet the above requirement. Since the commercial power systems operate at constant frequency, variation of frequency for speed control purpose is necessarily achieved by using either rotary (e.g. motor-generator sets) or solid state frequency conversion equipments. A typical frequency control scheme for induction motor using converter-inverter arrangement employing SCR circuitry is shown schematically in Fig. 3.31 which is self-explanatory. Fig. 3.32 shows typical speed-torque curves of an induction motor for two different frequencies.

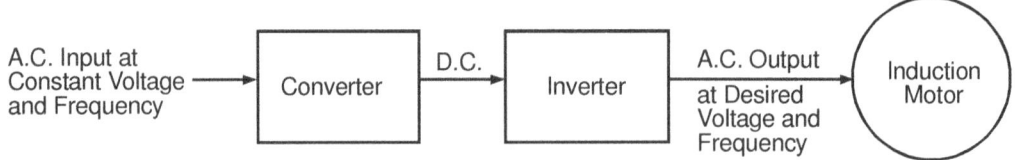

Fig. 3.31 : A typical frequency control scheme for an induction motor

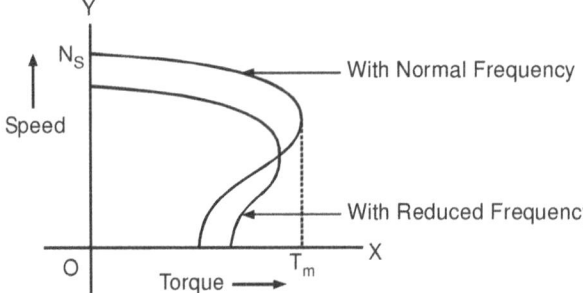

Fig. 3.32 : Speed-torque curves of an induction motor for two different frequencies

It will be observed that as the operating frequency decreases, apart from reduction in synchronous speed and consequent reduction in running speed of the motor for the given torque, the maximum torque gets reduced slightly and the starting torque increases.

The large expenditure that is involved on frequency conversion equipments makes the frequency control method very expensive. Therefore this method, so far, was very rarely used in actual practice except in few cases where independent power supplies were used e.g. in the electric propulsion of ships. But with the recent developments in semiconductor devices and reduction in their cost, frequency control method is becoming popular.

(b) Pole Changing : This method is generally used for obtaining multi-speed, squirrel-cage induction motor. For that, it is provided with some simple switching means for changing the number of poles on the stator winding. The basic principle of pole changing can be explained as given below.

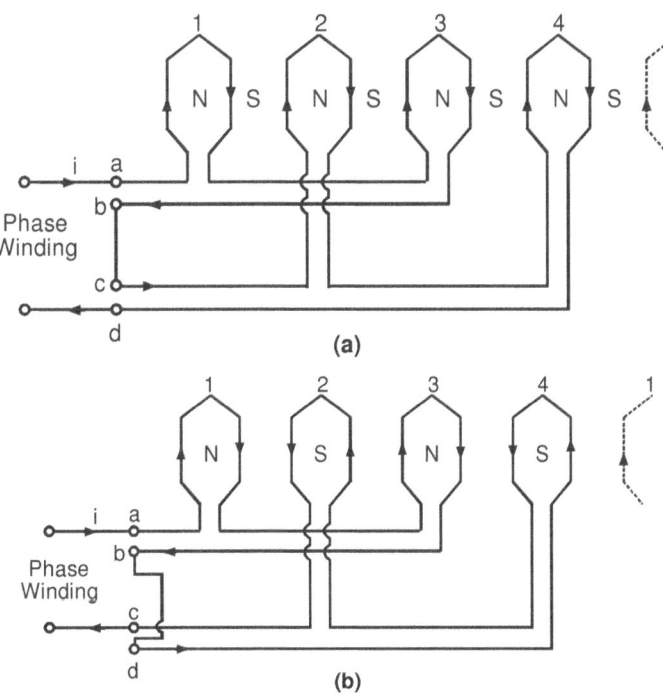

Fig. 3.33 : Simple series connections of phase circuits for obtaining
(a) 8 poles, (b) 4 poles

Fig. 3.33 (a) shows developed winding diagram for one phase of a three-phase winding. Coils 1 and 3 connected in series form one coil group (or circuit) while coils 2 and 4 connected in series form another coil group. These two coil groups are connected in series in such a fashion that all four coils are magnetized in the same direction (indicated by same directions of instantaneous values of currents in these coils in the diagram). Hence, these coils form four North poles. Four *consequent poles* of opposite polarity i.e. South poles are produced midway between the coils. Thus, this arrangement gives total eight poles. But if the two coil groups are connected in series as shown in Fig. 3.33 (b), there will be in all four poles only. Obviously, the synchronous speed in this case will be double of that in the first case. The corresponding speed-torque curves are shown in Fig. 3.34. Two-speed motors with the speed ratios other than 1 : 2 are obtained by the use of two separate motor windings. By a combination of two stator windings, each with the provision of pole changing, a four-speed motor may be obtained.

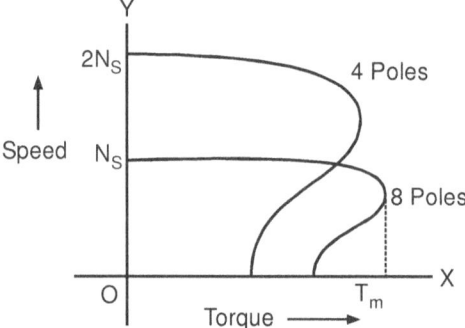

Fig. 3.34 : Typical speed-torque curves of a pole changing induction motor

This method of speed control is more suitable for squirrel-cage induction motors rather than slip-ring induction motors. This is because a cage type rotor is adaptable to any number of stator poles. But this is not the case with a wound rotor. To avoid negative torque development by some rotor conductor belts, a slip-ring induction motor requires a pole changing arrangement on the stator as well as on the rotor.

(c) Voltage Control : The slip and therefore the speed of the induction motor can be varied by changing the applied stator voltage. From Equation (3.34), we know that for an induction motor operating at or near full-load slip,

$$T \propto SV^2$$

That is torque developed by an induction motor varies as the square of the applied voltage. Therefore if the voltage is reduced, the torque is also reduced. Consequently, the speed drops down i.e. slip increases until the increased rotor current and hence the increased current drawn by the motor compensates for the reduction in torque due to reduced applied voltage. Thus, the motor produces the required load torque at a lower speed. Fig. 3.35 shows the typical speed-torque curves with stator-voltage control.

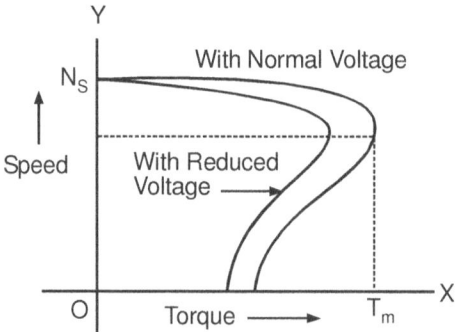

Fig. 3.35 : Speed-torque curves of an induction motor with stator-voltage control

Inspite of being most simple, this method is rarely used in actual practice except for small single-phase induction motors used for fans, home appliances, etc. The principal reasons are as follows :

- A large change in voltage is required for a relatively small change in speed.

- When the supply voltage is reduced by a large percentage of the rated voltage, the induction motor gets overheated due to increase in the current drawn under constant load torque condition.

- A large change in supply voltage seriously affects the magnetic conditions of the motor.

- Need of additional voltage changing auxiliary equipment makes the method expensive.

(d) Rotor-Resistance Control : We have seen earlier (refer to Equation 3.38) that for an induction motor working at or near full-load slip, the torque and slip are related approximately as

$$T \propto \frac{S}{R_2}$$

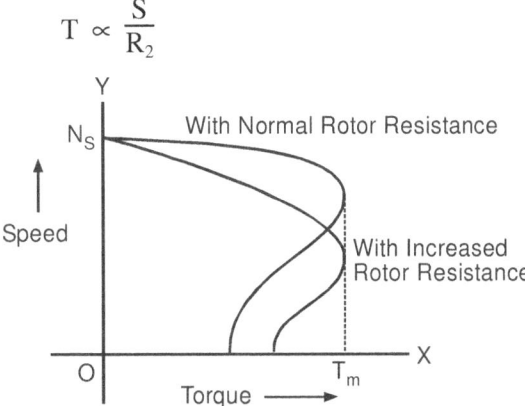

Fig. 3.36 : Speed-torque curves of an induction motor with rotor-resistance control

For a given torque, therefore, the slip at which the motor works is proportional to the rotor resistance. Using this fact, in the case of slip-ring induction motors, the slip can be artificially increased and hence the speed can be decreased by introducing the external resistance in series with each phase of the rotor winding. By this method, any speed below the normal value down to the crawling can be obtained. Fig. 3.36 shows the typical speed-torque curves of a slip-ring induction motor using rotor-resistance control. The rotor-resistance starter (Fig. 3.29) if continuously rated may be used for the speed control purposes. Even though this method of speed control is simple, it has following drawbacks :

- This method can be applied for only slip-ring induction motor.

- It cannot give speeds above normal.

- Reduction in speed is at the cost of efficiency.

- With a large resistance in the rotor circuit, the speed regulation of the motor is very poor i.e. a small change in load produces a large change in speed. Hence the motor under this condition acts almost as a variable-speed drive.

- Due to cooling arrangement needed, the resistance controllers i.e. external rotor resistors are comparatively bulky and expensive.

Because of the above limitations, this method is used only in those cases where motors are to be started against heavy loads and where speed control is needed for short periods or the reduction is only a few per cent of normal speed.

(e) **Injection of an E.M.F. in the Rotor Circuit :** Slip and therefore the running speed of an induction motor can be varied by injecting an e.m.f. (E_j) of slip frequency into the rotor circuit through slip-rings. If this injected e.m.f. is in phase opposition to the rotor induced e.m.f. (E_2), the net e.m.f. in the rotor circuit reduces. Consequently, the rotor current and hence the torque developed by the motor reduces. This ultimately results into reduction in speed of the motor. Reverse is the case when the injected e.m.f. is in phase with the rotor induced e.m.f. Such an e.m.f. increases the rotor current, torque and hence the speed of the motor. Fig. 3.37 shows the speed-torque curves of an induction motor under the above two conditions. Injection of the desired e.m.f. of slip frequency into the rotor circuit can be carried out with the help of an auxiliary commutating machine or by providing the rotor itself with the commutator.

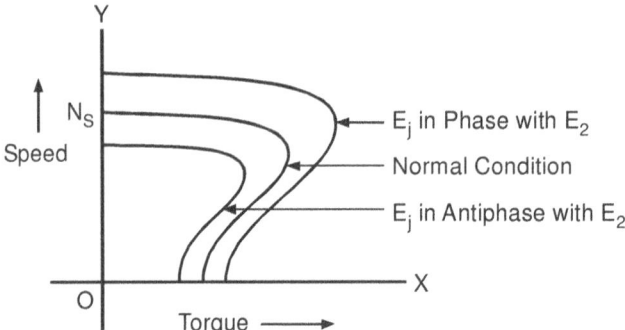

Fig. 3.37 : Speed-torque curves of an induction motor with injection of an e.m.f. in its rotor circuit

This method of speed control is efficient and has better speed regulation. However, need of an arrangement to inject an e.m.f. in the rotor circuit makes it very expensive. Hence, it is used only for the motors of very large rating.

(f) **Cascade, Concatenation or Tandem Operation :** This method requires two induction motors mechanically coupled together. At least one of these motors must have a wound rotor. This wound rotor induction motor is called the *main motor*, while the other (which may be either of slip-ring type or squirrel-cage type) is called the *auxiliary motor*. The stator of the main motor is connected to the supply while its rotor slip-rings are connected to the stator of the auxiliary machine (Fig. 3.38 a). In case both the motors are of slip-ring type, there is another way of electrically connecting them together through their rotors for cascade operation as illustrated in Fig. 3.38 (b).

Usually two motors are operated in cascade with their torques acting in the same direction. This operation is called *cumulative cascading*. But they can also be run with their torques acting in opposition. The operation is then called *differential cascading*.

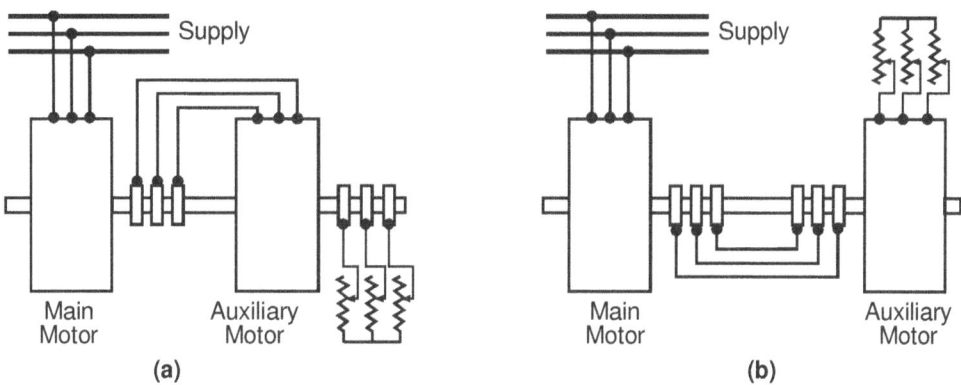

Fig. 3.38 : Cascade operation of two induction motors

If P_1 and P_2 are the number of poles of main and auxiliary motors respectively, f is the supply frequency, then cascade operation of two motors can give the following four synchronous speeds :

(i) By Using Main Motor Alone :

$$N_S = \frac{120\,f}{P_1} \text{ revolutions per minute}$$

(ii) By Using Auxiliary Motor Alone : The auxiliary motor may be run separately from the mains. Under this condition, we have

$$N_S = \frac{120\,f}{P_2} \text{ revolutions per minute}$$

(iii) By Using Both Motors in Cumulative Cascade :

$$N_S = \frac{120\,f}{P_1 + P_2} \text{ revolutions per minute}$$

(iv) By Using Both Motors in Differential Cascade :

$$N_S = \frac{120\,f}{P_1 - P_2} \text{ revolutions per minute}$$

Cascade operation is very rarely used in actual practice because it suffers from the following disadvantages :

(i)   Necessity of two motors. This makes the method expensive.

(ii)   Low power factor, efficiency and pull-out torque.

(iii) Complicated operation.

(iv)   Limited number of speeds.

Example 3.24 : *The rotor of a 4-pole, 50 Hz, 3-phase induction motor has a resistance of 0.2 Ω per phase and its full-load speed is 1440 r.p.m. If the load torque remains unchanged, calculate the approximate value of the additional resistance to be inserted in the rotor circuit to reduce the motor speed by 10%.*

Solution : For an induction motor working at or near full-load slip, the torque and slip are related approximately as

$$T \propto \frac{S}{R_2}$$ (Refer to Equation 3.38)

$\therefore$ $T_1 \propto \dfrac{S_1}{R_2}$ and $T_2 \propto \dfrac{S_2}{R_2 + r}$

Or, $\dfrac{T_1}{T_2} = \dfrac{S_1}{S_2} \times \dfrac{(R_2 + r)}{R_2}$

where suffixes represent the two sets of conditions, one with normal rotor resistance R_2 and the other with external resistance r added in the rotor circuit. Under the given condition, since

$$T_1 = T_2$$

$$\frac{S_1}{S_2} = \frac{R_2}{R_2 + r}$$

Now, Synchronous speed, $N_S = \dfrac{120\,f}{P} = \dfrac{120 \times 50}{4} = 1500$ r.p.m.

$$S_1 = \frac{1500 - 1440}{1500} = 0.04$$

When the speed is reduced by 10 %, the new speed will be

$$N_2 = 0.90 \times 1440 = 1296 \text{ r.p.m.}$$

$\therefore$ $S_2 = \dfrac{1500 - 1296}{1500} = 0.136$

Also, $R_2 = 0.2\ \Omega$

Substituting these values in the above expression, we have

$$\frac{0.04}{0.136} = \frac{0.2}{0.2 + r}$$

$\therefore$ **r = 0.48 Ω**   **... Ans.**

Hence, external resistance of 0.48 Ω must be added to the rotor circuit to reduce the speed by 10 %.

Example 3.25 : *A 3-phase, 440 V, 50 Hz, 110 kW, 24-pole, 245 r.p.m., star-connected, slip-ring induction motor has a stator to rotor turns ratio of 1.25. The resistance measured between each pair of slip-rings is 0.04 Ω. This motor drives a fan which requires 110 kW at the full-load speed of the motor. The torque required to drive the fan varies as the square of the speed. What resistance should be connected in series with each slip-ring so that the fan will run at 175 r.p.m.? Neglect stator resistance, stator leakage reactance and rotational losses of the motor.*

Solution : Synchronous speed, $N_S = \dfrac{120\,f}{P} = \dfrac{120 \times 50}{24} = 250$ r.p.m.

Let S_1 and T_1 represent the slip and the torque at the initial speed of N_1 = 245 r.p.m. under full-load conditions and S_2 and T_2 represent the slip and the torque at the desired speed of N_2 = 175 r.p.m. Then

$$\text{Full-load slip, } S_1 = \frac{250 - 245}{250} = 0.02$$

$$\text{Torque at full load, } T_1 = \frac{110 \times 10^3 \times 60}{2\pi \times 245} = 4287.44 \text{ Nm}$$

Since the rotor is star connected, the resistance between a pair of slip-rings will be equal to twice the rotor resistance per phase.

∴   Rotor resistance per phase,

$$R_2 = \frac{0.04}{2} = 0.02 \ \Omega$$

Now, from Equation (3.45),

$$T_1 = \frac{3}{2\pi n_s} \times \frac{S_1 E_2^2 R_2}{R_2^2 + (S_1 X_2)^2}$$

Here,

$$n_s = \frac{250}{60} = 4.167 \text{ r.p.s., } S_1 = 0.02$$

$$E_2 = \frac{440}{\sqrt{3} \times 1.25} = 203.227 \text{ V}, \quad R_2 = 0.02$$

Substituting these values in the above equation, we have

$$4287.44 = \frac{3}{2\pi \times 4.167} \times \frac{0.02 \times (203.227)^2 \times 0.02}{(0.02)^2 + (0.02 \times X_2)^2}$$

∴ $X_2 = 0.322 \ \Omega$

Further, slip at 175 r.p.m.

$$S_2 = \frac{250 - 175}{250} = 0.3$$

Since $T \propto N^2$ (given), the torque T_2 at 175 r.p.m. will be given by

$$T_2 = T_1 \left(\frac{N_2}{N_1}\right)^2 = 4287.44 \times \left(\frac{175}{245}\right)^2 = 2187.469 \text{ Nm}$$

Let r be the external resistance to be added in each phase of the rotor circuit to achieve the slip S_2 = 0.3. Then again from Equation (3.45),

$$T_2 = \frac{3}{2\pi n_s} \times \frac{S_2 E_2^2 (R_2 + r)}{(R_2 + r)^2 + (S_2 X_2)^2}$$

Substituting the values of the various quantities in the above equation, we get

$$2187.469 = \frac{3}{2\pi \times 4.167} \times \frac{0.3 \times (203.227)^2 \times (0.02 + r)}{(0.02 + r)^2 + (0.3 \times 0.322)^2}$$

Simplifying this expression, we have

   $1.541 \ r^2 - 0.938 \ r - 0.005 = 0$

Solution of the above quadratic equation gives,

$$r = \frac{0.938 \pm \sqrt{(0.938)^2 + 4 \times 1.541 \times 0.005}}{2 \times 1.541}$$

$$= 0.614 \ \Omega \text{ or } -0.005 \ \Omega$$

Rejecting the negative value, we get

External resistance to be added in each rotor phase,

$$r = 0.614 \, \Omega \qquad \text{... Ans.}$$

Example 3.26 : *Two 3-phase, slip-ring induction motors, one having 4 poles and the other having 20 poles are operated in cascade from 3-phase, 50 Hz supply. Find the synchronous speeds which can be obtained from this operation.*

Solution : The following synchronous speeds are obtainable from the cascade operation of the two given induction motors.

(i) With 4-Pole Motor Alone :

$$N_S = \frac{120 \, f}{P_1} = \frac{120 \times 50}{4} = \textbf{1500 r.p.m.} \qquad \text{... Ans.}$$

(ii) With 20-Pole Motor Alone :

$$N_S = \frac{120 \, f}{P_2} = \frac{120 \times 50}{20} = \textbf{300 r.p.m.} \qquad \text{... Ans.}$$

(iii) With Two Motors in Cumulative Cascade :

$$N_S = \frac{120 \, f}{P_1 + P_2} = \frac{120 \times 50}{(4 + 20)} = \textbf{250 r.p.m.} \qquad \text{... Ans.}$$

(iv) With Two Motors in Differential Cascade :

$$N_S = \frac{120 \, f}{P_1 - P_2} = \frac{120 \times 50}{(4 - 20)} = \textbf{-375 r.p.m.} \qquad \text{... Ans.}$$

Here, negative sign indicates that in this case the set will rotate in the opposite direction.

3.30 COMPARISON OF SQUIRREL-CAGE AND SLIP-RING INDUCTION MOTORS

The comparison between squirrel-cage and slip-ring induction motors in a tabular form given below will be helpful in understanding the suitability of these motors for different applications discussed in the next section :

Table 3.1

	Points for Comparison	Squirrel-Cage Induction Motor	Slip-Ring Induction Motor
1.	Construction	Simple and robust construction.	Less simple construction.
2.	Cost	Cheaper.	Costlier.
3.	Starting	The motor can be started by (i) star-delta starter (ii) stator-resistance starter (iii) auto-transformer starter.	The motor requires rotor-resistance starter.
4.	Starting torque	Low starting torque. It cannot be increased in an ordinary way.	High starting torque. It can be increased by the insertion of external resistance in each phase of the rotor.
5.	Pull-out torque	Pull-out torque greater.	Pull-out torque less.
6.	Efficiency	More efficiency.	Comparatively less efficiency.
7.	Power factor	Better power factor on full load.	Poor power factor on full load.
8.	Speed control	Speed control difficult.	Speed control easier.
9.	Maintenance	Requires less maintenance.	Requires more maintenance.
10.	Fire hazards	Safe from the point of view of fire hazards as there are no rubbing contacts.	Risk of fire hazards due to sparking at the brushes.

3.31 APPLICATIONS OF THREE-PHASE INDUCTION MOTORS

- **Squirrel-Cage Induction Motors :** Being the simplest, most robust, cheapest and highly efficient type, it is the most widely used type of a.c. motors. Following are some of the applications of these motors.

Lathes, drilling machines, grinders, various types of presses, compressors, fans, blowers, conveyors, water pumps, laundry washing machines, wood working equipments, printing machinery, cement and textile mills, etc.

- **Slip-Ring or Wound-Rotor Induction Motors :** These motors are most suitable for the applications requiring a high starting torque and smooth speed control over a limited range, e.g. lifts, hoists, cranes, elevators, rolling mills, various types of presses, compressors, propulsion of ships, winding machines, etc.

3.32 POINTS TO REMEMBER

- In general, if a stationary system of coils suitably wound is supplied with polyphase a.c., then a uniformly rotating magnetic field of constant magnitude is produced.

- When the three phase windings displaced in space through 120° electrical are supplied with three-phase a.c., they produce uniformly rotating magnetic field of constant magnitude. The resultant field in space at any instant has magnitude equal to 1.5 times the maximum flux produced by one phase. The speed with which the flux rotates bears a fixed relation with the supply frequency and the number of poles (N = 120 f/P).

- Speed of the rotating magnetic field produced by the stator winding of a three-phase induction motor is known as *synchronous speed* of the motor. It is always denoted by N_S.

- The speed of the rotor relative to that of the rotating magnetic field produced by the stator is known as *absolute slip* or only *slip* (or sometimes slip speed). In other words, slip is the difference between the synchronous speed (N_S) and the actual speed (N) of the rotor. It is usually expressed as a fraction or percentage of the synchronous speed.

- Frequency of the rotor e.m.f. is proportional to the relative speed (i.e. $N_s - N$) of the rotating stator field to rotor.

- Under standstill condition, the induction motor acts as a simple polyphase static transformer, the stator being the primary and the short-circuited rotor being the secondary, the frequency on either side remaining the same (equal to supply frequency f).

- Under running condition, the rotor frequency is equal to the stator supply frequency multiplied by the slip and therefore it is sometimes referred to as slip frequency.

- The average torque produced by an induction motor depends not only on the flux per stator pole and rotor current but also on the rotor power factor.

- The torque produced by an induction motor is maximum when the reactance per phase of the rotor at any slip S (i.e. SX_2) is equal to the resistance per phase of the rotor (i.e. R_2).

- Maximum torque (also known as pull-out or break-down torque) is inversely proportional to the standstill rotor reactance (i.e. X_2). Further, the value of the maximum torque is independent of the rotor resistance, but the slip at which the maximum torque occurs is a function of the rotor resistance.

- Starting torque of an induction motor is proportional to the square of the applied voltage. Hence, it is very sensitive to any changes in the supply voltage.

- When the torque (T) is plotted against the slip (S) from S = 1 (standstill condition) to S = 0 (synchronous speed condition), the curve obtained is known as *toque-slip characteristic* of an induction motor.

- Motors with low resistance cage type rotors have inherently low starting torque.

- Induction motor starter mainly limits the starting current to a safe value without at the same time, reducing the starting torque to a value less than that required to start and accelerate the motor and the load. In addition to this, it also provides protection to the motor against overload, low voltage and single phasing.

- The reversal of rotation can be easily achieved in a three-phase induction motor simply by interchanging the supply connections to any two of the three terminals of the stator.

- The speed of the induction motor can be controlled by varying any one of the two basic factors, namely the synchronous speed of the motor and its slip. The synchronous speed of the motor can be changed by changing the supply frequency or the number of poles. The slip may be changed by changing the supply voltage, introducing extra resistance in the rotor circuit, injecting e.m.f. in the rotor circuit or by operating the motor in tandem or cascade with another induction motor.

3.33　IMPORTANT FORMULAE AT A GLANCE

- $$\text{Synchronous speed, } N_S = \frac{120\,f}{P} \text{ r.p.m.}$$

where　f = Frequency of the supply, in hertzs

　　　　P = Number of poles

- $$\text{Fractional slip, } S = \frac{N_S - N}{N_S}$$

$$\text{Percentage slip} = \frac{N_S - N}{N_S} \times 100$$

where　N_S = Synchronous speed of the motor, in r.p.m

　　　　N = Actual rotor speed, in r.p.m.

- $$\text{Actual rotor speed, } N = N_S\,(1 - S) \text{ r.p.m.}$$

where　N_S = Synchronous speed of the motor, in r.p.m.

　　　　S = Fractional slip

Standstill Condition :

- $$\text{Rotor frequency, } f_2 = f \text{ hertzs}$$

$$\text{Rotor current per phase, } I_2 = \frac{E_2}{Z_2} = \frac{E_2}{\sqrt{R_2^2 + X_2^2}} \text{ amperes}$$

$$\text{Rotor power factor, } \cos \phi_2 = \frac{R_2}{Z_2} = \frac{R_2}{\sqrt{R_2^2 + X_2^2}} \text{ lagging}$$

where　f = Supply frequency, in hertzs

　　　E_2 = Rotor e.m.f. per phase at standstill, in volts

　　　R_2 = Rotor resistance per phase, in ohms

　　　X_2 = Rotor reactance per phase at standstill, in ohms

　　　ϕ_2 = Phase difference between the rotor e.m.f. E_2 and rotor current I_2

Running Condition (At Slip = S) :

-
$$\text{Rotor frequency, } f_{2S} = S \cdot f \text{ hertzs}$$

$$\text{Rotor e.m.f. per phase, } E_{2S} = S \cdot E_2 \text{ volts}$$

$$\text{Rotor current per phase, } I_{2S} = \frac{E_{2S}}{Z_{2S}} = \frac{SE_2}{\sqrt{R_2^2 + (S \cdot X_2)^2}} \text{ amperes}$$

$$\text{Rotor power factor, } \cos \phi_{2S} = \frac{R_2}{Z_{2S}} = \frac{R_2}{\sqrt{R_2^2 + (S \cdot X_2)^2}} \text{ lagging}$$

where S = Fractional slip

f = Supply frequency, in hertz

E_2 = Rotor e.m.f. per phase at standstill, in volts

R_2 = Rotor resistance per phase, in ohms

X_2 = Rotor reactance per phase at standstill, in ohms

ϕ_{2S} = Phase difference between the rotor e.m.f. E_{2S} and rotor current I_{2S}

- Gross torque developed by an induction motor,

$$T = \frac{K S E_2^2 R_2}{R_2^2 + (SX_2)^2}$$

where K = Constant of proportionality

S = Fractional slip

E_2 = Rotor e.m.f. per phase at standstill, in volts

R_2 = Rotor resistance per phase, in ohms

X_2 = Rotor reactance per phase at standstill, in ohms

- Slip corresponding to the maximum torque,

$$S_m = \frac{R_2}{X_2}$$

where R_2 = Rotor resistance per phase, in ohms

X_2 = Rotor reactance per phase at standstill, in ohms

-
$$\text{Maximum torque, } T_m = \frac{KE_2^2}{2X_2}$$

where K = Constant of proportionality

E_2 = Rotor e.m.f. per phase at standstill, in volts

X_2 = Rotor reactance per phase at standstill, in ohms

-
$$\text{Starting torque, } T_{st} = \frac{K E_2^2 R_2}{R_2^2 + X_2^2}$$

where K = Constant of proportionality

E_2 = Rotor e.m.f. per phase at standstill, in volts

R_2 = Rotor resistance per phase, in ohms

X_2 = Rotor reactance per phase at standstill, in ohms

-
$$\frac{T_f}{T_m} = \frac{2S_m \cdot S_f}{S_m^2 + S_f^2}$$

where T_f = Full-load torque

T_m = Maximum torque

S_m = Slip corresponding to maximum torque

S_f = Slip at full load

- $$\frac{T_{st}}{T_m} = \frac{2S_m}{S_m^2 + 1}$$

where T_{st} = Starting torque

T_m = Maximum torque

S_m = Slip corresponding to maximum torque

- P_2 : (Rotor copper loss : P_m = 1 : S : (1 – S)

where P_2 = Rotor input, in watts

P_m = Total mechanical power developed by the rotor, in watts

S = Slip of the motor

- Torque developed by an induction motor

$$T = \frac{3}{2\pi n_s} \times \frac{SE_2^2 R_2}{R_2^2 + (SX_2)^2} \text{ newton-metres}$$

where n_s = Synchronous speed of the motor, in r.p.s.

S = Slip of the motor

E_2 = Rotor e.m.f. per phase at standstill, in volts

R_2 = Rotor resistance per phase, in ohms

X_2 = Rotor reactance per phase at standstill, in ohms

- Maximum torque developed by an induction motor,

$$T_m = \frac{3}{2\pi n_s} \times \frac{E_2^2}{2X_2} \text{ newton-metres}$$

where n_s = Synchronous speed of the motor, in r.p.s.

E_2 = Rotor e.m.f. per phase at standstill, in volts

X_2 = Rotor reactance per phase in standstill, in ohms

- Efficiency of an induction motor,

$$\eta = \frac{\text{Net power output at the shaft}}{\text{Power input to the motor}}$$

3.34 EXERCISES

3.34.1 Review Questions

1. What is a rotating magnetic field ? How does it differ from an alternating field ?
2. Prove mathematically or otherwise, how the application of a symmetrical 3-phase supply to the 3-phase stator winding of an induction motor gives rise to a rotating magnetic field.
3. State the essential conditions to be satisfied for obtaining a rotating magnetic field.
4. Explain the operating principle of a 3-phase induction motor.
5. Define the term slip of an induction motor. How does slip vary with the load ? Describe the commonly used methods of measuring slip.
6. How can the direction of rotation of a 3-phase induction motor be reversed ?
7. Describe in brief, the constructional features of a 3-phase squirrel-cage induction motor and a slip-ring induction motor. State relative merits and demerits of the rotor constructions used in these two types of motors.

8. Deduce the expressions for the rotor frequency, rotor e.m.f., rotor current and rotor power factor in the case of a 3-phase induction motor under :
   (i) Standstill condition   (ii) Running condition.

9. Derive from first principles, the generalized expression for gross torque developed by a three-phase induction motor.

10. Sketch a typical torque-slip characteristic of an induction motor. Explain its nature. What is the effect of increasing the rotor circuit resistance on this characteristic ?

11. Show that in a three-phase induction motor with negligible stator impedance, maximum torque is developed at slip $S = \dfrac{R_2}{X_2}$, where R_2 and X_2 are rotor resistance and standstill reactance respectively.

12. Show that in a three-phase induction motor, the ratio of full-load torque (T_f) to maximum torque (T_m) is given by

$$\frac{T_f}{T_m} = \frac{2\, S_m \cdot S_f}{S_m^2 + S_f^2}$$

   where, S_m = Slip corresponding to maximum torque, and
                 S_f = Full-load slip.

13. Show that for three-phase induction motor : $\dfrac{T_{st}}{T_m} = \dfrac{2S_m}{1 + S_m^2}$

   where S_m is the slip at which maximum torque occurs.

14. When the mechanical load on the induction motor shaft is increased, how does the motor meet with the new conditions ?

15. List the losses that take place in an induction motor. State the different factors on which these losses depend.

16. Draw the power-flow diagram of a 3-phase induction motor and comment on it.

17. Derive the relationship between the rotor input, rotor copper loss, total mechanical power developed by the rotor and slip in the case of an induction motor.

18. In the case of an induction motor, define the terms : Efficiency, Synchronous-watt.

19. Why starters are necessary for starting the induction motors ? Discuss the various types of starters used for starting three-phase induction motors.

20. Discuss briefly the different methods of speed control of three-phase induction motors.

21. Compare a squirrel-cage induction motor with a slip-ring induction motor with reference to construction, performance and applications.

3.34.2 Examples for Practice

1. A 3-phase, 400 V, 6-pole, 50 Hz induction motor runs at 940 r.p.m.
   Calculate : (i) Slip, (ii) Frequency of rotor e.m.f.

   (0.06 or 6%, 3 Hz)

2. The resistance and standstill reactance of a star-connected rotor of a 3-phase, 400 V, 50 Hz slip-ring induction motor are 0.02 Ω and 0.35 Ω per phase respectively. The stator of the motor is also star connected and the stator to rotor turns ratio is 2. Calculate :
   (a) Starting current per phase of the rotor and its power factor when the slip-rings are

short-circuited, the stator being connected to normal supply voltage, (b) Necessary external resistance per phase in the rotor circuit to limit the starting current drawn by the motor to 70 A, (c) Rotor phase current and power factor at 3% slip.

(362.32 A, 0.057, 0.82 Ω, 168.7 A, 0.89)

3. The power input to the rotor of a 440 V, 50 Hz, 3-phase, 6-pole induction motor is 60 kW. It is found that the rotor e.m.f. makes 90 complete cycles per minute. Calculate : (a) Slip, (b) Rotor speed, (c) Rotor copper loss per phase, (d) Total mechanical power developed, (e) The rotor resistance per phase if the rotor current is 60 A.

(0.03, 970 r.p.m., 600 W, 58.2 kW, 0.167 Ω)

4. The power input to a 230 V, 50 Hz, 4-pole, mesh-connected, 3-phase induction motor running at 1440 r.p.m. and power factor 0.8 is 10 kW. The stator losses are 0.6 kW, and friction and windage losses are 0.8 kW. Calculate : (a) The current in each stator phase, (b) Slip, (c) The efficiency of the motor.

(18.12 A, 0.04, 82.24 %)

5. A 3-phase, 6 pole, 500 V, 50 Hz, induction motor has a slip of 0.04 per unit while delivering its full-load output of 20 kW. If under this condition, stator copper loss is equal to rotor copper loss, stator iron loss is 20% higher than stator copper loss, and mechanical losses are one-half of the no-load losses, calculate the efficiency of a motor.

(84%)

6. A 3-phase, 6-pole, 50 Hz induction motor has the rotor resistance of 0.2 Ω per phase and develops the maximum torque at a speed of 875 r.p.m. Calculate its starting torque as a percentage of maximum torque.   (T_{st} = 24.62% of T_m)

7. A 400 V, 4-pole, 50 Hz, 3-phase, star-connected induction motor has a wound rotor of resistance 0.02 Ω per phase and standstill reactance of 0.3 Ω per phase. Full-load torque is obtained at a speed of 1455 r.p.m. Calculate : (i) the ratio of full-load torque to maximum torque, (ii) the speed at maximum torque and, (iii) the ratio of starting torque to full-load torque.   (0.7482, 1400 r.p.m., 0.1775)

8. A 4-pole, 50 Hz, 3-phase induction motor has wound rotor with a resistance and standstill reactance of 0.1 Ω and 1 Ω per phase respectively. Find the amount of resistance to be inserted in each rotor phase to obtain full-load torque at starting. The slip at full load is 4 per cent.   (0.3 Ω)

9. A 3-phase induction motor has a rotor resistance and standstill reactance of 0.05 Ω and 0.25 Ω per phase respectively. While working at normal voltage, its full-load slip is 4 percent. Calculate : (i) Percentage reduction in stator voltage to develop full-load torque at half of the full-load speed, (ii) Corresponding power factor.

(24.24%, 0.359 lagging)

10. A 3-phase, 8-pole, 50 Hz, slip-ring induction motor has the rotor circuit resistance of 0.02 Ω per phase and runs on full load at 720 r.p.m. If an extra resistance of 0.02 Ω per phase is added in the rotor circuit, what will be the new full-load speed ?

CHAPTER

FOUR

SPECIAL PURPOSE MOTORS

4.1 INTRODUCTION

Increased use of automatic control systems for both military and industrial purposes has caused a marked increase in the importance of the smaller rotating electrical machines and components. Basically, a *system* is an assembly of interacting components or parts which function together to perform a specific task. The system used for maintaining or altering, in accordance with a desired manner, any quantity of interest in a machine, mechanism or other equipment is called a *control system*. If the controlling action is made automatic, the system is said to be *automatic control system* or *feedback control system*.

System Classification : Depending upon the nature of the control action, control systems are classified as *open-loop systems* and *closed-loop systems*.

Open-Loop System : Any physical system having the control action independent of its output is called a *open-loop system*. Hence, in such a system, there is no automatic correction for variation in its output from the desired value. Fig. 4.1 represents an open-loop system with the help of a block diagram. Field or armature controlled d.c. shunt motor, the manual control of the generator field to produce the required output voltage are the few examples of an open-loop system. Though open-loop control is economically advantageous, it is inaccurate and quite unreliable.

Fig. 4.1 : General block diagram of an open-loop system

Closed-Loop System : A system having the control action dependent on its output is called a *closed-loop system*. Such a system can be represented by the general block diagram as shown in Fig. 4.2. It consists of three basic elements namely the feedback element, controller and controlled system (a plant or process). Feedback element provides the feedback signal which is a function of the output. Comparator (or error detector) compares this signal with reference input and generates the actuating signal thereby actuating the control elements. The control elements consisting of an amplifier and other elements in turn manipulate the actuating signal and produce control signal suitable for the drive used in the controlled system. Finally, conditions in the controlled system are altered in such a manner as to produce the desired output.

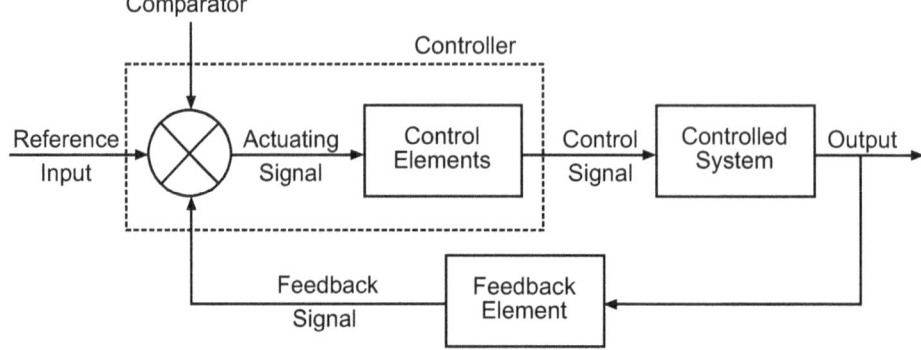

Fig. 4.2 : General block diagram of a closed-loop control system

Though costlier, closed-loop control, is more accurate and reliable. Hence, it is used for all modern sophisticated equipments.

This chapter is mainly devoted to a brief study of stepper motors and servo motors used as drive in the various control systems. Other types of motors commonly used in the applications requiring high starting torque and light weight are a.c. series motors, universal motors, brushless d.c. motors, linear induction motors and single-phase induction motors. These types of motors are also briefly studied in this chapter. Detailed study of all these motors is beyond the scope of this book.

4.2 STEPPER MOTORS

A *stepper motor* is an electrical motor which converts electrical input in the form of series of pulses into discrete angular movements, commonly called as *steps*. This conversion is on one to one basis i.e. the motor moves through one step for each input pulse.

4.3 TYPES OF STEPPER MOTORS

Following three types of stepper motors are in common use :

(i) Variable-reluctance motors, (ii) Permanent-magnet motors, (iii) Hybrid motors.

4.3.1 Variable-Reluctance Stepper Motors

Constructional Features : This is the most basic type of stepper motor. Fig. 4.3 schematically represents such a motor. The stator usually made of laminated silicon steel has six salient poles or teeth and is wound for three phases located 120° apart. The two coils wound around diametrically opposite poles and connected in series form a stator phase. The three phases thus formed are energised from a d.c. source in a specified sequence through an electronic switching device. The rotor is also normally made of silicon steel laminations and has four salient poles (or teeth) without any exciting winding as shown.

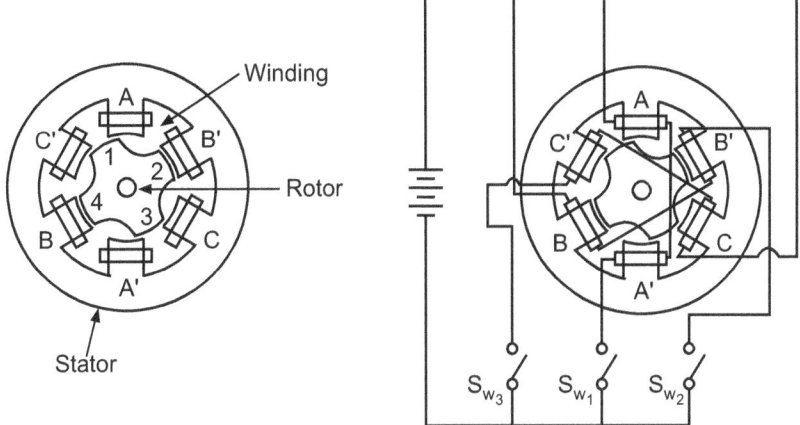

Fig. 4.3 : Schematic representations of a variable-reluctance stepper motor

(a) Cross-sectional view, (b) Winding arrangement

Operation : When phase A is excited (with coil A forming a North-pole and coil A' forming a South-pole), the rotor in its attempt to seek the position of minimum reluctance between the stator and rotor, is subjected to an electromagnetic torque and thereby rotates until its axis coincides with the axis of phase A (Fig. 4.4 a). If now, phase B is excited (with coil B forming a North-pole and coil B' forming a South-pole), disconnecting the supply to phase A, the rotor will move through 30° in an anticlockwise direction and take up the minimum reluctance position shown in Fig. 4.4 (b). Next, if phase C is energised while disconnecting the supply to phase B, the rotor will move through another 30° in an anticlockwise direction and take the position indicated in Fig. 4.4 (c). Thus, if three phases are successively excited in the above manner by supplying the voltage pulses, the motor will take one step of 30° with each voltage pulse and will require 12 pulses to make one complete revolution.

Further, it will be observed that if the three stator phases are supplied with voltage pulses adopting a switching sequences as A - C - B - A - ... , the rotor will move in the clockwise direction.

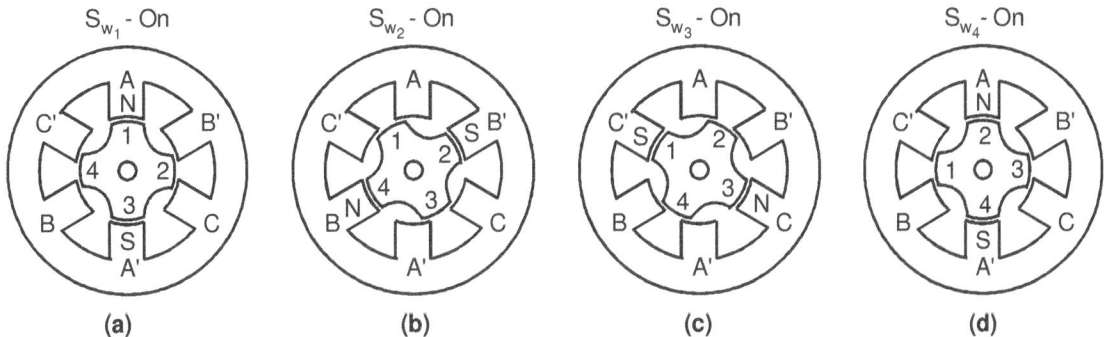

Fig. 4.4 : Step motions as switching sequence proceeds in a three-phase variable-reluctance stepper motor

Reduction in Step Angles : The 30° step angle obtained in the motor of Fig. 4.3 is not a small angle. It can be shown that if the rotor of the motor under consideration had 8 salient poles, the rotor would move 15° for each voltage pulse. Thus, with 8 rotor poles and stator wound for three phases, 24 steps would be required for making one complete revolution. A further reduction in step angle can be achieved either by increasing the number of poles of the stator and rotor or by adopting different constructional techniques such as :

(a) Using *reduction-gear* stepper motor.

(b) Using *multi-stack* or *cascade* type stepper motor.

(a) Using Reduction-Gear Stepper Motor : Fig. 4.5 shows the cross-sectional view of this type of variable-reluctance motor. The stator has 8 salient poles and is wound for 4 phases. Each salient pole of the stator has two teeth. The rotor has 18 equally spaced teeth. The general relationship between step angle θ_s, number of stator phases m and rotor teeth N_r is given by

$$\theta_s = \frac{360°}{m \cdot N_r} \qquad\qquad \dots (4.1)$$

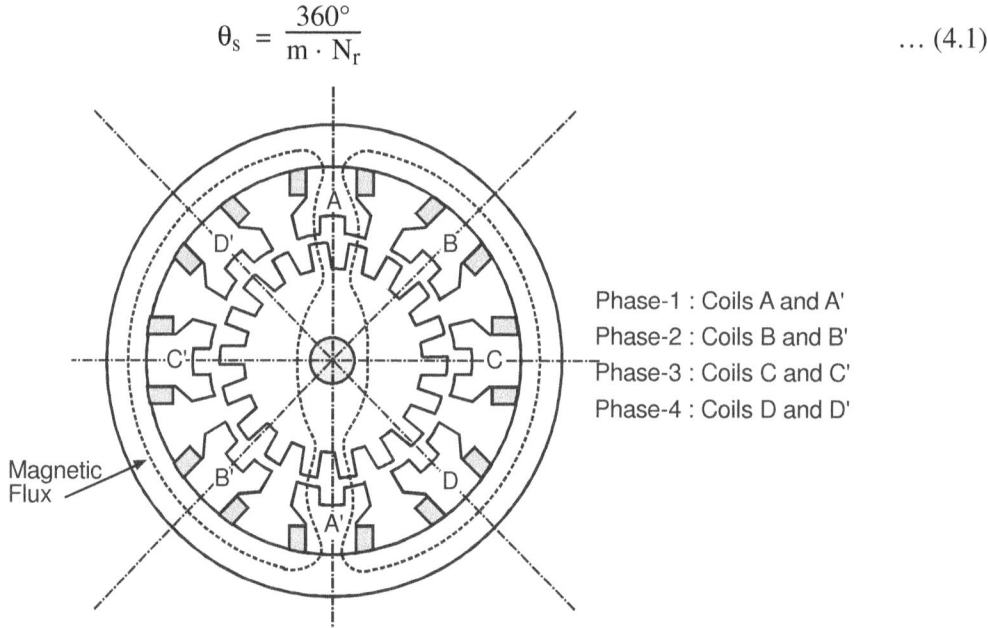

Phase-1 : Coils A and A'
Phase-2 : Coils B and B'
Phase-3 : Coils C and C'
Phase-4 : Coils D and D'

Fig. 4.5 : Reduction-gear stepper motor (with phase-1 excited)

Hence, with the type of construction shown in Fig. 4.5, motor will have step angle of 5%. By choosing different combinations of number of rotor teeth and/or stator phases, any desired step angle can be obtained.

(b) Using Multi-Stack or Cascade type Stepper Motor : The variable-reluctance motors shown in Figs. 4.3 and 4.5 are *single-stack type* motors. An outstanding feature of this type of motor is that three or four phases are arranged in a single stack i.e. in the same plane. Another type of variable-reluctance motors is the *multi-stack* type or *cascade* type. Fig. 4.6 shows a three stack (sometimes also called 3-phase) motor.

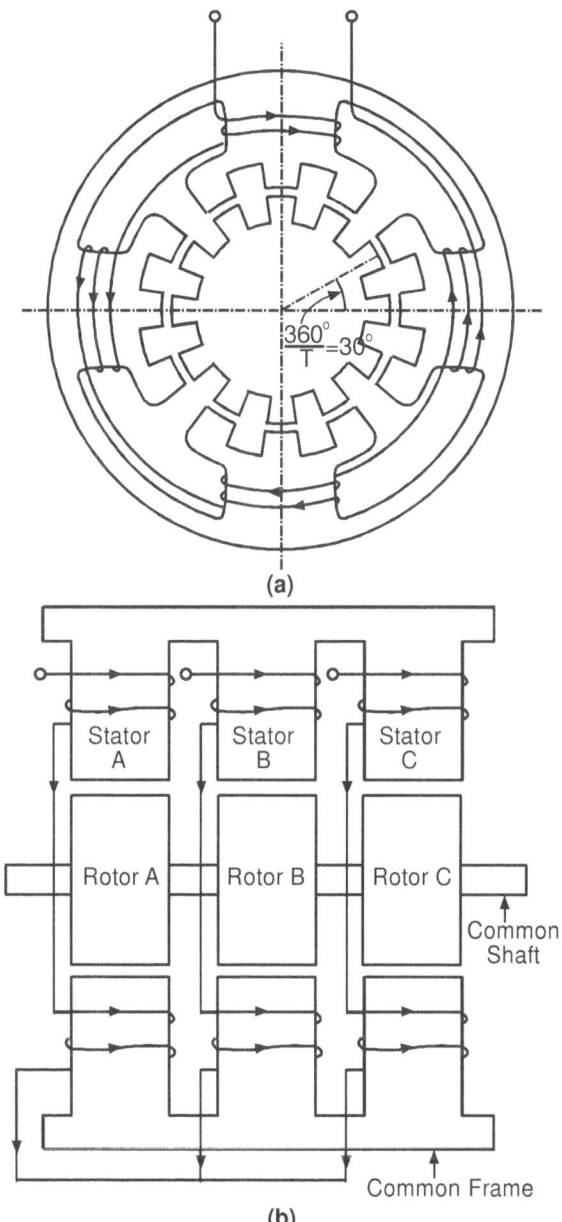

$$\frac{360^\circ}{T} = 30^\circ$$

(a)

(b)

**Fig. 4.6 : (a) End view of stator and rotor of one stack of a variable-reluctance motor,
(b) Longitudinal cross-sectional view of a 3-stack variable reluctance motor**

In this type of motor, both stator and rotor have a toothed structure with the same tooth pitch. The stators of the three stacks have a common frame while the rotors have a common shaft. The teeth of all the rotors are perfectly aligned with respect to each other, while the stator teeth of various stacks are arranged to have a progressive angular displacement of

$$\beta = \frac{360^\circ}{q \cdot T} \qquad \qquad \dots (4.2)$$

where, q = Number of stacks, T = Number of teeth

To begin with, let us assume that the winding of stator C is excited and the stator and rotor teeth in that stack are in alignment for minimum reluctance. Obviously, at this moment, the teeth of both the members of other stacks will be misaligned due to progressive angular displacement of β between the stator stacks. Now, if the excitation is switched from the winding of stator C to the winding of stator A, the rotor will move by angle β so that the stator and rotor teeth of that stack are aligned. Next, the excitation of the winding of stator B will cause further movement of the rotor through β. Thus, if the stator windings are excited in sequence A - B - C - A - ... , the rotor moves in steps of β in one direction. The direction of rotation will be reversed if the switching sequence is changed to A - C - B - A - ...

Typical step angles of stepper motors are 15°, 7.5°, 2° and 0.72°, the choice being dependent upon the angular resolution required for the particular application.

4.3.2 Permanent-Magnet Stepper Motors

● **Constructional Features :** Since, this type of a stepper motor employs a permanent magnet in its rotor construction, it is called a *permanent-magnet stepper motor*. Fig. 4.7 (a) shows a schematic representation of a basic four-phase, 2-pole, permanent-magnet stepper motor. The stator has four poles (or teeth) around which exciting coils are wound. The rotor is of cylindrical type and made of ferrite material which is permanently magnetized. The basic scheme for the driving circuit is shown in Fig. 4.7 (b).

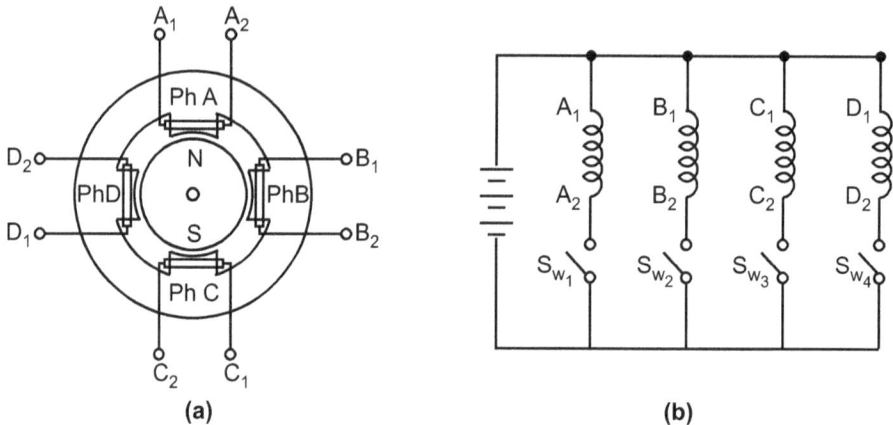

Fig. 4.7 : (a) Cross-sectional view of a four-phase, permanent-magnet stepper motor,
(b) Basic drive circuit

● **Operation :** If the phases are excited in sequence A - B - C - D - ... , due to electromagnetic torque developed by the interaction between the magnetic field set up by the exciting winding and the permanent magnet, the rotor will be driven in clockwise direction as shown in Fig. 4.8. In this case, the step angle will be obviously 90°.

● **Reduction in Step Angles :** The reduction in step angle can be achieved by increasing the number of stator phases and rotor poles. However, due to difficulties in construction, stepper motors with permanent magnet rotors cannot be manufactured in small size with large number of poles, hence small steps are not possible. As an alternative, *hybrid motors* operating under the combined principles of the permanent-magnet and variable-reluctance motors are widely employed for small step angles.

The special feature of the permanent-magnet stepper motor is that when on no load, the rotor comes to rest at a fixed position even if excitation ceases. Such positions are referred to as the *detent positions*. In general, these positions coincide with the rest positions (or equilibrium positions) under excited conditions, as long as only one phase is excited.

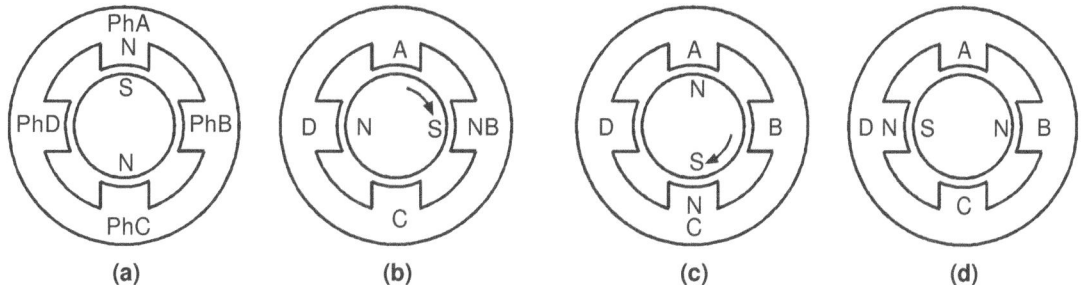

Fig. 4.8 : Steps in a four-phase, permanent-magnet stepper motor

There are two obvious disadvantages in the use of a permanent magnet in the construction of the motor :

(i) The magnet is costly.

(ii) The maximum flux density level and hence the torque developed by the motor are limited by the level of magnetic remanence of the magnet.

4.3.3 Hybrid Stepper Motors

These motors operating under the combined principles of the permanent-magnet and variable reluctance motors are widely employed for small step angles.

Constructional Features : Fig. 4.9 shows cross-sectional view of a typical hybrid motor. The stator core structure is similar to that of the variable reluctance motor. The stator is generally wound for two or four phases. Important feature of the hybrid motor is its rotor structure. The rotor consists of cylindrically shaped permanent magnet magnetized parallel to the shaft axis. Each pole of this magnet is covered with laminated silicon steel end caps. These end caps are uniformly toothed. The teeth on the two end caps are misaligned with respect to each other by a half tooth pitch.

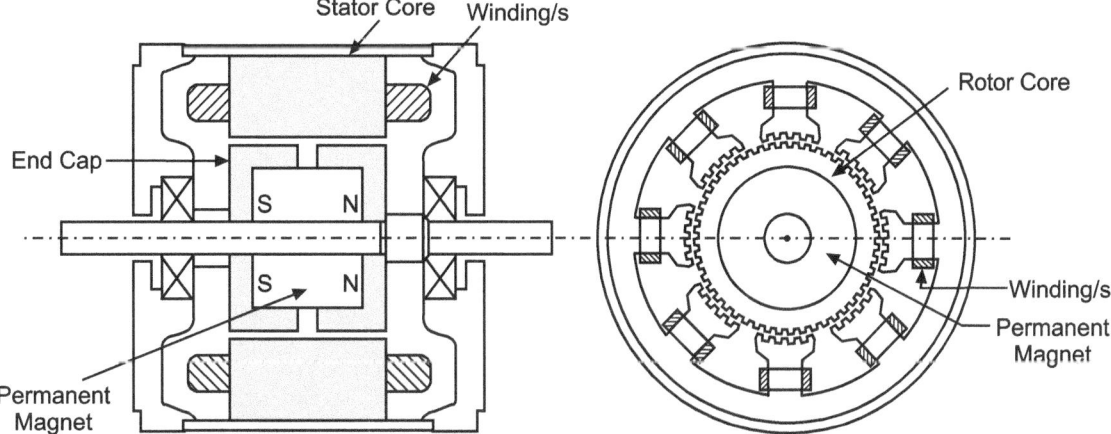

Fig. 4.9 : Construction of a typical hybrid stepper motor

Operation : The permanent magnet in the rotor structure of the motor produces a unipolar field, while the stator of the motor produces a distributed magnetic field due to the currents supplied to its windings. The torque is created by the interaction of these two magnetic fields in the toothed structure in the air-gaps. In this type of motor, by studying the resultant field pattern in the toothed structure in the air-gaps, it can be shown that no effective torque is generated by the stator magnetic field alone as in the variable reluctance motor but the permanent magnet in the rotor play an important role in creating the driving force. Thus the motor works on the combined principles of the permanent magnet and variable reluctance motors. Stepping action of the motor is caused by the sequential switching of supply to the phases of the motor.

In order to raise the torque, multi-stack hybrid motors are employed.

Advantages of Hybrid Stepper Motors :

Following are the main advantages of the hybrid stepper motors :

- Step angle as low as 1.8°.

- High torque per unit volume.

- Availability of some detent torque due to the presence of permanent magnet in the rotor structure.

4.4 STEPPER MOTOR CHARACTERISTICS

The characteristics of the stepper motors are classified as :

(i) Static characteristics, (ii) Dynamic characteristics.

These characteristics are discussed briefly in the following articles.

4.4.1 Static Characteristics

The characteristics relating to a motor under stationary condition are called its *static characteristics*. They include :

(i) Torque-displacement characteristics, (ii) Torque-current characteristics.

(i) Torque-Displacement Characteristics : If the stepper motor (without any load) is first kept stationary at a rest (or equilibrium) position with one of the stator phase windings excited in a specified mode and an external torque (T) is applied (say by means of a pulley, string and weight arrangement) to its shaft, some angular displacement (θ) will occur. The relation between this external torque (which is a measure of the corresponding opposing electromagnetic torque developed by the motor) and the angular displacement is called the *torque-displacement characteristic* of a motor. Fig. 4.10 shows the torque-displacement characteristic of a stepper motor.

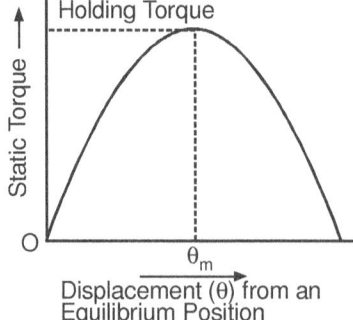

Fig. 4.10 : Torque-displacement characteristic of a stepper motor

From the figure, it will be observed that initially the static torque increases with the angular displacement reaching a maximum value at $\theta = \theta_m$ and then falls to zero. Thus, the nature of variation of torque versus displacement is almost sinusoidal. The maximum static torque which occurs at $\theta = \theta_m$ is termed the *holding torque.*

(ii) Torque-Current Characteristics : The maximum static torque that can be applied to the shaft of an excited motor without causing a continuous rotation (i.e. the holding torque of the motor) increases with the exciting current. The relation between this maximum static torque and the current in the specified excitation scheme is called the *torque-current characteristic.* Fig. 4.11 shows the torque-current characteristics for variable-reluctance and permanent-magnet stepper motors.

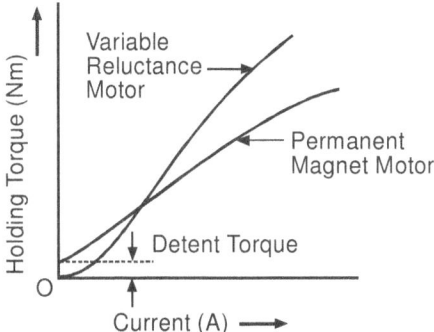

Fig. 4.11 : Torque-current characteristics of stepper motors

The torque in a variable-reluctance motor is zero when it is not excited. On excitation, initially it increases with the current parabolically and then the relation between the two becomes almost linear due to magnetic saturation. In a permanent-magnet motor, a static torque appears even if it is not excited. This specific torque is referred to as *detent torque.* Further, the static torque increases linearly with the current in such a motor.

Some Important Definitions :

*   **Holding Torque :** It is defined as the maximum static torque that can be applied to the shaft of an excited motor without causing a continuous rotation.

*   **Detent Torque :** This torque is defined as the maximum static torque that can be applied to the shaft of an unexcited motor without causing a continuous rotation. It appears only in permanent-magnet stepper motors.

4.4.2 Dynamic Characteristics

The characteristics relating to a motor under running condition or which is about to start, are called its *dynamic characteristics.* The dynamic characteristics of a stepper motor include :

(i) Pull-in torque characteristics,

(ii) Pull-out torque characteristics.

(i) Pull-in Torque Characteristics : *Pull-in torque* of a stepper motor for a given stepping rate measured in pulses per second (p.p.s.) is defined as the maximum load torque at which the motor can start and stop without losing its synchronism i.e. without missing any step. The pull-in torque versus stepping rate curve is called the *pull-in torque characteristic* or *starting characteristic* of a stepper motor. It is shown in Fig. 4.12.

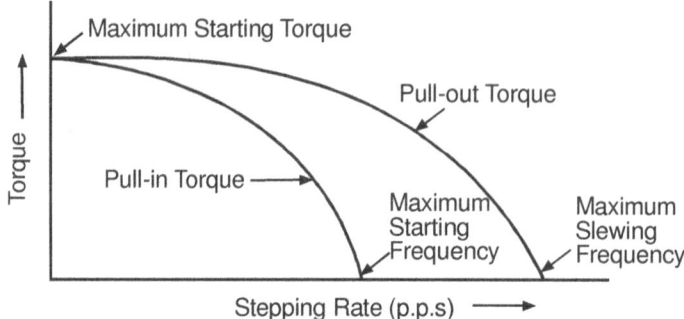

Fig. 4.12 : Torque versus stepping rate curves for a stepper motor

(ii) Pull-out Torque Characteristics : *Pull-out torque* of a stepper motor is defined as the maximum torque load that a motor can drive before losing synchronism at a specified stepping rate in pulses per second. The relation between the pull-out torque and stepping rate is called the *pull-out torque characteristic* or *slewing characteristic* of a stepper motor. (Fig. 4.12)

Some Important Definitions :

- **Maximum Starting Frequency Or Maximum Pull-in Rate :** It is defined as the maximum frequency (or stepping rate) at which the unloaded motor can start and stop without losing steps.

- **Maximum Slewing Frequency Or Maximum Pull-out Rate :** It is defined as the maximum frequency (or stepping rate) at which the unloaded motor can run without losing steps.

- **Maximum Starting Torque Or Maximum Pull-in Torque :** It is defined as the maximum load torque with which the motor can start and synchronize with the pulse train of a frequency as low as 10 p.p.s.

- **Slew Range :** It is the range of stepping rate in which the load velocity follows the pulse rate without losing a step, but the motor cannot start, stop or reverse on command.

4.5 DRIVE SYSTEMS OF STEPPER MOTORS

Generally, stepper motors are operated by electronic circuits, mostly on a d.c. power supply. The drive systems of stepper motors are classified into *open-loop* and *closed-loop* drives.

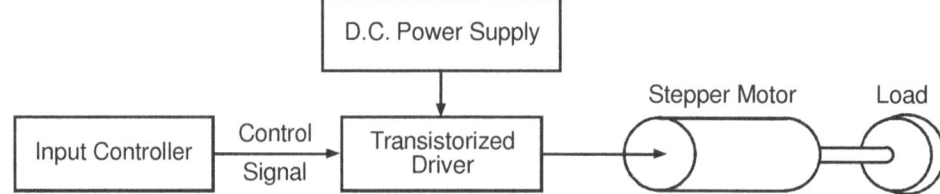

Fig. 4.13 : Modern driving system for a stepper motor in open-loop mode

Fig. 4.13 illustrates the block diagram of a modern driving system for a stepper motor in open-loop mode. The *input controller* consisting of integrated circuits or microprocessor performs various functions such as generating and governing the number of step command pulses and their timings, logic sequencing, etc. The output signals of the input controller are transmitted to the input terminals of a *power driver* by which the turning on/off of the motor winding is governed. The power driver may be called a *motor driver* or simply a *driver*.

The open-loop drive is an economically advantageous driving method and widely accepted in applications of speed and position controls. However, there are certain limitations of this type of drive. For instance, a stepper motor driven in the open-loop mode may fail to follow a pulse command when stepping rate is too high or the inertial load is too heavy. Moreover, the motor motion tends to be oscillatory.

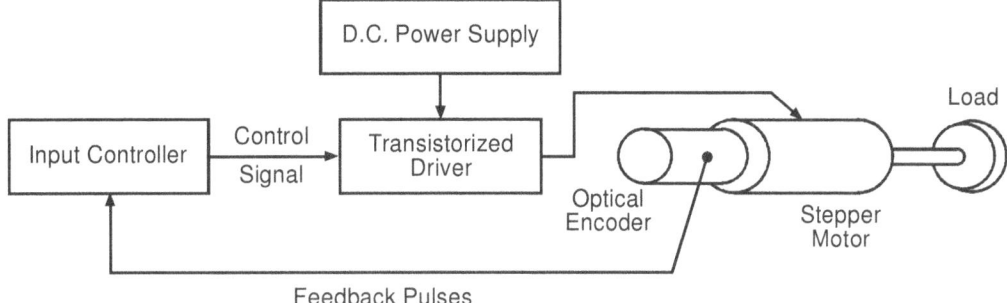

Fig. 4.14 : Block diagram of closed-loop drive for a stepper motor

The performance of a stepper motor can be improved to a great extent by employing position feedback and/or speed feedback to determine the proper phase(s) to be switched at proper timings. This type of control is called the *closed-loop drive*. For this, now-a-days, a rotor position sensor such as optical encoder usually coupled to the rotor shaft is used (Fig. 4.14). Closed-loop control not only prevents the step failure but it also gives motor motion much quicker and smoother.

The detailed discussion on different electronic components involved in the drive circuit for a stepper motor is beyond the scope of this book.

4.6 APPLICATIONS OF STEPPER MOTORS

The stepper motors are very widely used in computer peripherals such as serial printers, floppy disc drives, etc. Another big application field for stepper motors is found in the numerical controls of machine tools and workpieces. Other applications include process control systems, facsimiles, space-crafts, watches, semi-automatic wiring machines for printed circuit boards, etc.

4.7 SERVOMOTORS

A *servomechanism* in simple words, is an automatic control system (or a feedback system) which in response to an input signal carries out various functions such as moving a shaft to a certain position, moving a load in a particular direction at a particular speed, etc. *Servomotors* are used as drive in servomechanisms. These motors can be of electrical, hydraulic or pneumatic types. Discussion that follows, is restricted to electrical type of servomotors only.

4.8 SPECIAL FEATURES OF SERVOMOTORS

Servomotors which are specially designed and built primarily for use in feedback control systems, in general, have the following special features :

* Low inertia. For this, these motors normally have light-in-weight construction with large length-to-diameter ratio for rotors. Servomotors, therefore, are distinguished by relatively small-diameter rotors for their frame size.

- High speed of response. This results from high torque-to-weight ratio of a servomotor. Hence, these motors can be started, stopped and reversed very quickly.

- Linear torque-speed characteristic i.e. torque for any control voltage decreases at a definite uniform rate with speed.

- The output torque of the motor at any speed is roughly proportional to the applied control voltage. This is true more particularly in respect of starting torque (also called stall torque or locked-rotor torque).

- The motor operates stably i.e. it does not oscillate or overshoot.

4.9 TYPES OF SERVOMOTORS

Servomotors are classified as :

(i) A.C. servomotors,

(ii) D.C. servomotors.

Both these types of servomotors are briefly discussed in the following articles.

4.9.1 A.C. Servomotors

Most of the servomotors used in servomechanisms are a.c. and are of the two-phase induction motor type. Fig. 4.15 schematically represents a two-phase servomotor.

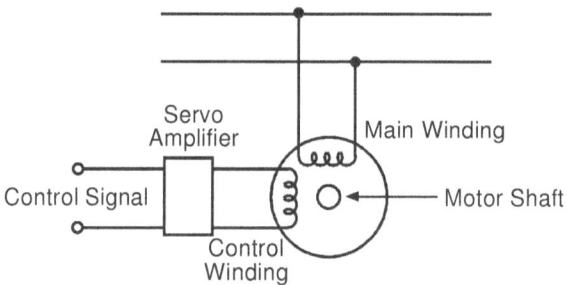

Fig. 4.15 : Schematic representation of a two-phase servomotor

Constructional Features : Similar to a normal induction motor, this motor comprises of a stator and a rotor.

Stator : The stator of this motor which has a laminated structure, is wound with its two windings placed 90 electrical degrees apart in space. One of the windings called the *main winding* (also called as *reference* or *fixed phase*) is excited from the constant-voltage supply source. The other winding called the *control winding* (or *control phase*) is energised by the variable control voltage which is 90 electrical degrees out of phase with respect to the voltage across the main winding. This control voltage is supplied from a servo amplifier.

Rotor : The rotor is usually of the squirrel cage type with small diameter and large length to keep the mechanical inertia as low as possible. It has high resistance in order to obtain a torque-speed characteristic as linear as possible. Inertia of the rotor is further reduced using drag-cup rotor (Fig. 4.16) for very low power applications. This type of rotor is a special form of squirrel-cage rotor in which conductors are in the form of a drag-cup made of a non-magnetic conducting material such as copper, aluminium, or an alloy. The slotted rotor laminations are replaced by a set of stationary ring shaped laminations that provide a low-reluctance path for the magnetic flux.

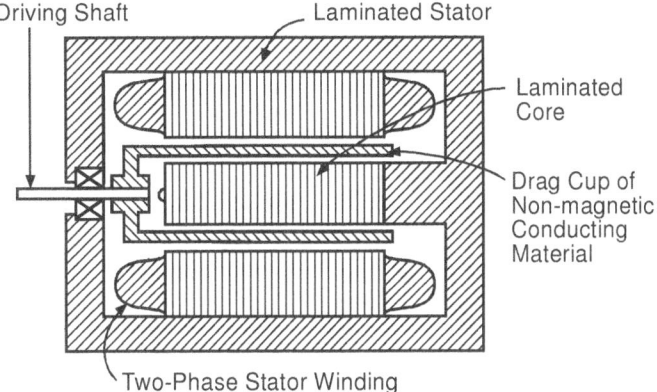

Fig. 4.16 : Cross-section of a two-phase servomotor with drag-cup type rotor

To minimize rotor kinetic energy, servomotors are wound with as many poles as possible so that they operate at low speeds. This also provides corresponding increase in torque. These motors have small air gaps to reduce magnetizing current and consequent losses.

Principle of Operation : Principle of operation of two-phase servomotor is same as that of an ordinary two-phase induction motor. When two voltages with time phase difference of 90 electrical degrees are applied to the two stator phases 90 electrical degrees apart in space, a rotating magnetic field is produced. As the field sweeps over the rotor, e.m.f.s and hence the currents are induced in the rotor conductors forming a closed path. The rotating magnetic field interacts with these currents producing a torque on the rotor in the direction of field rotation.

Characteristics of A.C. Servomotors :

• **Torque-Speed Characteristics :** We know that the general shape of the torque-speed characteristic of a two-phase induction motor depends largely on the value of rotor resistance (Fig. 4.17). Increasing the rotor resistance linearizes the speed-torque characteristics. Because of this, the rotor of the servomotor is built with high resistance so that its torque-speed characteristic is nearly linear. Fig. 4.18 (a) shows the torque-speed characteristics of a servomotor for various control voltages (V_1, V_2, V_3, V_4 etc.).

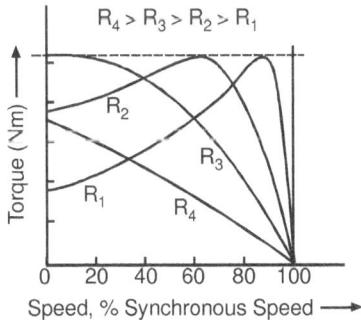

Fig. 4.17 : Variation of torque-speed characteristics of an induction motor with rotor resistance

It will be observed that the torque (particularly stall or starting torque) varies almost linearly with speed as well as with control voltage. The torque for any particular value of control voltage is high in the zero speed range and decreases as the motor speeds up. The drop in torque serves as a stabilising feature for the control system. Fig. 4.18 (b) shows the no-load speed and stall torque versus control voltage curves (with fixed-phase voltage constant).

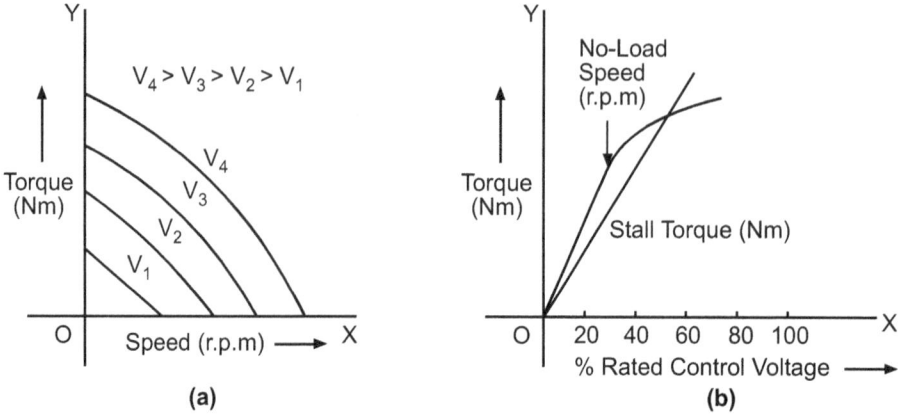

(a) | (b)

**Fig. 4.18 : (a) Typical torque-speed characteristics of a servomotor (a.c.)
for various control voltages,**

(b) No-load speed and stall-torque versus control-voltage curves

● **Other Performance Characteristics :** Fig. 4.19 illustrates some other performance characteristics of a typical a.c. servomotor.

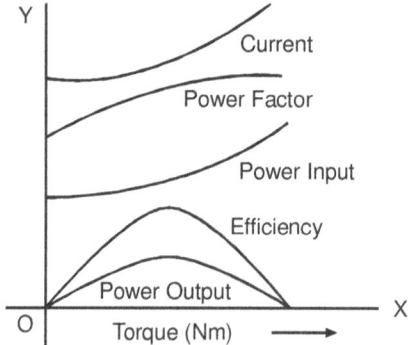

Fig. 4.19 : Performance characteristics of a typical a.c. servomotor

● **Applications :** Because of their ruggedness, light-in-weight construction, high torque-to-weight ratio, reliability, freedom from radio noise and the simplicity of their driving circuits, a.c. servomotors are widely used particularly in instrument servos, computers, tracking and guidance systems, self-balancing recorders, remote-positioning devices, process controllers, robotics, machine tools, special purpose machines and in other numerous applications where precision angular motion is required.

4.9.2　D.C. Servomotors

Except some minor differences in constructional features, a d.c. servomotor is essentially an ordinary d.c. motor (usually shunt). To meet the requirement of low inertia, d.c. servomotors are designed with large length-to-diameter ratio for their armatures. Further, to attain linear torque-speed characteristics, they are generally separately excited.

Classification of D.C. Servomotors : D.C. servomotors can be controlled by using either the current of the field winding or the armature current. Accordingly, they are classified as :

(i) Field controlled d.c. servomotors,

(ii) Armature controlled d.c. servomotors.

(i) Field Controlled D.C. Servomotors : In this type of motor, the output (i.e. control signal) from the servo-amplifier is applied to the field winding keeping the armature current constant (Fig. 4.20).

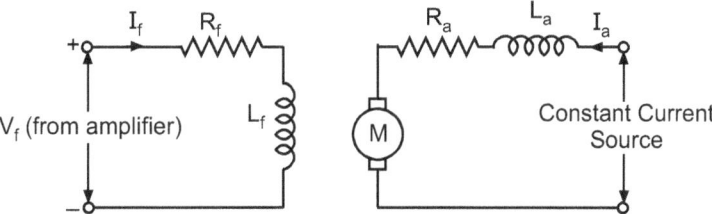

Fig. 4.20 : Field controlled d.c. servomotor

Even though the power required for field control is only a fraction of the power required for armature control, it is less common. This is because the time constant of the field circuit (L_f/R_f) is large compared with the armature circuit time constant (L_a/R_a). Consequently, field control does not give as rapid response as armature control. Also, the torque-speed characteristics under field control are not as linear as under armature control. Field control is normally used for small size motors as only a low power servo-amplifier is required, while the armature current which is not large can be supplied from an inexpensive constant-current source.

(ii) Armature Controlled D.C. Servomotors : Fig. 4.21 illustrates this type of d.c. servomotor. In this case, the output (i.e. control signal) of the servo-amplifier is applied to the armature winding and the field current is kept constant. As already mentioned earlier in comparison with field control, armature control gives nearly, ideal linear performance with rapid response. For large size motors, use of armature control becomes on the whole more economical.

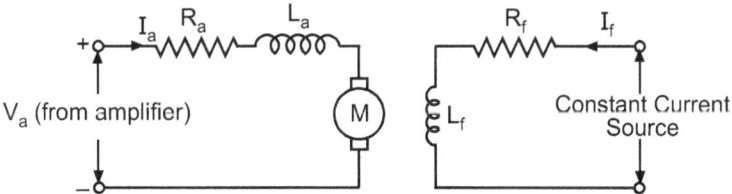

Fig. 4.21 : Armature controlled d.c. servomotor

The constant field in the above case can be supplied using a permanent magnet. Such a motor is then called the *permanent-magnet motor*. Since no field coils are required, these motors are rugged, relatively less expensive and have better efficiency and overall performance (with straighter speed-torque characteristics).

Characteristics of D.C. Servomotors :

● **Torque-Speed Characteristics :** Torque-speed characteristics of d.c. servomotors are quite similar to those for a.c. servomotors (Fig. 4.22). Comments made earlier regarding starting torque and stability consideration in respect of torque-speed characteristics of a.c. servomotors are therefore equally applicable to torque-speed characteristics of d.c. servomotors.

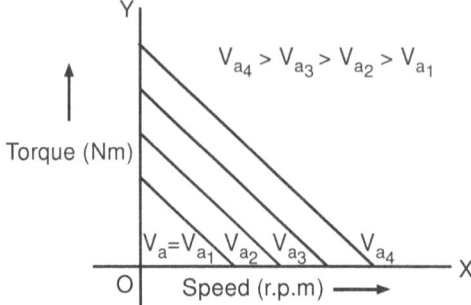

Fig. 4.22 : Family of torque-speed curves for an armature controlled d.c. servomotor with varying control voltage

• **Other Performance Characteristics :** Fig. 4.23 shows some other performance characteristics of a typical d.c. servomotor.

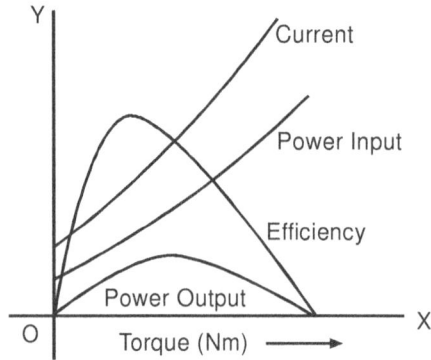

Fig. 4.23 : Performance characteristics of a typical d.c. servomotor

• **Applications of D.C. Servomotors :** The inertia of d.c. servomotor tends to be larger than that of squirrel-cage a.c. motors. This and added frictional drag of brushes are the main factors which discourage their use in instrument servos. In small sizes, d.c. servomotors are primarily used in air-craft control systems where weight and space limitations require motors to deliver maximum power per unit volume. They are often used for intermittent duty or where unusually high starting torques are required e.g. for fan and blower drives. They may also be used for electromechanical actuators, process controllers, programming devices, robotics, machine tools, special purpose machines and for a host of other applications of a similar nature.

4.10 SINGLE-PHASE A.C. SERIES MOTORS

Operation of a D.C. Series Motor on A.C. Supply : If an ordinary d.c. series motor is connected to an a.c. supply, because of simultaneous reversal of field and armature currents, it will develop a unidirectional torque and as a result of this, its armature will rotate. However, performance of such a motor when operated on a.c. supply will not be satisfactory, mainly for the following reasons :

• Excessive eddy currents induced in the solid parts like yoke and pole cores due to alternating flux would cause overheating of the motor and a distinct lowering of its efficiency.

- Relatively large reactance of field circuit will reduce the power factor and output to such low values as to make the motor impractical.

- E.M.F. induced by transformer action (called as *transformer e.m.f.*) in the short circuited armature coils during their commutation period* would cause vicious sparking at the brushes.

Design Considerations for an A.C. Series Motor : For operating the d.c. series motor satisfactorily on a.c. supply, following modifications in the design are generally incorporated :

- Eddy-current loss is minimized by laminating the entire field structure.

- The field flux cannot be reduced or neutralized drastically for the purpose of improving the power factor, for its presence is essential to produce the required torque. Still, it is necessary to reduce the reactance of the field winding if the power factor is to be reasonably high. Hence, to reduce the reactance of the field winding, if possible, a low-frequency (as low as $16\frac{2}{3}$, 25 Hz) supply is used ($\because X_L = 2\pi fL$). Further, inductance of the field winding is also made as low as is practical. For this, the field is wound with fewer turns than an equivalent d.c. motor ($\because L = N^2/S$). But this change reduces the field flux for a given current. To some extent, this reduction in flux is compensated by minimizing the reluctance (S) of the magnetic circuit ($\because \phi = \text{m.m.f.}/S$). This is achieved by operating the iron at low flux densities (using increased pole area) and, therefore, at high permeabilities and by using a very short air gap.

- In order to obtain the required torque with low field flux, number of armature coils is increased. Naturally, the armature of an a.c. series motor becomes unusually larger than the corresponding d.c. series motor. Increased number of armature coils increases the armature reaction**. This creates commutation troubles and results in high armature reactance. To neutralize the increased armature reaction, a compensating winding is embedded in the pole faces. If this compensating winding is connected in series with the armature as shown in Fig. 4.24 (a), the motor is said to be *conductively compensated*. For the motors which are to be operated on a.c. as well as d.c. supply system, conductive compensation is necessary. If the compensating winding is short-circuited on itself as shown in Fig. 4.24 (b), the motor is said to be *inductively compensated*. In this case, the compensating winding acts as a short-circuited secondary of a transformer, the armature being the primary. Hence, ampere-turns of the compensating winding nearly neutralize the ampere-turns of the armature.

---

*   *The brief period during which reversal of current takes place in the armature coil when its active sides pass from the influence of one pole to the other is called **commutation period**. The coil remains short circuited by a brush during this period. This entire process is called **commutation**.*

** *The effect of armature flux on the flux produced by the main poles of the machine is called **armature reaction**.*

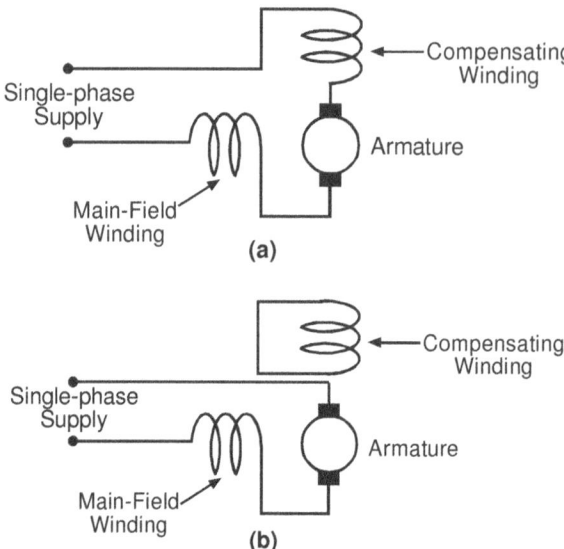

Fig. 4.24 : (a) Conductively compensated single-phase a.c. series motor,

(b) Inductively compensated single-phase a.c. series motor

• E.M.F. induced by transformer action in the short-circuited armature coil undergoing commutation (Fig. 4.25 a) is reduced by taking following measures :

(i) Preferably single-turn armature coils are used. This necessitates a large number of segments and correspondingly large commutator.

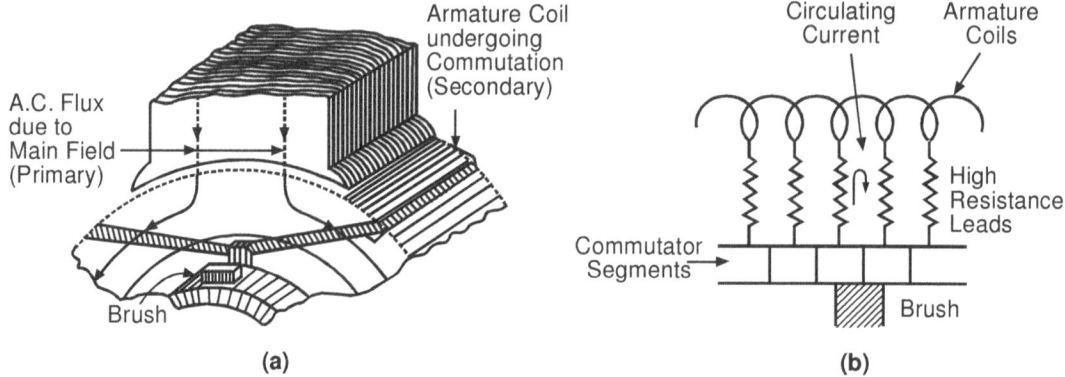

Fig. 4.25 : (a) Transformer e.m.f. in the armature coil undergoing commutation,

(b) Resistance leads to improve commutation

(ii) Flux per pole is made as small as possible. Hence, for having sufficient flux to develop the required torque, the number of poles is increased.

(iii) Frequency of the supply is reduced.

The large short-circuit current caused by transformer e.m.f. in the armature coil undergoing commutation ultimately results into severe sparking at the brushes. This current may be reduced by inserting resistance leads between the armature coils and the commutator segments as illustrated in Fig. 4.25 (b). However, by providing interpoles* (Fig. 4.26), use of such resistance leads can be completely eliminated.

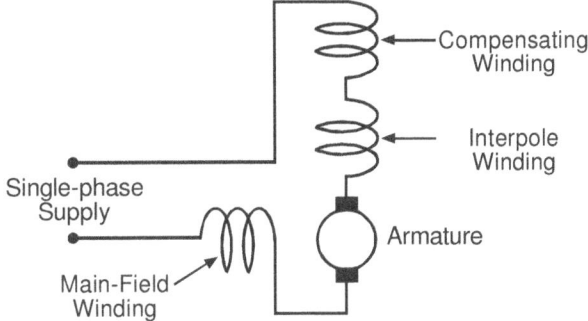

Fig. 4.26 : Series motor with interpoles

- **Performance Characteristics :** Operating characteristics of an a.c. series motor are similar to those of a d.c. series motor as illustrated in Figs. 4.27 (a) and (b). Torque varies nearly as square of the armature current and speed varies inversely as the armature current. The starting torque of such a motor is generally 3 to 4 times its full-load torque. The speed of this motor attains dangerously high value on no load or light load. Hence, it is always used with some load on it.

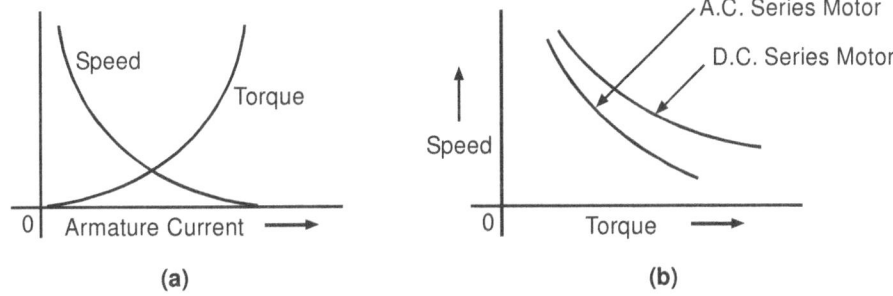

Fig. 4.27 : (a) Torque versus armature current and speed versus armature current characteristics of a.c. series motor,

(b) Speed-torque characteristics of a.c. and. d.c. series motors

- **Reversal of Rotation :** The motor of this type may be reversed by reversing the connections to either the field or the armature winding. When interpoles and series connected compensating winding are used, these should be treated as part of the armature.

- **Applications :** Because of high starting torque, large capacity single-phase a.c. series motors are commonly employed in traction, hoists and similar other services.

---

* *These are the small auxiliary poles placed mid-way between the main poles to improve the performance of the machine. The exciting coils of the interpoles are connected in series with the armature.*

4.11 UNIVERSAL MOTORS

These are small capacity series motors designed to operate on either direct current or single-phase alternating current supply of approximately the same voltage, with nearly similar operating characteristics. Normally the frequency of the a.c. supply used is upto 50 Hz.

- **Constructional Features :** General constructional features of single-phase a.c. series motors have already been discussed in detail in the previous section. Two types of universal motors are in use, namely, *non-compensated* and *compensated*. The non-compensated motor is usually built with concentrated or salient poles (Fig. 4.28). On the other hand, compensated motor has distributed field windings (main field and compensating winding). Hence, the stator of such a motor resembles to that of a split-phase induction motor[*]. Both these types of motors have a wound armature similar to that of a small d.c. motor. Fig. 4.29 shows the connection diagrams for these motors.

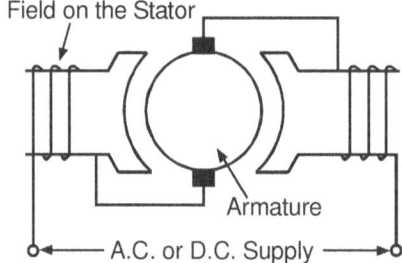

Fig. 4.28 : Cross-sectional view of a non-compensated type universal motor

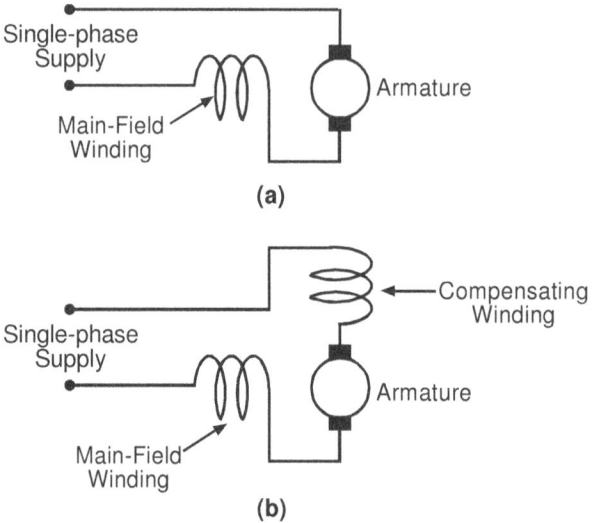

Fig. 4.29 : Connection diagram of an universal motor

(a) Non-compensated type, (b) Compensated type

---

[*]   *Refer to Section 4.15.1.*

• **Speed-Torque Characteristics :** Speed-torque characteristics of a non-compensated universal motor, for both a.c. and d.c. operations are shown in Fig. 4.30 (a). Similarly, Fig. 4.30 (b) shows the speed-torque characteristics of a compensated universal motor. From these figures, it will be observed that the compensated motor has better *universal characteristics* i.e. it has nearly the same operating characteristics on d.c. as well as on a.c. supply. Depending upon their ratings, universal motors are usually designed for full-load operating speeds ranging between 3000 to 20000 r.p.m. and if necessary, are provided with in built speed reduction gears for low speed applications. Normally, the friction and windage losses in small universal motors are sufficient to limit their no-load speeds to a safe value.

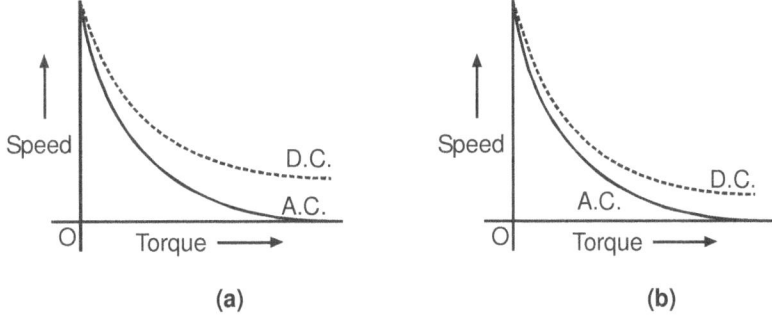

Fig. 4.30 : (a) Speed-torque characteristics of a non-compensated universal motor, (b) Speed-torque characteristics of a compensated universal motor

• **Reversal of Rotation :** As already mentioned previously for single-phase series motors, for universal motors also, reversal can be achieved by reversing the connections to either the field or the armature winding.

• **Applications :** Even though compensated type universal motors have more superior characteristics, non-compensated motors are in more general use, particularly for small power applications. This is because they are less expensive and simpler in construction. Being high-speed motors, universal motors are smaller in size than other types for a given output. Hence, these motors are used where light weight is important. High starting torque is also their outstanding feature. The usual applications of the universal motors are for domestic appliances like vacuum cleaners, food mixers, coffee grinders, sewing machines, hair driers, electric shavers, etc. Their other applications include blowers, mechanical computing machines, portable tools like drilling machines and other small power drives.

4.12 BRUSHLESS D.C. MOTORS

With the advent of variable frequency inverters, it has become possible to free the synchronous motors[*] from the fixed-speed constraint imposed by mains-frequency operation. Inverter-fed self-controlled permanent magnet synchronous motor is one such motor. There being

---

[*]   *Similar to d.c. generator, an alternator (i.e. a.c. generator) is a reversible machine. When supplied with a.c., it can work as a motor. The alternator operated in this fashion is known as a synchronous motor. It always runs at a fixed speed called synchronous speed determined by the number of poles and line frequency ($N_S = 120\ f/P$).*

overall similarity between this motor (which is basically an a.c. motor) and conventional d.c. motor except the requirement of brushes and the commutator, it is named as *brushless or commutatorless d.c. motor.*

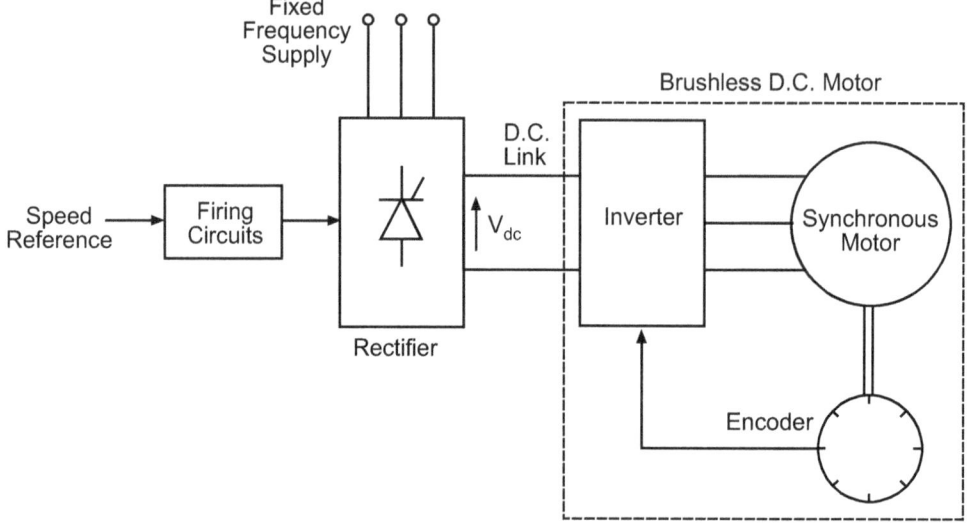

Fig. 4.31 : Brushless d.c. motor drive

- **Constructional Features :** Fig. 4.31 illustrates this type of motor with the help of a simple block diagram. In conventional d.c motor, field magnets are placed on the stator and armature winding is placed on the rotor. However, brushless d.c. motor has a polyphase winding (armature) on the stator and permanent magnets on the rotor. The motor is fed through a rectifier, d.c. link and inverter. Either an optical or Hall element sensor (encoder) is suitably mounted on the rotor shaft.

- **Principle of Operation :** The drive functions similar to d.c. motor. In a d.c. motor, we know that the mechanical commutator reverses the direction of the current in each (rotating) armature coil at the appropriate point such that, regardless of speed, the current under each (stationary) field pole is always in the right direction to produce the desired unidirectional torque. In a brushless d.c. motor, the roles of stator and rotor are reversed i.e. in the case of this motor, the field is rotating and the armature winding consisting of three phases is stationary. The timing and direction of current in each phase is governed by the inverter switching which in turn is determined by the rotor position-dependent signals obtained from an encoder mounted on the rotor shaft. Hence, regardless of speed, the torque is always in the right direction. Thus, the combination of the rotor position sensor and inverter performs effectively the same function as the commutator in a conventional d.c. motor. Hence, such a motor is also sometimes referred to as an *electronically commutated motor.*

- **Operating Characteristics :** Speed-torque characteristics of brushless d.c. motor are similar to the conventional d.c. motor.

- **Speed Control :** The speed of brushless d.c. motor can be controlled by controlling the d.c. link voltage to the inverter. The d.c. link is usually provided by a controlled rectifier. Hence, the motor speed can be controlled by varying the input converter firing angle as illustrated in Fig. 4.31.

• **Applications :** Due to absence of brushes and commutator, brushless d.c. motors require practically no maintenance, have long life, high reliability, high efficiency (exceeding 75%), low inertia and friction, and low radio frequency interference and noise. Due to low inertia and friction, these motors have a faster acceleration and can be run at much higher speeds (upto 30,000 r.p.m. or even higher). Armature windings being on the stator, cooling is more effective. However, as compared to conventional d.c. motors, these motors have low starting torque and high cost. But now-a-days, as inverter costs have fallen, lower power drives using brushless d.c. motors are becoming more and more attractive especially where very high speeds are required.

The brushless d.c. motors are used in numerous applications which include turn table drives in record players, tape drives for video recorders, spindle drives in hard disc drives for computers, lower cost and low power drives in computer peripherals, instruments and control systems. They are also used in the fields of aerospace (e.g. gyroscope motors) and biomedical (e.g. in cryogenic coolers and artificial heart pumps).

4.13 LINEAR INDUCTION MOTORS

Linear induction motor is essentially a special type of a polyphase induction motor with its stator (primary) and rotor (secondary) cut by a radial plane and then unrolled (Figs. 4.32 a and b) so that instead of producing a torque (causing rotation), it produces a linear force (causing linear motion) along its length.

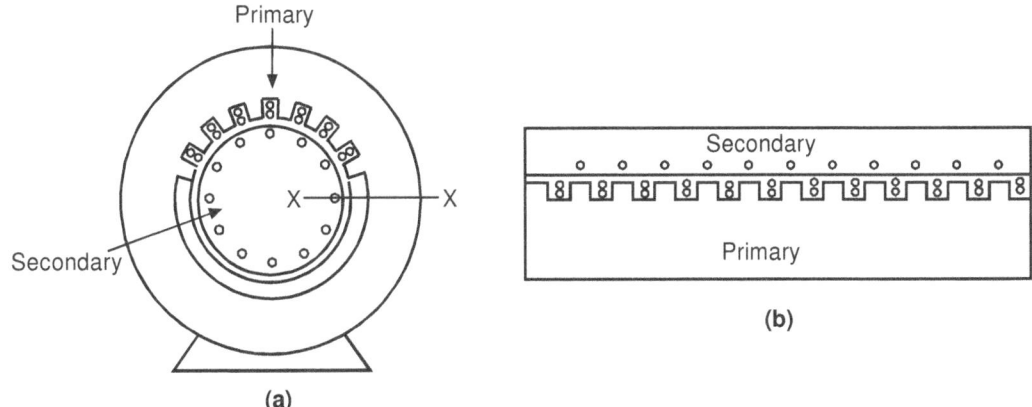

Fig. 4.32 : (a) A conventional cage-type three-phase induction motor in cylindrical form,
(b) Primitive linear induction motor

In principle, there are as many different types of linear electric motors as there are rotary electric machines. However, induction type linear electric motors are the most popular one.

• **Constructional Features :** In its simplest form, a linear induction motor consists of a field system having a three-phase distributed primary winding housed in slots. The field system may have one primary or two primaries as shown in Figs. 4.33 (a) and (b) or (c) and (d) respectively. Linear induction motor having one primary is called *single-sided linear induction motor (SLIM)* whereas linear induction motor having two primaries is known as a *double-sided linear induction motor (DSLIM)*. The secondary of a linear induction motor is normally in the form of a conducting plate made of either copper or aluminium. In single-sided linear induction motor, a ferromagnetic plate is generally placed on the other side of the conducting plate to provide a low reluctance path for the main flux.

Depending on the use, the linear induction motor may have a short primary (Figs. 4.33 a and b) or a short secondary (Figs. 4.33 c and d).

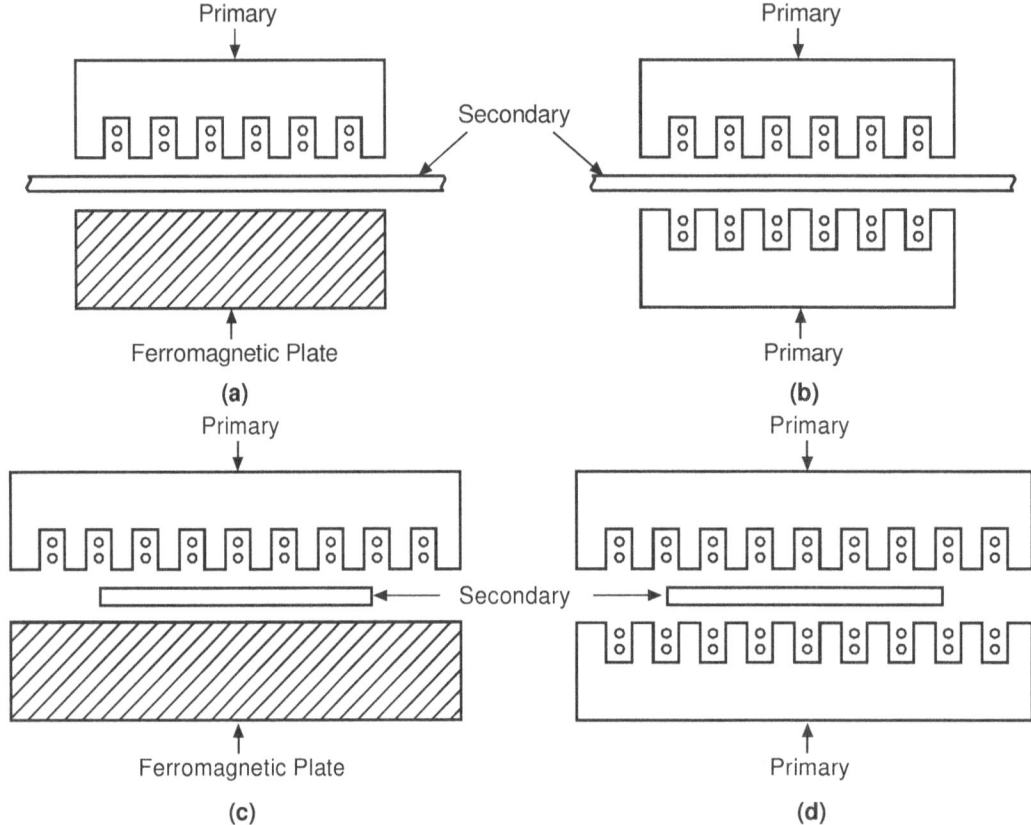

Fig. 4.33 : Diagrammatic representation of
(a) Single-sided linear induction motor with short primary
(b) Double-sided linear induction motor with short primary
(c) Single-sided linear induction motor with short secondary
(d) Double-sided linear induction motor with short secondary

Unlike a polyphase induction motor, a linear induction motor may have moving primary with fixed secondary or moving secondary with fixed primary.

• **Principle of Operation :** When the three-phase primary winding of a linear induction motor is excited from a balanced three-phase supply, a linearly travelling field is produced. The velocity (linear) of this field is given by

$$v_S = 2f \text{ (pole-pitch)} = f\lambda \text{ metres/s} \qquad \dots (4.3)$$

where λ is the wavelength of the travelling field and is equal to two pole pitches.

This linear travelling field induces eddy currents in the secondary. The interaction between the primary and secondary fields results in the production of the linear force, thus forcing the secondary (if movable) away from the primary and carrying it along in the direction of the linearly travelling magnetic field. As in the case of a conventional induction motor, the velocity (linear) with which the secondary moves is less than v_S and is given by

$$v = v_S (1 - S) \text{ metres/s} \qquad \dots (4.4)$$

- **Thrust-Speed Characteristics :** In the case of a linear induction motor, a force producing the linear motion is called *thrust*. The thrust-speed characteristic of a linear induction motor is as shown in Fig. 4.34. It is similar to the torque-speed characteristic of a conventional induction motor.

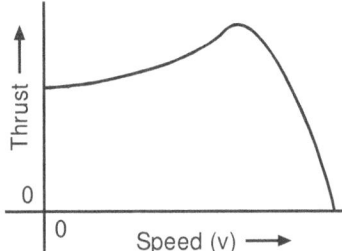

Fig. 4.34 : Thrust-speed characteristic of a linear induction motor

- **Applications :** There are numerous applications of the linear induction motors. Some of them are as listed below :

Aircraft launch system, weaponry, roller coasters, shuttle propulsion, stop valves, induction stirrers for molten metals, automatic sliding doors in electric trains, conveyors, haulers, electromagnetic pumps, travelling cranes, high-speed traction, accelerating cars and lorries for indoor crash tests, actuators for h.v. circuit breakers, impact extruders for metals, etc.

4.14 SINGLE-PHASE INDUCTION MOTORS

A single-phase induction motor is similar in construction to the three-phase squirrel-cage induction motor except that the stator has distributed single-phase winding. Fig. 4.35 schematically represents 2-pole, single-phase induction motor.

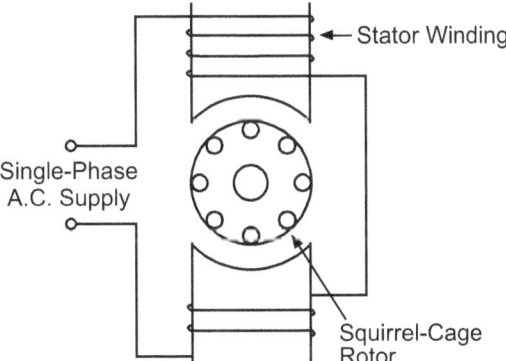

Fig. 4.35 : Schematic representation of a 2-pole, single-phase induction motor

- **Operating Principle :** When a single-phase stator winding is connected to a source of alternating voltage, the current flowing through this winding produces a resultant field which alternates along the axis of the winding. Such a field, varying or pulsating sinusoidally with the time along a fixed space axis while acting on a stationary cage rotor cannot produce its rotation. To understand this, consider a single-phase induction motor shown in Fig. 4.36 with the rotor at rest. When single-phase supply is given to the stator winding, current flowing through this winding produces an alternating flux ϕ_s acting along the axis of the winding. This alternating field induces an e.m.f. in the rotor conductors by transformer action. The rotor circuit being closed, this e.m.f. called *transformer e.m.f.* sets up current through the rotor conductors.

If it is assumed that the stator flux ϕ_s is acting in the downward direction and increasing positively at a particular instant as shown in Fig. 4.36, then the current in the rotor conductors must flow in such a direction as to oppose this flux ϕ_s (Lenz's law). The direction of the current in the rotor conductors, therefore, will be as shown in Fig. 4.36. The application of Fleming's left hand rule shows that under this condition, the force experienced by the conductors on the left side of the rotor is just opposite to that experienced by the conductors on the right side of the rotor. The rotor will, therefore, experience no torque and the motor thus develops no inherent starting torque. As a result, it is not self-starting.

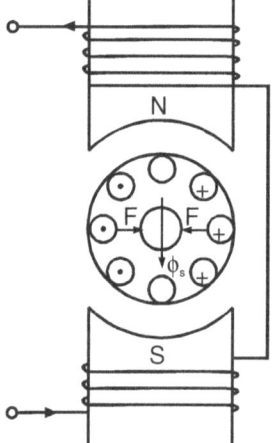

Fig. 4.36 : Transformer e.m.fs in the rotor of a single-phase induction motor

However, it has been observed that if the rotor is given an initial rotation in any direction, the single-phase induction motor develops torque and the rotor continues to pick up speed in that particular direction. This typical behaviour of a single-phase induction motor can be explained with the help of the following theory :

• **Double Revolving Field Theory :** As already mentioned previously, when a single-phase stator winding is connected to a source of alternating voltage, the current flowing through this winding produces a field which varies sinusoidally with time along a fixed space axis. According to double revolving field theory, such a flux can be resolved into two equal sinusoidal fields rotating in opposite directions at synchronous speeds*, each having a maximum value equal to one half that of the given field as illustrated in Fig. 4.37 (a).

---

*   *Synchronous speed, $N_S = \dfrac{120\,f}{P}$ r.p.m.*

   where f = Supply frequency, in Hz, P = Number of poles.

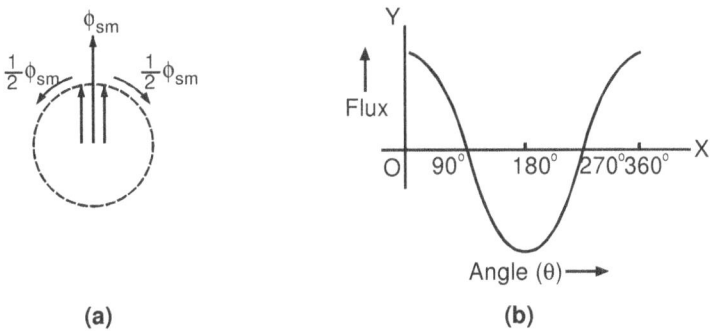

(a)   (b)

Fig. 4.37 : (a) Single-phase alternating stator field represented by two oppositely rotating fields, (b) Resultant of two oppositely rotating fields

Here, ϕ_{sm} is assumed to be the maximum value of the stator field, ϕ_s. From Fig. 4.37 (b), it can be easily verified that the resultant of these two component fields gives the original alternating stator field. Each of the component rotating fields of the stator field produces a torque in a manner similar to that described for three-phase induction motor in Section 3.3, but these torques are in opposite directions. The total torque developed by the motor is given by the resultant of these two torques. The complete torque-speed curves (extended into the other quadrant) for the two oppositely rotating component fields considered independently are shown with the help of dotted lines in Fig. 4.38. The resultant torque-speed curve (solid line) given by the sum of the two component curves is also shown in the figure. From this resultant torque-speed curve, it can be observed that at starting when the rotor is at standstill, the torques developed by two component rotating fields are exactly equal and opposite. Therefore, the torque developed by the motor is zero. Consequently, the single-phase induction motor is not self-starting. However, if the rotor is given an initial rotation in any direction, the net torque developed causes the rotor to continue to rotate in the direction in which it is initially rotated and the motor gives the same type of performance as three-phase induction motor.

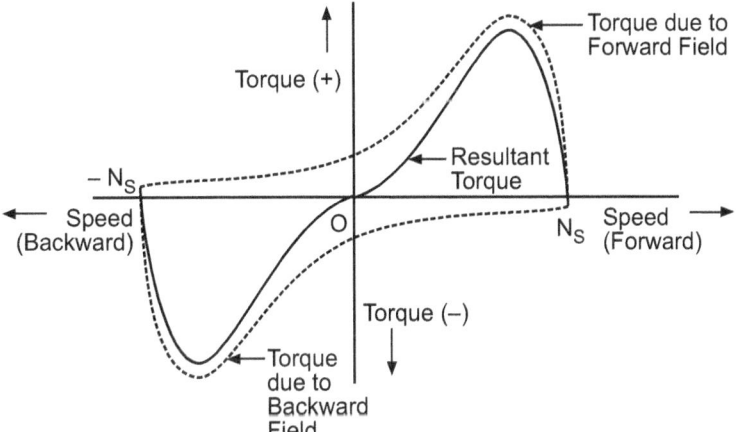

Fig. 4.38 : Torque-speed curves for the two oppositely rotating component fields and resultant torque-speed curve in a single-phase induction motor

4.15 TYPES OF SINGLE-PHASE INDUCTION MOTORS

We have seen that a single-phase induction motor has an alternating field and not a rotating field and, therefore, has no starting torque at all. However, they are made self-starting by providing the various special arrangements which enable them to have a rotating magnetic field at least at starting. Accordingly, the motors are of the following commonly used types.

4.15.1 Resistance Split-Phase Motors

These motors are commonly known as *split-phase motors*. The stator of this type of motor carries two windings, one called the *main winding* (M) and the other known as *auxiliary winding* (A) or *starting winding*. The axes of these windings are displaced from each other usually by an angle of 90 electrical degrees in space. The rotor (G) of the motor is of normal cage type. Fig. 4.39 (a) shows the motor schematically and Fig. 4.39 (b) shows its connection diagram.

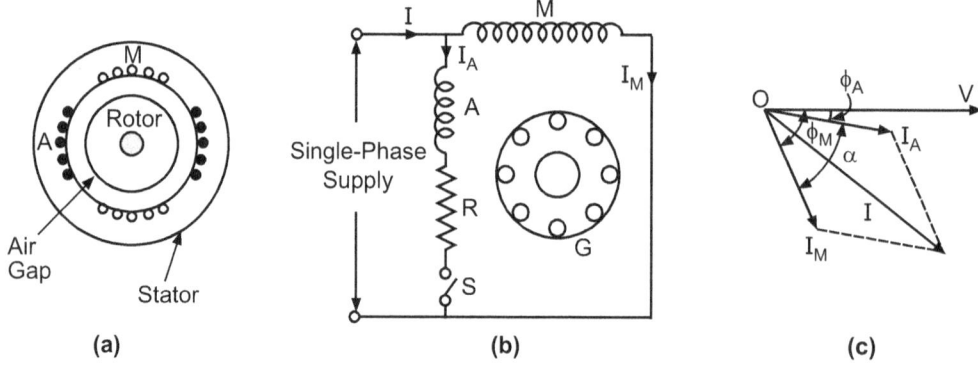

(a)	(b)	(c)

Fig. 4.39 : (a) Schematic representation of a split-phase type single-phase induction motor, (b) Connection diagram, (c) Phasor diagram

The auxiliary winding along with the series resistor (R) is connected across the main winding. Instead of connecting externally such a high resistance in series with an auxiliary winding, its resistance may be increased by choosing a high resistance fine copper wire for winding purposes. The resistance to reactance ratio of the auxiliary winding circuit being higher than the main winding, currents through them are nearly in quadrature (Fig. 4.39 c). The resulting fluxes due to these currents are, therefore, displaced in space through 90° and have considerable time phase difference. A rotating magnetic field is, therefore, produced   (as in a two-phase motor). The motor thus develops a starting torque. Once the motor is started, the auxiliary winding is disconnected with the help of a centrifugal switch (S) at about 75 to 80% of the synchronous speed.

• **Torque-Speed Characteristic :** Fig. 4.40 shows the torque-speed characteristic of a resistance split-phase motor. The starting torque of this type of motor is generally 125 to 150 % of full-load torque.

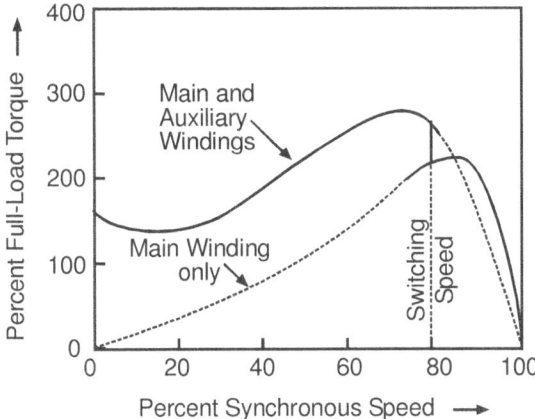

Fig. 4.40 : Typical torque-speed characteristic of a resistance split-phase motor

• **Reversal of Rotation :** The direction of rotation of this type of motor can be reversed by reversing the terminal connections of either the main or the auxiliary winding.

• **Applications :** These motors are commonly used in small electric tools, fans, blowers, centrifugal pumps, domestic refrigerator units, oil burners, washing machines, etc.

4.15.2 Capacitor Split-Phase Motors

These motors are commonly called as *capacitor motors.* This type of motor is similar in construction to resistance split-phase type single-phase induction motor considered above, except that the resistance in series with the auxiliary winding is replaced by a capacitor. The high starting torque is the outstanding feature of a capacitor motor because the fluxes produced by two windings on the stator can be made to have a time phase difference of practically 90°. Thus, this type of motor becomes essentially a two-phase motor. Due to use of a capacitor, the motor also has better power factor. Following are the three main types of the capacitor motors :

(i) Capacitor-Start Motors : In this case, the auxiliary winding (A) in series with a capacitor (C) is in the circuit only during the starting period and then disconnected with the help of a centrifugally operated starting switch (S) after the motor reaches 75 to 80 % of synchronous speed. This type of motor is shown schematically in Fig. 4.41 (a) and Fig. 4.41 (b) shows the phasor diagram.

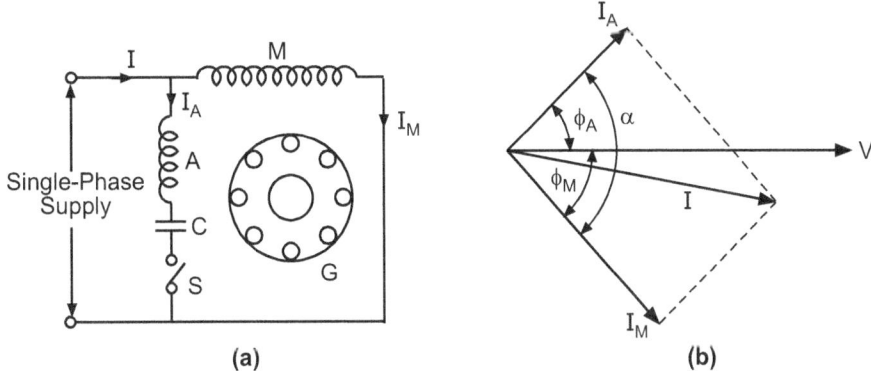

Fig. 4.41 : (a) Schematic representation of a capacitor-start, single-phase induction motor, (b) Phasor diagram

• **Torque-Speed Characteristic :** Torque-speed characteristic of this type of motor is shown in Fig. 4.42. The starting torque of this type of motor is generally of the order of 350 to 400 % of full-load torque. Thus, high starting torque is the outstanding feature of this motor.

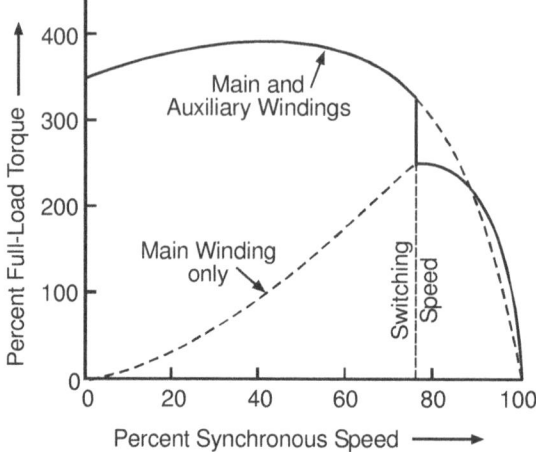

Fig. 4.42 : Typical torque-speed characteristic of a capacitor-start motor

(ii) Permanent-Split or Single-Value Capacitor Motors : In this type of motor, the auxiliary winding (A) along with the capacitor (C) is in the circuit for both, starting and running (Fig. 4.43 a).

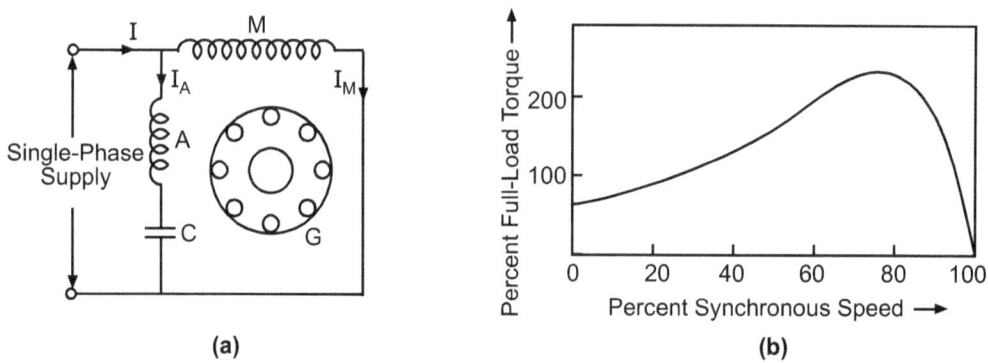

(a)   (b)

Fig. 4.43 : (a) Schematic representation of a permanent-split, capacitor

type single-phase induction motor, (b) Typical torque-speed characteristic

• **Torque-Speed Characteristic :** Since the capacitor and auxiliary winding remains permanently in the circuit, this improves the power factor and running performance of the motor. However, the starting torque of this type of motor is not good (it is only 50 to 100 % of full-load torque) as the value of the capacitor has to be chosen as a compromise between best starting and best running conditions. The resulting torque-speed characteristic of this type of motor is shown in Fig. 4.43 (b).

(iii) Capacitor Start and Run Or Two-Value Capacitor Motors : This type of motor uses two capacitors (C_1 and C_2) for starting, one of them (C_2) being cut out for running by means of a centrifugal switch (S) when the motor reaches about 75 to 80 % of synchronous speed.

Fig. 4.44 (a) schematically illustrates this type of motor.

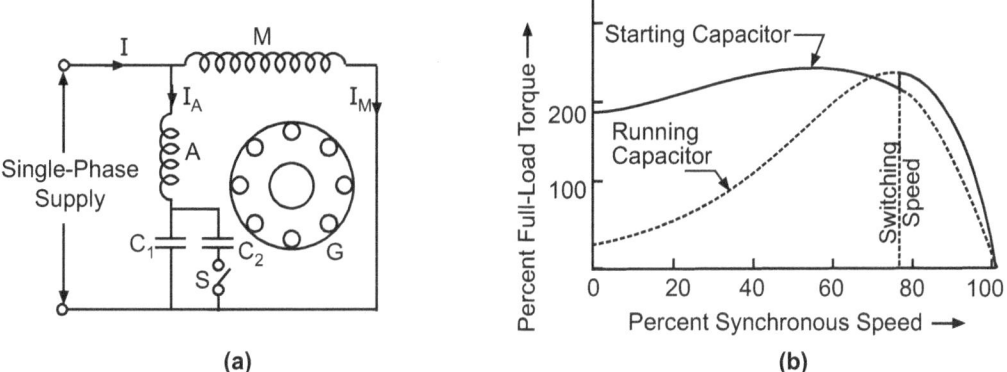

(a)	(b)

**Fig. 4.44 : (a) Schematic representation of a capacitor start and
run, single-phase induction motor, (b) Typical torque-speed characteristic**

• **Torque-Speed Characteristic :** This type of motor has better starting and running performance with improved power factor. Fig. 4.44 (b) shows the typical torque-speed characteristic for such a motor.

• **Reversal of Rotation in Capacitor Split-Phase Motors :** Reversal of direction of rotation can be obtained in all types of capacitor split-phase motors by changing the terminal connections of one of the windings.

• **Applications of Capacitor Split-Phase Motors :** These motors are in very common use for fans, blowers, drilling machines, grinders, compressors, conveyors, refrigerators, air conditioners, washing machines, domestic water pumps, etc.

4.15.3 Shaded-Pole Motors

The most usual form of a motor of this type has a rotor (G) of squirrel cage type and the stator (M) with salient poles (P_1, P_2). In addition to its own exciting coil (C_1, C_2), each pole carries a copper shading coil, band or ring (B_1, B_2) on one of its unequally divided parts (Fig. 4.45). Production of torque in this type of motor can be explained as below :

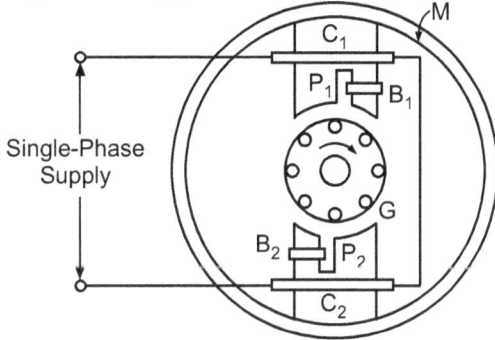

Fig. 4.45 : Shaded-pole type, single-phase induction motor

• **Operating Principle :** When the single-phase supply is given to the stator winding, an alternating flux is produced. Fig. 4.46 (a) shows the waveform for the sinusoidally varying alternating stator current and the flux produced by it. The distribution of this flux in the pole area is greatly influenced by the magnitude of the induced e.m.f. in the shading ring by transformer action. To examine this, let us consider three instants of time, namely t_1, t_2 and t_3 on the waveform for the stator current. At the instant when $t = t_1$, the rate of rise of stator current and hence that of stator flux being high, large e.m.f. is induced in the shading ring. The direction of this induced e.m.f. and hence the current set up by it in the short-circuited shading ring will be such as to oppose the rise of the stator current (Lenz's law). The opposing flux produced by the induced current in the shading ring makes stator flux distribution in the pole area non-uniform. There is crowding of flux in the non-shaded portion of the pole and magnetic axis (MA) lies along the middle of this part (Fig. 4.46 b).

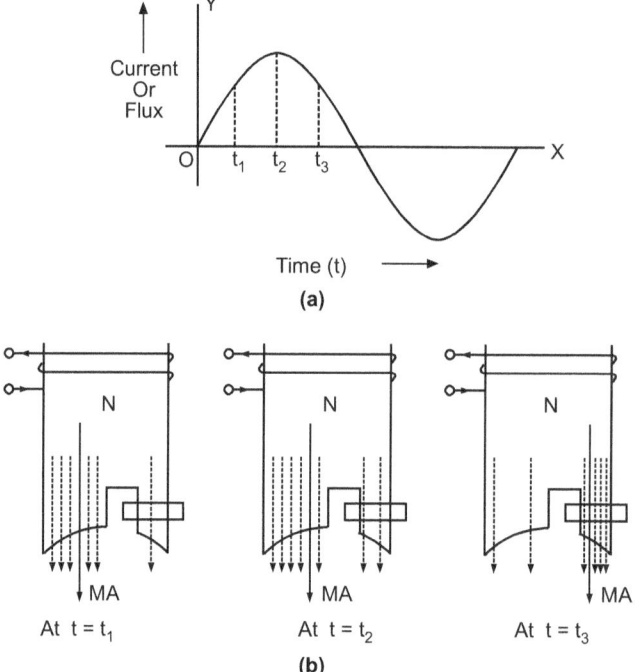

Fig. 4.46 : Production of torque in a shaded-pole type, single-phase induction motor

At the instant when $t = t_2$, even though the stator current is at its maximum, the rate of change of current and hence that of stator flux is minimum. Under this condition, the induced e.m.f. in the shading ring is negligible and there being practically no opposing flux, stator flux distribution in the pole area will be uniform. As a result of this, the position of magnetic axis (MA) is shifted towards the centre line of the pole.

At the instant when $t = t_3$, the stator current which is rapidly decreasing, again induces large e.m.f. in the shading ring. The direction of this e.m.f. and resulting induced current in the shading ring is now such as to oppose the decrease in the stator current. The flux produced by a current in the shading ring, therefore, strengthens the flux in the shaded portion of the pole. Consequently, the magnetic axis gets shifted to the middle of the shaded part of the pole. This sequence is repeated even in the negative half cycle of the stator current. This periodic shift in the stator flux from the unshaded to the shaded part of the pole gives to some extent rotating field effect and produces a low-starting torque.

• **Torque-Speed Characteristic :** Fig. 4.47 shows the typical torque-speed characteristic of this type of motor. The starting torque of this type of motor is only about 40 to 50 % of full-load torque.

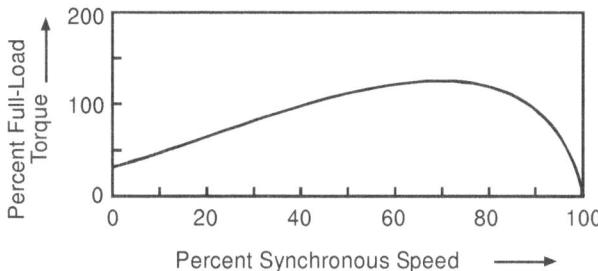

Fig. 4.47 : Typical torque-speed characteristic of a shaded-pole motor

• **Reversal of Rotation :** The shaded-pole motor generally has a definite direction of rotation which cannot be reversed. However, if such reversal is essential, it can be achieved by providing two shading coils, one on each end of every pole. Then by open-circuiting one set of shading coils and short-circuiting the other set, desired direction of rotation can be achieved.

• **Applications :** Due to absence of centrifugal switch, construction of the motor of this type is simple and robust. However, the motor has low efficiency and low power factor and its starting torque is very poor. Therefore, such motors are suitable for only small powers and where the starting conditions are easy e.g. they are commonly employed for driving small fans, motorised valves, recording instruments, record players, gramophones, toy motors, photocopying machines, hair dryers, advertising displays, etc.

4.16 POINTS TO REMEMBER

• A stepper motor is an electrical motor which converts electrical input in the form of series of pulses into discrete angular movements, commonly called as *steps*.

• A servomechanism in simple words, is an automatic control system (or a feedback system) which in response to an input signal carries out various functions such as moving a shaft to a certain position, moving a load in a particular direction at a particular speed, etc. Servomotors are used as drive in servomechanisms.

• Most of the servomotors used in servomechanisms are a.c and of the two-phase induction motor type.

• Except some minor differences in constructional features, a d.c. servomotor is essentially an ordinary d.c. motor (usually shunt type).

• If an ordinary d.c. series motor is connected to an a.c. supply, because of simultaneous reversal of field and armature currents, it develops a unidirectional torque. As a result of this, its armature will rotate. However, performance of such a motor when operated on a.c. supply will not be satisfactory. For satisfactory performance, it needs many design modifications.

- Universal motors are small capacity series motors designed to operate on either direct current (d.c.) or single-phase alternating current supply of approximately the same voltage with nearly similar operating characteristics.

- There being overall similarity between the inverter-fed self-controlled permanent-magnet synchronous motor (which is basically an a.c. motor) and conventional d.c. motor except the requirement of brushes and the cummutator, it is named as *brushless* or *commutatorless* d.c. motor.

- Linear induction motor is essentially a special type of a polyphase induction motor with its stator (primary) and rotor (secondary) cut by a radial plane and then unrolled so that instead of producing a torque (causing rotation), it produces a linear force (causing linear motion) along its length.

- Single-phase induction motors are designed to operate on a single-phase supply.

- When the stator winding of a single-phase induction motor is connected to a single-phase supply, the current flowing through it produces resultant field which alternates along the axis of the winding. Such a field varying sinusoidally with time along a fixed space axis while acting on a stationary cage rotor, cannot produce its rotation. Consequently, a single-phase induction motor is not inherently self-starting. However, if the rotor is given an initial rotation in any direction, the single-phase induction motor develops torque and rotor continues to pick up speed in that particular direction.

- Single-phase induction motors are made self-starting by providing various special arrangements which enable them to have a nearly rotating magnetic field at least at starting.

- The direction of rotation of resistance split-phase and capacitor split-phase motors can be reversed by reversing the terminal connections of either the main or the auxiliary winding.

- The shaded-pole motor generally has a definite direction of rotation which cannot be reversed.

4.17 EXERCISES

4.17.1 Review Questions

1. What is a stepper motor ? Explain the construction and principle of working of (i) Variable-reluctance stepper motor, (ii) Permanent-magnet stepper motor, (iii) Hybrid stepper motor.

2. Discuss the different characteristics of stepper motors and state their applications.

3. Define the following terms in relation to stepper motors : (i) Holding torque, (ii) Detent torque, (iii) Pull-in torque, (iv) Pull-out torque, (v) Maximum starting torque, (vi) Maximum starting frequency, (vii) Maximum slewing frequency.

4. Write briefly on drive systems of stepper motors.

5. What are the special features of servomotors ? State their types.

6. Discuss briefly, the constructional features, working and characteristics of

   (i) A.C. servomotors,

   (ii) D.C. servomotors.

   State the applications of these motors.

7. Will a d.c. series motor work satisfactorily when connected across an a.c. supply ? Explain your answer with reasons.

8. Mention the modifications in the design to be incorporated to enable a d.c. series motor to work satisfactorily on a.c. supply.

9. What is the difference between a conductively compensated single-phase a.c. series motor and an inductively compensated single-phase a.c. series motor ?

10. Draw and explain the performance characteristics of an a.c. series motor. Comment briefly on these characteristics and mention the applications of this type of motor.

11. Why are the a.c. series motors preferred for electric traction ?

12. What is an universal motor ? Comment briefly on its constructional features and speed-torque characteristics. Mention its applications.

13. How is the direction of rotation of each of the following types of motors reversed ?

    (i) Series motors, (ii) Universal motors.

14. Explain the principle of operation of a brushless d.c. motor. What are the advantages of this motor over conventional d.c. motor ? State its applications.

15. What is a linear induction motor ? Give its principle of operation.

16. State the applications of linear induction motors.

17. Explain the principle of working of a single-phase induction motor with the help of double revolving field theory.

18. Discuss why single-phase induction motors do not have a starting torque. Describe with the aid of diagram of connections and phasor diagrams, various methods used to obtain a starting torque in the case of single-phase induction motors.

19. Compare different types of single-phase induction motors and state their applications.

20. Explain the principle of split-phasing used in single-phase induction motors. Name the different methods employed. Explain each of them.

21. Draw a neat circuit diagram and explain the working of resistance split-phase induction motor. State the use of a centrifugal switch in it.

22. Why are single-phase induction motors not self-starting ? With the help of a diagram, explain the working of the capacitor-start induction motor. Also draw the phasor diagram.

23. Explain the capacitor-start and run, single-phase induction motor. Draw its connection diagram and phasor diagram. Also sketch the torque-speed characteristic. State its any two applications.

24. Explain why the starting torque of a capacitor split-phase type single-phase induction motor is better than a resistance split-phase type single-phase induction motor.

25. How is the direction of rotation of resistance split-phase type and capacitor split-phase type single-phase induction motors reversed ?

26. Explain the principle of working of a shaded-pole, single-phase induction motor. Draw its torque-speed characteristic and state its applications.

27. Is it possible to change the direction of rotation of a shaded-pole type single-phase induction motor ? Explain your statement.

CHAPTER

FIVE

INTRODUCTION TO MICROCONTROLLERS

5.1 INTRODUCTION TO MICROCONTROLLERS AND MICROPROCESSORS

5.1.1 Microprocessor

Microprocessors are regarded as one of the most important devices in our everyday machines called computers. Before we start, we need to understand what exactly microprocessors are and their appropriate implementations. Microprocessor is an electronic circuit that functions as the central processing unit (CPU) of a computer, fabricated on a very small chip capable of performing ALU operations and communicating with the external devices connected to it. Providing computational control. Microprocessors are also used in other advanced electronic systems, such as computer printers, automobiles, and jet airliners.

The first microprocessor was the Intel 4004, produced in 1971. Originally developed for a calculator and revolutionary for its time, it contained 2,300 transistors on a 4-bit microprocessor that could perform only 60,000 operations per second. The first 8-bit microprocessor was the Intel 8008, developed in 1972 to run computer terminals. The Intel 8008 contained 3,300 transistors. The first truly general-purpose microprocessor, developed in 1974, was the 8-bit Intel 8080, which contained 4,500 transistors and could execute 200,000 instructions per second. By 1989, 32- bit microprocessors containing 1.2 million transistors and capable of executing 20 million instructions per second had been introduced.

The microprocessor is heart of any electronics system which contains the following functional block:

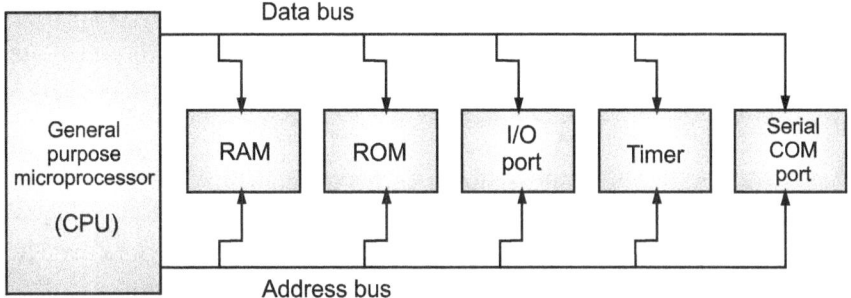

Fig. 5.1: Microprocessor based system

CPU/ALU is used to process the data or to perform arithmetic and logical operation like addition, subtraction, multiplication division etc. it include **RAM/ROM** are the memory element to store the data, then Input/output **(I/O)** ports are required to connect the external devices along with **timer** and **serial** port. All these blocks are interfaced separately to microprocessor.

5.1.2 Microcontroller

A microcontroller is a small device used to process data and control the application. Microcontroller contains one or more CPUs (processor cores) along with memory and programmable input/output ports on a single chip. Microcontrollers are designed for embedded applications, in contrast to the microprocessors used in personal computers or other general purpose applications consisting of various discrete chips. Typical microcontroller system is shown in Fig. 5.2

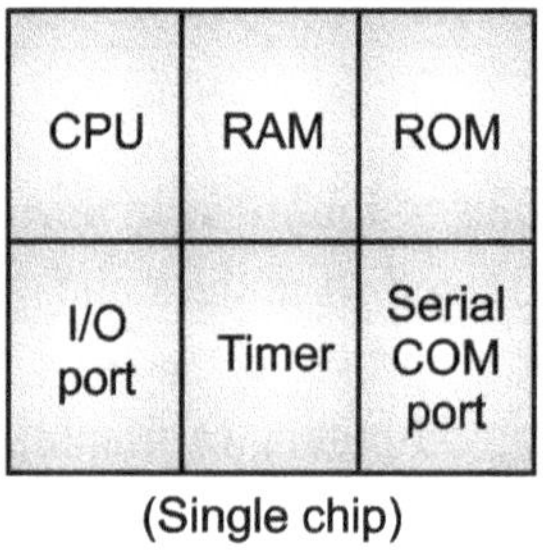

CPU	RAM	ROM
I/O port	Timer	Serial COM port

(Single chip)

Fig. 5.2: Microcontroller system

A microcontroller can be compared to a Swiss knife with multiple functions incorporated in the same IC.

- A microprocessor requires an external memory for program/data storage. Instruction execution requires movement of data from the external memory to the microprocessor or vice versa. Usually, microprocessors have good computing power and they have higher clock speed to facilitate faster computation.

- A microcontroller has required on-chip memory with associated peripherals. A microcontroller can be thought of a microprocessor with inbuilt peripherals.

- A microcontroller does not require much additional interfacing ICs for operation and it functions as a standalone system. The operation of a microcontroller is multipurpose, just like a Swiss knife.

Microcontrollers are also called embedded controllers. A microcontroller clock speed is limited only to a few tens of MHz. Microcontrollers are numerous and many of them are application specific.

Intel first produced a microcontroller in 1976 under the name MCS-48, which was an 8 bit microcontroller. Later in 1980 they released a further improved version (which is also 8 bit), under the name MCS-51. The most popular microcontroller 8051 belongs to the MCS-51 family of microcontrollers by Intel. Following the success of 8051, many other semiconductor manufacturers released microcontrollers under their own brand name but using the MCS-51 core.

Global companies and giants in semiconductor industry like Microchip, Zilog, Atmel, Philips, Siemens released products under their brand name. The specialty was that all these devices could be programmed using the same MCS-51 instruction sets. They basically differed in support device configurations like improved memory, presence of an ADC or DAC etc. Intel then released its first 16 bit microcontroller in 1982, under name MCS-96.

Microcontrollers are used in automatically controlled products and devices, such as automobile engine control systems, implantable medical devices, remote controls, office machines, appliances, power tools, toys and other embedded systems. By reducing the size and cost compared to a design that uses a separate microprocessor, memory, and input/output devices, microcontrollers make it economical to digitally control even more devices and processes.

5.1.3 Difference Between Microcontroller and Microprocessor

Microprocessor	Microcontroller
Microprocessor is heart of Computer system.	Microcontroller is a heart of embedded system.
It is just a processor. Memory and I/O components have to be connected externally	Microcontroller has external processor along with internal memory and I/O components
Since memory and I/O has to be connected externally, the circuit becomes large.	Since memory and I/O are present internally, the circuit is small.
Cannot be used in compact systems and hence inefficient	Can be used in compact systems and hence it is an efficient technique
Cost of the entire system increases	Cost of the entire system is low

5.2 ROLE OF EMBEDDED SYSTEM

If we look around, we will find ourselves to be surrounded by computing systems. Every year millions of computing systems are built destined for desktop computers (Personal Computers, workstations, mainframes and servers) but surprisingly, billions of computing systems are built every year embedded within larger electronic devices and still goes unnoticed. Any device running on electric power either already has computing system or will soon have computing system embedded in it.

Today, **embedded systems** are found in cell phones, digital cameras, camcorders, portable video games, calculators, and personal digital assistants, microwave ovens, answering machines, home security systems, washing machines, lighting systems, fax machines, copiers, printers, and scanners, cash registers, alarm systems, automated teller machines, transmission control, cruise control, fuel injection, anti-lock brakes, active suspension and many other devices/ gadgets.

A precise *definition of embedded systems* is not easy. Simply stated, all computing systems other than general purpose computer (with monitor, keyboard, etc.) are embedded systems.

System is a way of working, organizing or performing one or many tasks according to a fixed set of rules, program or plan. In other words, an arrangement in which all units assemble and work together according to a program or plan. An embedded system is a system that has software embedded into hardware, which makes a system dedicated for an application (s) or specific part of an application or product or part of a larger system. It processes a fixed set of pre-programmed instructions to control electromechanical equipment which may be part of an even larger system (not a computer with keyboard, display, etc).

A general-purpose definition of embedded systems is that they are devices used to control, monitor or assist the operation of equipment, machinery or plant. "Embedded" reflects the fact that they are an integral part of the system. In many cases, their "embeddedness" may be such that their presence is far from obvious to the casual observer. *Block diagram of a typical embedded system* is shown in fig 5.3.

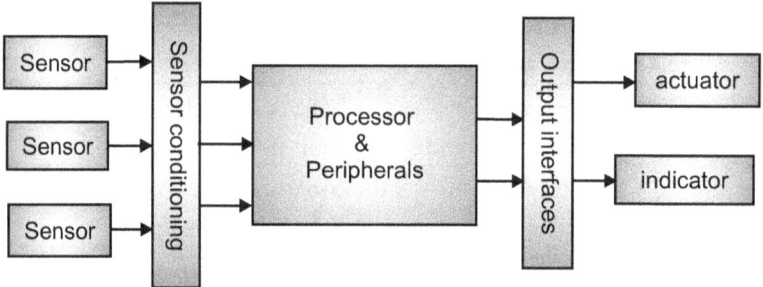

Fig. 5.3 : Typical embedded system

An embedded system is an engineering artinvolving computation that is subject to physical constraints (reaction constraints and execution constraints) arising through interactions of computational processes with the physical world. Reaction constraints originate from the behavioral requirements & specify deadlines, throughput, and jitter whereas execution constraints originate from the implementation requirements & put bounds on available processor speeds, power, memory and hardware failure rates. The key to embedded systems design is to obtain desired functionality under both kinds of constraints.

Characteristics of Embedded System:

- Embedded systems are application specific & single functioned; application is known a priori, the programs are executed repeatedly.

- Efficiency is of paramount importance for embedded systems. They are optimized for energy, code size, execution time, weight & dimensions, and cost.

- Embedded systems are typically designed to meet real time constraints; a real time system reacts to stimuli from the controlled object/ operator within the time interval dictated by the environment. For real time systems, right answers arriving too late (or even too early) are wrong.

- Embedded systems often interact (sense, manipulate & communicate) with external world through sensors and actuators and hence are typically reactive systems; a reactive system is in continual interaction with the environment and executes at a pace determined by that environment.

- They generally have minimal or no user interface.

- Embedded systems are designed to do some specific task, rather than be a general-purpose computer for multiple tasks. Some also have real-time performance constraints that must be met, for reasons such as safety and usability; others may have low or no performance requirements, allowing the system hardware to be simplified to reduce costs.

- Embedded systems are not always standalone devices. Many embedded systems consist of small, computerized parts within a larger device that serves a more general purpose. For example, the Gibson Robot Guitar features an embedded system for tuning the strings, but the overall purpose of the Robot Guitar is, of course, to play music.[7] Similarly, an embedded system in an automobile provides a specific function as a subsystem of the car itself.

- The program instructions written for embedded systems are referred to as firmware, and are stored in read-only memory or Flash memory chips. They run with limited computer hardware resources: little memory, small or non-existent keyboard or screen.

5.3 OPEN SOURCE EMBEDDED PLATFORMS

For any embedded system development we required hardware and software tools so this entire line of embedded products is based on the visionary concept of open source hardware and software platform. That is, hardware and software developments are openly shared among users to stimulate new ideas and advance the embedded concept. The vendor (manufacturer) of any embedded development board openly shares the schematic of it and also required software to it. Embedded system open source software includes compilers, assemblers, and debuggers to develop embedded system.

Software Tools can come from Several Sources :

- Software companies that specialize in the embedded market

- Ported from the GNU software development tools

- Sometimes, development tools for a personal computer can be used if the embedded processor is a close relative to a common PC processor

As the complexity of embedded systems grows, higher level tools and operating systems are migrating into machinery where it makes sense. For example, cellphones, personal digital assistants and other consumer computers often need significant software that is purchased or provided by a person other than the manufacturer of the electronics. In these systems, an open programming environment such as Linux, NetBSD, OSGi or Embedded Java is required so that the third-party software provider can sell to a large market.

Compiler:

A compiler is a computer program (or set of programs) that transforms source code written in a programming language (the source language) into another computer language (the target language, often having a binary form known as object code).[1] The most common reason for wanting to transform source code is to create an executable program.

The name "compiler" is primarily used for programs that translate source code from a high-level programming language to a lower level language (e.g., assembly language or machine code). If the compiled program can run on a computer whose CPU or operating system is different from the one on which the compiler runs, the compiler is known as a cross-compiler.

A program that translates from a low level language to a higher level one is a decompiler. A program that translates between high-level languages is usually called asource-to-source compiler or transpiler. A language rewriter is usually a program that translates the form of expressions without a change of language. More generally, compilers are sometimes called translators. A compiler is likely to perform many or all of the following operations:lexical analysis, preprocessing, parsing, semantic analysis (Syntax-directed translation), code generation, and code optimization.

Program faults caused by incorrect compiler behavior can be very difficult to track down and work around; therefore, compiler implementers invest significant effort to ensure compiler correctness.

Assembler

An assembler is a program which creates object code by translating combinations of mnemonics and syntax for operations and addressing modes into their numerical equivalents. This representation typically includes an operation code ("opcode") as well as other control bits.[1] The assembler also calculates constant expressions and resolvessymbolic names for memory locations and other entities.[2] The use of symbolic references is a key feature of assemblers, saving tedious calculations and manual address updates after program modifications. Most assemblers also include macro facilities for performing textual substitution e.g., to generate common short sequences of instructions as inline, instead of called subroutines.

Some assemblers may also be able to perform some simple types of instruction set-specific optimizations.

Debugger

A debugger or debugging tool is a computer program that is used to test and debug other programs (the "target" program). The code to be examined might alternatively be running on an instruction set simulator (ISS), a technique that allows great power in its ability to halt when specific conditions are encountered but which will typically be somewhat slower than executing the code directly on the appropriate (or the same) processor. Some debuggers offer two modes of operation—full or partial simulation—to limit this impact.

A special program used to find errors (bugs) in other programs. A debugger allows a programmer to stop a program at any point and examine and change the values of variables.Embedded debugging may be performed at different levels, depending on the facilities available. From simplest to most sophisticate they can be roughly grouped into the following areas:

- Interactive resident debugging, using the simple shell provided by the embedded operating system (e.g. Forth and Basic)

- External debugging using logging or serial port output to trace operation using either a monitor in flash or using a debug server like the Remedy Debugger which even works for heterogeneous multicore systems.

- An in-circuit debugger (ICD), a hardware device that connects to the microprocessor via a JTAG or Nexus interface. This allows the operation of the microprocessor to be controlled externally, but is typically restricted to specific debugging capabilities in the processor.

The most commonly used embedded platforms are:

- Arduino is an open source embedded platform based on easy to use hardware and software. it's mostly used application based system.

- The Raspberry Pi is also comes in open source platforms which can be used to design develop embedded systems and practical Iot devices.

Advantages of open-source embedded platforms

- **Lower Costs:** Open source platform usually does not require a licensing fee and its lower cost is generally one of the key reasons why small businesses choose to adopt this platform.

- **Flexibility:** A programmer can take a standard software package which include compiler,debugger etc. and modify it to better as per design needs.

- **Availability of External Support:** External technical support is available for many of the open source embedded platform. Some vendors offer support contracts and there are service providers that install, configure and maintain a software and hardware system. Many open source products also have active online community support that may be able to answer your questions through online blogs.

- **Qualitiy:** It's continually evolving in real time as developers add to it and modify it, which means it can be better quality and more secure and less prone to bugs than proprietary systems, because it has so many users poring over it and weeding out problems.

5.4 ATMEGA 328P MICROCONTROLLER

Atmega 328p (AVR) is low power CMOS 8-bit microcontroller from Atmel.TheAtmega 328p core combines a rich instruction set with 32 general purpose working registers. All the 32 registers are directly connected to the Arithmetic Logic Unit (ALU), allowing two independent registers to be accessed in a single instruction executed in one clock cycle. The resulting architecture is more code efficient while achieving throughputs up to ten times faster than conventional microcontrollers .This microcontroller has following features:

Features:

- It has 131 powerful instructions which most of instructions execute in single clock cycle

- 32Kbytes of In-System Programmable Flash Memory with Read-Write capabilities, 1Kbytes EEPROM, 2Kbytes SRAM

- It has 23 general purpose I/O lines for connecting external device. 32 general purpose working registers.

- It has Real Time Counter (RTC), three flexible Timer/Counters with compare modes and PWM, programmable Watchdog Timer with internal Oscillator

- It has 6- channel 10-bit ADC, 1 serial programmable USARTs , 1 byte-oriented 2-wire Serial Interface (I2C) and SPI serial port

- It has special microcontroller features like Power-on Reset and Programmable Brown-out Detection, Internal Calibrated Oscillator, External and Internal Interrupt Sources, Six Sleep Modes: Idle, ADC Noise Reduction, Power-save, Power-down, Standby, and Extended Standby

- Operating voltage of microcontroller varies in 1.8 - 5.5V

- Operating speed of microcontroller depends on supply voltage range and it is given as:

  0 - 4MHz @ 1.8 - 5.5V –

  0 - 10MHz @ 2.7 - 5.5V

  0 - 20MHz @ 4.5 - 5.5V.

- Atmel offers the QTouch® library for embedding capacitive touch buttons, sliders and wheels functionality into AVR microcontrollers.

- The ATmega328/P is supported with a full suite of program and system development tools including: C Compilers, Macro Assemblers, Program Debugger/Simulators, In-Circuit Emulators, and Evaluation kits.

5.5 BLOCK DIAGRAM OF ATMEGA 328P

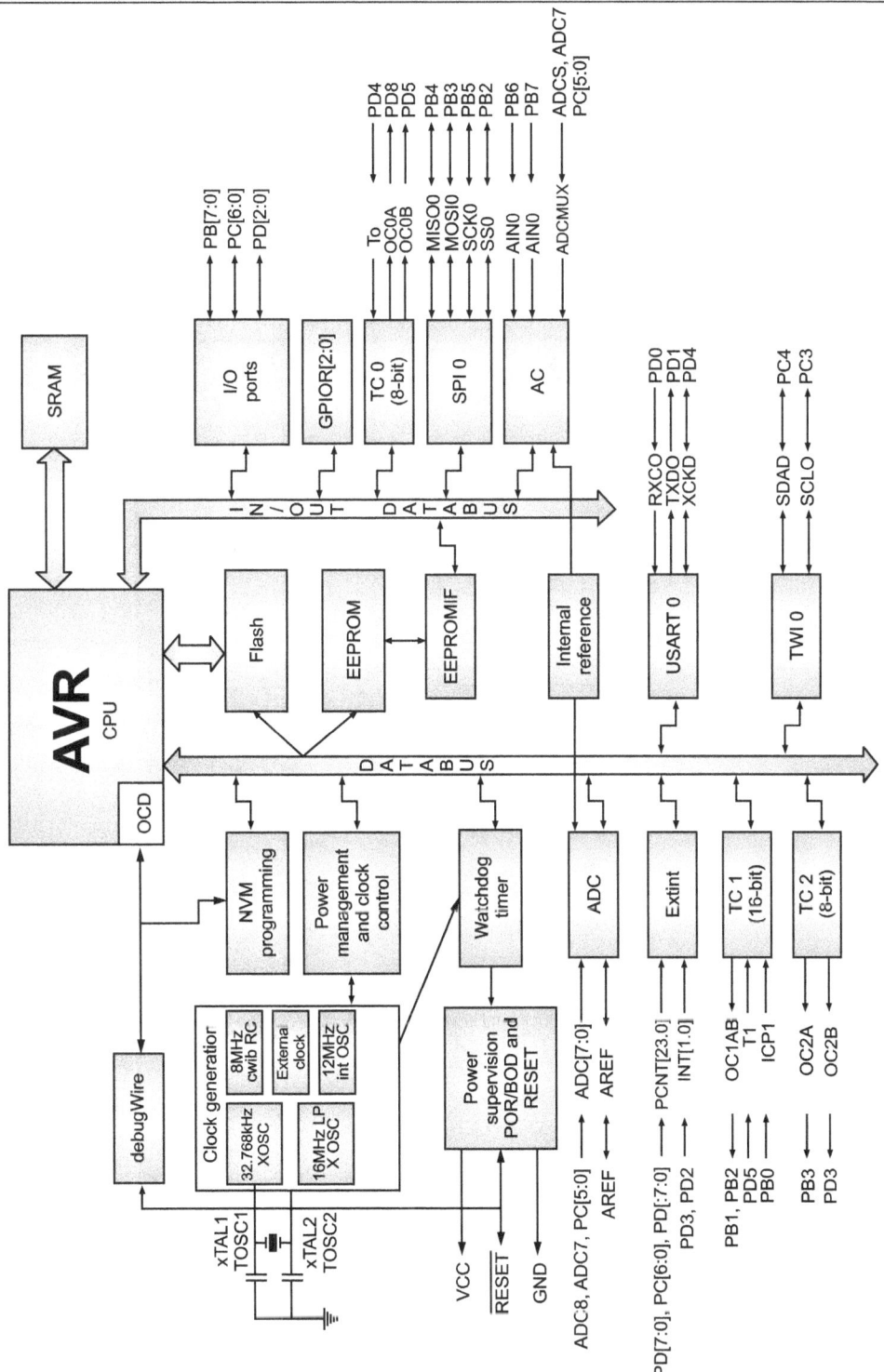

Fig. 5.4 : Block diagram of Atmega 328p

The above Fig. shows Block diagram of Atmega 328p microcontroller which includes following functional devices.

AVR (CPU)

This is 8-bit data processing unit used to perform arithmetic and logic operation and also it communicate to all devices which are connected to it through data bus. AVR architecture is shown In Fig. 5.5.

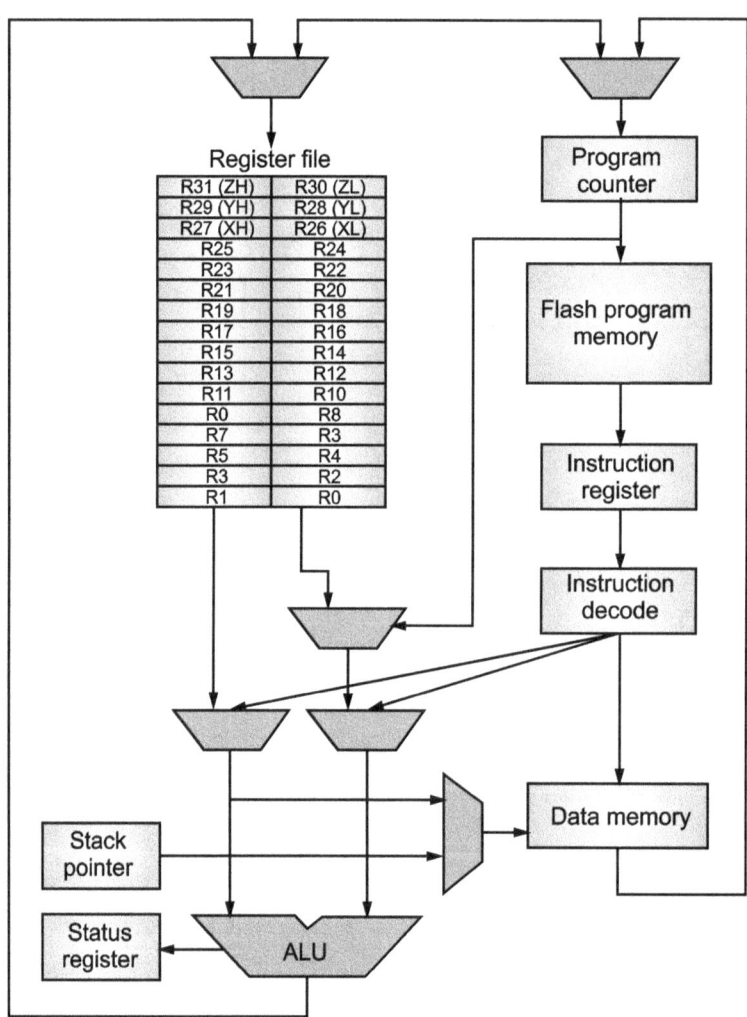

Fig. 5.5 :AVR CPU Architecture

ALU-Arithmetic Logic Unit

The ALU used to perform arithmetic and logical operation between registers or between a constant and a register. In typical ALU operations, two operands are taken from the register file, the operation is executed, and the result is stored back in the register file in one clock cycle.

Register File

As shown in Fig. 5.6 the register file in AVR CPU are fast access Register File contains 32 x 8-bit general purpose working registers with a single clock cycle access time. Six of the 32 registers can be used as three 16-bit indirect address register pointers for Data Space addressing – enabling efficient address calculations. One of the these address pointers can also be used as an address pointer for look up tables in Flash program memory

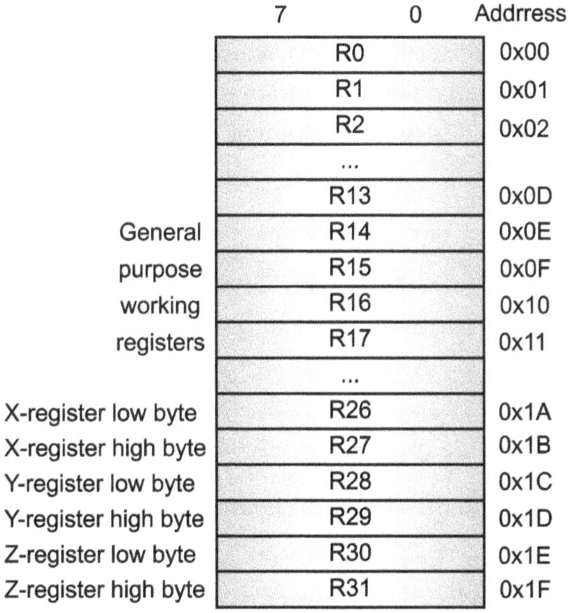

	7 0	Addrress
	R0	0x00
	R1	0x01
	R2	0x02
	...	
	R13	0x0D
General	R14	0x0E
purpose	R15	0x0F
working	R16	0x10
registers	R17	0x11
	...	
X-register low byte	R26	0x1A
X-register high byte	R27	0x1B
Y-register low byte	R28	0x1C
Y-register high byte	R29	0x1D
Z-register low byte	R30	0x1E
Z-register high byte	R31	0x1F

Fig 5.6: AVR General Purpose working registers.

Most of the instructions operating on the Register File have direct access to all registers, and most of them are single cycle instructions.

Memory

The ATmega328 is divided with three main memory sections:

- Flash electrically erasable programmable read only memory (EEPROM)

- Static random access memory (SRAM)

- Byte addressable EEPROM for data storage.

Flash electrically erasable programmable read only memory (EEPROM): Flash EEPROM is used to store programs. The ATmega328 is equipped with 32Kbytes of on board reprogrammable flash memory it can be erased and programmed as a single unit. Flash EEPROM is nonvolatile memory contents are retained when microcontroller power is lost. This memory component is organized into 16K locations with 16 bits at each location.

Static random access memory (SRAM): Static RAM memory is volatile. That is, if the microcontroller loses power, the contents of SRAM memory are lost. It used to store temporary data and It can be written to and read from during program execution. The ATmega328 has 2K bytes of SRAM. A small portion of the SRAM is set aside for the general purpose registers used by the processor and also for the input/output and peripheral subsystems aboard the microcontroller.

Byte addressable EEPROM for data storage: This memory is used to permanently store data which required during program execution. It is nonvolatile. It is especially useful for logging system malfunctions and fault data during program execution. It is also useful for storing data that must be retained during a power failure but might need to be changed periodically.

Status Register

The Status Register contains information about the result of the most recently executed arithmetic instruction. This information can be used for altering program flow in order to perform conditional operations. The Status Register is updated after all ALU operations,

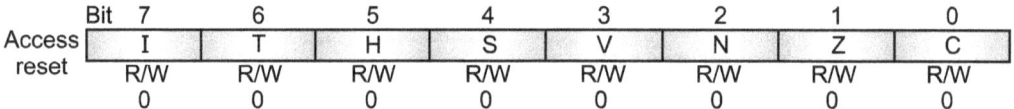

Fig. 5.7 : Status register bit pattern

- **Bit 7 – I : Global Interrupt Enable** : The Global Interrupt Enable bit must be set for the interrupts to be enabled. The individual interrupt enable control is then performed in separate control registers The I bit is cleared by hardware after an interrupt has occurred, and is set by the RETI instruction to enable subsequent interrupts. The I-bit can also be set and cleared by the application with the SEI and CLI instructions.

- **Bit 6 – T: Copy Storage** The Bit Copy instructions BLD (Bit LoaD) and BST (Bit STore) use the T-bit as source or destination for the operated bit. A bit from a register in the Register File can be copied into T by the BST instruction, and a bit in T can be copied into a bit in a register in the Register File by the BLD instruction.

- **Bit 5 – H: Half Carry Flag** The Half Carry Flag H indicates a Half Carry in some arithmetic operations. Half Carry Flag is useful in BCD arithmetic.

- **Bit 4 – S: Sign Flag** :S = N $\oplus$ V The S-bit is always an exclusive or between the Negative Flag N and the Two's Complement Overflow Flag V.

- **Bit 3 – V: Two's Complement Overflow Flag** The Two's Complement Overflow Flag V supports two's complement arithmetic.

- **Bit 2 – N: Negative Flag** The Negative Flag N indicates a negative result in an arithmetic or logic operation.

- **Bit 1 – Z: Zero Flag**The Zero Flag Z indicates a zero result in an arithmetic or logic operation.

- **Bit 0 – C: Carry Flag**The Carry Flag C indicates a carry in an arithmetic or logic operation.

Program Counter (PC)

The Program counter used to store the address value of the current instruction, commonly called as Instruction Pointer (IP) .It is 14-bits wide thus it can access up to 16kb program memory locations.

Stack Pointer

The Stack is mainly used for storing temporary data, for storing local variables and for storing return addresses after interrupts and subroutine call. The Stack Pointer Register always points to the top of the Stack. Some of the stack related instructions is given in Fig.5.8.

Instruction	Stack Pointer	Description
PUSH	Decremented by 1	Data is pushed onto the stack
CALL ICALL RCALL	Decremented by 2	Return address is pushed onto the stack with a subroutine call or interrupt
POP	Incremented by 1	Data is popped from the stack
RET RETI	Incremented by 2	Return address is popped from the stack with return from subroutine or return from interrupt.

Fig. 5.8 : Stack Pointer Instructions

Instructions Register and Decoder

An Instruction Register (IR) is used to holds the instruction currently being executed or decoded. The Instruction Register is a part of CPU's control unit.The instruction decoder is the circuit that decodes an opcode.

5.6 PORT STRUCTURE

The Atmel ATmega328 is equipped with four, 8-bit general purpose, digital input/output (I/O) ports designated PORTA, PORTB, PORTC and PORTD. All of these ports also have alternate functions which will be described later. The Fig. 5.9 shows the pin configuration of Atmega328p microcontroller.

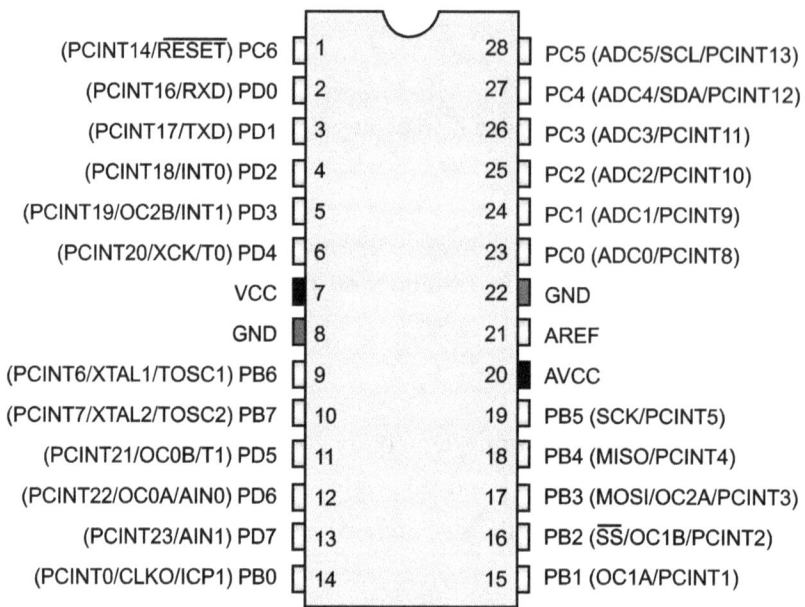

Fig. 5.9: Pin configuration of ATmega328p

All AVR ports have true Read-Modify-Write functionality when used as general digital I/O ports. This means that the direction of one port pin can be changed without unintentionally changing the direction of any other pin with the SBI and CBI instructions.

All port pins have individually selectable pull-up resistors with a supply-voltage invariant resistance. All I/O pins have protection diodes to both VCC and Ground as indicated in the following Fig. 5.10.

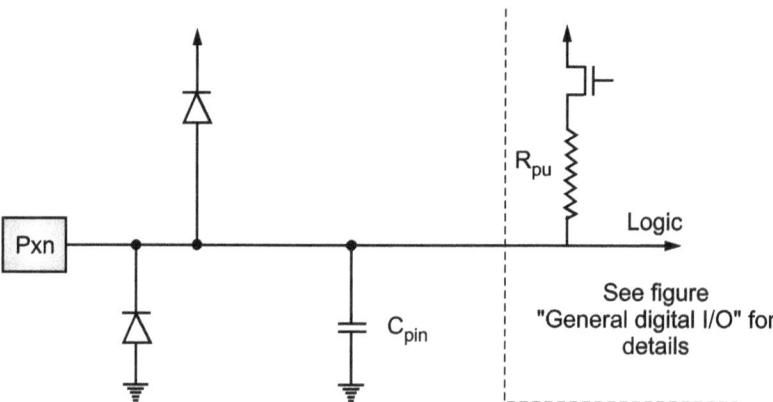

Fig. 5.10: I/O Pin Equivalent schematic

Each port pin can be read and write using set of registers which will given as below

- Data Register PORTx - used to write output data to the port.

- Data Direction Register DDRx – used to set a specific port pin to either output(1) or input (0).

- Input Pin Address PINx —- used to read input data from the port.

A lower case "x" represents the numbering letter for the port, and a lower case "n" represents the bit number. However, when using the register or bit defines in a program, the precise form must be used. For example, PORTB3 for bit no. 3 in Port B, here documented generally as PORTxn.

Fig. 5.11 describes the settings required to configure a specific port pin to either input or output. If selected for input, the pin may be selected for either an input pin or to operate in the high impedance (Hi-Z) mode. In Hi-Z mode, the input appears as high impedance to a particular pin. If selected for output, the pin may be further configured for either logic low or logic high. Port pins are usually configured at the beginning of a program for either input or output and their initial values are then set. Usually all eight pins for a given port are configured simultaneously.

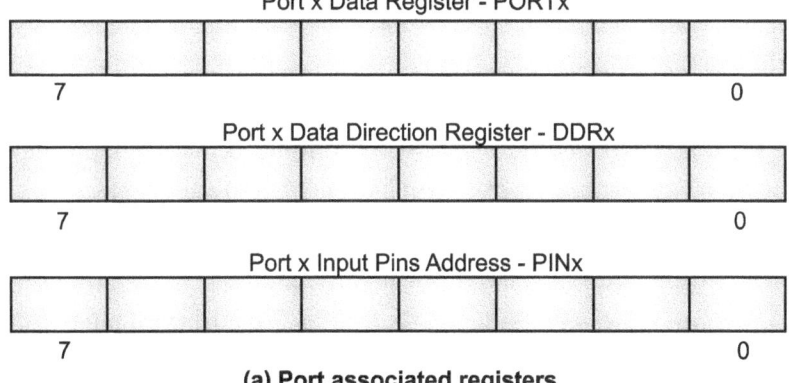

(a) **Port associated registers**

DDxn	PORTxn	I/O	Comment	Pullup
0	0	input	Tri-state (Hi-Z)	No
0	1	input	Source current if externally pulled low	Yes
1	0	output	Output low (Sink)	No
1	1	output	Output high (Source)	No

x: port designator (A, B, C, D)
n: pin designator (0 - 7)

(b) **Port pin configuration**

Fig. 5.11: ATmega328p port configuration registers

5.7 SENSOR AND ACTUATORS

Sensors and actuators are two components used widely in *mechatronics system*. Mechanical systems are continue to be controlled with electronic systems due to this over the past 30 years, vehicle electronic systems have changed significantly The evolution of microcontroller and sensor technology is allowing automobile industry to create complex systems that can provide higher levels of vehicle control and safety.

5.7.1 Sensors

Sensor is a device that when exposed to a physical phenomenon (temperature, displacement, force, etc.) produces a proportional output signal (electrical, mechanical, magnetic, etc.).

The term transducer is often used synonymously with sensors. However, ideally, a sensor is a device that responds to a change in the physical phenomenon. On the other hand, a transducer is a device that converts one form of energy into another form of energy. This is shown in block diagram 5.12

Fig. 5.12: Shows the sensor used as transducer

A sensor contains some signal conditioning circuits(Transduction element) to amplify weak signal and can refine raw signals.

Selection of Sensor

A number of static and dynamic factors must be considered in selecting a suitable sensor to measure the desired physical parameter. Following is a list of typical factors:

- **Range:** Difference between the maximum and minimum value of the sensed parameter
- **Resolution:** The smallest change the sensor can differentiate
- **Accuracy:** Difference between the measured value and the true valuePrecision—Ability to reproduce repeatedly with a given accuracy
- **Sensitivity:** Ratio of change in output to a unit change of the input
- **Zero Offset:** A nonzero value output for no input
- **Linearity:** Percentage of deviation from the best-fit linear calibration curve
- **Zero Drift:** The departure of output from zero value over a period of time for no input
- **Response Time:** The time lag between the input and output
- **Bandwidth:** Frequency at which the output magnitude drops by 3 dB
- **Resonance:** The frequency at which the output magnitude peak occurs
- **Operating Temperature:** The range in which the sensor performs as specified Dead band—The range of input for which there is no output
- **Signal-to-Noise Ratio:** Ratio between the magnitudes of the signal and the noise at the output.

Types of Sensors

1. Linear and Rotational Sensors

Linear and rotational position sensors are two of the most fundamental of all measurements used in a typical mechatronics system. In general, the position sensors produce an electrical output that is proportional to the displacement they experience. There are contact type sensors such as strain gage, LVDT, RVDT, tachometer, etc.

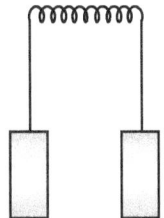

Fig. 5.13 : Bonded strain gauge

They can be classified based on the range of measurement. Usually the high-resolution type of sensors such as *hall effect, fiberoptic inductance, capacitance*, and *strain gage* are suitable for only very small range (typically from 0.1 mmto 5 mm). Among many linear displacement sensors, strain gage provides high resolution at low noise level and is least expensive. A typical resistance strain gage consists of resistive foil arranged as shown in the Fig. 5.13.

2. Acceleration Sensors

Measurement of acceleration is important for systems subject to shock and vibration. Although acceleration can be derived from the time history data obtainable from linear or rotary sensors, the accelerometers whose output is directly proportional to the acceleration is preferred. Two common types include the *seismic mass* type and the *piezoelectric* accelerometer. The seismic mass type accelerometer is based on the relative motion between a mass and the supporting structure. The natural frequency of the seismic mass limits its use to low to medium frequency applications. The piezoelectric accelerometer, however, is compact and more suitable for high frequency applications.

3. Force, Torque, and Pressure Sensors

Among many type of force/torque sensors, the *strain gage dyanamo meters* and *piezoelectric type* are most common. Both are available to measure force and/or torque either in one axis or multiple axes. The dynamometers make use of mechanical members that experiences elastic deflection when loaded. These types of sensors are limited by their natural frequency. On the other hand, the piezoelectric sensors are particularly suitable for dynamic loadings in a wide range of frequencies. They provide high stiffness, high resolution over a wide measurement range, and are compact.

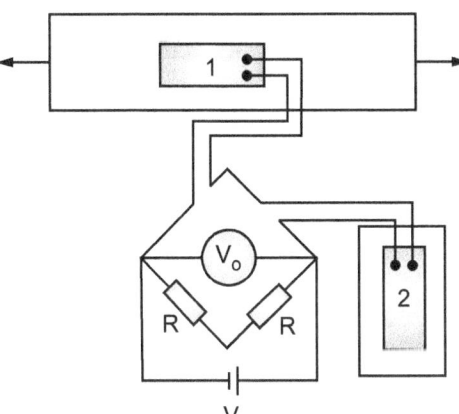

Fig. 5.14 : Shows the experimental setup for pressure measurement

Flow sensing is relatively a difficult task. The fluid medium can be liquid, gas, or a mixture of the two. Furthermore, the flow could be laminar or turbulent and can be a time-varying phenomenon. The venturimeter and orifice plate restrict the flow and use the pressure difference to determine the flow rate. Thepitot tube pressure probe is another popular method of measuring flow rate. When positioned against the flow,they measure the total and static pressures. The flow velocity and in turn the flow rate can then be determined. The rotameter and the turbine meters when placed in the flow path, rotate at a speed proportional to the flow rate. The electromagnetic flow meters use noncontact method. Magnetic field is applied in the transverse direction of the flow and the fluid acts as the conductor to induce voltage proportional to the flow rate.

Ultrasonic flow meters measure fluid velocity by passing high-frequency sound waves through fluid. Aschematic diagram of the ultrasonic flow meter is as shown in Fig. 5.15. The transmitters (T) provide the sound signal source. As the wave travels towards the receivers (R), its velocity is influenced by the velocity of the fluid flow due to the doppler effect. The control circuit compares the time to interpret the flow rate. This can be used for very high flow rates and can also be used for both upstream and downstream flow. The other advantage is that it can be used for corrosive fluids, fluids with abrasive particles, as it is like a noncontact sensor.

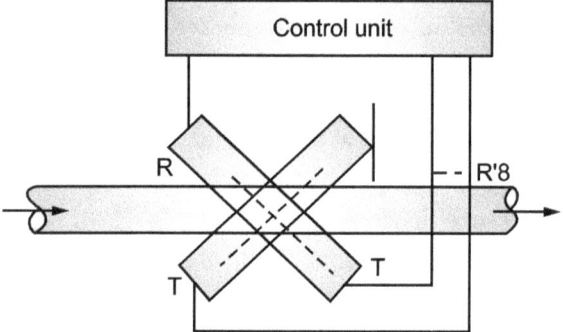

Fig. 5.15 : Flow Measurement Setup

4. Temperature Sensors

A variety of devices are available to measure temperature, the most common of which are thermocouples, thermisters, resistance temperature detectors (RTD), and infrared types.

Thermocouples are the most versatile, inexpensive, and have a wide range (up to $1200\infty C$ typical). Athermocouple simply consists of two dissimilar metal wires joined at the ends to create the sensing junction. When used in conjunction with a reference junction, the temperature difference between the reference junction and the actual temperature shows up as a voltage potential. *Thermisters* are semicon-ductor devices whose resistance changes as the temperature changes. They are good for very high sensitivity measurements in a limited range of up to 100∞ C. The relationship between the temperature and the resistance is nonlinear. The *RTD*s use the phenomenon that the resistance of a metal changes with temperature. They are, however, linear over a wide range and most stable.

Infrared type sensors use the radiation heat to sense the temperature from a distance. These noncontactsensors can also be used to sense a field of vision to generate a thermal map of a surface

5. Proximity Sensors

They are used to sense the proximity of an object relative to another object. They usually provide a on or off signal indicating the presence or absence of an object. *Inductance, capacitance, photoelectric*, and *hall effect*types are widely used as proximity sensors. Inductance proximity sensors consist of a coil woundaround a soft iron core. The inductance of the sensor changes when a ferrous object is in its proximity. This change is converted to a voltage-triggered switch. Capacitance types are similar to inductance except the proximity of an object changes the gap and affects the capacitance. Photoelectric sensors are normally aligned with an infrared light source. The proximity of a moving object interrupts the light beam causing the voltage level to change. Hall effect voltage is produced when a current-carrying conductor is exposed to a transverse magnetic field. The voltage is proportional to transverse distance between the hall effect sensor and an object in its proximity.

6. Light Sensors

Light intensity and full field vision are two important measurements used in many control applications. Phototransistors, photoresistors, and photodiodes are some of the more common type of light intensitysensors. A common photoresistor is made of cadmium sulphide whose resistance is maximum when the sensor is in dark. When the photoresistor is exposed to light, its resistance drops in proportion to the intensity of light. When interfaced with a circuit as shown in Fig. 6.26 and balanced, the change in light intensity will show up as change in voltage. These sensors are simple, reliable, and cheap, used widely for measuring light intensity.

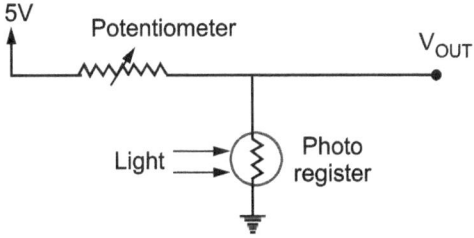

Fig. 5.16 : Light sensing with Photoresistor

7. Smart Material Sensors

There are many new smart materials that are gaining more applications as sensors, especially in distributed sensing circumstances. Of these, *optic fibers, piezoelectric,* and *magnetostrictive* materials have found appli-cations. Within these, optic fibers are most used.

Optic fibers can be used to sense strain, liquid level, force, and temperature with very high resolution. Since they are economical for use as *in situ* distributed sensors on large areas, they have found numerous applications in smart structure applications such as damage sensors, vibration sensors, and cure-monitoring sensors. These sensors use the inherent material (glass and silica) property of optical fiber to sense the environment. Fig 5.17 illustrates the basic principle of operation of an embedded optic fiber used to sense displacement, force, or temperature. The relative change in the transmitted intensity or spectrum is proportional to the change in the sensed parameter.

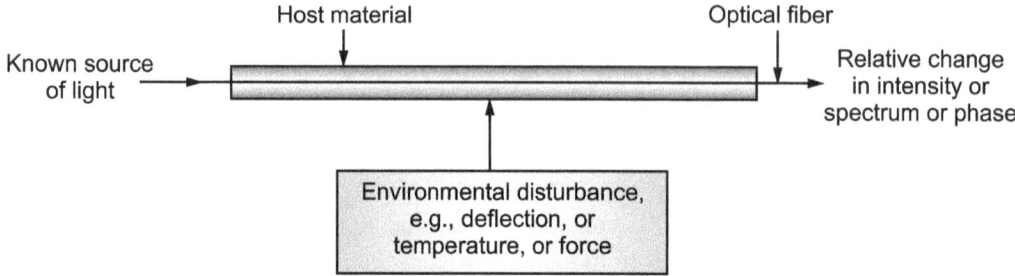

Fig. 5.17 : Principle of operation of optic fiber sensing

8. Micro- and Nanosensors

Microsensors (sometimes also called MEMS) are the miniaturized version of the conventional macrosensors with improved performance and reduced cost. Silicon micromachining technology has helped the development of many microsensors and continues to be one of the most active research and development topics in this area.

Vision microsensors have found applications in medical technology. A *fiberscope* of approximately 0.2 mm in diameter has been developed to inspect flaws inside tubes. Another example is a *microtactile sensor*, which uses laser light to detect the contact between a catheter and the inner wall of blood vessels during insertion that has sensitivity in the range of 1 mN. Similarly, the progress made in the area of nanotech-nology has fuelled the development of nanosensors. These are relatively new sensors that take one step further in the direction of miniaturization and are expected to open new avenues for sensing applications

5.7.2 Actuators

Actuators are basically the muscle behind a mechatronics system that accepts a control command (mostly in the form of an electrical signal) and produces a change in the physical system by generating force, motion, heat, flow, etc. Normally, the actuators are used in conjunction with the power supply and a coupling mechanism as shown in Fig. 5.18. The power unit provides either AC or DC power at the rated voltage and current. The coupling mechanism acts as the interface between the actuator and the physical system. Typical mechanisms include rack and pinion, gear drive, belt drive, lead screw and nut, piston, and linkages.

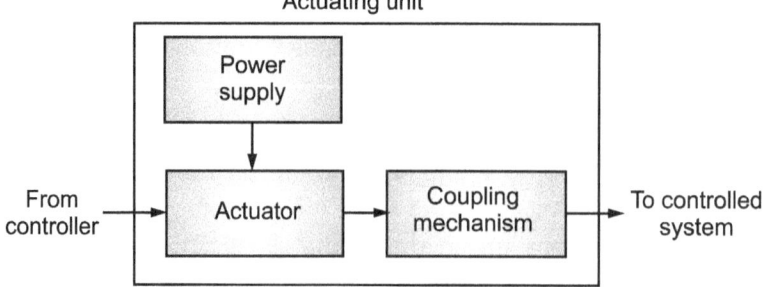

Fig. 5.18 : A Typical actuating unit

5.7.3 Selection of Actuator

The selection of the proper actuator is more complicated than selection of the sensors, primarily due to their effect on the dynamic behavior of the overall system. Furthermore, the selection of the actuator dominates the power needs and the coupling mechanisms of the entire system.

In general, the following performance parameters must be addressed before choosing an actuator for a specific need:

- **Continuous Power Output:** The maximum force/torque attainable continuously without exceeding thetemperature limits

- **Range of Motion:** The range of linear/rotary motion

- **Resolution :** The minimum increment of force/torque attainable

- **Accuracy :** Linearity of the relationship between the input and output

- **Peak Force/Torque :** The force/torque at which the actuator stalls

- **Heat Dissipation:** Maximum wattage of heat dissipation in continuous operation

- **Speed Characteristics:** Force/torque versus speed relationship

- **No Load Speed :** Typical operating speed/velocity with no external load.

- **Frequency Response:** The range of frequency over which the output follows the input faithfully, appli-cable to linear actuators

- **Power Requirement :** Type of power (AC or DC), number of phases, voltage level, and current capacity

5.7.4 Types of Actuators

1. **Electrical Actuators:**

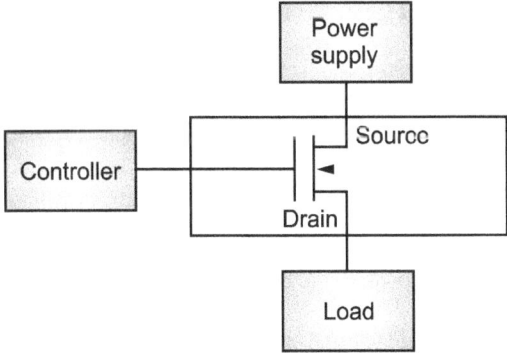

Fig. 5.19 : n-channel power MOSFET

Electrical switches are the choice of actuators for most of the on-off type control action. Switching devices such as diodes, transistors, triacs, MOSFET, and relays accept a low energy level command signal from the controller and switch on or off electrical devices such as motors, valves, and heating elements. For example, a MOSFET switch is shown in Fig. 5.19.The gate terminal receives the low energy control signal from the controller that makes or breaks the connection between the power supply and the actuator load. When switches are used, the designer must make sure that switch bounce problem is eliminated either by hardware or software.

2. Electromechanical Actuators

The most common electromechanical actuator is a motor that converts electrical energy to mechanical motion. Motors are the principal means of converting electrical energy into mechanical energy in industry. Broadly they can be classified as DC motors, AC motors, and stepper motors.

DC motors operate on DC voltage and varying the voltage can easily control their speed. They are widely used in applications ranging from thousands of horsepower motors used in rolling mills to fractional horsepower motors used in automobiles (starter motors, fan motors, windshield wiper motors, etc.).

AC motors are the most popular since they use standard AC power, do not require brushes and commu-tator, and are therefore less expensive. AC motors can be further classified as the induction motors, synchro-nous motors, and universal motors according to their physical constructionThe induction motor is simple,rugged, and maintenance free. They are available in many sizes and shapes based on number of phases used. For example, a three-phase induction motor is used in large-horsepower applications, such as pump drives, steel mill drives, hoist drives, and vehicle drives. The two-phase servomotor is used extensively in position control systems. Single-phase induction motors are widely used in many household appliances.

The stepper motor is a discrete (incremental) positioning device that moves one step at a time for each pulse command input. Since they accept direct digital commands and produce a mechanical motion, the stepper motors are used widely in industrial control applications. They are mostly used in fractional horsepower applications. With the rapid progress in low cost and high frequency solid-state drives, they are finding increased applications.

3. Electromagnetic Actuators

The solenoid is the most common electromagnetic actuator. A DC solenoid actuator consists of a soft iron core enclosed within a current carrying coil. When the coil is energized, a magnetic field is established that provides the force to push or pull the iron core. AC solenoid devices are also encountered, such as AC excitation relay.

A solenoid operated directional control valve is shown in Fig. 5.20. Normally, due to the spring force, the soft iron core is pushed to the extreme left position as shown. When the solenoid is excited, the soft iron core will move to the right extreme position thus providing the electromagnetic actuation.

Another important type is the electromagnet. The electromagnets are used extensively in applications that require large forces.

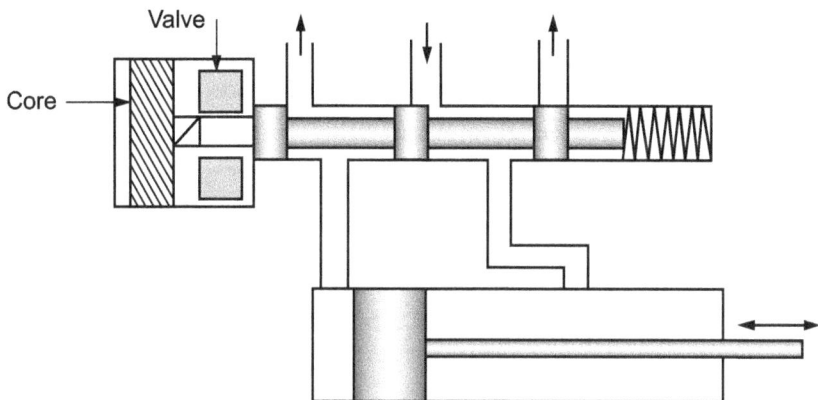

Fig. 5.20 : Solenoid operated directional control

4. Hydraulic and Pneumatic Actuators

Hydraulic and pneumatic actuators are normally either *rotary motors* or *linear piston/cylinder* or *controlvalves*. They are ideally suited for generating very large forces coupled with large motion. Pneumaticactuators use air under pressure that is most suitable for low to medium force, short stroke, and high-speed applications. Hydraulic actuators use pressurized oil that is incompressible. They can produce very large forces coupled with large motion in a cost-effective manner. The disadvantage with the hydraulic actuators is that they are more complex and need more maintenance.

5. Smart Material Actuators

Unlike the conventional actuators, the smart material actuators typically become part of the load bearing structures. This is achieved by embedding the actuators in a distributed manner and integrating into the load bearing structure that could be used to suppress vibration, cancel the noise, and change shape. Of the many smart material actuators, *shape memory alloys, piezoelectric (PZT), magnetostrictive, Electrorheo-logical fluids*, and *ion exchange polymers* are most common.

The PZT actuators are essentially piezocrystals with top and bottom conducting films as shown in   Fig. 5.21.When an electric voltage is applied across the two conducting films, the crystal expands in the transverse direction as shown by the dotted lines. When the voltage polarity is reversed, the crystal contracts thereby providing bidirectional actuation.

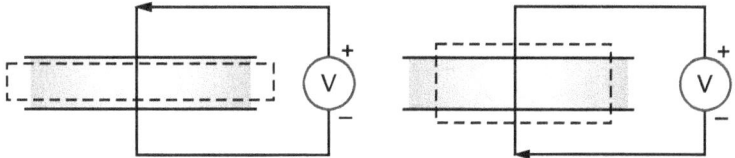

Fig. 5.21 : Piezoelectric actuator

Magnetostrictivematerial is an alloy of terbium, dysprosium, and iron that generates mechanical strainsup to 2000 microstrain in response to applied magnetic fields. They are available in the form of rods, plates, washers, and powder. Fig 5.22 shows a typical magnetostrictive rod actuator that is surrounded by a magnetic coil. When the coil is excited, the rod elongates in proportion to the intensity of the magnetic field established.

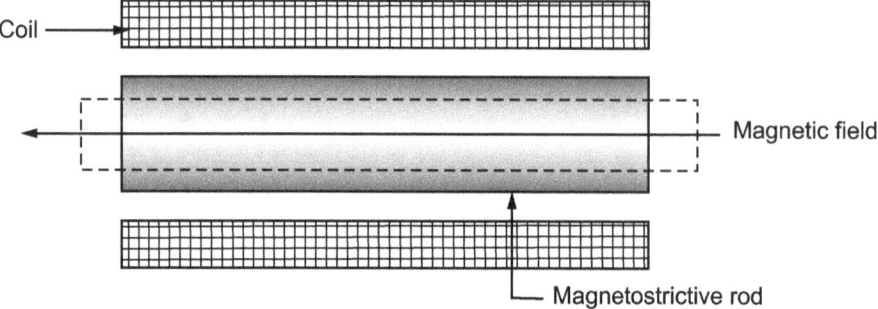

Fig. 5.22 : Magnetostrictive rod actuator

6. Micro- and Nanoactuators

Microactuators, also called micromachines, microelectromechanical system (MEMS), and microsystems are the tiny mobile devices being developed utilizing the standard microelectronics processes with the integration of semiconductors and machined micromechanical elements. Another definition states that any device produced by assembling extremely small functional parts of around 1–15 mm is called a micromachine.

In *electrostatic motors*, electrostatic force is dominant, unlike the conventional motors that are based on magnetic forces For smaller micromechanical systems the electrostatic forces are well suited as an actuating force. Fig 5.23shows one type of electrostatic motor. The rotor is an annular disk with uniform permitivity and conductivity. In operation, a voltage is applied to the two conducting parallel.

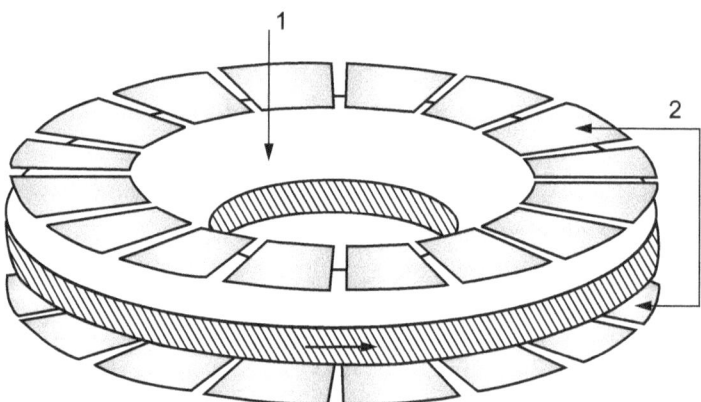

Fig. 5.23 : Shows one type of electrostatic motor

5.8 DATA ACQUISITION SYSTEMS

Data Acquisition Systems are used by most engineers and scientists for laboratory research, industrial control, test and measurement to input and output data to and from a computer. A Data Acquisition and control system typically consist of the followings block

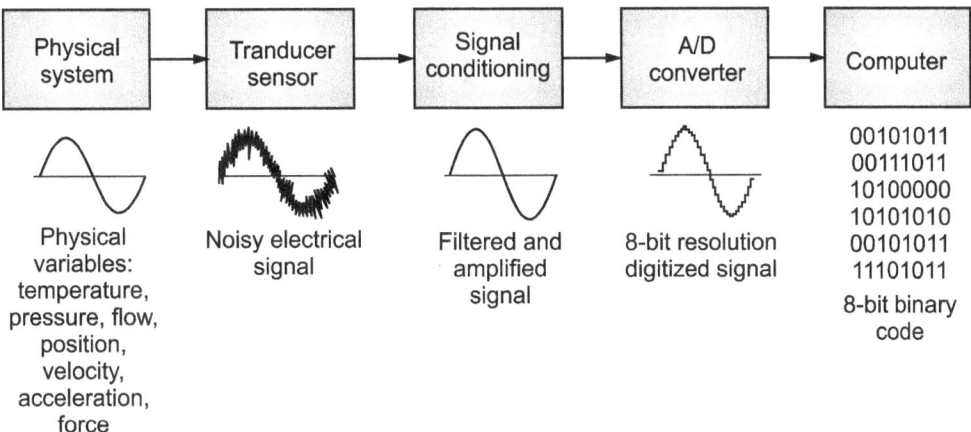

Fig. 5.24

Data acquisition systems measure, store, display, and analyze information collected from a variety of devices.

The data acquisition system consists of following functional components:

- **Transducers/Sensors**- Most measurements require a transducer or a sensor, a device that converts a measurable physical quantity into an electrical signal. Examples include temperature, strain, acceleration, pressure, vibration, and sound. Yet others are humidity, flow, level, velocity, charge, pH, and chemical composition. Sensors come in numerous shapes, sizes, and specifications. They connect between the measured physical device and the signal conditioner's input

- **Signal Conditioners** accept sensor output signals and convert them into a form that the data acquisition system can manipulate. Signal conditioners typically amplify, filter, isolate, and linearize these signals. They also convert current to voltage and voltage to frequency, provide other functions such as simultaneous sample and hold (SS&H), and supply a bias voltage or signal excitation for certain transducers. They may come with single-ended inputs or differential inputs for improving signal-to-noise ratios.

- **A/D Converter** - The output of the signal conditioner, in turn, connects to the input of an analog-to-digital converter (ADC). the ADC converts the conditioned analog signal to a digital signal that can be transferred out of the data acquisition system to a computer for processing, graphing, and storing.

- **Computer:** A computer with the appropriate application software to process, analyze and log the data to disk. Such software may also provide a graphical display of the data.

- **Output Interface** to provide appropriate process control response.it may be printer display or recording unit.

5.9 INTRODUCTION TO ARDUINO IDE

Arduino is an open-source platform used for building electronics projects. Arduino consists of both a physical programmable circuit board (often referred to as a microcontroller) and a piece of software, or IDE (Integrated Development Environment) that runs on your computer, used to write and upload computer code to the physical board.

The Arduino platform has become quite popular with people just starting out with electronics, and for good reason. Unlike most previous programmable circuit boards, the Arduino does not need a separate piece of hardware (called a programmer) in order to load new code onto the board – you can simply use a USB cable. Additionally, the Arduino IDE uses a simplified version of C++, making it easier to learn to program. Finally, Arduino provides a standard form factor that breaks out the functions of the micro-controller into a more accessible package.

Features of Arduino IDE Platform

- ArduinoIDE comes in multiplatform environment it can run on windows,linux and Macintosh.

- Arduino IDE is a user friendly interface to allow one to quickly write, load, and execute code on a microcontroller.

- A barebones programneed only consist of a setup() and loop() function.

- The ArduinoIDE adds the other required pieces such as header files and the main program construct .

- We can program hardware via USB cable this is key features added to use modern computers for IDE.

- The hardware available of arduino is cheap and available different version with additional features.

- The arduinoprojects were developed in an educational environment and are therefore great for new designer to get things quickly.

- Although there are many different types of Arduino boards available on of the Arduinouno is popular one having ATmega328p microcontroller.

Arduino IDE Overview

The Arduino Development Environment is illustrated in Fig. 5.24 TheADE contains a text editor, a message area for displaying status, a text console, a toolbar of common functions, and an extensive menuing system. The ADE also provides a user friendly interface to the ArduinoDuemilanove which allows for a quick upload of code. This is possible because the ArduinoDuemilanove is equipped with a bootloader program.

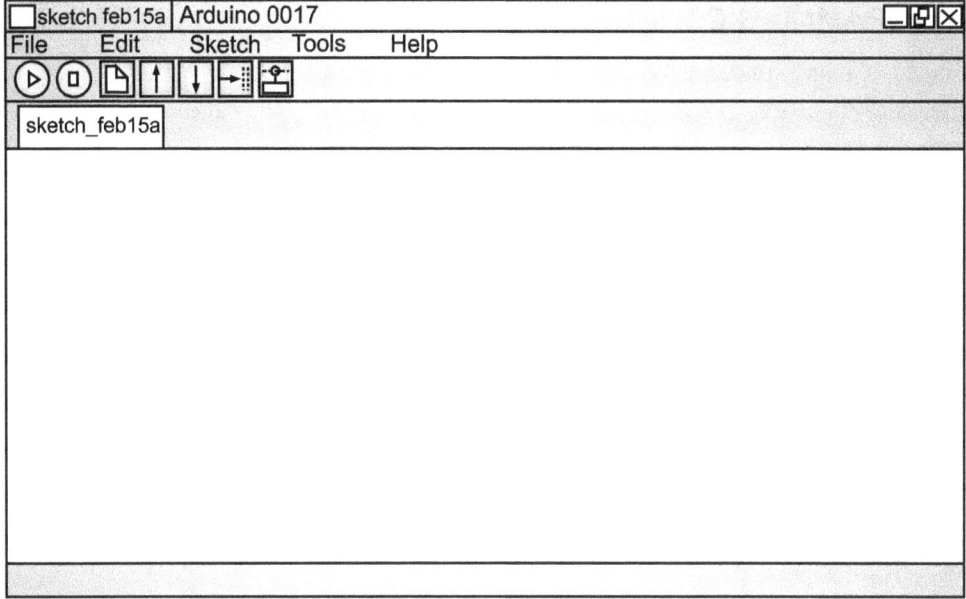

Fig. 5.25 : Arduino development Environment

A close up of the Arduino toolbar is provided in Fig. 5.25.The tool bar provides single button access to the more commonly used menu features. Most of the features are self-explanatory. The "Upload to I/O Board" button compiles your code and uploads it to the Arduino Duemilanove. The "Serial Monitor" button opens the serial monitor feature. The serial monitor feature allows text data to be sent to and received from the Arduino Duemilanove. The serial monitor feature is halted with the "Stop" button.

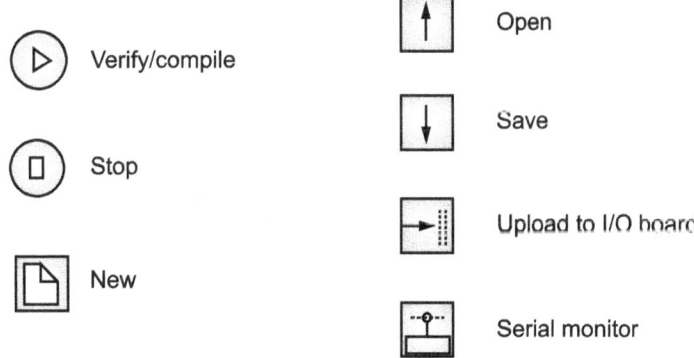

Fig. 5.26 : Arduino IDE buttons

Sketchbook Concept

In keeping with a hardware and software platform for students of the arts, the Arduino environment employs the concept of a sketchbook. An artist maintains their works in progress in a sketchbook. Similarly, we maintain our programs within a sketchbook in the Arduino environment. Furthermore, we refer to individual programs as sketches. An individual sketch within the sketchbook may be accessed via the Sketchbook entry under the file tab.

5.10 PROGRAMMING CONCEPTS

We covered many fundamental concepts. In this section we discuss operators, programming constructs, and decision processing constructs to complete our fundamental overview of programming concepts.

5.10.1 Variables

There are two types of variables used within a program: global variables and local variables. A global variable is available and accessible to all portions of the program. Whereas, a local variable is only known and accessible within the function where it is declared.

When declaring a variable in C, the number of bits used to store the operator is also specified below, we provide a list of common C variable sizes used with the ImageCraft ICC AVR compiler.

Type	Size	Range
unsigned char	1	0.255
signed char	1	−128.127
unsigned int	2	0.65535
signed int	2	−32768 ... 32767
float	4	+/−1.175e−38 .. + /−3.40e + 38
double	4	+/−1.175e−38...+/−3.40e + 38

When programming microcontrollers, it is important to know the number of bits used to store the variable and also where the variable will be assigned. For example, assigning the contents of an unsigned char variable, which is stored in 8-bits, to an 8-bit output port will have a predictable result.

5.10.2 Operators

There are a wide variety of operators provided in the C language. An abbreviated list of common operators are provided in coming sectionsThe operators have been grouped by general category. The symbol, precedence, and brief description of each operator are provided.

General Operators

General		
Symbol	**Precedence**	**Description**
{ }	1	Brackets, used to group program statements
( )	1	Parenthesis, used to establish precedence
=	12	Assignment

Within the general operations category are brackets, parenthesis, and the assignment operator. We have seen in an earlier example how bracket pairs are used to indicate the beginning and end of the main program or a function.The parenthesis is used to boost the priority of an operator.

The assignment operator (=) is used to assign the argument(s) on the right-hand side of an equation to the left-hand side variable. It is important to insure that the left and the right-hand side of the equation have the same type of arguments

Arithmetic Operators

The arithmetic operations provide for basic math operations using the operators given .the assignment operator (=) is used to assign the argument(s) on the right-hand side of an equation to the left-hand side variable.the description is given in below Fig.

In this example, a function returns the sum of two unsigned int variables passed tothe function.

```
unsignedintsum_two(unsigned int variable1, unsigned int variable2)


{


unsignedint sum;

sum = variable1 + variable2;

return sum;

}
```

Arithmetic Operations		
Symbol	Precedence	Description
*	3	Multiplication
/	3	Division
+	4	Addition
−	4	Subtraction

Logical Operators

The logical operators provide Boolean logic operations. They can be viewed as comparison operators. One argument is compared against another using the logical operator provided.The result is returned as a logic value of one (1, true, high) or zero (0 false, low). The description is given below.

Arithmetic Operations		
Symbol	**Precedence**	**Description**
<	6	Less than
< =	6	Less than or equal to
>	6	Greater
> =	6	Greater than or equal to
= =	7	Equal to
! =	7	Not equal to
&&	9	Logical AND
||	10	Logical OR

Bit Manipulation Operators

There are two general types of operations in the bit manipulation category: shifting operations and bitwise operations the description is given in below.

Bit Manipulation Operations		
Symbol	**Precedence**	**Description**
<<	5	Shift left
>>	5	Shift right
&	8	Bitwise AND
^	8	Bitwise exclusive OR
		8	Bitwise OR

Unary Operators

The unary operators, as their name implies, require only a single argument.

For example, in the following code segment, the value of the variable "i" is incremented. This is a shorthand method of executing the operation "$i = i + 1$;".The description of operator is given as.

Unary Operations		
Symbol	**Precedence**	**Description**
!	2	Unary negative
~	2	One's complement (bit-by-bit inversion)
+	2	Increment
--	2	Decrement
type (argument)	2	Casting operator (data type conversion)

5.10.3 Programming Control Structures (Costructs)

In this section, we discuss several methods of looping through a code example.

1. For Loop : The for loop provides a mechanism for looping through the same portion of code a fixed number of times The for loop consists of three main parts:

loop initiation

loop termination testing and

the loop increment.

In the following code fragment the for loop is executed ten times.

```
unsignedint    loop_ctr;
for(loop_ctr = 0; loop_ctr< 10; loop_ctr++)
{


//loop body
}
```

The for loop begins with the variable "loop_ctr" equal to 0. During the first pass through the loop, the variable retains this value. During the next pass through the loop, the variable "loop_ctr" is incremented by one. This action continues until the "loop_ctr" variable reaches the value of ten. Since the argument to continue the loop is no longer true, program execution continues after the close bracket for the for loop.

2. While Loop: The **while** loop is another programming construct that allows multiple passes through a portion of code. The while loop will continue to execute the statements within the open and close brackets while the condition at the beginning of the loop remains logically true. The code snapshot below will implement a ten iteration loop. Note how the "loop_ctr" variable is initialized outside of the loop and incremented within the body of the loop. As before, the variable may be initialized to a greater value and then decremented within the loop body.

```
unsignedint    loop_ctr;
loop_ctr = 0;


while(loop_ctr< 10)


{
//loop body
loop_ctr++;

}
```

Frequently, within a microcontroller application, the program begins with system initialization actions. Once initialization activities are complete, the processor enters a continuous loop. This may be accomplished using the following code fragment.

```
while(1)

{
}
```

The if statement :

The **if** statement will execute the code between an open and close bracket set should the condition within the if statement be logically true for example.

```
If(condition)
{
    ///do if condition is true
}
```

There is another two constructs under if is used for false condition these are

if-else and if-else-if for example

If(somecondition)
 	
{
    ///do if condition is true
}
else
{
    ///do if condition is false
}
	If(first condition)
	
	{
	    ///do if first condition is true
	}
	else if(second condition)
	{
	    ///do if second condition is
	true
	}

Switch/case Statement:

The **switch** statement is used when multiple if-else conditions exist. Each possible condition is specified by a case statement. When a match is found between the switch variable and a specific case entry, the statements associated with the case are executed until a **break** statement is encountered.

Example: Suppose eight pushbutton switches are connected to PORTD. Each switch willimplement a different action. A switch statement may be used to process the multiple possible decisions as shown in the following code fragment.

```c
voidread_new_input(void)

{

new_PORTD = PIND;
if(new_PORTD != old_PORTD)//check for status change PORTD
switch(new_PORTD)
{
case 0x01://process change in PORTD input
//PD0

//PD0 related actions
break;
case 0x02://PD1
//PD1 related actions
break;

.

.

.

.

.

case 0x80://PD7
//PD7 related actions
break;
                default:    //all other cases
}                           //end switch(new_PORTD)
}                           //end if new_PORTD
old_PORTD=new_PORTD;    //update PORTD
}
```

5.10.4 Functions

- At the highest level is the main program which calls functions that have a defined action. When a function is called, program control is released from the main program to the function. Once the function is complete, program control reverts back to the main program.

Functions may in turn call other functions as shown in Fig. 5.26. This approach results in a collection of functions that may be reused over and over again in various projects. Most importantly, the program is now subdivided into doable pieces, each with a defined action. This makes writing the program easier but also makes it much easier to modify the program since every action is in a known location.

```
void main(void)
{
:

function1( ); → void function1(void)
{

:

:

}
function2( );→ void function2(void)
{

:

:

}
}
```

There are three different pieces of code required to properly configure and call the function:

1. The function prototype,
2. The function call, and
3. The function body.

- **Function Prototypes** are provided early in the program as previously shown in the programtemplate. The function prototype provides the name of the function and any variables required by the function and any variable returned by the function.

The function prototype follows this format

return_variablefunction_name(required_variable1, required_variable2);

- **Function Call** is the code statement used within a program to execute the function. The function call consists of the function name and the actual arguments required by the function. If the function does not require arguments to be delivered to it for processing, the parenthesis containing the variable list is left empty.

The function call follows this format:

function_name(required_variable1, required_variable2);

A function that requires no variables follows this format:

function_name( );

- **Function Body** is a self-contained "mini-program." The first line of the function body contains the same information as the function prototype: the name of the function, any variables required by the function, and any variable returned by the function. The last line of the function contains a "return" statement. Here a variable may be sent back to the portion of the program that called the function. The processing action of the function is contained within the open ({) and close brackets (}). If the function requires any variables within the confines of the function, they are declared next. These variable are referred to as local variables. The actions required by the function follow.

The function prototype follows this format:

return_variablefunction_name(required_variable1, required_variable2) {

```
//local variables required by the function
unsignedint     variable1;
unsigned char variable2;
//program statements required by the function
//return variable
returnreturn_variable;
}
```

5.10.5 Constants

The #define statement is used to associate a constant name with a numerical value in a program. It can be used to define common constants such as pi. It may also be used to give terms used within a program a numerical value. This makes the code easier to read. For example, the following constants may be defined within a program:

```
//program constants
#define          TRUE  1
#define          FALSE 0
#define          ON  1
#define          OFF 0
```

5.11 EXERCISES

1. Write a short note on Microprocessor based system?

2. Draw the block diagram of microprocessor and state the application.

3. What is microcontroller stat it's applications?

4. What is the difference between microprocessor and microcontroller.

5. What is the Role of Embedded system?

6. Draw and Explain typical Embedded system?

7. State the characteristics of Embedded system?

8. What is the advantages of open-source embedded platforms.

9. What is open-source embedded platform.

10. Write a short note on Assembler, compiler and debugger.

11. Write the features of ATmega328P microcontroller?

12. Draw the block diagram of ATmega328P microcontroller.

13. Explain AVR CPU Architecture?

14. Write a short note on port structure.

15. Explain PORTx, PINx, and DDRx Registers and it's use in digital I/O.

16. What is sensor? State few types of sensor?

17. What is actuator? Sate few types of actuator.

18. What are the features of Arduino IDE.

19. Which are variable used in Arduino program.

20. Explain different operators in Arduino program.

21. Explain following constructs used in programming

    (i) for loop

    (ii) while loop

    (iii) if

22. What is function? What is function call and function body with example

◈ ◈ ◈

PERIPHERAL INTERFACE - I

6.1 CONCEPT OF GPIO IN ATMEGA 328P BASED ARDUINO BOARD

Arduino/Genuino Uno is a microcontroller board based on the ATmega328P. It has 14 digital input/output pins of which 6 can be used as PWM outputs, 6 analog inputs, a 16 MHz quartz crystal, a USB connection, a power jack, an ICSP header and a reset button. It contains everything needed to support the microcontroller; simply connect it to a computer with a USB cable or power it with a AC-to-DC adapter or battery to get started.

Each of the 14 digital pins on the Uno can be used as an input or output, using pinMode(), digitalWrite(), and digitalRead() functions.

They operate at 5 volts. Each pin can provide or receive 20 mA as recommended operating condition and has an internal pull-up resistor (disconnected by default) of 20-50k ohm. A maximum of 40mA is the value that must not be exceeded on any I/O pin to avoid permanent damage to the microcontroller.

In addition, some pins have **specialized functions**:

● **Serial**: **0** (RX) and **1** (TX). Used to receive (RX) and transmit (TX) TTL serial data. These pins are connected to the corresponding pins of the ATmega8U2 USB-to-TTL Serial chip

● **External Interrupts: 2 and 3**. These pins can be configured to trigger an interrupt on a low value, a rising or falling edge, or a change in value. See the attachInterrupt() function for details.

● **PWM**: **3, 5, 6, 9, 10, and 11**. Provide 8-bit PWM output with the analogWrite() function.

● **SPI: 10 (SS), 11 (MOSI), 12 (MISO), 13 (SCK).** These pins support SPI communication using the SPI library.

● **LED: 13**. There is a built-in LED driven by digital pin 13. When the pin is HIGH value, the LED is on, when the pin is LOW, it's off.

● **TWI: A4 or SDA pin and A5 or SCL pin**. Support TWI communication using the Wire library.

The Uno has 6 analog inputs, labeled A0 through A5, each of which provide 10 bits of resolution (i.e. 1024 different values). By default they measure from ground to 5 volts, though is it possible to change the upper end of their range using the AREF pin and the analogReference() function.

There are a couple of other pins on the board:

AREF: Reference voltage for the analog inputs. Used with analogReference().

Reset: Bring this line LOW to reset the microcontroller. Typically used to add a reset button to shields which block the one on the board.

6.2 DIGITAL INPUT AND OUTPUT

Each of 14 digital I/O pins can be either *inputs* or *outputs*. Inputs are used to read information from sensors or any outside devices, while outputs are used to control actuators or external device may be LED, Motor and display. To do this first we required to specify the direction (in or out) in the sketch you create in the IDE. Digital inputs can only read one of two values, and digital outputs can only output one of two values (HIGH and LOW). These operations can be done using following functions

6.2.1 pinMode() function

This function used to configure port pin(direction) for either input or output.

Syntax pinMode(pin, mode)

Where pin provides number of port pin and mode is either INPUT or OUTPUT.

pins configured as pinMode(pin, INPUT) with nothing connected to them, or with wires connected to them that are not connected to other circuits, will report seemingly random changes in pin state, picking up electrical noise from the environment, or capacitive coupling the state of a nearby pin.Often it is useful to steer an input pin to a known state if no input is present. This can be done by adding a pull-up resistor (to +5V), or a pull-down resistor (resistor to ground) on the input. A 10K resistor is a good value for a pull-up or pull-down resistor.

Example

```
void setup()
{
  pinMode(ledPin, OUTPUT);    // sets the digital pin as output
}
```

6.2.2 digitalWrite() function

This function is used to Write a logic HIGH('1') or a logic LOW ('0') value to a digital pin.

If the pin has been configured as an OUTPUT with pinMode(), its voltage will be set to the corresponding value: 5V (or 3.3V on 3.3V boards) for HIGH, 0V (ground) for LOW.

If the pin is configured as an INPUT, digitalWrite() will enable (HIGH) or disable (LOW) the internal pullup on the input pin. It is recommended to set the pinMode() to INPUT_PULLUP to enable the internal pull-up resistor. See the digital pins tutorial for more information.

if you do not set the pinMode() to OUTPUT, and connect an LED to a pin, when calling digitalWrite(HIGH), the LED may not glow properly.

Syntax **digitalWrite(pin, value)**

Where pin=the pin number,value=HIGH or LOW

Example

```
int ledPin = 13;              // LED connected to digital pin 13
void setup()
{
  pinMode(ledPin, OUTPUT);    // sets the digital pin as output
}
void loop()
{
  digitalWrite(ledPin, HIGH);  // sets the LED on
  delay(100);                  // waits for a second
  digitalWrite(ledPin, LOW);   // sets the LED off
  delay(100);                  // waits for a second
}
```

6.2.3 digitalRead() function

This function used to Reads the value from a specified digital pin, either HIGH or LOW after reading of value it will return HIGH or LOW.

Syntax digitalRead(pin)

Where Pin=the number of the digital pin you want to read

Example

```
int ledPin = 13; // LED connected to digital pin 13
int inPin = 7;   // pushbutton connected to digital pin 7
int val = 0;     // variable to store the read value

void setup()
{
  pinMode(ledPin, OUTPUT);    // sets the digital pin 13 as output
  pinMode(inPin, INPUT);      // sets the digital pin 7 as input
}

void loop()
{
  val = digitalRead(inPin);   // read the input pin
  digitalWrite(ledPin, val);  // sets the LED to the button's value
}
```

6.3 UART CONCEPT

The microcontroller is parallel device that transfers eight bits of data simultaneously over eight data lines to parallel I/O devices. However, in many situations, parallel data transfer is impractical for example, parallel data transfer over a long distance is very expensive. Hence, serial communication is widely used in long distance communication.

In serial data communication, 8-bit data is converted to serial bits using a parallel in serial out (PISO) shift register and then it is transmitted over a single data line. The data byte is always transmitted with least significant bit (LSB) first.

The universal asynchronous receiver/transmitter (UART) takes bytes of data and transmits the individual bits in a sequential fashion. At the destination, a second UART re-assembles the bits into complete bytes. Each UART contains a shift register, which is the fundamental method of conversion between serial and parallel forms. Serial transmission of digital information (bits) through a single wire or other medium is less costly than parallel transmission through multiple wires.

The UART usually does not directly generate or receive the external signals used between different items of equipment. Separate interface devices are used to convert the logic level signals of the UART to and from the external signaling levels. External signals may be of many different forms. Examples of standards for voltage signaling are RS-232, RS-422 and RS-485 from the EIA. Historically, current (in current loops) was used in telegraph circuits. Some signaling schemes do not use electrical wires. Examples of such are optical fiber, IrDA (infrared), and (wireless) Bluetooth in its Serial Port Profile (SPP). Some signaling schemes use modulation of a carrier signal (with or without wires). Examples are modulation of audio signals with phone line modems, RF modulation with data radios, and the DC-LIN for power line communication.

6.3.1 Types of Serial Communication

Serial data communication uses two types of communication.

(a) Synchronous Serial Data Communication: In this transmitter and receiver are synchronized. It uses a common clack to synchronize the receiver and the transmitter. First the synch character is sent and then the data is transmitted. This format is generally used for high speed transmission. In Synchronous serial data communication a block of data is transmitted at a time.

(b) Asynchronous Serial Data Transmission: In this, different clock sources are used for transmitter and receiver. In this mode, data is transmitted with start and stop bits. A transmission begins with start bit, followed by data and then stop bit. For error checking purpose parity bit is included just prior to stop bit. In Asynchronous serial data communication a single byte is transmitted at a time.

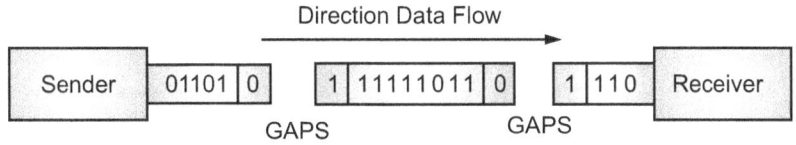

Asynchronous Transmission

Fig. 6.1 : Asynchronous Serial data transmission

6.3.2 Serial Communication is Classified into Three Types of Communication

(a) **Simplex Communication Link:** In simplex transmission, the line is dedicated for transmission. The transmitter sends and the receiver receives the data.

(b) **Half Duplex Communication Link:** In half duplex, the communication link can be used for either transmission or reception. Data is transmitted in only one direction at a time.

(c) **Full Duplex Communication Link:** If the data is transmitted in both ways at the same time, it is a full duplex i.e. transmission and reception can proceed simultaneously. This communication link requires two wires for data, one for transmission and one for reception.

6.3.4 Baud Rate

The rate at which the bits are transmitted is called baud or transfer rate. The baud rate is the reciprocal of the time to send one bit. In asynchronous transmission, baud rate is not equal to number of bits per second. This is because; each byte is preceded by a start bit and followed by parity and stop bit. But in case of synchronous transmission, if data is transmitted with 9600 baud, it means that 9600 bits are transmitted in one second. For bit transmission time = 1 second/ 9600 = 0.104 ms.

6.3.5 Serial Data Format

The serial data format includes one start bit, between five and eight data bits, and one stop bit. A parity bit and an additional stop bit might be included in the format as well. The Fig. 4.1 below illustrates the serial data format.

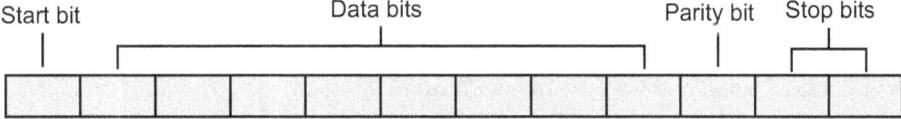

Fig. 6.2 : Data format

The format for serial port data is often expressed using the following notation: Number of data bits - parity type - number of stop bits.

6.4 TIMERS

A timer / counter is a piece of hardware built in the Arduino controller (other controllers have timer hardware, too). Used to generate time delay or counting external pulses It is like a clock, and can be used to measure time events.

The controller of the Arduino is the Atmel AVR ATmega168 or the ATmega328. These chips are pin compatible and only differ in the size of internal memory. Both have 3 timers, called timer0, timer1 and timer2. Timer0 and timer2 are 8bit timer, where timer1 is a 16bit timer. The most important difference between 8bit and 16bit timer is the timer resolution. 8bits means 256 values where 16bit means 65536 values for higher resolution.

The controller for the Arduino Mega series is the Atmel AVR ATmega1280 or the ATmega2560. Also identical only differs in memory size. These controllers have 6 timers. Timer 0, timer1 and timer2 are identical to the ATmega168/328. The timer3, timer4 and timer5 are all 16bit timers, similar to timer1.

All timers depends on the system clock of your Arduino system. Normally the system clock is 16MHz, but for the Arduino Pro 3,3V it is 8Mhz. So be careful when writing your own timer functions.

The timer hardware can be configured with some special timer registers. In the Arduino firmware all timers were configured to a 1kHz frequency and interrupts are gerally enabled

Timer0:

Timer0 is a 8bit timer. In the Arduino world timer0 is been used for the timer functions, like delay(), millis() and micros(). If you change timer0 registers, this may influence the Arduino timer function. So you should know what you are doing.

Timer1:

Timer1 is a 16bit timer. In the Arduino world the Servo library uses timer1 on Arduino Uno (timer5 on Arduino Mega).

Timer2:

Timer2 is a 8bit timer like timer0. In the Arduino work the tone() function uses timer2.

Timer3, Timer4, Timer5:

Timer 3,4,5 are only available on Arduino Mega boards. These timers are all 16bit timers.

Now we will see the timer modules and their features

6.4.1 TC0 - 8-bit Timer/Counter0 with PWM

Timer/Counter0 (TC0) is a general purpose 8-bit Timer/Counter module, with two independent Output Compare Units, and PWM support. It allows accurate program execution timing (event management) and waveform generation.

Features

- Two independent Output Compare Units
- Double Buffered Output Compare Registers
- Clear Timer on Compare Match (Auto Reload)
- Glitch free, phase correct Pulse Width Modulator (PWM)
- Variable PWM period
- Frequency generator
- Three independent interrupt sources (TOV0, OCF0A, and OCF0B)

1. Registers

We can change the Timer behaviour through the timer register. The most important timer registers are :

TCCRx - Timer/Counter Control Register. The prescaler can be configured here.

TCNTx - Timer/Counter Register. The actual timer value is stored here.

OCRx - Output Compare Register

ICRx - Input Capture Register (only for 16bit timer)

TIMSKx - Timer/Counter Interrupt Mask Register. To enable/disable timer interrupts.

TIFRx - Timer/Counter Interrupt Flag Register. Indicates a pending timer interrupt.

2. Clock Select and Timer Frequency

The TC can be clocked internally, via the prescaler, or by an external clock source on the T0 pin. The Clock Select logic block controls which clock source and edge is used by the Timer/Counter to increment (or decrement) its value. The TC is inactive when no clock source is selected. The output from the Clock Select logic is referred to as the timer clock (clkT0).

Different clock sources can be selected for each timer independently. To calculate the timer frequency (for example 2Hz using timer1) you will need:

1. CPU frequency 16Mhz for Arduino

2. Maximum timer counter value (256 for 8bit, 65536 for 16bit timer)

3. Divide CPU frequency through the choosen prescaler (16000000 / 256 = 62500)

4. Divide result through the desired frequency (62500 / 2Hz = 31250)

Verify the result against the maximum timer counter value (31250 < 65536 success) if fail, choose bigger prescaler.

Table 6.1 shows the clock select bit description

CS12	CS11	CS10	Description
0	0	0	No clock source (Timer/Counter stopped)
0	0	1	$clk_{10}/1$ (No prescaling)
0	1	0	$clk_{10}/8$ (From prescaler)
0	1	1	$clk_{10}/64$ (From prescaler)
1	0	0	$clk_{10}/256$ (From prescaler)
1	0	1	$clk_{10}/1024$ (From prescaler)
1	1	0	External clock source on T_1 pin. Clock on falling edge.
1	1	1	External clock source on T_1 pin. Clock on rising edge.

3. Counter Unit

The main part of the 8-bit Timer/Counter is the programmable bi-directional counter unit. Fig 6.3 is the block diagram of the counter and its surroundings.

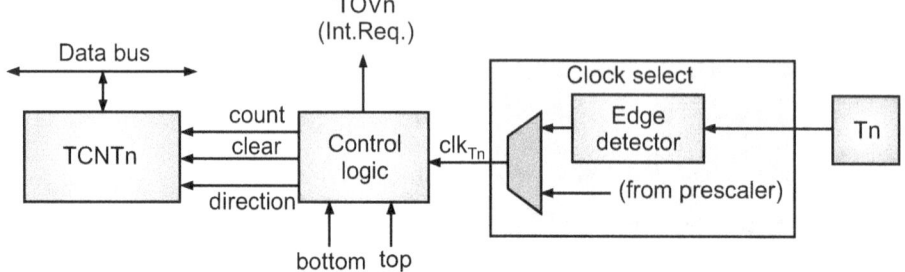

Fig. 6.3 : Block diagram of counter unit

Table 6.2 shows the signal description of counter unit

Signal Name	Description
count	Increment or decrement TCNT0 by 1.
direction	Select between increment and decrement.
clear	Clear TCNT0 (set all bits to zero).
clk_{Tn}	Timer/Counter clock, referred to as clk_{T0} in the following
top	Signalize that TCNT0 has reached maximum value.
bottom	Signalize that TCNT0 has reached minimum value (zero).

Depending of the mode of operation used, the counter is cleared, incremented, or decremented at each timer clock (clkT0). clkT0 can be generated from an external or internal clock source, selected by the Clock Select bits (CS0[2:0]). When no clock source is selected (CS0=0x0) the timer is stopped. However, the TCNT0 value can be accessed by the CPU, regardless of whether clkT0 is present or not. A CPU write overrides (has priority over) all counter clear or count operations.

The counting sequence is determined by the setting of the WGM01 and WGM00 bits located in the Timer/ Counter Control Register (TCCR0A) and the WGM02 bit located in the Timer/Counter Control Register B (TCCR0B).

4. Output Compare Unit

The 8-bit comparator continuously compares TCNT0 with the Output Compare Registers (OCR0A and OCR0B). Whenever TCNT0 equals OCR0A or OCR0B, the comparator signals a match. A match will set the Output Compare Flag (OCF0A or OCF0B) at the next timer clock cycle. If the corresponding interrupt is enabled, the Output Compare Flag generates an Output Compare interrupt. The Output Compare Flag is automatically cleared when the interrupt is executed. Alternatively, the flag can be cleared by software by writing a '1' to its I/O bit location.

The Waveform Generator uses the match signal to generate an output according to operating mode set by the WGM02, WGM01, and WGM00 bits and Compare Output mode (COM0x[1:0]) bits. The max and bottom signals are used by the Waveform Generator for handling the special cases of the extreme values in some modes of operation

Table 6.3 Shows the waveform generator bit setting

Mode	WGM02	WGM01	WGM00	Timer/Counter Mode of Opeation
0	0	0	0	Normal
1	0	0	1	PWM, Phase Correct
2	0	1	0	CTC
3	0	1	1	Fast PWM
4	1	0	0	Reserved
5	1	0	1	PWM, Phase Correct
6	1	1	0	Reserved
7	1	1	1	Fast PWM

6.4.2 TC1 - 16-bit Timer/Counter1 with PWM

The 16-bit Timer/Counter unit allows accurate program execution timing (event management), wave generation, and signal timing measurement.

Features

- True 16-bit Design (i.e., allows 16-bit PWM)

- Two independent Output Compare Units

- Double Buffered Output Compare Registers

- One Input Capture Unit

- Input Capture Noise Canceler

- Clear Timer on Compare Match (Auto Reload)

- Glitch-free, Phase Correct Pulse Width Modulator (PWM)

- Variable PWM Period

- Frequency Generator

- External Event Counter

- Independent interrupt Sources (TOV, OCFA, OCFB, and ICF)

1. **Registers**

The Timer/Counter (TCNT1), Output Compare Registers (OCRA/B), and Input Capture Register (ICR1) are all 16-bit registers.

The Timer/Counter Control Registers (TCCR1A/B/C) are 8-bit registers and have no CPU access restrictions. Interrupt requests signals are all visible in the Timer Interrupt Flag Register (TIFR1).

The Timer/Counter can be clocked internally, via the prescaler, or by an external clock source on the T1 pin. The Clock Select logic block controls which clock source and edge the Timer/Counter uses to increment (or decrement) its value.

The double buffered Output Compare Registers (OCR1A/B) are compared with the Timer/Counter value at all time. The result of the compare can be used by the Waveform Generator to generate a PWM or variable frequency output on the Output Compare pin (OC1A/B).

Note: To perform a 16-bit write operation, the high byte must be written before the low byte. For a 16-bit read, the low byte must be read before the high byte. Not all 16-bit accesses uses the temporary register for the high byte. Reading the OCR1A/B 16-bit registers does not involve using the temporary register.

2. Timer/Counter Clock Sources

The Timer/Counter can be clocked by an internal or an external clock source. The clock source is selected by the Clock Select logic which is controlled by the Clock Select bits in the Timer/Counter control Register B (TCCR1B.CS[2:0]).

3. Counter Unit

The main part of the 16-bit Timer/Counter is the programmable 16-bit bi-directional counter unit which is shown in Fig.

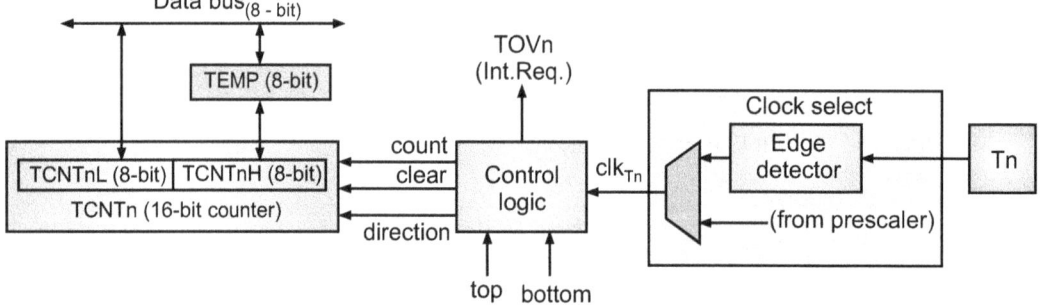

Fig. 6.4 : 16-bit counter unit

Table 6.4 Signal Description of counter unit

Signal Name	Description
Count	Increment of decrement TCNT1 by 1.
Direction	Select between increment and decrement.
Clear	Clear TCNT1 (set all bits to zero)
clk_{T1}	Timer/Counter clock.
TOP	Signalize that TCNT1 has reached maximum value.
BOTTOM	Signalize that TCNT1 has reached minimum value (zero).

The 16-bit counter is mapped into two 8-bit I/O memory locations: Counter High (TCNT1H) containing the upper eight bits of the counter, and Counter Low (TCNT1L) containing the lower eight bits. The TCNT1H Register can only be accessed indirectly by the CPU.

When the CPU does an access to the TCNT1H I/O location, the CPU accesses the high byte temporary register (TEMP). The temporary register is updated with the TCNT1H value when the TCNT1L is read, and TCNT1H is updated with the temporary register value when TCNT1L is written. This allows the CPU to read or write the entire 16-bit counter value within one clock cycle via the 8-bit data bus.

6.4.3 TC2 - 8-bit Timer/Counter2 with PWM and Asynchronous Operation

Timer/Counter2 (TC2) is a general purpose, channel, 8-bit Timer/Counter module

Features

- Channel Counter

- Clear Timer on Compare Match (Auto Reload)

- Glitch-free, Phase Correct Pulse Width Modulator (PWM)

- Frequency Generator

- 10-bit Clock Prescaler

- Overflow and Compare Match Interrupt Sources (TOV2, OCF2A, and OCF2B)

- Allows Clocking from External 32kHz Watch Crystal Independent of the I/O Clock

1. Registers

The Timer/Counter (TCNT2) and Output Compare Register (OCR2A and OCR2B) are 8-bit registers. Interrupt request (shorten as Int.Req.) signals are all visible in the Timer Interrupt Flag Register (TIFR2).

The Timer/Counter can be clocked internally, via the prescaler, or asynchronously clocked from the TOSC1/2 pins .

The double buffered Output Compare Register (OCR2A and OCR2B) are compared with the Timer/ Counter value at all times. The result of the compare can be used by the Waveform Generator to generate a PWM or variable frequency output on the Output Compare pins (OC2A and OC2B).

2. Timer/Counter Clock Sources

The Timer/Counter can be clocked by an internal synchronous or an external asynchronous clock source: The clock source clkT2 is by default equal/synchronous to the MCU clock, clkI/O. When the Asynchronous TC2 bit in the Asynchronous Status Register (ASSR.AS2) is written to '1', the clock source is taken from the Timer/Counter Oscillator connected to TOSC1 and TOSC2.

3. Counter Unit

The main part of the 8-bit Timer/Counter is the programmable bi-directional counter unit

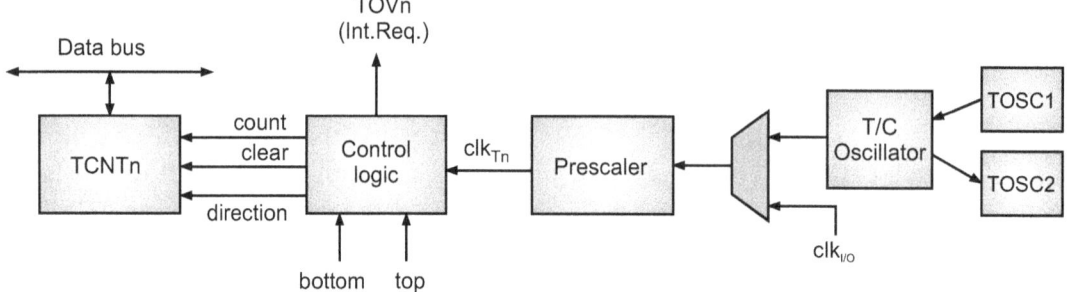

Fig. 6.5 : Counter Unit

Table 6.5 Signal Description of counter unit

Signal Name	Description
count	Increment of decrement TCNT2 by 1.
direction	Select between increment and decrement.
clear	Clear TCNT2 (set all bits to zero)
clk_{Tn}	Timer/Counter clock, referred to as clk_{T2} in the following.
top	Signalize that TCNT2 has reached maximum value.
bottom	Signalize that TCNT2 has reached minimum value (zero).

Depending on the mode of operation used, the counter is cleared, incremented, or decremented at each timer clock (clkT2). clkT2 can be generated from an external or internal clock source, selected by the Clock Select bits (CS2[2:0]). When no clock source is selected (CS2[2:0]=0x0) the timer is stopped. However, the TCNT2 value can be accessed by the CPU, regardless of whether clkT2 is present or not. A CPU write overrides (has priority over) all counter clear or count operations.

The counting sequence is determined by the setting of the WGM21 and WGM20 bits located in the Timer/ Counter Control Register (TCCR2A) and the WGM22 bit located in the Timer/Counter Control Register B (TCCR2B).

The Timer/Counter Overflow Flag (TOV2) is set according to the mode of operation selected by the TCC2B.WGM2[2:0] bits. TOV2 can be used for generating a CPU interrupt.

6.4.4 Mode of Operation

All timer modules (Timer0,1,2) are working in following modes

1. Normal Mode

The simplest mode of operation is the Normal mode). In this mode the counting direction is always up (incrementing), and no counter clear is performed. The counter simply overruns when it passes its maximum value (8-bt or 16-bi)(MAX=0xFFFF) and then restarts from 0x0000. In normal operation the Timer/Counter Overflow Flag (TIFRx.TOV) will be set in the same timer clock cycle as the TCNTx becomes zero

There are no special cases to consider in the Normal mode, a new counter value can be written anytime.

(Note –'x' stands for timer module no.0,1or2)

2. Clear Timer on Compare Match (CTC) Mode

In Clear Timer on Compare or CTC modes), the OCRxA or ICRx registers are used to manipulate the counter resolution: the counter is cleared to ZERO when the counter value (TCNTx) matches either the OCRxA or the ICRx.The OCRxA or ICRx define the top value for the counter, hence also its resolution. This mode allows greater control of the compare match output frequency. It also simplifies the operation of counting external events.

(Note –'x' stands for timer module no.0,1or2)

3. Fast PWM Mode

The Fast Pulse Width Modulation or Fast PWM modes,provide a high frequency PWM waveform generation option. The Fast PWM modes differ from the other PWM options by their single-slope operation. The counter counts from BOTTOM to TOP, then restarts from BOTTOM. TOP is defined as 0xFF when WGM0[2:0]=0x3. TOP is defined as OCR0A when WGM0[2:0]=0x7.

In Fast PWM mode, the counter is incremented until the counter value matches the TOP value. The counter is then cleared at the following timer clock cycle.

4. Phase Correct PWM Mode

The Phase Correct PWM mode provides a high resolution, phase correct PWM waveform generation. The Phase Correct PWM mode is based on dual-slope operation: The counter counts repeatedly from BOTTOM to TOP, and then from TOP to BOTTOM. When WGM0[2:0]=0x1 TOP is defined as 0xFF. When WGM0[2:0]=0x5, TOP is defined as OCR0A.

6.5 INTERFACING OF LED

A LED is an acronym for Light Emitting Diode and is basically an electronic device which emits light when an electric current flows through it. Light-emitting diodes are used in applications as diverse as aviation lighting, automotive lighting, advertising, general lighting and traffic signals. LEDs have allowed new text, video displays, and sensors to be developed, while their high switching rates are also useful in advanced communications technology.

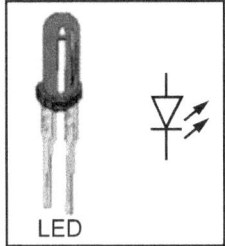

Fig. 6.6

Interfacing of LED with any arduino board is simplest one. Now as shown in below Fig. 6.6 the simplest way of LED interfacing is shown. LED is connected to the digital pin 13 and ground with series resistor the one end of resistor is connected to the digital pin 13 the other end of the resistor is connected to long leg of the LED (the positive leg called anode).the short end of LED (negative called cathode) is connected to the GND.

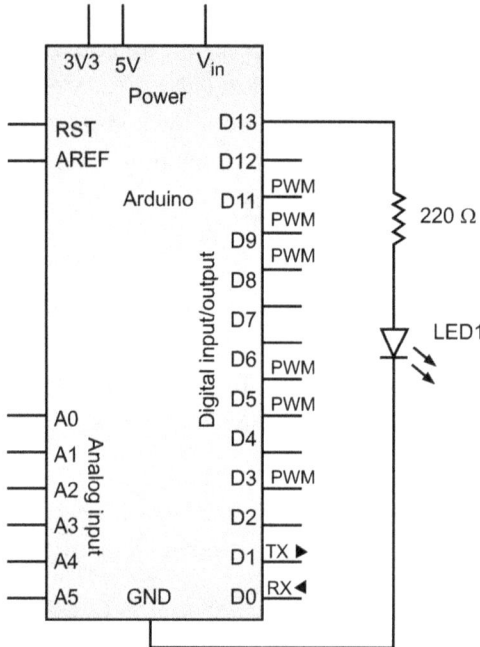

Fig. 6.7 : Interfacing of LED to arduino

6.5.1 Code for Blinking LED

After Circuit connection we can plug the arduino board into our computer through USB or JTAG cable,start the Arduino Software (IDE) and use the algorithm and code as explained.

Example

Now try this program, which will flash the LED at 1.0 Hz. Everything after the 1000ms. It is always good to add comments to a program.

Algorithm

1. Start.

2. Configure Port pin for Output using pinMode()

3. Turn ON LED.by sending logic HIGH

4. Wait for some time (1000ms).

5. Turn OFF LED by sending logic LOW

6. Wait for some time (1000ms).

Code

```
/*------------------------ Blinking LED, 1.0 Hz on pin 13------------------------*/


void setup()          // one-time actions
{
   pinMode(13,OUTPUT);                    // define pin 2 as an output
}
void loop()          // loop forever
{
   digitalWrite(13,HIGH);          // pin 2 high (LED on)
   delay(1000);                    // wait 1000 ms
    digitalWrite(13,LOW);          // pin 2 low (LED off)
   delay(1000);                    // wait 1000 ms
}
```

6.6 INTERFACING WITH LCD

In recent years the LCD(liquid crystal display) is finding widespread use replacing LED's. This is due to the following reason:

- The declining prices of LCD.

- The ability to display numbers, characters, and graphics. This is in contrast to LEDs, which are limited to numbers and few characters.

- In corporation of a refreshing controller into the LCD, thereby reliving the CPU of the task of refreshing the LCD. In contrast, the LED must be refreshed by the CPU to keep displaying the data.

- Ease of programming for characters and graphics.

Most of LCD's available in the market are based on controller HD44780. The LCD display can be interfaced either in 4-bit interface or 8-bit interface mode.

The LCDs have a parallel interface, meaning that the microcontroller has to manipulate several interface pins at once to control the display. The interface consists of the following pins:

- **Vcc, Vss and Vee:** While Vcc and Vss provide +5V and ground, repectively, Vee is used for controlling LCD contrast.

- **Register Select (RS):** There are two very important registers inside the LCD. The RS pin is used for their selection as follows.

(a) RS = 0: the instruction command code register is selected, allowing the user to send a command such as clear display, cursor at home.

(b) RS = 1: the data register is selected, allowing the user to send the data to be displayed on the LCD.

- **Read/write (R/W):** R/W input allows the user to write information to the LCD or read information from it. R/W = 1 when reading, R/W = 0 when writing.

- **Enable (EN):** The enable pin is used by the LCD to latch information presented to its data pins.

- **Data bus (D0 – D7):** The 8-bit data pins, D0-D7 are used to send the information to the LCD or read the contents of the LCD's internal registers. To display the numbers and letters, we send ASCII codes to these pins while making RS=1.

The process of controlling the display involves putting the data that form the image of what you want to display into the data registers, then putting instructions in the instruction register. The LiquidCrystal Library simplifies this for you so you don't need to know the low-level instructions.

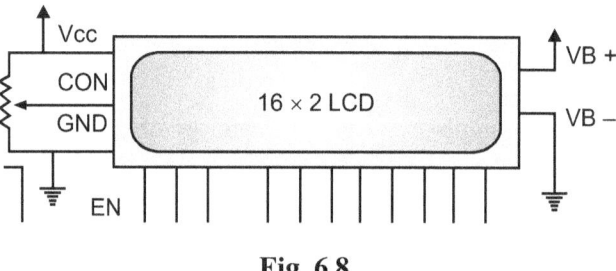

Fig. 6.8

The Hitachi-compatible LCDs can be controlled in two modes: 4-bit or 8-bit. The 4-bit mode requires seven I/O pins from the Arduino, while the 8-bit mode requires 11 pins. For displaying text on the screen, you can do most everything in 4-bit mode, so example shows how to control a 2x16 LCD in 4-bit mode.

Fig. 6.9 shows the schematic diagram of LCD interface with arduino.LCD RS pin is connected to digital pin 12, LCD Enable pin is connected to digital pin 4,11,LCD D7-D4 is connected to pins(2-5)

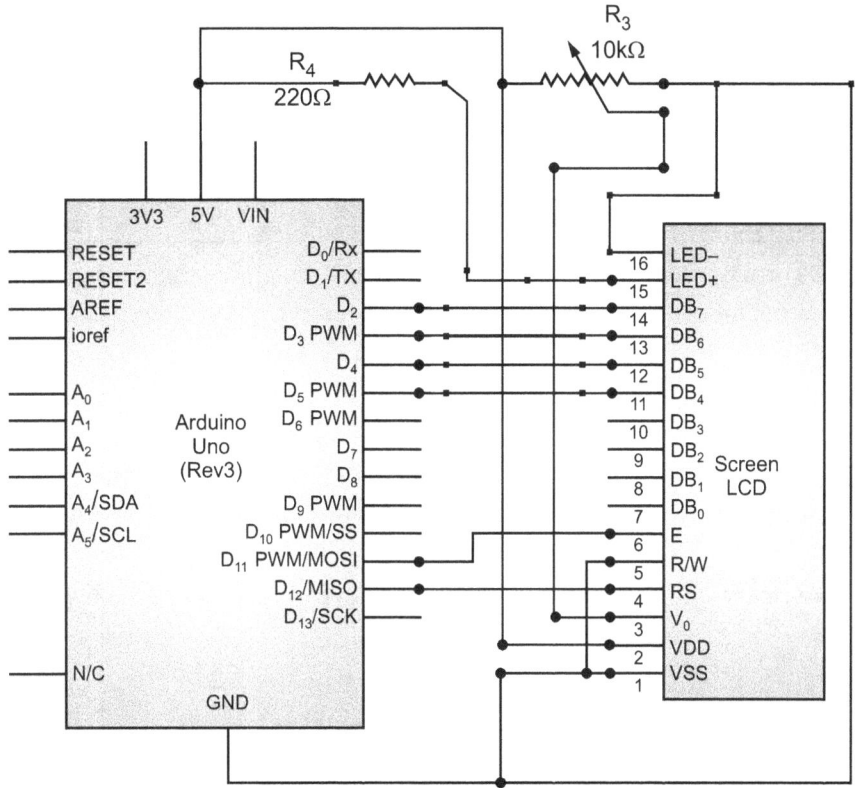

Fig. 6.9 : Shows the schematic of LCD with arduino

Code for LCD display

The following code displays "Hello World!" on LCD module and shows the time in seconds since the arduino was reset.

```
#include<LiquidCrystal.h>                // include the library code:

LiquidCrystal lcd(12,11,5,4,3,2);        // initialize the library with the numbers of the
interface ins

void setup()

{
  lcd.begin(16, 2);          // set up the LCD's number of columns and rows:
  lcd.print("hello, world!");   // Print a message to the LCD.


}


void loop()

{
  lcd.setCursor(0, 1);    // set the cursor to column 0, line 1
```

lcd.print(millis() / 1000);   // print the number of seconds since reset:
}

Output on LCD

hello,world!

6.7 INTERFACING WITH KEYPAD

A keypad is often needed to provide input to an Arduino system, and membrane-type keypads are an economical solution for many applications. They are quite thin and can easily be mounted wherever they are needed.

We demonstrate how to use a 12-button(3x4) numeric keypad, similar to what you might find on a telephone. A 12-button keypad has three columns and four row. Pressing a button will short one of the row outputs to one of the column outputs. From this information, the Arduino can determine which button was pressed. For example, when key 1 is pressed, column 1 and row 1 are shorted. The Arduino will detect that and input a 1 to the program.

How the rows and column are arranged inside the keypad is shown in the Fig.6.8.

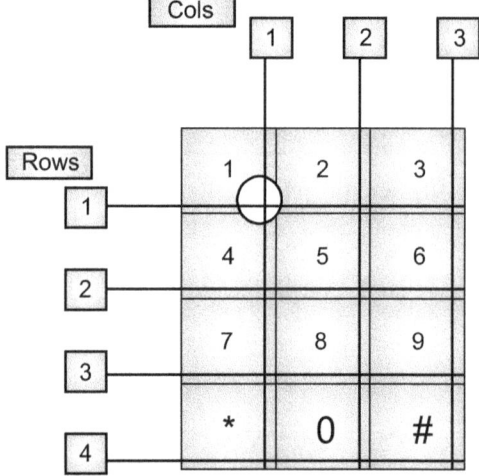

Fig. 6.10 : 3x4 Keypad matrix

Now we can see its a 12 button keypad so it has total 3 columns and 4 rows and similarly there are 7 pins to control these 12 buttons. So, the simple formula is total number of pins = Number of Rows + Number of Columns.

Columns and rows are connected with each other now suppose I press button "1" on the keypad then first row and the first column will get short and I will get to know that button "1" is pressed.

Same is the case with other buttons, for example I press button "8" then second column and the third row will get short so this code will remain unique for each button.

In simple words, on each button press different column and row will get short we need to detect which one gets short in order to get the pressed button.

Now we can interface the rows and columns connections from keypad to the arduino.

We can Connect the keypad to the Arduino as shown in Fig. 6.11.

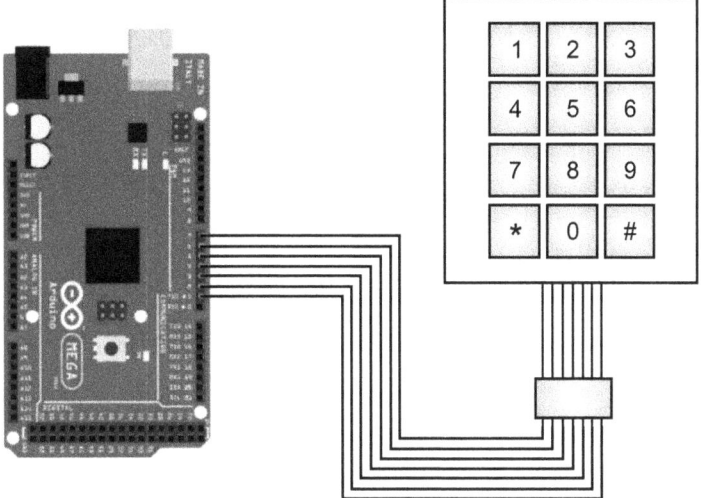

Fig. 6.11 : keypad interfacing to arduino

Code Example

We demonstrate the "keypad.h" Arduino library. When a user presses a button on the keypad, the program will display the value the serial monitor. The code for 3x4 Matrix Keypad with Arduino is as This code prints the key pressed on the keypad to the serial port.

```
#include "Keypad.h"
const byte Rows= 4; //number of rows on the keypad i.e. 4
const byte Cols= 3; //number of columns on the keypad i,e, 3
//we will definne the key map as on the key pad:
char keymap[Rows][Cols]=
{
{'1', '2', '3'},
{'4', '5', '6'},
{'7', '8', '9'},
{'*', '0', '#'}
};                         //  a char array is defined as it can be seen on the
above
//keypad connections to the arduino terminals
byte rPins[Rows]= {A6,A5,A4,A3};                         //Rows 0 to 3
```

```
byte cPins[Cols]= {A2,A1,A0}; /                                    /Columns 0 to 2

Keypad kpd= Keypad(makeKeymap(keymap), rPins, cPins, Rows, Cols);   //initializes
an instance of the Keypad class

void setup()
{
    Serial.begin(9600);                                // initializing serial monitor
}

//If key is pressed, this key is stored in 'keypressed' variable

//If key is not equal to 'NO_KEY', then this key is printed out

void loop()
{
    char keypressed = kpd.getKey();
    if (keypressed != NO_KEY)
    {
        Serial.println(keypressed);
    }
}
```

6.8 SERIAL COMMUNICATION WITH ARDUINO IDE

Serial communication is used for communication between the arduino board and a computer or other device. All Arduino board have one or two serial port which is controlled through UART or USART protocol.

In an asynchronous serial communication system, such as the USART aboard the ATmega328, framing bits are used at the beginning and end of a data byte. These framing bits alert the receiver that an incoming data Byte has arrived and also signals the completion of the data byte reception. The data rate for an asynchronous serial system is typically much slower than the synchronous system, but it only requires a single wire between the transmitter and receiver.

Serial communication provides an easy and flexible way for our arduino board to interact with our computer and other device.

Implementing serial communications involves hardware and software .the hardware provides the electrical signaling between Arduino and the device it is communicating .The software uses the hardware to send bytes or bits that the connected hardware understands. The arduino serial libraries simplify our most of the hardware complexity.

6.8.1 Serial Hardware

Serial hardware sends and receives data as electrical pulses that represent sequential bits. The zeros and ones that carry the information that makes up a byte can be represented in various ways. the scheme used by arduino is 0 volts to represent a bit value of 0,and 5volts(or 3.3 volts) to represent a bit value of 1.

Some serial devices use the RS-232 standard for serial connection. These usually have a nine-pin connector, and an adapter is required to use them with the Arduino. RS-232 is an old and venerated communications protocol that uses voltage levels not compatible with Arduino digital pins.

Serial communication on pins TX/RX uses TTL logic levels (5V or 3.3V depending on the board).We cannot connect these pins directly to RS-232 serial port;they operate at +/- 12 V and can damage Arduino Board. RS-232 adapters that connect RS-232 signals to Arduino 5V (or 3.3V) pins these adapters take care of the signal levels.

6.8.2 Software Serial

We will usually use the built-in Arduino serial library to communicate with the hardware serial ports. Serial libraries simplify the use of the serial ports by insulating you from hardware complexities.

Sometimes you need more serial ports than the number of hardware serial ports available. If this is the case, you can use an additional library that uses software to emulate serial hardware

The following code that will make the Arduino ECHO anything you send to it.

Therefore, if you type a 4 the arduino will send back a 4. If you type a letter F the arduino will send back letter F.

```
byte byteRead;
void setup()
{
  Serial.begin(9600);    // Turn the Serial Protocol ON
}
void loop()
{  /*  check if data has been sent from the computer: */
    if (Serial.available())
                      {
                      /* read the most recent byte */
                      byteRead = Serial.read();
      /*ECHO the value that was read, back to the serial port. */
                      Serial.write(byteRead);

  }
}
```

Once the Arduino sketch has been uploaded to the Arduino. Open the Serial monitor, which looks like a magnifying glass at the top right section of the Arduino IDE. Please note, that you need to keep the USB connected to the Arduino during this process, as the USB cable is your communication link between your computer and the Arduino.

Type anything into the top box of the Serial Monitor and press <Enter> on your keyboard. This will send a series of bytes to the Arduino. The Arduino will respond by sending back your typed message in the larger textbox.which is shown as shown in sketch.

Our sketch must call the Serial.begin() function before it can use serial input or output. The function takes a single parameter: the desired communication speed. You must use the same speed for the sending side and the receiving side, or you will see gobbledygook (or nothing at all) on the screen. This example and most of the others in this book use a speed of 9,600 baud (baud is a measure of the number of bits transmitted per second). The 9,600 baud rate is approximately 1,000 characters per second. You can send at lower or higher rates (the range is 300 to 115,200), but make sure both sides use the same speed.

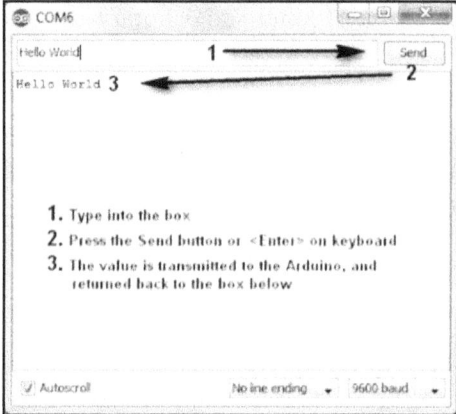

Fig. 6.12

Now we will see two important functions which used mostly in serial communication with arduino.

1. Serial.print()

Prints data to the serial port as human-readable ASCII text. This command can take many forms. Numbers are printed using an ASCII character for each digit. Floats are similarly printed as ASCII digits, defaulting to two decimal places. Bytes are sent as a single character.

Syntax: Serial.print(val)

      Serial.print(val, format)

2. Serial.printIn():

Prints data to the serial port as human-readable ASCII text followed by a carriage return character (ASCII 13, or '\r') and a newline character (ASCII 10, or '\n'). This command takes the same forms as Serial.print()

Syntax: Serial.println(val)

Serial.println(val, format)

Characters and strings are sent as is with examples

- Serial.print(78) gives "78"

- Serial.print(1.23456) gives "1.23"

- Serial.print('N') gives "N"

- Serial.print("Hello world.") gives "Hello world."

An optional second parameter specifies the base (format) to use; permitted values are BIN (binary, or base 2), OCT (octal, or base 8), DEC (decimal, or base 10), HEX (hexadecimal, or base 16). For floating point numbers, this parameter specifies the number of decimal places to use. For example:

Serial.print(78, BIN) gives "1001110"

Serial.print(78, OCT) gives "116"

Serial.print(78, DEC) gives "78"

Serial.print(78, HEX) gives "4E"

Serial.println(1.23456, 0) gives "1"

Serial.println(1.23456, 2) gives "1.23"

Serial.println(1.23456, 4) gives "1.2346"

Now we will see code to send text and data to be displayed on your PC or Mac using the Arduino IDE or the serial terminal program of your choice.

Following programe/ sketch prints sequential numbers on the Serial Monitor

Code Example

```
void setup()
{
Serial.begin(9600); // send and receive at 9600 baud
}
int number = 0;
void loop()
{ Serial.print("The number is ");
Serial.println(number);   // print the number
  delay(500); // delay half second between numbers
 number++; // to the next number
}
```

Click the Serial Monitor icon in the IDE and you should see the output displayed as follows:

The number is 0

The number is 1

The number is 2

Fig. 6.13

6.9 EXERCISES

1. Explain the concept of GPIO in ATmega328P.

2. What is the use of digital Input and output pin?

3. Explain the function used in digital I/O pin.

4. What is UART? Applications of UART.

5. Explain the types of serial communication.

6. Write a short note on timer in ATmega328P.

7. State the registers used in Timer.

8. What are the different modes of timer.

9. Draw and Explain interfacing of LED.

10. Write a program to ON/OFF LED after 1000ms.

11. Draw and explain interfacing of LCD with arduino.

12. Write a program to display "Hello world" on 16×2 LCD display.

13. Draw and Explain Interfacing of keypad to arduino.

14. What is serial Hardware and software serial.

15. Write a short Note on.

    (i) Serialprint()

    (ii) SerialprintIn ().

◇ ◇ ◇

CHAPTER

SEVEN

PERIPHERAL INTERFACE - II

7.1 CONCEPT OF ADC IN ATMEGA 328P BASED ARDUINO BOARD

Microcontrollers are capable of detecting binary signals: is the button pressed or not? These are digital signals. When a microcontroller is powered from five volts, it understands zero volts (0V) as a binary 0 and a five volts (5V) as a binary 1. The world however is not so simple and likes to use shades of gray. What if the signal is 2.72V? Is that a zero or a one? We often need to measure signals that vary; these are called analog signals

7.1.1 What is the ADC?

An Analog to Digital Converter (ADC) is a very useful feature that converts an analog voltage on a pin to a digital number. By converting from the analog world to the digital world, we can begin to use electronics to interface to the analog world around us.

The ATmega 328p based arduino board has ADC device in it. The device features a 10-bit successive approximation ADC. The ADC is connected to an 8-channel Analog Multiplexer which allows eight single-ended voltage inputs constructed from the pins of Port A. The single-ended voltage inputs refer to 0V (GND).

Features

- 10-bit Resolution
- 13 - 260µs Conversion Time
- Six Multiplexed Single Ended Input Channel
- Temperature Sensor Input Channel
- 0 - VCC ADC Input Voltage Range
- Selectable 1.1V ADC Reference Voltage
- Free Running or Single Conversion Mode
- Interrupt on ADC Conversion Complete

7.1.2 ADC Input Channels

In Single Conversion mode, always select the channel before starting the conversion. The channel selection may be changed one ADC clock cycle after writing one to ADSC. However, the simplest method is to wait for the conversion to complete before changing the channel selection

In Free Running mode, always select the channel before starting the first conversion. The channel selection may be changed one ADC clock cycle after writing one to ADSC. However, the simplest method is to wait for the first conversion to complete, and then change the channel selection

7.1.3 ADC Voltage Reference

The reference voltage for the ADC (VREF) indicates the conversion range for the ADC. Single ended channels that exceed VREF will result in codes close to 0x3FF. VREF can be selected as either AVCC, internal 1.1V reference, or external AREF pin.

The main function of the analog pins for most Arduino users is to read analog sensors, the analog pins also have all the functionality of general purpose input/output (GPIO) pins. Consequently, if a user needs more general purpose input output pins, and all the analog pins are not in use, the analog pins may be used for GPIO.

Now we will see functions used to configure ADC in Arduino.

7.1.4 analogRead() Function

analogRead() function reads the value from the specified analog pin. The Arduino board contains a 6 channels (8 channels on the Mini and Nano, 16 on the Mega), 10-bit analog to digital converter. This means that it will map input voltages between 0 and 5 volts into integer values between 0 and 1023. This yields a resolution between readings of: 5 volts / 1024 units or, .0049 volts (4.9 mV) per unit. The input range and resolution can be changed using analogReference().

It takes about 100 microseconds (0.0001 s) to read an analog input, so the maximum reading rate is about 10,000 times a second.

Syntax analogRead(pin)

Where pin: the number of the analog input pin to read from (0 to 5 on most boards, 0 to 7 on the Mini and Nano, 0 to 15 on the Mega).

It returns value int(0 to 1023)

Note : If the analog input pin is not connected to anything, the value returned by analogRead() will fluctuate based on a number of factors (e.g. the values of the other analog inputs, how close your hand is to the board, etc.).

7.1.5 analogWrite() Function

analogWrite() function writes an analog value (PWM wave) to a pin. Can be used to light a LED at varying brightnesses or drive a motor at various speeds. After a call to analogWrite(), the pin will generate a steady square wave of the specified duty cycle until the next call to analogWrite() (or a call to digitalRead() or digitalWrite() on the same pin). The frequency of the PWM signal on most pins is approximately 490 Hz. On the Uno and similar boards, pins 5 and 6 have a frequency of approximately 980 Hz. Pins 3 and 11 on the Leonardo also run at 980 Hz.

On most Arduino boards (those with the ATmega168 or ATmega328), this function works on pins 3, 5, 6, 9, 10, and 11. On the Arduino Mega, it works on pins 2 - 13 and 44 - 46. Older Arduino boards with an ATmega8 only support analogWrite() on pins 9, 10, and 11.

The *analogWrite* function has nothing to do with the analog pins or the *analogRead* function.

Syntax analogWrite(pin, value)

Where pin: the pin to write to.

value: the duty cycle: between 0 (always off) and 255 (always on).

7.1.6 analogRefrence() function

Configures the reference voltage used for analog input (i.e. the value used as the top of the input range). The options are:

- DEFAULT: the default analog reference of 5 volts (on 5V Arduino boards) or 3.3 volts (on 3.3V Arduino boards)

- INTERNAL: an built-in reference, equal to 1.1 volts on the ATmega168 or ATmega328 and 2.56 volts on the ATmega8 (*not available on the Arduino Mega*)

- INTERNAL1V1: a built-in 1.1V reference (*Arduino Mega only*)

- INTERNAL2V56: a built-in 2.56V reference (*Arduino Mega only*)

- EXTERNAL: the voltage applied to the AREF pin (0 to 5V only) is used as the reference

Syntax analogReference(type)

Where type: which type of reference to use (DEFAULT, INTERNAL, INTERNAL1V1, INTERNAL2V56, or EXTERNAL).

7.1.7 Example Code ADC interfacing with Arduino

We want to read the voltage on an analog pin. Perhaps you want a reading from a potentiometer (pot) or a device or sensor that provides a voltage between 0 and 5 volts.

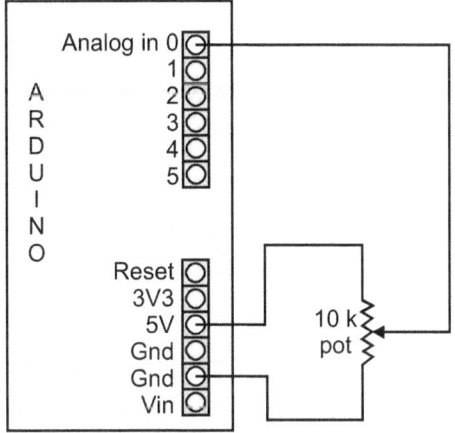

Fig. 7.1: Analog voltage Interface to Arduino

This sketch reads the voltage on an analog pin and flashes an LED in a proportional rate to the value returned from the analogRead function. The voltage is adjusted by a potentiometer connected as shown in Fig. 7.1

code

```
/* Pot sketch blink an LED at a rate set by the position of a potentiometer */
const int potPin = 0;   // select the input pin for the potentiometer
const int ledPin = 13;   // select the pin for the LED
int val = 0;           // variable to store the value coming from the sensor
void setup()
{  pinMode(ledPin, OUTPUT);  // declare the ledPin as an OUTPUT
}
void loop()
{  val = analogRead(potPin);   // read the voltage on the pot
digitalWrite(ledPin, HIGH);  // turn the ledPin on
delay(val);            // blink rate set by pot value (in milliseconds)
digitalWrite(ledPin, LOW);  // turn the ledPin off
delay(val);            // turn led off for same period as it was turned on
}
```

7.2 INTERFACING WITH TEMPERATURE SENSOR (LM35)

LM35 is an analog, linear temperature sensor whose output voltage varies linearly with change in temperature. LM35 is three terminal linear temperature sensors from National semiconductors. It can measure temperature from-*55 degree Celsius to +150 degree Celsius.* The voltage output of the LM35 increases 10mV per degree Celsius rise in temperature. LM35 can be operated from a 5V supply and the stand by current is less than 60uA. The pin out of LM35 is shown in the Fig. below.

So that's all info you need about LM35 for this particular temperature display project using arduino uno. So let's get to LM35 temperature sensor interfacing with arduino!

LM35 is an analog temperature sensor. This means the output of LM35 is an analog signal. Microcontroller's don't accept analog signals as their input directly. We need to convert this analog output signal to digital before we can feed it to a microcontroller's input. For this purpose, we can use an ADC (Analog to Digital Converter).

The following Fig. 7.2 shows the interfacing of LM35 to Arduino

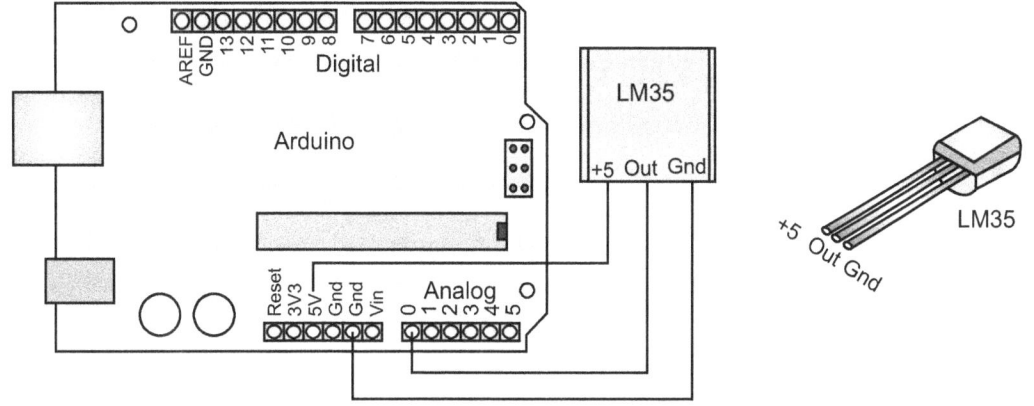

Fig. 7.2: LM35 interface to Arduino

7.2.1 Example code for LM35 interface

The program displays the temperature in Fahrenheit and Celsius (Centigrade) using the popular LM35 heat detection sensor. The sensor looks similar to a transistor and is connected as shown in Fig. 7.2:

code

```
/* lm35 sketch prints the temperature to the Serial Monitor */
const int inPin = 0;        // analog pin
void setup()
{ Serial.begin(9600);
}
void loop()
{
 int value = analogRead(in Pin);
Serial.print(value);
Serial.print(" > ");
float millivolts = (value / 1024.0) * 5000;
float Celsius = millivolts / 10;   // sensor output is 10mV per degree Celsius
Serial.print(Celsius);
Serial.print(" degrees Celsius, ");
Serial.print( (Celsius * 9)/ 5 + 32 );        // converts to Fahrenheit
Serial.println(" degrees Fahrenheit");
  delay(1000);                                 // wait for one second
}
```

The LM35 temperature sensor produces an analog voltage directly proportional to temperature with an output of 1 millivolt per 0.1°C (10 mV per degree). The sketch converts the analogRead values into millivolts and divides this by 10 to get degrees. The sensor accuracy is around 0.5°C, and in many cases you can use integer math instead of floating point.

7.3 LVDT

The term LVDT stands for the linear variable differential transformer. It is the most widely used inductive transducer that covert the linear motion into the electrical signals.

The output across secondary of this transformer is the differential so it is called so. They are very accurate inductive transducers as compared to other inductive transducers.

7.3.1 Construction of LVDT

Main Features of Construction are as,

- The transformer consists of a primary winding P and two secondary winding S1 and S2 wound on a cylindrical former (which is hollow in nature and will contain core).
- Both the secondary windings have equal number of turns and are identically placed on the either side of primary winding
- The primary winding is connected to an AC source which produces a flux in the air gap and voltages are induced in secondary windings.
- A movable soft iron core is placed inside the former and displacement to be measured is connected to the iron core.
- The iron core is generally of high permeability which helps in reducing harmonics and high sensitivity of LVDT.
- The LVDT is placed inside a stainless steel housing because it will provide electrostatic and electromagnetic shielding.
- The both the secondary windings are connected in such a way that resulted output is the difference of the voltages of two windings.

Principle of Operation and Working

As the primary is connected to an AC source so alternating current and voltages are produced in the secondary of the LVDT. The output in secondary S_1 is e_1 and in the secondary S_2 is e_2. So the differential output is, $e_{out} = e_1 - e_2$ This equation explains the **principle of Operation of LVDT**.

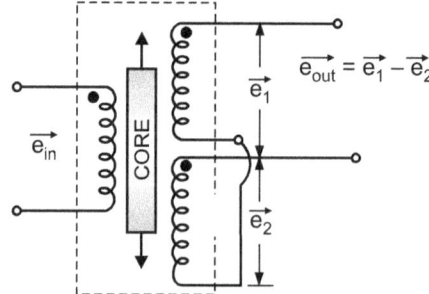

Fig. 7.3 : The LVDT Operation

Usually the primary of the LVDT is excited from a 50Hz, 230V AC supply through a step down transformer. Two terminals of the secondary windings are connected in series opposition and secondary output is rectified by a rectifier and the DC voltage output is measured between the other two terminals.

7.3.2 LVDT Interfacing

In electronics System LVDT is generally used with rectifier and signal conditioning device this shown in Fig. 7.4 the rectified output is given to the signal conditioning circuit and the output of signal conditioning is the applied to the analog input pin of microcontroller which has built in ADC.

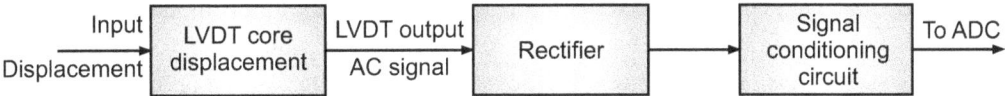

Fig. 7.4 : Block diagram of LVDT interface

The circuit shown in Fig. 7.5 is a complete adjustment -free linear variable differential transformer (LVDT) signal conditioning circuit. This circuit can accurately measure linear displacement (position).The LVDT is a highly reliable sensor because the magnetic core can move without friction and does not touch the inside of the tube.

Therefore, LVDTs are suitable for flight control feedback systems, position feedback in servomechanisms, automated measurement in machine tools, and many other industrial and Scientific electromechanical applications where long term reliability is important.

This circuit uses the AD698 LVDT signal conditioner that contains a sine wave oscillator and a power amplifier to generate the excitation signals that drive the primary side of the LVDT. The AD698 also converts the secondary output into a dc voltage. The AD8615 rail-to-rail amplifier buffers the output of the AD698 and drives a low power 12-bit successive approximation analog-To-digital converter (ADC). The system has a dynamic range of 82 dB and a system bandwidth of 250 Hz, making it ideal for precision industrial position and gauging applications. The signal conditioning circuitry of the system consumes only 15mA of current from the ±15V supply and 3 mA from the +5V supply.

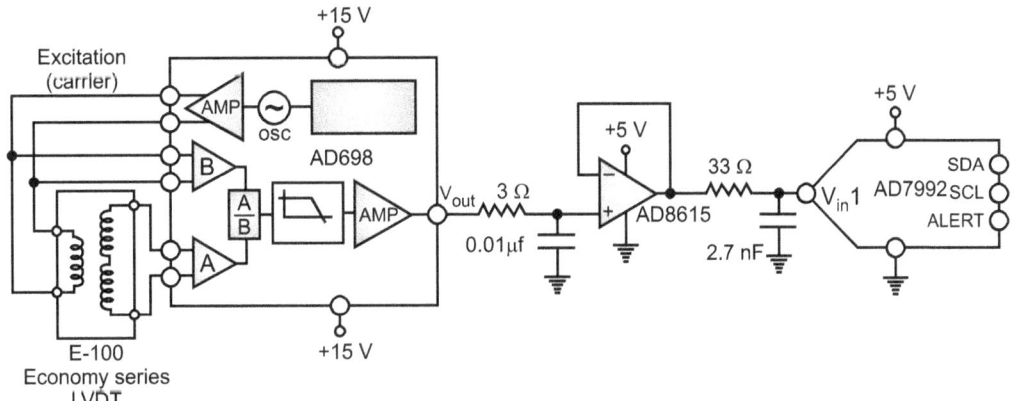

Fig. 7.5 : Circuit Diagram of LVDT with AD698

7.4 STAIN GAUGE

A strain gauge is a register used to measure strain on an object. When an external force is applied on an object, due to which there is a deformation occur in the shape of the object. This deformation in the shape either compressive or tensile is called strain, and it is measured by the strain gauge. When an object deforms within the limit of elasticity, either it becomes narrower and longer or it become shorter and broadens. As a result of it, there is a change in resistance end-to-end. The strain gauge is sensitive to that small changes occur in the geometry of an object. By measuring the change in resistance of an object, the amount of induced stress can be calculated. The change in resistance normally has very small value, and to sense that small change, strain gauge has a long thin metallic strip arrange in a zig-zag pattern on a non-conducting material called the carrier, as shown below, so that it can enlarge the small amount of stress in the group of parallel lines and could be measured with high accuracy. The gauge is literally glued onto the device by an adhesive.

When an object shows physical deformation, its electrical resistance gets change and that change is then measured by gage.

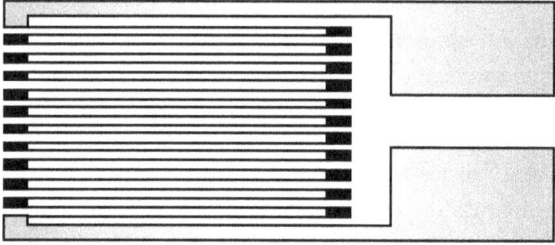

Fig. 7.6

7.4.1 Strain Gauge Bridge Circuit

Strain gauge bridge circuit shows the measured stress by the degree of discrepancy, and uses a voltmeter in the center of the bridge to provide an accurate measurement of that imbalance:

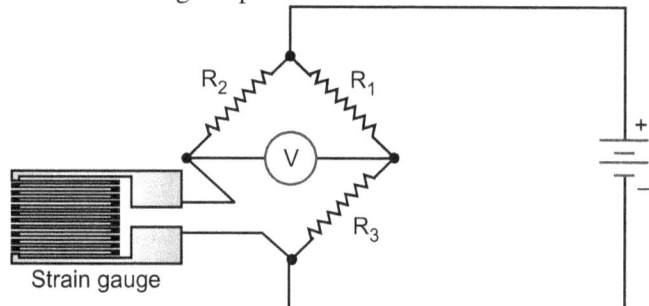

Fig. 7.7 : Strain Gauge with wheatstone bridge

In this circuit, R_1 and R_3 are the ratio arms equal to each other, and R_2 is the rheostat arm has a value equal to the strain gage resistance. When the gauge is unstrained, the bridge is balanced, and voltmeter shows zero value. As there is a change in resistance of strain gauge, the bridge gets unbalanced and producing an indication at the voltmeter. The output voltage from the bridge can be amplified further by a differential amplifier.

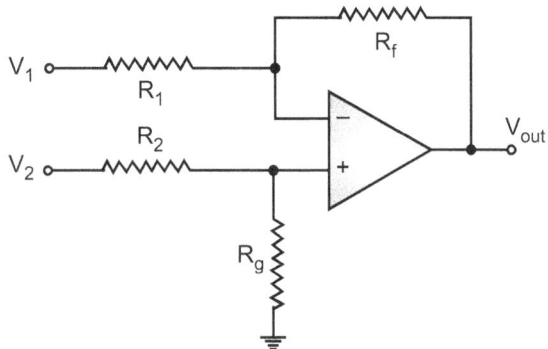

Fig. 7.8 : Differential Amplifier

7.4.2 Differential Amplifier

A differential amplifier is the combination of inverting and non-inverting amplifier. A differential amplifier is a type of electronic amplifier that amplifies the difference between two input voltages but suppresses any voltage common to the two inputs.

The output of differential amplifier can be read through the analog signal input of the Arduino board and after proper calibration it is possible to display actual strain on the serial monitor or on LCD display. This output can be further used to control some other parameter according to the application.

7.5 ACCELEROMETER

An accelerometer is a device that measures proper acceleration; proper acceleration is not the same as coordinate acceleration (rate of change of velocity). For example, an accelerometer at rest on the surface of the Earth will measure acceleration due to Earth's gravity, straight upwards (by definition) of g ≈ 9.81 m/s2. By contrast, accelerometers in free fall (falling toward the center of the Earth at a rate of about 9.81 m/s^2) will measure zero.

An accelerometer is an electro-mechanical device that is used to measure the specific force of an object, a force obtained due to the phenomenon of weight exerted by an object that is kept in the frame of reference of the accelerometer.

In the case of static acceleration, the device is mainly used to find the degrees at which an object is tilted with respect to the ground. In dynamic acceleration, the movement of the object can be foreseen.

Accelerometers have multiple applications in industry and science. Highly sensitive accelerometers are components of inertial navigation systems for aircraft and missiles. Accelerometers are used to detect and monitor vibration in rotating machinery.

7.5.1 Types of Accelerometer

Piezoelectric Accelerometer

The most commonly used device is the piezoelectric accelerometer. As the name suggests, it uses the principle of piezoelectric effect. The device consists of a piezoelectric quartz crystal on which an accelerative force, whose value is to be measured, is applied.

Due to the special self-generating property, the crystal produces a voltage that is proportional to the accelerative force. The working and the basic arrangement is shown in the Fig. 7.9.

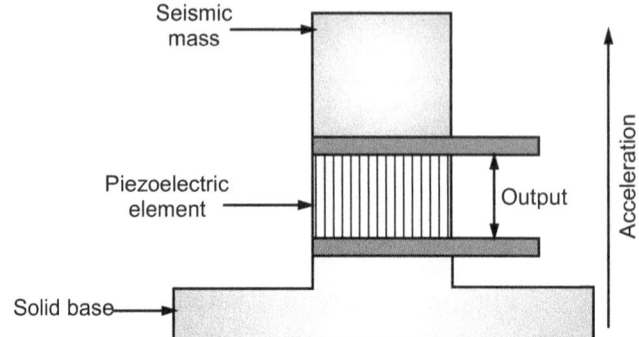

Fig. 7.9 : Piezoelectric Accelerometer

As the device finds its application as a highly accurate vibration measuring device, it is also called a vibrating sensor. Vibration sensors are used for the measurement of vibration in bearings of heavy equipment and pressure lines. The piezoelectric accelerometer can be classified into two. They are high impedance output accelerometer and low impedance accelerometer.

In the case of high impedance device, the output voltage generated in proportion to the acceleration is given as the input to other measuring instruments. The instrumentation process and signal conditioning of the output is considered high and thus a low impedance device cannot be of any use for this application. This device is used at temperatures greater than 120 degree Celsius.

Capacitive Accelerometer

Capacitive Accelerometers sense a change in electrical capacitance in response to acceleration. The sensing element of a Capacitive Accelerometer is made up of two parallel plate capacitors acting in differential mode.

These parallel capacitors operate in a bridge circuit with two fixed capacitors and alter the peak voltage which is generated by an oscillator when the sensor is under acceleration. Detection circuits will capture the peak voltage which is fed to a summing amplifier to process the final output signal.

Piezoresistive Accelerometers

Piezoresistive Accelerometers design for high frequency, high g shock measurement. Instead of sensing the capacitance changes in the seismic mass, a piezoresistive accelerometer takes advantage of the resistance change of piezoresistive materials to covert mechanical strain to a DC output voltage. Most of the Piezoresistive designs are either MEMS type (gas damped) or bonded strain gauge type (fluid damped) and they are suitable for impact measurements where frequency range and g level are considerably high.

Piezoresistive accelerometers are widely used in automobile safety testing including anti-lock braking system, safety air-bags and traction control system as well as weapon testing and seismic measurements. In addition, micro machined accelerometers are available and used in various applications, such as sub millimeter piezoresistive accelerometers in extremely small dimensions used for biomedical applications.

7.5.2 Interfacing of Accelerometer with Arduino

The most popular accelerometer used is ADXL335 small, thin, low power, 3axis accelerometer that contains signal conditioned voltage outputs. It is designed to measure the acceleration with a full scale range of ±3 g. It measures two kinds of motion. First kind of motion that it measures is the static acceleration of gravity when the accelerometer is tilted. So during the diamond polishing phase if the arm tilts it will send a signal. The second kind of acceleration it measures is the dynamic acceleration which will help to detect the change is vibration that may occur when the diamond polishing machine is at work.

The ADXL3xx outputs the acceleration on each axis as an analog voltage between 0 and 5 volts. To read this, all you need is the analogRead() function.

The accelerometer uses very little current, so it can be plugged into your board and run directly off of the output from the digital output pins. To do this, you'll use three of the analog input pins as digital I/O pins, for power and ground to the accelerometer, and for the self-test pin. You'll use the other three analog inputs to read the accelerometer's analog outputs is shown in Fig. 7.10.

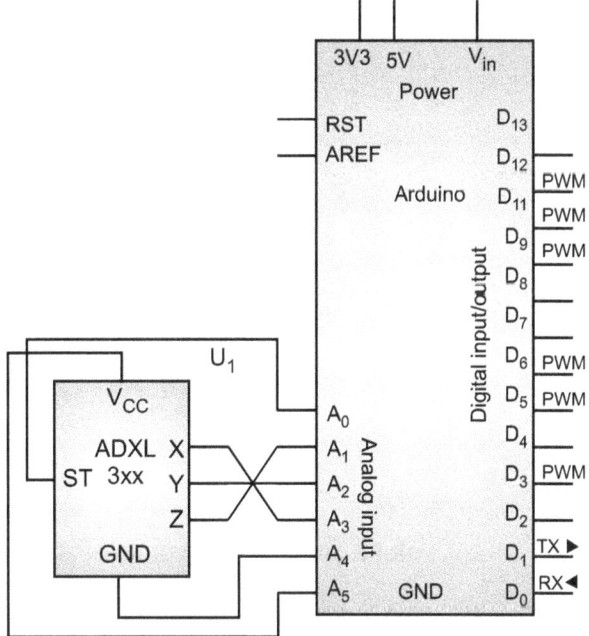

Fig. 7.10 : Interfacing of Accelerometer to Arduino

Here are the pin connections for the configuration shown above:

Breakout Board Pin	Self-Test	Z-Axis	Y-Axis	X-Axis	Ground	VDD
Arduino Analog Input Pin	0	1	2	3	4	5

Or, if you're using just the accelerometer:

ADXL3xx Pin	Self-Test	ZOut	YOut	XOut	Ground	VDD
Arduino Pin	None (unconnected)	Analog Input 1	Analog Input 2	Analog Input 3	GND	5V

Please, be aware that some accelerometers use 3.3V power supply and might be damaged by 5V. Check the supplier's documentation to find out which is the correct voltage.

Code

We want to respond to acceleration; for example, to detect when something starts or stops moving. Or you want to detect how something is oriented with respect to the Earth's surface (measure acceleration due to gravity).

The simple sketch here uses the ADXL320 to display the acceleration in the x- and y-axes:

```
/*  accel sketch  simple sketch to output values on the x- and y-axes  */
const int xPin = 0;          // analog input pins
const int yPin = 1;
void setup()
{
Serial.begin(9600);          // note the higher than usual serial speed
}
void loop()
{
    int xValue;                // values from accelerometer stored here
    int yValue;
    xValue = analogRead(xPin);
```

```
yValue = analogRead(yPin);

    Serial.print("X value = ");

Serial.println(xValue);

Serial.print("Y value = ");

Serial.println(yValue);

delay(100);

}
```

We can use techniques to extract information from the accelerometer readings. we might need to check for a threshold to work out movement. we may need to average values like the sound example to get values that are of use. If the accelerometer is reading horizontally, you can use the values directly to work out movement.

7.6 CONCEPT OF PWM

Pulse Width Modulation, or PWM, is a technique for getting analog results with digital means. Digital control is used to create a square wave, a signal switched between on and off. This on-off pattern can simulate voltages in between full on (5 Volts) and off (0 Volts) by changing the portion of the time the signal spends on versus the time that the signal spends off. The duration of "on time" is called the pulse width. To get varying analog values, you change, or modulate, that pulse width.

Duty Cycles

To describe the amount of "on time", we use the concept of duty cycle. Duty cycle is measured in percentage. The percentage duty cycle specifically describes the percentage of time a digital signal is on over an interval or period of time. This period is the inverse of the frequency of the waveform.

If a digital signal spends half of the time on and the other half off, we would say the digital signal has a duty cycle of 50% and resembles an ideal square wave. If the percentage is higher than 50%, the digital signal spends more time in the high state than the low state and vice versa if the duty cycle is less than 50%. Here is a graph that illustrates these three scenarios:

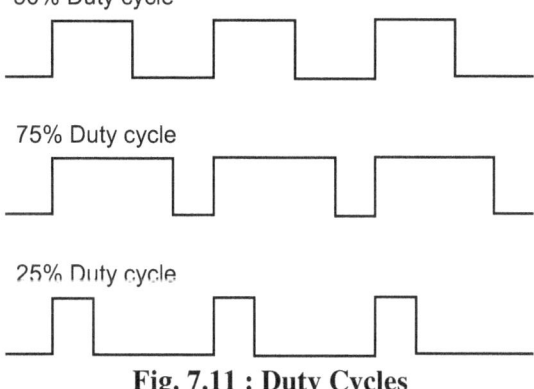

Fig. 7.11 : Duty Cycles

A call to analogWrite() is on a scale of 0 - 255, such that analogWrite(255) requests a 100% duty cycle (always on), and analogWrite(127) is a 50% duty cycle (on half the time) and so on . This is illustrated in Fig 7.12 given below.

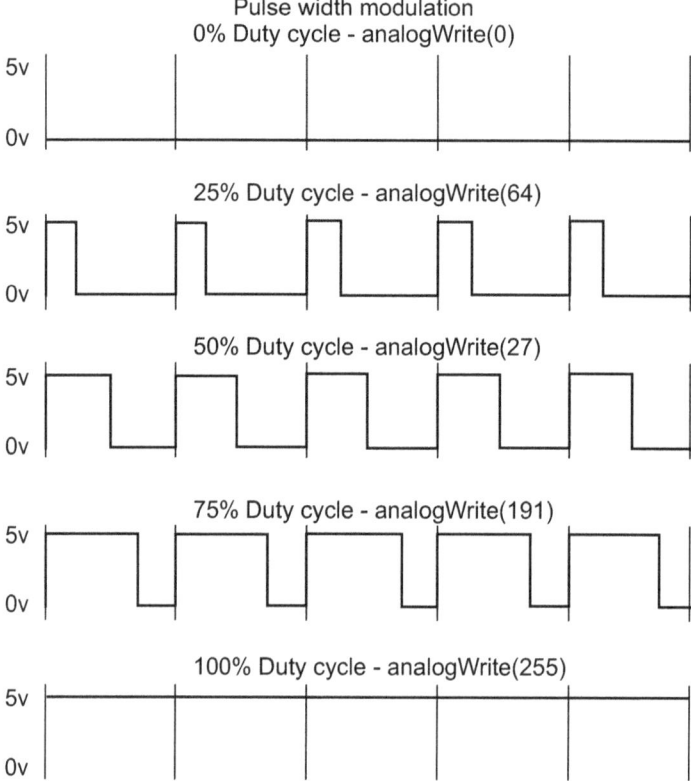

Fig. 7.12 : Generating PWM signal on Arduino board

7.7 DC MOTOR INTERFACE USING PWM

A direct current (DC) motor is another widely used device that translates electrical pulses into mechanical movement. In the DC motor we have only + and – leads. Connecting them to a DC voltage source moves the motor in one direction. By reversing the polarity, the DC motor will move in the opposite direction. One can easily experiment with the DC motor. For example, small fans used in many motherboards to cool the CPU are run by DC motors.

The speed of the DC motor increases with increase in the supply voltage. However we cannot exceed supply voltage beyond the rated voltage. The speed of the DC motor also depends on the load. At no load speed is highest. As we increase the load the speed decreases.

Direction Control of DC Motor

There two types generally used to control the direction which as:

1. Unidirectional control

2. Bidirectional control

The Fig. 7.13 shows the unidirectional DC motor rotation for clockwise (CW) and counterclockwise (CCW) rotations.

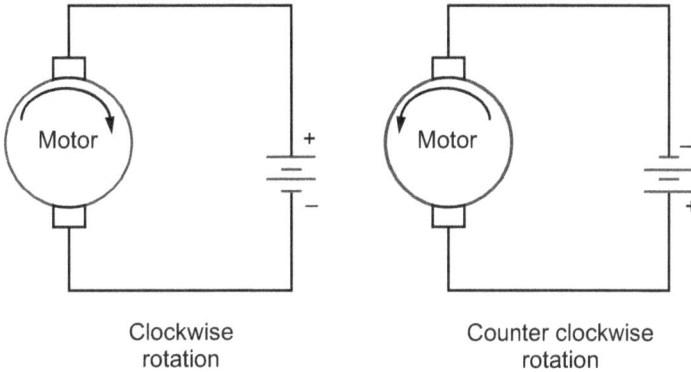

Clockwise
rotation

Counter clockwise
rotation

Fig. 7.13 : Unidirectional motor control

The direction will change when we reverse the power supply polarity.

With the help of switches or relays or some specially designed chips we can change the direction of the DC motor rotation. This is shown in Fig. 7.14.

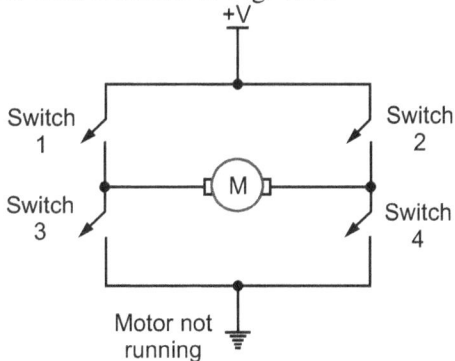

Fig. 7.14 : Bidirectional control of DC motor

Table 7.1 Switch Configuration

Motor Operation	SW1	SW2	SW3	SW4
Off	Open	Open	Open	Open
Clockwise	Closed	Open	Open	Closed
Counter Clockwise	Open	Closed	Closed	Open
Invalid	Closed	Closed	Closed	Closed

This type of controlling is generally called as H-bridge control only precaution required is when using relays and transistors; we must ensure that invalid configurations do not occur.

7.7.1 Speed control using PWM(Pulse width modulation)

The speed of the motor depends on three factors: (a) load, (b) voltage, and (c) current. For a given fixed load we can maintain a steady speed by using a method called *pulse width modulation* (PWM). By changing (modulating) the width of the pulse applied to the DC motor we can increase or decrease the amount of power provided to the motor, thereby increasing or decreasing the motor speed.

PWM is so widely used in DC motor control that some microcontrollers come with the PWM circuitry embedded in the chip. In such microcontrollers all we have to do is load the proper registers with the values of the high and low portions of the desired pulse, and the rest is taken care by the microcontroller.

The Fig. 7.15 shows the PWM signal comparison to generate different duty cycle

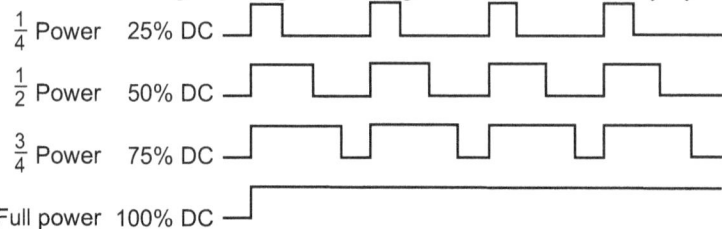

Fig. 7.15 : Power Variation using PWM

7.7.2 DC motor interface using Arduino

There are generally different ways we can connect DC motor to microcontroller depending upon types of driver we used which as.

   1.   Driving a DC Motor Using a Transistor

   2.   Driving a DC Motor using h-bridge IC (L293)

1.   Driving a DC Motor Using a Transistor

When PWMing a transister,the higher the PWM value,the faster the motor will spin.the lower the value,the slower it will spin.let us see how we can connect trnsistor TIP120 (NPN-type transistor) To drive motor.

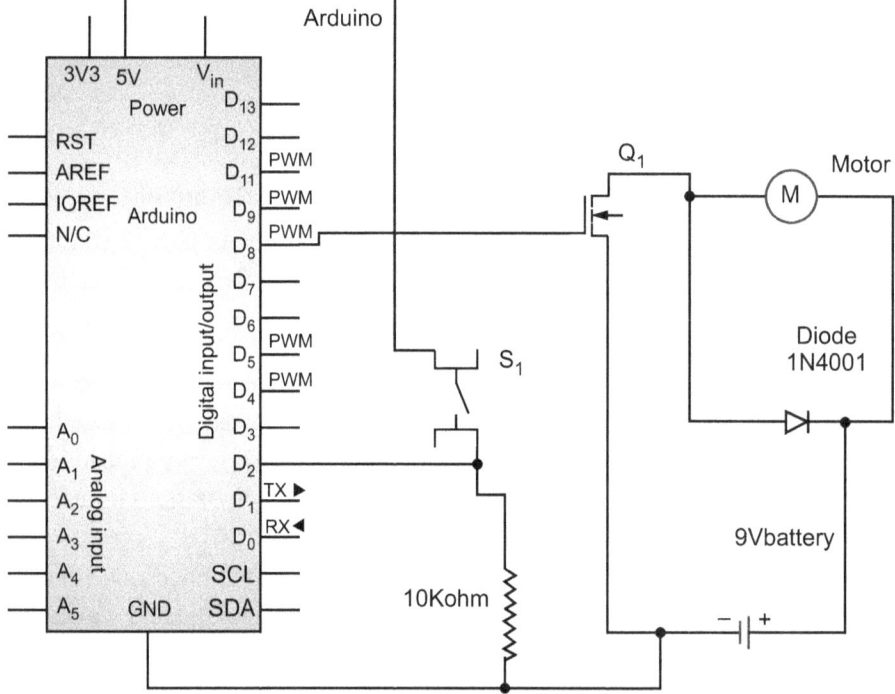

Fig. 7.16 : DC motor interface with Arduino

The Arduino can only provide 40mA at 5V on its digital pins. Most motors require more current and/or voltage to operate. A transistor can act as a digital switch, enabling the Arduino to control loads with higher electrical requirements. The transistor in this example completes the motor's circuit to ground. This example uses a TIP120, which can switch up to 60V at 5A.

When PWMing a transistor, it's similar to pulsing an LED. The higher the PWM value, the faster the motor will spin. The lower the value, the slower it will spin.

Transistors have three pins. For Bipolar Junction Transistors (BJT), like the one used in this example, the pins are called *base*, *collector*, and *emitter*. A small amount of current on the base pin closes a circuit between the collector and emitter pins. BJTs come in two different types, NPN and PNP. The TIP120 is a NPN-type transistor, which means the collector will connect to the motor, and the emitter will connect to ground.

Example Code for DC motor

```
int pushButton = 2;      // give a name to digital pin 2, which has a pushbutton
attached
int motorControl = 9;   // transistor which controls the motor will be attached to
digital pin 9

// the setup routine runs once when you press reset:
void setup()
{
  pinMode(pushButton, INPUT);            // make the pushbutton's pin an input
  pinMode(motorControl, OUTPUT);         // make the transistor's pin an output
}
// the loop routine runs over and over again forever:

void loop()
{

  if(digitalRead(pushButton) == HIGH) // read the status of button and check if it
is pressed
{
    for(int x = 0; x <= 255; x++)                          // ramp up the motor speed
{
    analogWrite(motorControl, x);
                      delay(50);
  }
    for(int x = 255; x >= 0; x--)                          // ramp down the motor speed
```

```
{
    analogWrite(motorControl, x);
          delay(50);
    }
 }
 delay(1);                     // delay in between reads for stability
}
```

2. Driving a DC Motor using h-bridge IC (L293)

We want to control the direction and speed of a brushed motor. This extends the functionality by controlling both motor direction and speed through commands from the serial port.

Connect a DC motor to the output pins of the H-Bridge as shown in Fig. 7.17.

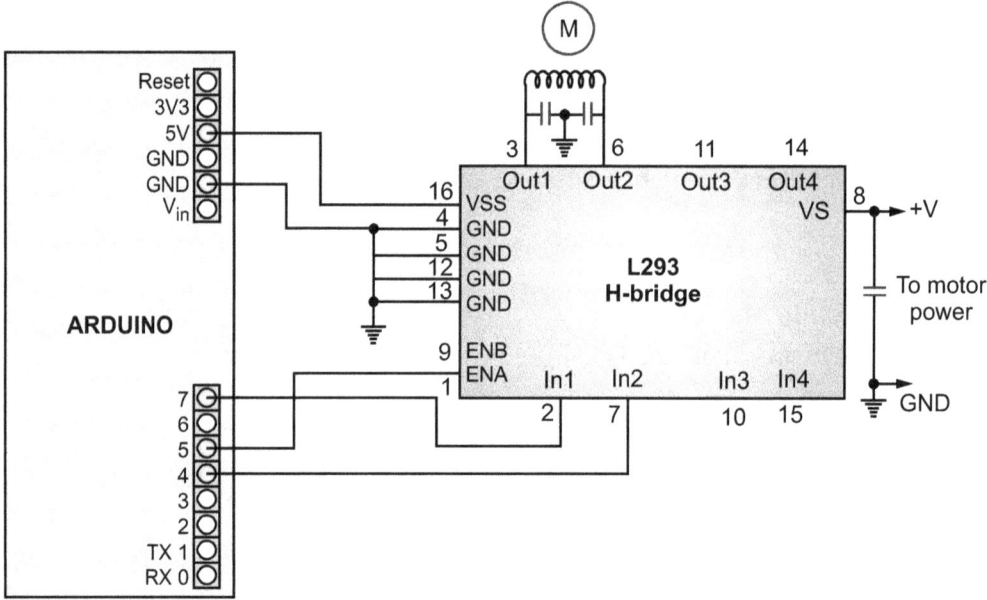

Fig. 7.17 : Connecting DC motor using L293 with arduino

The motor direction is controlled by the levels on the IN1 and IN2 pins. But in addition, speed is controlled by the analogWrite value on the EN pin. Writing a value of 0 will stop the motor; writing 255 will run the motor at full speed. The motor speed will vary in proportion to values within this range.

Example Code

```
/* * Brushed_H_Bridge sketch
 * commands from serial port control motor speed and direction
 * digits '0' through '9' are valid where '0' is off, '9' is max speed
```

```
* + or - set the direction */
const int enPin  = 5;  // H-Bridge enable pin
const int in1Pin = 7;  // H-Bridge input pins
const int in2Pin = 4;
void setup()
{
Serial.begin(9600);
pinMode(in1Pin, OUTPUT);
 pinMode(in2Pin, OUTPUT);
Serial.println("Speed (0-9) or + - to set direction");
}
void loop()
{
 if ( Serial.available())
    {
            char ch = Serial.read();
            if(ch >= '0' && ch <= '9')            // is ch a number?
                        {
                            int speed = map(ch, '0', '9', 0, 255);
                    analogWrite(enPin, speed);
                        Serial.println(speed);
                    }
            else if (ch == '+')
                    {
                            Serial.println("CW");
                            digitalWrite(in1Pin,LOW);
                                digitalWrite(in2Pin,HIGH);
                        }
                else if (ch == '-')
                            {
```

```
                    Serial.println("CCW");
                    digitalWrite(in1Pin,HIGH);
                    digitalWrite(in2Pin,LOW);
                    }
        else
        {
        Serial.print("Unexpected character ");
        Serial.println(ch);
        }
    }
}
```

7.8 EXERCISES

1. What is ADC? Write features of ADC in ATmega328p microcontroller.

2. Explain following functions used in ADC.

    (i) analogRead() function

    (ii) analogwrite() function

    (iii) analogReference() function.

3. Draw and Explain Interfacing of ADC with Arduino.

4. Draw and Explain temperature sensor (LM35) to Arduino.

5. Write the program to display temperature using LM35 heat detection sensor.

6. What is LVDT? Write main feature of LVDT.

7. Explain operation and working of LVDT.

8. What is strain gauge and strain gauge bridge circuit.

9. What is accelerometer and it's types.

10. Draw and Explain Interfacing of Accelerometer with Arduino.

11. Explain the concept of PWM with waveform.

12. Draw and Explain Interfacing of DC motor with arduino for speed control.

SAMPLE QUESTION PAPER I

End-Sem. Theory Examination

Time : 2 Hours   **Max. Marks : 50**

Instructions to the candidates :

(1) Answer Q. 1 or Q.2, Q. 3 or Q. 4, Q. 5 or Q. 6, Q. 7 or Q. 8.

(2) Neat diagrams must be drawn wherever necessary.

(3) Figures to the right side indicate full marks.

(4) Assume suitable data if necessary.

---

1. **(a)** Write the features of ATmega328p. **[6]**

   (b) What is digital I/O pin? Explain the functions used in digital I/O. **[6] OR**

2. **(a)** What is sensor ? What are the types of sensor explain any three. **[6]**

   (b) Draw and Explain Interfacing of (16 × 2) LCD to arduino. **[6]**

3. **(a)** State the factors on which electromagnetic torque developed in a D.C. motor depends. Deduce the expression for the torque developed in a D.C. motor. **[7]**

   (b) A 4-pole d.c. motor has lap connected armature winding with 576 conductors and draws an armature current of 25 A. If the flux per pole is 0.02 Wb, calculate the gross torque developed by the motor. **[6] OR**

4. **(a)** Compare a squirrel cage induction motor with a slip-ring induction motor with reference to construction, performance and applications. **[7]**

   (b) The rotor of a 4-pole, 50 Hz, 3-phase induction motor has a resistance of 0.2 Ω per phase and its full-load speed is 1440 r.p.m. If the load torque remains unchanged, calculate the approximate value of the additional resistance to be inserted in the rotor circuit to reduce the motor speed by 10%. **[6]**

5. **(a)** Write a short note on following function

   (i) Serialprint() (ii) serialprintIN() **[6]**

   (b) Write program to measure temperature using LM35 with arduino microcontroller. **[6]OR**

6. **(a)** What is ADC ? Explain use of ADC function in arduino programming. **[6]**

   (b) Draw and Explain interfacing of accelerometer (ADXL335) to arduino microcontroller.**[6]**

7. **(a)** Why starters are necessary for starting the induction motors? With a neat diagram, Explain the auto-transformer starter. **[7]**

   (b) The input to a 400 V, 6-pole, 50 Hz, 3-phase, star-connected induction motor is 10 kW while running at 950 r.p.m. The stator losses total 600 W and friction and windage losses amount to 400 W. Find the output and efficiency of the motor. **[6] OR**

8. **(a)** What is a stepper motor? With a neat diagram, explain the permanent magnet stepper motor. State its two applications. **[7]**

   (b) What is linear induction motor? Give its principle of operations state its two applications **[6]**

◈ ◈ ◈

SAMPLE QUESTION PAPER II

End-Sem. Theory Examination

Time : 2 Hours   **Max. Marks : 50**

Instructions to the candidates :
(1) Answer Q. 1 or Q.2, Q. 3 or Q. 4, Q. 5 or Q. 6, Q. 7 or Q. 8.
(2) Neat diagrams must be drawn wherever necessary.
(3) Figures to the right side indicate full marks.
(4) Assume suitable data if necessary.

1. **(a)** Write the difference between microprocessors and microcontollers? List advantages of microcontroller. **[6]**
    (b) Write a short note on Arduino IDE? List features of arduino IDE? **[6] OR**
2. **(a)** Draw and Explain block diagram of Data Acquisition system. **[6]**
    (b) Write a short note on Timer modes in ATmega328p. **[6]**
3. **(a)** Draw neat labelled diagram of the cross-section of a four pole, D.C. shunt connected generator. What are essential functions of the field coils, armature, commutator and brushes. **[7]**
    (b) A d.c. series motor has an armature resistance of 0.25 Ω and a field resistance of 0.5 Ω. The speed is 700 r.p.m. when the current is 24 A and the terminal voltage 230 V. Assuming the flux to be proportional to current, calculate the speed of the motor when it takes 40 A from the supply. **[6] OR**
4. **(a)** Explain the different methods of controlling the speed a D.C. shunt motor. **[7]**
    (b) A 230 V, d.c. shunt motor takes an armature current of 20 A on a certain load. Resistance of the armature is 0.5 Ω. Find the resistance required in series with the armature to halve the speed, if the load torque is proportional to the square of the speed. **[6]**
5. **(a)** Draw and Explain Interfacing of LM35 Temperature sensor to arduino. **[6]**
    (b) Write program to measure temperature using LM35 with arduino microcontroller. **[6] OR**
6. **(a)** Write a program to display "Hello world" on 16×2 LCD. **[6]**
    (b) Draw and Explain the Interfacing diagram of ATmega328p to control DC motor using PWM. **[6]**
7. **(a)** Sketch a typical torque slip characteristics of an induction motor. Explain its nature. What is the effect of increasing the rotor circuit resistance on this characteristic? **[7]**
    (b) A 6-pole, 50 Hz, 3-phase, induction motor is developing a maximum torque of 30 Nm at 960 r.p.m. Determine the torque exerted by the motor at 5 % slip. Rotor resistance per phase is 0.6 Ω. **[8] OR**
8. **(a)** What are the special features of servometers? State their types. Give two applications of each type. **[7]**
    (b) Draw a neat circuit diagram and explain the working of resistance split-phase induction motor. State the use of a centrifugal switch in it. **[6]**

Notes